GRAVE DANGER

ALSO BY JAMES GRIPPANDO

GRAVE DANGER

A JACK SWYTECK NOVEL

JAMES GRIPPANDO

HARPER

An Imprint of HarperCollins*Publishers*

GRAVE DANGER. Copyright © 2025 by James Grippando, Inc. All rights reserved. Printed in the United States of America. No part of this book may be used or reproduced in any manner whatsoever without written permission except in the case of brief quotations embodied in critical articles and reviews. For information, address HarperCollins Publishers, 195 Broadway, New York, NY 10007.

HarperCollins books may be purchased for educational, business, or sales promotional use. For information, please email the Special Markets Department at SPsales@harpercollins .com.

FIRST EDITION

Designed by Michele Cameron

Library of Congress Cataloging-in-Publication Data has been applied for.

ISBN 978-0-06-335803-4

24 25 26 27 28 LBC 5 4 3 2 1

For Tiffany

GRAVE DANGER

PROLOGUE

Ava Bazzi hurried across Keshavarz Boulevard in the center of Tehran, her daughter's tiny fingers clamped tightly in her own. The asphalt was warm beneath the thin leather soles of her tan pumps, and the sidewalk was even hotter. A headscarf would not have been her personal preference on this unusually warm autumn morning, but religious law required it.

The Bazzi family—Ava, her husband, Farid, and their four-year-old daughter, Yasmin—had been living in London since Yasmin was an infant, so the return to Iran was a bit of an adjustment. Still, it wasn't the way her friends in London thought, all with the Western misconception that black was the only acceptable color for head coverings. Ava favored fashionable and colorful compliance with the Islamic Republic's modesty laws. A yellow scarf with a hint of jasmine flowers. Capri pants cut just above the ankle. And a loose-fitting silk blouse with three-quarter-length sleeves, a neckline that showed no cleavage, and a tail long enough to cover the curve of her behind.

The street vendors were in good spirits, singing and calling out to potential customers. The familiar aroma of thick black coffee wafted from a small café. Some things in Tehran never change, but so much of what Ava remembered from her childhood had become almost unrecognizable. Keshavarz was once a tree-lined boulevard of pristine beauty and elegance, home to the elite of the Islamic Republic. But now many of the magnificent trees had been cut down, and the grandiose buildings had been turned into government offices and classrooms.

"You're hurting my hand, Mommy," said Yasmin.

Ava was squeezing too tight, for sure. It was an overreaction to the more worrisome changes she'd noticed on her return from London.

Barely a month had passed since the arrest of Mahsa Amini, a twenty-two-year-old woman who committed the crime of showing her hair in violation of the modesty laws. Her senseless death in custody, at the hands of the brutal morality police, triggered worldwide outrage and mass protests across the country. The Iranian regime's ruthless crackdown on demonstrators only fueled further protests. Right on Keshavarz, not far from Yasmin's school, sixteen-year-old Nika Shakarami had joined street protesters and was last seen being shoved into a police van. Ten days later, the morality police delivered her battered body to her family, claiming that Shakarami had committed suicide by jumping off a building. Soon after, Sarina Esmailzadeh, also sixteen, was bludgeoned to death with batons by security forces at a protest in Karaj. The crackdown then moved from the streets to the classrooms as security forces raided the Shahid girls' high school in Ardabil and demanded that a group of students sing a pro-regime song. Sixteen-year-old Asra Panahi refused and was beaten to death. Human rights groups estimated that, since Amini's arrest on September 13, victims of the regime numbered in the hundreds, and the murder of schoolgirls had every mother in Iran worried sick—including Ava.

"Walk faster," said Ava.

"I can't go any faster," said Yasmin.

An old woman dressed in a black charoud passed Ava on the sidewalk, clicking her tongue in disapproval of the younger woman's interpretation of "modest" attire. A rectangular opening in her black veil revealed only the woman's eyes, though in just that passing glance, Ava felt the weighty glare of an entire society: a tradition that must be kept, a truth that cannot be questioned, a morality whose nature is absolute, a law that cannot be broken, changed, or resisted.

They stopped at the iron gate just off the boulevard. The sign at the entrance to the playground read GIRLS' SCHOOL, SHAHID. Compulsory education in Iran did not begin until age six, but Ava and her husband were in agreement that Yasmin would start pre-primary at four. The large two-story building was made of white bricks, with heavy entrance doors and orange shutters that flanked the windows. The second floor was for older girls, ages nine to thirteen. A black hijab was mandatory starting in kindergarten. A simple white headscarf with a red headband singled out Yasmin and her classmates as preschoolers.

As they entered through the gate, the atmosphere in the schoolyard was noticeably tense. The teachers seemed nervous, and the girls were huddled together in small groups, whispering.

"I don't want to go to school," said Yasmin.

Ava took a deep breath, trying to push away the fear that had become a permanent fixture in her mind. She knew that Yasmin's education was crucial, but she also knew that the safety and well-being of her daughter could not be guaranteed in a place where girls were beaten and killed for simply expressing themselves.

"Mommy, did you hear me? I don't want to go to school."

Ava gently stroked Yasmin's hair and crouched down to meet her daughter's eyes. "I know it's scary right now, but it's important to keep going to school and learning. You're going to be strong and smart, and if you go to school, you can be anything you want to be when you grow up."

Yasmin's expression softened. "Can I be an astronaut?"

"Sure."

"A doctor?"

"Without a doubt."

"A lawyer?"

"We'll talk."

Yasmin's teacher came to greet them in the yard. Ava gave her daughter a kiss, handed her over to the teacher, and watched with trepidation as they disappeared into the building through the double doors.

As Ava turned to leave, she caught sight of a familiar face. Javad, a childhood friend she hadn't seen in years, was dropping off his daughter. They made eye contact, and a smile spread across Javad's face.

"Ava, it's good to see you!" Javad said. "I thought you and Farid were living in London."

"We just moved back."

"How did Farid's hotel business work out?"

Farid and his business partners owned six boutique hotels in Iran that catered to international travelers, each with a high-end Persian restaurant. With Ava's support and encouragement, he'd developed a business plan to expand to London.

"Not well enough for the UK to renew our entrepreneur visa, I'm afraid."

"I'm so sorry," said Javad.

"It's a shame, really," said Ava. "Just when the pilot hotel was getting traction, COVID shut down the whole industry. There was no way to recover."

"How is Farid taking it?"

"About as you'd expect," said Ava.

He nodded slowly, as if knowing exactly what she meant. "I'll be sure to steer clear. Hey, I have to run, but let's have coffee one morning after drop-off, okay?"

Javad was the first boy ever to tell her she was beautiful, but that was at the age of eleven. She had, in fact, grown into a truly beautiful woman, with shoulder-length raven hair, soft brown eyes, and captivating eyebrows that shone in the sunlight like filigrees of silk thread. Getting together for coffee would be harmless, even if they were both married—as long as Farid approved.

"Yes, let's try and do that," said Ava.

They said goodbye, and Ava took a slightly different route home for a stop at the bazaar. One of the joys of returning to Tehran was the outdoor market near ValiAsr Square, which was a culinary delight. Metal pots and pans hung from hooks, holding dried spices and onions. Colorful displays of fresh fruit and vegetables filled block after block of tented vendor stands. The air was alive with the aromas of roasted saffron and chives, sweet carrot, bitter melon, and fresh herbs. That morning, however, Ava couldn't get near the market. The street was impassable. In the time it had taken Ava to walk Yasmin to school, thousands of demonstrators had crowded the street.

"Zan, zendegi, azadi," they chanted in unison. *Women, life, freedom.* It was the rallying cry of the grassroots movement against oppression.

Vehicular traffic was at a standstill, horns blasting. A small fire was burning in the crosswalk. Young women were publicly removing their head coverings and tossing them into the flames. Across the way, a woman was standing atop a mailbox. The crowd around her chanted even louder—"Zan, zendegi, azadi"—in support.

Ava stopped for a moment and watched as the woman took a pair of scissors from her bag, cut off her long ponytail, and then held it defiantly over her head. The crowd around her erupted. It was an act of political symbolism, at once a statement against the rules of compulsory hijab for women, and an act of defiance in honor of Mahsa Amini, the young woman whose death had sparked so many demonstrations like the one in which Ava had suddenly found herself. Ava believed in everything the demonstrators were fighting for. But the street was not her battleground of choice. She turned away from the crowds and continued toward home.

Her apartment building was one of the newest in the neighborhood, five stories of concrete and steel, with a rooftop garden. Outside the gleaming glass doors, a doorman dressed in a black suit and a red cravat bid Ava good morning as she entered the lobby. Ava took the elevator to the eighth floor and entered their corner apartment, a two-bedroom unit with plenty of space for a family of three. It was actually nicer than their flat in London, though the surrounding neighborhood was not nearly as interesting—older stucco apartment buildings painted in dirty white and faded shades of green or yellow. From a window in the living room, Ava could see the demonstrations in the square below. She removed her scarf slowly, watching, and then returned to the door to make sure she'd locked it. Her heels clicked on the wood floor in the hallway to the master bedroom. She stopped at the bureau and unlocked the top drawer. Her cell phone was inside. She'd left it behind, under lock and key, because the morality police had been stopping women on the street and checking their phones. If "seditious" messages were found, they would be arrested on the spot.

Ava had one text message: What did you have for dinner?

She texted the coordinated reply that told the sender that it was safe to communicate: Soup.

Ava was part of a growing grassroots effort by Iranian women whose common objective was to keep information flowing after the government's shutdown of the internet in response to the demonstrations. The network was too unstructured to have formal "rules," but it was common sense and commonly understood that if you received a text, you read it, passed it along to the next woman, and then deleted it. It wasn't safe to keep the messages on a cell phone. If the morality police found them, both the sender and recipient would be arrested.

Her phone chimed with the arrival of another text message. It was a photograph of an ugly circular bruise on a woman's leg. The message read: Rubber bullet. I was doing nothing. Riot police shot me.

Ava texted back. Why the crowds on Keshavarz? Did something bad happen?

Some of the women who were brave enough to participate just stuck to the facts, no questions asked or answered. But when trouble was so close to home, it was impossible not to start a conversation and fish for more.

The reply came quickly. 315 protesters indicted this morning. 4 as mohareb.

Mohareb. "Enemy of God." It is the worst possible crime in Shiite Muslim law. The regime had resorted to desperate measures, charging demonstrators as *mohareb*. Ava had studied enough of her country's history to know that even Ayatollah Ruhollah Khomeini, the founder of the Islamic regime in the late 1970s, had only *threatened* to accuse his opponents of being "enemies of God." The penalty was public execution.

Another text appeared on Ava's screen, but it was a different sender. After the introductory exchange—dinner and soup—the news followed.

School raid in District 6. I'm taking my daughter home now.

Ava assumed the sender meant the girls' high school. Teenage girls had been among the most vocal opponents of the regime, and while at school they were easy targets for the morality police. Ava texted back:

Mine is too young to know what is going on.

A quick response came: Not too young to be caught in the crossfire.

So true, and the message chilled Ava. The last tally circulated by text said that 27 children were among the reported total of 215 demonstrators killed since September. Ava put her cell phone back in the locked drawer, covered her head with a scarf, and hurried out the door to the elevator. The ride to the lobby seemed to take forever, and she ran out of the building, hitting full speed by the time she passed the doorman on the sidewalk. The demonstration on the street seemed to have grown even larger, the cries for justice even louder.

Ava's heart was pounding like a jackhammer, the blood rushing to her head, as she ran as fast as she could past the demonstrators. The smell of tear gas filled the air as she approached Yasmin's school, which only heightened her concern. Ava continued straight ahead, pushing through the crowd, determined to reach the school at any cost, nearly breathless as she arrived. A dozen other mothers were already waiting outside the entrance gate to the school grounds. Like Ava, they had come to pull their daughters out and take them home, where it was safe. Yasmin was only in prekindergarten, but the primary school was adjacent to the girls' high school, and the text message was burned into Ava's mind: *Not too young to be caught in the crossfire.*

The schoolmaster was standing on the other side of the iron gate. She was clearly sympathetic to the pleas of distressed parents who had come for their daughters. The gates creaked open as girls, one by one, were passed to waiting arms outside the schoolyard. Ava caught sight of Yasmin coming through the door, escorted by her teacher.

"Mommy's here!" Ava shouted.

Yasmin broke free from her teacher and ran to the gate. The head of school passed her to Ava.

"May Allah keep you safe," the school head whispered.

Ava took her daughter in her arms, just long enough to make her feel safe, and then put her back on the sidewalk. Other mothers at the gate called for their daughters and prayed aloud.

"We must hurry," Ava shouted, and she started running, leading Yasmin along with her.

"Are we going home?"

"Daddy's office," said Ava. "It's closer."

Ava made a turn down a side street. Demonstrators sprinted past her and Yasmin, and Ava could see the utter panic on their faces. A gunshot rang out somewhere in the surrounding neighborhood. The crowd scattered in all directions, people screaming in confusion, and the race down the street became a stampede of civilians in search of any safe place to hide from the police. Ava's husband had his office on the north side of the boulevard, but barricades blocked their way. Armed members of Tehran's Guidance Patrol had closed off the square. Yasmin could run no farther. Crying and exhausted, she forced her mother to stop.

"What now, Mommy?"

Their apartment wasn't as close as Farid's office, but there was no other choice. Ava picked up Yasmin and carried her, running a half block and then walking to catch her breath, then running again toward home. Another canister of tear gas exploded behind them, propelling Ava forward. Gunshots cracked in rapid succession—*pow, pow, pow!*—unleashing screams and more panic.

"Stop right there, woman!" a police officer shouted.

Ava froze. Two officers rushed toward her. The bigger one grabbed her by the arm.

"Where is your hijab?" he demanded.

Ava reached for it, only to discover that her scarf was gone.

"It must have fallen off," she said. "I was running with my daughter, trying to get home safely."

"You cut your hair," said the other officer accusingly.

"No," said Ava. "I wear it short."

"You lie!"

"No, it's true. Our family just returned from London. We lived there for my husband's work. I wear my hair short with his permission."

"You were one of those women who cut their hair in protest."

"No, that's not true!" said Ava, her voice shaking. "I obey the laws."

"Liar!"

Ava didn't see it coming, but the sudden crack of his baton against her arm made her cry out in pain.

"Mommy!" Yasmin shrieked.

"Where is your husband?"

"At work," she said, which drew another smack of the baton.

"The address!"

Ava gave it to him. The officer told his partner to "take the girl to her father," and then he cuffed Ava's hands behind her back.

"You're under arrest."

"No, please!"

Yasmin called out to her mother, but they were being pulled in opposite directions. The arresting officer dragged Ava toward the police van, where more officers, batons swinging, were shoving men, women, and teenagers into the back of the van like mob criminals. Ava checked over her shoulder again and again, calling to her daughter, until Yasmin disappeared into the back of a squad car. Her heart sank as the beacons flashed and the car pulled away.

"This is all a mistake!" Ava said, as they reached the police van.

"Yes, and you made it," said the officer.

He shoved her inside the van, and the double doors slammed shut.

CHAPTER 1

You are experiencing mirror image syndrome," the marriage counselor said from behind her desk. Dr. Stanger's office furnishings were ultramodern, and the oval desktop was solid glass. Beneath the halogen lighting, it glistened like a puddle of her clients' tears.

"What does that mean?" asked Jack.

Jack Swyteck and his wife of nine years, FBI agent Andie Henning, were seated in matching wing chairs facing their counselor. Jack was dressed in a dark suit and tie, having just come from the courthouse. Andie was wearing FBI khaki pants, the standard blue polo shirt, and an empty holster. Weapons were strictly forbidden in Dr. Stanger's sessions, and no one had to ask why. Counseling had been Jack's idea—one last attempt to find an alternative to Andie's solution to the "rough patch" in their marriage.

Dr. Stanger folded her hands atop her desk. "Mirror image syndrome means that the two of you are looking at the exact same reality and each seeing your spouse as the unreasonable one."

"That's not a syndrome," said Jack. "That's life."

"'Life without parole,' a criminal lawyer might say," Andie said, teasing, with an exaggerated sigh.

"Criminal *defense* lawyer," said Jack. "I'm not a criminal."

"This is not constructive," Dr. Stanger said.

"Actually, it is," said Andie. "Our *life* for the last nine years has been doing things Jack's way. I've lost count of the number of times his work as a criminal lawyer—"

"Criminal *defense* lawyer."

"—has caused me professional embarrassment at the bureau. If our marriage and our daughter are the most important things in our life, why can't we try it my way?"

"Can I respond?" asked Jack.

"Of course," Dr. Stanger said.

"Because it's not reasonable to ask me to stop doing what I do best. I can't suddenly slap my mug on billboards and ask, 'Have You Been Injured in an Accident?'"

"To be fair, that's not what Andie is saying, Jack. Her point is that the essential nature of her work is to put criminals behind bars. She can't be an FBI agent and *not* do that. But a lawyer doesn't have to defend accused criminals to be a lawyer. There are a multitude of ways to practice law without being adverse to law enforcement."

"Thank you, Doctor," said Andie. "But my point is more than that: Why does it always have to be the woman who changes her career for the betterment of the marriage?"

"Why does either of us have to change their career?"

"Because this isn't working anymore, Jack."

The room went silent. Andie had uttered those words only once before, prior to counseling. But it was the first time she'd said it with such conviction.

The counselor broke the silence. "Would you like my take on what's not working?"

"By all means," said Jack.

"It's not the abstract possibility of a conflict of interest between a lawyer and a law enforcement agent that is straining your marriage. It's the self-imposed rule you've lived by to avoid any potential conflict."

The Rule. It was etched in stone: Andie didn't talk to Jack about her active investigations, and Jack didn't talk to Andie about his active cases. Jack's fear was that he might say something to land his client in jail; Andie's fear was that she might slip and reveal an FBI secret to one of Miami's top criminal defense lawyers.

"What's wrong with the Rule?" asked Andie, capital *R*.

"It's not healthy for two career-oriented people to muzzle themselves in that way," said Dr. Stanger. "I honestly don't know how you two have managed to stay together this long."

"Till death do us part," said Jack.

"Oh, give me a break, Jack. You've already been divorced once."

"She wasn't 'The One.'"

Dr. Stanger laid her pen on her notepad, as if they'd finally made a breakthrough. "If Andie is 'The One,' Jack, does that mean you're open to dropping the Rule?"

"I suppose that's better than dropping my career."

"I'm not asking you to drop—"

Dr. Stanger raised her hand like a traffic cop, stopping Andie in mid-sentence. "Andie, how about you? Are you willing to drop the Rule?"

Andie considered it, then spoke. "I'm open to it. But I have a condition."

"Go ahead," said Dr. Stanger.

Andie looked at Jack, then back at the counselor. "I want Jack to at least cut back on the criminal defense work. And not just a little."

Silence. Again, Dr. Stanger broke it.

"The ball is in your court, Counselor."

Jack breathed in and out. "You know, ninety-nine percent of civil cases never go to trial. They settle. And if you ask any mediator what's the best way to tell if a settlement is 'fair,' he'll tell you it's when neither side is happy."

"What are you saying?" asked Dr. Stanger.

Jack reached across the divide between the two wing chairs and took Andie's hand. "I'm saying yes. We drop the Rule. And I'll cut back on my criminal defense work."

"A lot," said Andie.

Jack swallowed hard. "Okay. A lot."

B iscayne Bay was black as night. As flashes of moonlight broke through the clouds, starlike twinkles rippled across the gentle waves beyond the seawall. Jack sat alone on the dock behind his house, keeping his buyer's remorse to himself. A lamp glowed in the window of the corner bedroom, where Andie was putting their daughter, Righley, to bed.

Criminal defense defined Jack as a lawyer. His first job out of law school had been with the Freedom Institute, where he spent four years defending death row inmates. He'd moved on from the institute by the time he met Andie, but his practice was still overwhelmingly criminal defense, and the occasional innocent client didn't stop her from asking, like everyone else, "How do you sleep at night knowing your client was guilty?" Truth was, Jack lost much more sleep defending the innocent, when his client faced prosecution for a crime someone else had committed. Too many of *those* cases would put any lawyer on the road to burnout. Over the years Jack had incorporated a few high-stakes civil lawsuits into his practice, mostly plaintiff's work that paid well enough to let him put something away for Righley's college fund and, even further off in the future, a comfortable retirement for him and Andie. The tension between Andie's career at the FBI and Jack's criminal defense practice was real, not imagined, and Jack understood her frustration. But there was no denying that what got Jack out of bed each morning and put a spring in his step was a trip to the criminal courthouse.

Jack's cell phone rang. He answered, and his father jumped straight to the point of his call.

"Hey, son, I hear you're finally coming over from the dark side."

A cop turned politician, Harry Swyteck had served two terms as the "law and order" governor of Florida. In his first term alone, he'd signed more death warrants than any governor in Florida's history, several for Jack's clients—including one who was innocent. Now one of Jack's closest friends, Theo Knight still walked this earth only because his lawyer wouldn't give up.

A seagull swept past Jack. "It sounds like you talked to Andie."

"Just got off the phone with her. Told me you're cutting back on your criminal practice. Way back."

"Did she tell you it was her idea?"

"She did."

Jack stepped to the edge of the dock, the waves splashing rhythmically below. "I suppose the two of you must be very happy."

"Not really."

"Oh, come off it. The heartburn I give Andie as an FBI agent doesn't begin to compare to the political damage I did to you as governor."

"That's water under the bridge, Jack. And even though I think this change can be a good thing, I always wanted it to be *your* idea. Like when I left politics. Agnes let it be my idea. Or at least she let me think it was my idea."

Agnes was Harry's late wife, Jack's stepmother. "Andie does things her own way," said Jack.

"Look, Jack. More than anything else, I want you and Andie to be happy. And I know this must be hard for you, redefining yourself as a lawyer."

"It is hard. Thank you for recognizing that."

"I want to make this easier for you. I have a case."

"What kind of case?"

"A civil case."

"Sounds like you're on Andie's side."

"I'm not on anybody's side. It's pro bono. And the stakes are higher than in any criminal case you've ever handled."

"Dad, I don't see how that's possible. I've done death penalty cases."

"I stand by my words: higher stakes."

"Okay. What's the case?"

"It was just filed in the United States District Court in Miami. *John Doe v. Jane Doe.*"

"Legal pseudonyms on both sides," said Jack. "I've had only one case like that. I represented the victim of a sexual assault suing her seventeen-year-old attacker."

"This case raises secrecy concerns of a different kind. The parties are Iranian citizens."

"Suing each other in federal court in Miami? How?"

"I wish I could tell you, but the complaint was filed under seal."

"You're asking me to take a case you know nothing about?"

"Not nothing. The case was filed under seal at the request of the US State Department. One of the parties—the woman who would be your client—is a political hot potato in US-Iranian relations."

"High stakes on a geopolitical level, is that it?"

"Aptly stated. I took the liberty of booking you a flight to Washington tomorrow morning."

"To do what?"

"Myra Weiss was my chief legal counsel when I was governor. She's now a big shot in Washington. She came to me because her firm has a conflict and can't accept the case. She needs a top-notch Miami trial lawyer who can take the heat from the White House, the US State Department, and the Iranian government. So of course I thought of you."

"That's music to my ears, Dad. But things are pretty rough with Andie right now. If I'm going to draw heat from the US government by representing an Iranian woman who's a political hot potato, I probably should talk to Andie."

"It's a pro bono case, Jack. 'For the good.'"

"So were my death penalty cases."

A deep sigh crackled over the line. "Jack, I'm not asking for a favor. I'm doing *you* a favor. This is the kind of stuff you live for. It's not a criminal case, but things could get just as bloody. If Andie doesn't like that, you can blame me."

Hiding behind his father was more like the offer Jack would never accept than the proverbial offer he couldn't refuse. But it was the old man's way of showing how much he cared, and for that, Jack was appreciative.

The moon broke through the clouds, and ripples of light rode across the waves toward the seawall. "All right, Dad. I'll pay Myra a visit."

CHAPTER 2

Jack's flight landed at Reagan National on Tuesday morning. Washington, DC, was ablaze with autumn color. Crisp air and cloudless blue skies greeted him as he stepped out of the taxi. It was the kind of October day that made south Floridians—stuck in heat and humidity until Halloween—wonder if life really was better north of the Mason-Dixon. Jack would reserve judgment until January. He entered the chrome-and-glass office building and was in the office of Myra Weiss before noon.

Myra was a partner at one of Washington's elite law firms, just a stone's throw from the White House. Her corner office on the twelfth floor offered what Big Law referred to as a "power vista," which Jack admired from a tufted leather armchair. Myra seemed immune to it, seated with her back to a floor-to-ceiling window that showcased Lafayette Square, the familiar Pennsylvania Avenue view of the White House, and, in the distance, the Washington Monument.

Myra was about ten years older than Jack, closer in age to him than to his father, but Jack had always thought of her as part of her former boss's generation. According to her bio on the American Bar Association website, she'd made it her mission as chair of the ABA's International Section to ensure that women sued in the United States under the Hague Convention had proper legal representation. Her firm handled as many as it could. For the rest, she recruited talented lawyers from all over the country to take cases on a pro bono basis.

"Do you have any experience with cases under the Hague Convention?" asked Myra.

"Not specifically. But I've had tons of trials with transnational implications, mostly under the Foreign Corrupt Practices Act."

"You'll take a mandatory training class," she said. "I look for highly skilled trial lawyers, not walking encyclopedias. You do at least know what the Hague Convention *is*, right?"

"A multilateral treaty," said Jack. "Something like a hundred signatory countries."

"Most important for our purposes, the convention governs court proceedings in which a parent alleges that his child was abducted by the other parent and removed from the usual country of residence."

"You say *his* child. I assume it works both ways. The mother or the father can sue under the Hague Convention if their spouse abducts the child."

"True. But my interest in these cases is narrower. All too often, the 'kidnapper' is a woman—a wife and mother fleeing an abusive husband. The Hague Convention provides a legal basis for the father to bring suit in the United States and secure the child's return to him in his home country."

"I presume it also provides some protection for the abused mother and her child," said Jack.

"Yes. *Some* protection. These cases are very difficult for a mother to win."

"How so?"

"The Hague Convention strongly disfavors kidnapping under any circumstances. Even proof that the mother was the victim of domestic abuse is not enough for her to win. She must prove that returning the child to the father under the Hague Convention would place *the child*—not the mother—in grave danger of 'physical or psychological harm.'"

"Sounds like a pretty nebulous standard," said Jack.

"You'll learn all about it in your training. For now, let's focus more specifically on the case that was filed in Miami. *John Doe v. Jane Doe*."

"I presume John Doe is the father."

"Yes. Farid Bazzi. He is Iranian and lives in Tehran. The mother is also Iranian but has lived in Miami with their daughter, Yasmin, for almost a year."

"That explains the Miami connection. But I'm still confused how this lawsuit is even in a US court. My understanding is that Iran is not a signatory to the Hague Convention."

"That's correct."

"So technically there is no legal basis for Farid to seek the return of the child to Iran."

"It's not that cut-and-dried."

"The law rarely is," said Jack.

"That goes double for international law. The Bazzi family moved to the UK when Yasmin was a newborn and stayed there until she was four. Yasmin lived less than a year in Iran before her mother took her to the United States. The UK is a signatory to the convention."

"But Farid wants the child returned to Iran, not the UK, right?"

"Of course he does," said Myra. "But Farid's lawyer pulled a clever legal move. Under the convention, a child can be returned only to his or her 'habitual place of residence.' Farid's lawyer is arguing that Yasmin's 'habitual place of residence' is the UK, where the family lived for most of her life."

"That's pure legal gamesmanship," said Jack. "The minute Yasmin sets foot in the UK, Farid will take her to Iran. Yasmin and her mother will never see each other again."

"You're a quick study, Jack. That's exactly the problem."

His father's words echoed in Jack's mind: *The stakes are higher than in any criminal case.* Jack's friends at the Freedom Institute might take issue. The case of *Doe v. Doe* wasn't life-or-death. But Jack took his father's meaning. Jack had never known his biological mother; she'd died in childbirth. Jack understood better than anyone that, for six-year-old Yasmin and her mother, the stakes could not be higher.

"Tell me more about Yasmin's mother," said Jack. "My father described her as a 'political hot potato.'"

"I see this as a humanitarian issue, not a political one."

"That makes the case even more interesting to me."

"Ultimately, it's up to Ava to decide whether she wants you to be her lawyer."

"Ava is her name?"

"She goes by the name Ava Bazzi," said Myra.

"Goes by? You mean she's using an alias?"

Myra drew a deep breath, as if there were so much more to the story. "Two years ago, Tehran's morality police arrested Ava Bazzi for taking part in a hijab protest. She was taken to an Iranian jail. That's the last anyone has seen of her."

"I remember hearing about the protests in the news."

"Ava did get news coverage at the time, but so did others. Over five hundred demonstrators were killed or disappeared. Amnesty International was very vocal about it. All those stories lost traction when the mainstream media turned to bigger international issues after Russia invaded Ukraine."

"And now, out of the blue, Ava Bazzi reappears in Miami as a respondent in a lawsuit filed under the Hague Convention?"

"Or does she? Most rational minds—governments excluded—believe Ava Bazzi died in custody at the hands of the morality police."

"So you're saying this is not the real Ava Bazzi? That this case is not about keeping a mother and her child together?"

"That's the threshold question. The Iranian government says Ava abandoned her husband and fled to the West with her daughter."

Jack finished Myra's point for her. "So, if the Iranian government is right, and this is, in fact, Ava Bazzi, the stakes could not be higher."

"Absolutely."

"But if you're right—the real Ava Bazzi is dead, and someone else abducted Yasmin—then what?"

"Then we have a potential international crisis that threatens to undermine the legitimacy of the Hague Convention and all the good work this organization does for abused mothers in desperate need of help all over the world—which both Harry and I entrust to you."

"I get the picture," said Jack.

"Either way, it should be a very interesting first meeting with your new client."

Jack looked past her, gazing through the window toward the White House. "Interesting, to say the least."

CHAPTER 3

J ack's day trip to Washington carried over to the next day. He landed in Miami late Wednesday afternoon and drove straight from the airport to his law office.

Myra Weiss had essentially locked him in a conference room with a Georgetown law professor for the required crash course on the Hague Convention, international child abduction, and child custody law. His training included case studies, which only confirmed that, way too often, the accused abductor was an abused woman fleeing domestic violence. The other point the professor impressed upon him was the speed at which the cases moved through the court system. "Six weeks from filing to finish," she'd told Jack. "In the world of jurisprudence, a Hague proceeding is a sprint, not a marathon."

There was no time to waste. Jack called Andie from the car and told her he would not be home for dinner; he had a seven o'clock meeting in his office. His client arrived early and was waiting on the front porch when his car pulled up in the driveway.

"I'm Jack," he said as he unlocked the front door.

"Do you live here?" she asked. "This looks more like a house than an office."

Jack smiled and showed her inside. It actually *was* a house that dated back to the 1920s, built in the old Florida style with external walls of coral rock, a gabled roof covered in Cuban barrel tile, and, on the inside, refurbished floors of Dade County pine. Over the years the neighborhood had transitioned from residential to commercial, one old house after another transformed into a doctor's office, a wine bar, a Pilates studio, or a cigar shop. The area was especially popular with criminal defense lawyers, who could practically walk to the courthouse along the Miami River. Jack's office was in the oldest house on the block, once home to Florida pioneer Julia Tuttle.

"Sometimes my wife does accuse me of living here," he said.

"I'm sorry. I'm keeping you away from your family, aren't I?"

"Not at all," he said, though, truthfully, she was.

Jack's personal office was once the dining room, his favorite room in the house. He switched on the lights and led his client past his desk to the matching armchairs in front of the fireplace, which Jack used about once every five years. He cleaned it once every ten.

"You didn't offer your name when I introduced myself," said Jack.

"Did you not read it in the court filing?" she asked.

"The complaint was filed under seal. I can't read it until you engage me as your attorney. That aside, I assume your real name is not Jane Doe."

"No," she said quietly.

"I understand you go by the name Ava Bazzi."

"Yes."

"Are you Ava Bazzi?"

She glanced away, toward the dark window, then back at Jack. "No."

"Who are you?"

"I am Zahra Bazzi. Ava was my sister. The pretty one."

She was being modest; the woman before him was quite striking. But Jack had more important things to address.

"I'm going to need a very good explanation why you're using your sister's name. But before we get there, I want to know more about Yasmin. Is she your child, or your sister's?"

"Yasmin is the biological child of Ava and Farid."

"Which makes her your niece," said Jack.

"She was my niece. Until . . ."

"Until what?"

"Until I married Farid."

Jack was taken aback. "You married your sister's husband?"

"I married her widower."

Farid as widower comported with what Jack had learned from Myra about Ava's encounter with the morality police. But he wanted Zahra's version of the story.

"May I explain?" asked Zahra.

"Please do."

"Ava is—was—my younger sister. Farid and I are almost the same age. We dated when I was eighteen and Farid was nineteen. It was serious, but he was a very jealous man."

"Was he abusive?" asked Jack.

"Never physically abusive, but he had a temper and could be verbally abusive. I broke off the relationship."

"And then?"

"A few years passed, and Ava blossomed into this beautiful young woman. Farid noticed. Everyone noticed. Ava asked me if it was okay with me if she dated him."

"What did you tell her?"

"I had no feelings for Farid. But I warned her about his temper. Ava said that he was no longer the jealous boy I'd dated as a teenager, and that he'd matured into a caring and understanding man."

"So they started dating."

"They fell in love and were married."

"When did Yasmin come along?"

"About a year after they married. She was just a few months old when they moved to London."

As Jack recalled, the UK connection was how Farid's lawyer had filed the case under the Hague Convention. "Tell me about that."

"Farid wanted to expand his hotel business to London. He got what's called a UK Tier 1 Entrepreneur visa, which allows foreigners from outside Europe to invest in and run a business. After five years, the visa holder and his family can apply for British citizenship."

"Was that their plan? To become British citizens?"

"I don't know. Whatever the plan was, it failed. Covid killed the hotel business."

"Is that why the family returned to Iran?"

"Yes. And everything changed."

"What do you mean by 'everything'?"

"Ava, for one. She liked the freedom she had as a woman in the UK. She didn't want to go back to Iran."

"Did Farid change as well?"

"From what I saw, yes. He was bitter and said the family would never go back to the UK. He never wanted to leave Iran again."

"Did he change toward Ava?"

"Again, I can only tell you what I saw, and I didn't like what I was seeing. He was verbally abusive to Ava, much like the way he treated me when we dated as teenagers."

Jack flipped the page on his notepad. Zahra was doing just fine with the chronological recital of events, but it was already late, and he hadn't seen his wife and daughter in two days. He skipped ahead in the story.

"How did Farid react to Ava's arrest by the morality police?"

"He was ready to divorce her before hearing her side of the story," said Zahra.

"What story did he hear that made him want to divorce her?"

"The government's story. They said she escaped from police custody, abandoned her husband and daughter, and returned to London to practice her wanton Western ways."

"You don't accept that story?"

"I don't, and I never will. It's a lie."

"How do you know?"

"Because I know my sister."

"Anything more specific than that?"

"Ava's dream was to return to London *with* her daughter. She would never have left Yasmin behind."

Jack tried to imagine Andie fleeing Miami, never to see Righley again. It was inconceivable. "So, it's your position that the government concocted the story that Ava escaped and fled the country."

"Yes. To cover up the fact that she was tortured and murdered in custody by the morality police. Like so many others who took to the streets in the hijab protests."

"But you can't prove that."

"No one will ever be able to prove it."

Jack flipped the page again in his notepad. "Let's circle back to where this conversation started: Why were you living under your sister's name?"

"Why don't you ask the US State Department that question?"

"I'm asking you."

"It was the best way to protect myself."

"From what?"

"When I took Yasmin and brought her to Miami, I knew that someone might find me and try to take her back."

"By 'someone,' you mean Farid."

"Yes. The only way to protect myself was to use Ava's passport and assume her identity."

"How did that protect you from Farid?"

"It made the Iranian government my ally."

"Your ally?"

"Not a formal alliance. But they would have no choice but to protect me."

"I don't follow your logic," said Jack.

"From the very beginning, the Iranian government has denied that the morality police murdered Ava while she was in custody. It's their position that she fled to the West and is still alive. When Zahra Bazzi became Ava Bazzi, I sent them a very clear message."

"What message?" asked Jack.

Her expression turned very serious. "If the Iranian government or anyone else tries to take Yasmin away from me, it will be war. I will throw an international spotlight on Ava's disappearance. I will make it my mission, to my last dying breath, to let the whole world know that the morality police *did* murder the real Ava Bazzi—a woman who did absolutely nothing wrong, and who lost her life only because she passed too close to a hijab protest while walking her daughter home from school."

Jack understood the full implication of her words. "Setting off a diplomatic crisis between the United States and Iran was not exactly the legal strategy I had in mind."

"The legal strategy is your department," said Zahra. "But now you know *my* strategy. And it's a good one."

"If you decide you want me to be your lawyer, we can talk more about whether it's a good one."

"It's already working, Mr. Swyteck. Why do you think Farid filed this case as *John Doe vs. Jane Doe*? Either the Iranian government forced him to keep the Bazzi name out of this, or he's trying to fly under the radar."

The use of pseudonyms was unusual in legal filings, which lent some credence to her explanation.

Zahra's cell rang, and she checked the incoming number. "It's Yasmin's babysitter," she told Jack. "I have to take this."

"Go right ahead." Jack rose to give her privacy and started toward the door, but the call was over before Jack was out of the room.

"I'm sorry," she said, tucking her phone into her purse. "I have to leave."

Jack stopped at the door. "Is everything okay?"

"Yes. Yasmin just needs her mommy."

For a split second, Jack thought she meant Ava, but "mommy" meant Zahra.

"If you're ready to retain me as your attorney, I can read the sealed court filings tonight, and we can have a more in-depth talk in the morning. It's your decision."

"Of course I want you," she said.

"Good. I'll walk you out."

Jack led her past the reception desk in what was once a living room, out the front door, and down the front steps. Flashes of moonlight broke through the sprawling limbs of a century-old oak tree as they crossed the lawn to Zahra's car.

"I look forward to meeting Yasmin," said Jack.

"She knows nothing about this."

"Understood. We'll keep it that way as long as we can."

She shook Jack's hand. "Thank you."

"I'll see you tomorrow morning," said Jack.

Zahra climbed into her car. Jack closed the door, the engine started, and she drove away. Jack watched until the red taillights rounded the corner and faded into the darkness.

Her mommy needs her.

Those words raised a host of questions. Apparently, "Zahra became Ava" was something his client meant quite literally. Or maybe the real explanation wasn't apparent at all. Either way, Jack knew exactly where their conversation would pick up in the morning.

Jack started back inside, across the lawn, and through the darkness. The moment he passed the oak's massive trunk, something—someone—appeared out of nowhere, flattening him like a passing bus. Before he could react, he was facedown in the grass. His attacker was sitting on his kidneys, and a cold steel blade was at his throat.

"Don't move," the man said. He had a wad of cotton or something in his mouth to distort his voice. "This is about Zahra, not Ava. You understand me?"

Jack heard his words, but he was too overwhelmed to understand. "Whatever you say."

The blade slid higher up Jack's neck. "No! Not 'whatever I say.' If you make this case about what happened to Ava, someone is going to get hurt. *Now* do you understand?"

The message was much clearer, and Jack burned those words into his memory: *What happened to Ava.*

"I understand," he said.

"Good. Now, keep looking at the ground. Don't get up till you count to a thousand. And don't you dare call the police. Got it?"

"Got it."

"Count out loud!"

"One, two—"

"Slower!"

"Three," he said, and with the short pause that followed, the blade pulled away from his neck. "Four," and the man's body weight lifted from the small of his back.

"Five . . . six," he continued, his count much slower than the echo of fleeing footfalls on pavement as his attacker faded into the night. He stopped counting at ten and sprinted across the lawn, up the front steps, and into his office. He grabbed his cell and dialed. Zahra answered.

"Zahra, it's Jack. Are you okay?"

"Yes. Fine. I just got home. Is something wrong?"

Jack quickly told her what happened.

"Oh, my God," she said. "Are you hurt?"

"I'm fine. Everything's going to be just fine. But let's not take any chances. I want you to lock your doors and stay inside. I'm calling the police now."

"No! Don't call the police! It will only make things worse!"

The attacker's warning was still in the back of his mind: *Don't you dare call the police.*

"Let's talk about this," said Jack. "I'll come to you. What's your address?"

She told him, and then reiterated her plea. "Please, Jack. For my sake and Yasmin's, don't call the police. Things will get so much worse. I know how he operates."

"How do you know who *he* is?"

"I don't. Not for certain. But every fiber in my body is telling me that you just met Farid."

Jack caught his breath. "I'll be at your house in five minutes."

"Okay. And, Jack?"

"Yeah?"

"There's an awful lot you don't know."

"I gathered that," he said, and hurried out the door.

CHAPTER 4

J ack's SUV skidded to a stop in the driveway outside Zahra's town house. Theo Knight pulled up right behind him.

He'd called Theo on the way over and told him to come. Theo was Jack's best friend, bartender, therapist, confidant, and sometime investigator. He was also a former client, a onetime gangbanger who easily could have ended up dead on the streets of Overtown or Liberty City. Instead he landed on death row for a murder he didn't commit. Jack literally saved his life. Theo was forever trying to return the favor. A case like this one—where the threat of physical injury was real—offered the perfect opportunity. Theo was six foot six and two hundred and fifty pounds of pure badass. Nowhere would Jack find a more loyal or capable bodyguard.

"You okay, bro?" asked Theo as they walked up the sidewalk.

"I'm fine. Got blindsided by some amateur trying to scare me."

"Every punk I met on death row was a fucking amateur."

Jack took his point. Zahra opened the door on the first knock. Jack introduced Theo, after which Zahra politely drew their attention to the mat beside the door, where both Zahra and her daughter kept their shoes.

"I normally offer slippers to guests," she said, "but not in his size."

"We're fine," said Jack, and they removed their shoes.

She led them through the small living room, and they sat at a round table in the dining area. Two court filings lay on the table side by side. Both were petitions under the Hague Convention and the International Child Abduction Remedies Act. One was captioned "John Doe v. Jane Doe" and marked FILED UNDER SEAL. The other was captioned "Farid Bazzi v. Zahra Bazzi," with no indication of being under seal. It was plainly marked AMENDED PETITION.

"Where did the amended petition come from?" asked Jack.

"The babysitter gave it to me. She said it was delivered while I was at your office."

Now that he was officially Zahra's attorney, he was free to review the petitions, sealed or not. Zahra made coffee while he compared the two filings. When she returned with three cups, he was ready to talk.

"Farid has completely changed strategies," said Jack.

"Obviously," said Zahra. "I'm the respondent, not Ava."

"I mean *completely*," said Jack. "Ava is not even mentioned in the amended petition."

"Why didn't he file that petition in the first place?"

Jack flipped to the last page of each petition, the attorneys' signature block. They were different.

"For one, he has a new lawyer. My guess is that Farid's first lawyer thought you would capitulate and hand over the child rather than try to defend the fact that you've been pretending to be Ava for the last year."

"I told you why I did that."

"It's still a crime. The key point is that after you hired me, Farid knew you weren't going to surrender."

"Trust me," said Theo, chiming in, "Jack doesn't wave white flags."

"Neither does Farid's new lawyer," said Jack. "Farid definitely traded up. He's found someone who can go blow for blow, the full fifteen rounds, Farid versus Zahra."

"And now the case is all about me, not Ava."

"Just like my attacker said it would be," said Jack.

"Which is another reason I think your attacker was Farid," said Zahra.

"That's possible," said Jack.

"Who else could it be?"

"It depends on what the guy meant by his threat, 'If you make this case about what happened to Ava, someone is going to get hurt.' If 'what happened to Ava' means what happened after she was arrested, then he could be some operative hired by the Iranian government to make sure no questions about Ava's disappearance are reopened."

"Maybe it was the Iranians who hired his new lawyer, too," said Theo.

"But if 'what happened to Ava' means what happened while she was married to Farid, then they are dealing with something very different. It might be Farid, and he doesn't want this case to be about the abuse he inflicted on your sister."

Zahra drank her coffee, but she was unconvinced. "Farid is a bully and an abuser. It was him."

"And yet you told me not to call the police."

"As I also told you, I know how Farid operates. If you hit him once, he hits you three times. If we call the police, there's no telling what he might do."

"I understand. But my issue with what you're telling me now is that you weren't honest with me in my office."

"I told you the truth."

"Not the whole truth. You led me to believe Farid's abuse was purely verbal. Nothing physical."

Zahra placed her cup in the saucer, and Jack noticed that it rattled a bit.

"I . . . I was afraid," she said softly. "I've always been afraid."

"I get that," said Jack. "I really do. But I have to ask the questions that Farid's lawyer might ask you in court: Why would an intelligent, beautiful, clear-thinking woman like you marry Farid if you knew he physically abused his first wife—your own sister?"

The sound of little footsteps emerged from the stairwell, and Yasmin entered the room. She hurried to Zahra and whispered, "Can I have a juice box, Mommy?"

Zahra hugged her, then looked across the table. "Does this answer your question, Jack?"

Jack replied with a sad, thin smile. Then he caught Yasmin's eye. "How old are you, Yasmin?"

"This many," she said, holding up six fingers.

"I have a daughter. Her name is Righley. She's this many," he said, holding up eight.

Yasmin smiled, then was suddenly bashful. She buried her face in Zahra's lap.

"No juice," said Zahra. "It's bedtime. I'll bring you water in a minute, Zahra. Now, say good night and go back to bed."

"Good night," Yasmin said softly, and scurried back up the stairs.

Jack's question had been answered, but Zahra laid it out even more plainly.

"I married Farid because I knew Ava was never coming back. She's dead. How could I leave that precious child alone with him?"

"That makes sense," said Jack. "I get why you married him. But why did Farid marry you? What did you say—'Hey, Farid, let's pick up where we left off when we were dating?'"

"It's more complicated than that," said Zahra. "Let me show you something."

She walked across the room to a black lacquer wall unit, pulled a framed photograph from the shelf, and handed it to Jack.

Jack looked at it carefully. "Is this you?"

"No. That's Ava."

Jack handed it to Theo, who did a double take. "You two could have been twins."

"Everybody says that," said Zahra.

"But you told me in my office that Ava was 'the pretty one.' You look just like her."

"Ava was the one everybody liked. It was her personality. Her sparkle. That's what made her 'the pretty one.'"

Theo handed the photograph back to Zahra, who laid it on the table.

"So, I have a little girl waiting on a cup of water," she said. "Are we agreed, no police?"

"I'll respect your choice," said Jack. "But I'm still concerned about your safety, staying here."

"There's always my place," said Theo.

"Excuse me?" said Zahra.

"I meant the apartment above my club," said Theo.

"Theo owns a jazz bar in Coconut Grove," added Jack.

"It's called Cy's Place," said Theo. "My great-uncle Cy used to live in the apartment above it. He's in his nineties now, and the stairs got to be too much for him. I live right across the hall."

"In other words, it's safe," said Jack.

"Thank you, but I'm not moving my daughter into an apartment above a bar."

"Fair enough," said Jack. "But Theo as your bodyguard is not a bad idea."

"I thought I was *your* bodyguard," said Theo.

"I'm married to an FBI agent who can shoot the cap off a Coke bottle from fifty yards away. I'll survive."

"I don't need a bodyguard," said Zahra.

"Two minutes ago, you told me Farid is a bully and an abuser."

"Okay, fine. If Farid and the Revolutionary Guard come crashing in here and take us hostage, I keep a spare key in the bird feeder on the back patio. You and Theo can come save us."

Jack didn't respond. She wasn't the first overstressed client to snap at him.

"I'm so sorry," said Zahra after taking a deep breath. "I know you're just trying to help."

"No apology needed," said Jack. "Actually, protection is only part of my thinking. This is going to be a difficult case. The legal hurdles for a mother accused of kidnapping her child are very high. We have to prove in court that returning Yasmin to her father would put her in grave danger of physical or psychological harm. And we have to prove it by 'clear and convincing evidence,' which is very close to the 'reasonable doubt' standard in criminal court."

"I can prove it," said Zahra. "Both physical and psychological. And it will be clear and convincing."

"Proof requires evidence," said Jack.

"Isn't my own testimony 'evidence'?"

"It will be your word against his," said Jack. "In any case of 'he said/she said,' you look for any little thing that can tip the balance. If Theo stays close to you and sees Farid stalking you outside your house or following you to the grocery store, he could be the witness at the hearing who tips the balance in your favor."

"I'll think about it," said Zahra.

Yasmin's little voice carried down the stairwell: "Mommy, are you bringing my juice?"

"On my way, sweetie," Zahra answered in a loud enough voice. "And I said water, not juice."

Jack and Theo walked with her to the foyer, and she opened the door.

"I'm going to be perfectly honest with you," said Jack. "I came here thinking I would probably have to tell you 'I'm out'—that you need to hire a new lawyer."

"Because you got roughed up?"

The whole truth was bigger than that: because he was roughed up, *and* because Andie wouldn't approve. "Yeah," he said. "Because I was roughed up."

"I'm glad you changed your mind."

"Mommy! My water!"

Jack glanced up the stairway toward Yasmin's bedroom. "I didn't change my mind. She changed it for me."

Zahra's big dark eyes shone with gratitude. Jack and Theo put their shoes on and stepped out, and the door closed behind them.

CHAPTER 5

Jack's first step as Zahra's lawyer was a Thursday-morning videoconference with the US Department of State, Office of Children's Issues, the central authority charged with the implementation of the Hague Convention in the United States.

Jack was at his desk in Miami. The real-time images of two division chiefs were on his split computer screen: Cheryl Comstock, Europe Abductions and Prevention, covering the UK; and Ben Davis, Eastern Hemisphere, covering Iran.

Jack began by sharing the key allegations in the amended petition, but Comstock interrupted. A Harvard-educated lawyer with salt-and-pepper hair and the discerning gaze of a powerful intellect, she looked to Jack more like a federal judge than a bureaucrat who'd spent her entire career on the ninth floor of the State Department.

"Chief Davis and I are intimately familiar with your client's case," said Comstock. "No need to brief us."

"Then I'll get right to the point," said Jack. "I intend to file an immediate motion asking the court to dismiss Mr. Bazzi's petition under the Hague Convention."

"What is the ground for dismissal?"

"Farid Bazzi is an Iranian citizen. Iran is not a signatory to the Hague Convention. There's no basis for him to bring this action under the convention."

Comstock showed no reaction. "What are you asking us to do?"

"Respectfully, I want the State Department to join in my motion and support my position."

"Is that the only purpose of this conference?"

"Yes."

"Then it's going to be a very short one. The answer is no."

Jack waited for her to say more, but she didn't. "May I ask why?"

"Before a foreign parent can file a petition in US court, he is required to file an application in the country of the child's habitual place of residence. Mr. Bazzi filed his Hague application in the United Kingdom."

"How?" asked Jack. "He's Iranian."

"Farid and his family lived in London under the UK Entrepreneur visa program. They lost their visa when his business failed, but Farid reapplied for British citizenship for himself and his daughter."

"Don't you see that as a clever legal maneuver to get around the fact that he's an Iranian citizen, with no rights under the Hague Convention?"

"The UK accepted his Hague application. That's their prerogative. As far as the US State Department is concerned, that's the end of the story."

Jack was not so naive as to think that politics didn't play a role. "I'm betting there's much more to it."

"We don't care to hear your speculation, Mr. Swyteck."

"Let me ask you this. I've been told that the State Department helped Mr. Bazzi find my client in Miami. Is that true?"

Jack was only half bluffing, having heard no specifics about the Bazzi case, but his mandatory Hague training had opened his eyes to the State Department's role in tracking down abused mothers accused of abducting their own children.

"I can't comment on this specific case, but that is an accommodation this office sometimes provides."

"Is it also true that you helped find Mr. Bazzi a new lawyer to file the amended petition?"

"Again, I can't comment on specific cases."

"I'll take that as a yes."

"Mr. Swyteck, just so you understand—the State Department takes a neutral position in suits under the Hague Convention."

"Neutral? It says right on your website that the State Department is 'a leader in US government efforts to prevent international parent child abduction.'"

Comstock remained composed, but her voice took on an edge. "Yes, and it can't be any other way. If the US fails to return children to a foreign country, then parents in the US will have a hard time getting their children back when they are abducted and taken abroad. Surely you can understand that."

Jack did. But he was also getting a taste of how, behind the scenes, the State Department stacked the deck against the abducting parent—even when she was an abused spouse. The original purpose of his call was a lost cause, but he needed to know how firmly the State Department was in Farid's camp.

"I want you to be aware that, as part of my client's case, I intend to prove that Farid Bazzi is an abuser," Jack said. "He was abusive to both Zahra Bazzi and her sister, Ava, before she disappeared."

Comstock showed no reaction, but Jack's words drew obvious concern from the division chief for the Eastern Hemisphere. Davis was a former US marine with the haircut of an enlisted man and the no-nonsense demeanor of a career officer.

"Let me offer you some friendly advice on that point," said Davis. "Perhaps friendlier than it would be if you were not Governor Swyteck's son."

"I'm listening."

"Ava Bazzi disappeared at a very low point in US-Iranian relations."

"That sounds like a very sanitized way of saying that she was one of over five hundred Iranians who were killed or disappeared for voicing their opposition to the hijab laws."

Davis continued, unfazed by Jack's point. "Since then, the State Department and the Iranian government have made important diplomatic advances. The most obvious was the disbanding of the clerical police. But there are other issues on the table being negotiated, not all related to human rights. In fact, there are very important negotiations underway at this very moment, which we are of course unable to discuss with you."

"What are you telling me?"

"The official position of the Iranian government is that Ava Bazzi escaped from jail in Tehran, fled the country, and is now living in the West."

"What is the State Department's position?" asked Jack.

"The State Department has never taken an official position."

"That's shameful."

"Your opinion is not germane to my point."

"What is your point?"

"Given the active and delicate diplomatic negotiations currently at stake here, right now would be a very inopportune time to resurrect the question of whether Ava Bazzi was among those killed by the clerical police."

Jack was taken aback. "Are you asking me to present my client's case in a way that does not conflict with the official position of the Iranian government?"

"No," said Davis. "I'm simply pointing out that what happened to Ava Bazzi during her marriage to Farid Bazzi is one thing. What happened to her after she was arrested by the clerical police is quite another. If you were to try to inject the latter into your case, it would be . . . shall we say, unfortunate."

It was eerily reminiscent of the threat from Jack's attacker: *If you make this case about what happened to Ava, someone is going to get hurt.* Jack had promised Zahra not to involve the police, but he had to call out this "coincidence."

"This doesn't sit well," he said.

"Excuse me?"

"Last night I hired a bodyguard to keep my client safe. Some thug put a knife to my throat and threatened me. Now I'm hearing the exact same message from the State Department."

"I hardly see the parallel," said Davis. "But I can assure you that we had nothing to do with any threats or thuggery."

It was a little like talking to Andie; or perhaps it was proof of Andie's point. *Really, Jack? A federal conspiracy under every rock?*

"I'll accept that," said Jack. "But let me be clear: I'm going to prove whatever I damn well need to prove to keep my client and her daughter together."

"I'm sorry you feel that way," said Davis.

"At the risk of sounding like an echo"—Jack deliberately used the director's own words—"your opinion is not germane."

He said goodbye and, with the click of a mouse, ended the video-conference.

CHAPTER 6

Jack and Zahra's first court appearance was Monday morning. Their troubles began on the courthouse steps. Dozens of demonstrators had gathered outside the Miami federal courthouse to protest the Iranian government's human rights abuses.

"Women, life, freedom!" they chanted in unison, the English translation of the Iranian rallying cry. Both men and women were among the demonstrators, but the women were more vocal. Some used megaphones. Others brandished posters that read WHERE IS AVA BAZZI?

Jack's advice to his client had been more like a firm warning: turning the case of *Farid Bazzi v. Zahra Bazzi* into a media circus about Ava Bazzi was not in the best interest of a six-year-old child. Over the weekend, he had ignored all inquiries from reporters, avoided social media, and done nothing to stimulate media interest. It was to no avail. Interest was both national and international. News vans were lined up on the street, one after another. Camera crews and reporters followed Jack and his client through the crowd, up the granite steps, and through the *whomp-whomp* of the revolving entrance doors. Cameras were not allowed in the federal courthouse, but reporters continued to pepper Jack and his client with questions all the way to the elevator.

Zahra, is your sister alive or dead?

Why did you use Ava's name?

What have you told your niece?

The elevator doors closed, shutting out the commotion. They rode in silence for a moment, but Jack had to ask the obvious question.

"Was this your doing?" he asked. "The protests. The media."

Zahra seemed surprised by his question. "You do realize that this is not just about Ava, don't you?"

"Obviously, it's also about you."

"No, no, no. Jack, hundreds of people, mostly women, were killed or disappeared during the hijab protests. Less than a handful of those murders got international attention. This lawsuit is a chance to shine a spotlight on the regime's crimes against its own people. Against humanity."

Jack felt like his eyes had finally opened. "So, when those demonstrators ask, 'Where is Ava Bazzi,' they are asking—"

"They're asking, Where is my niece? Where is my sister? Where is my daughter?"

The case had been assigned to US district judge Samuel Carlton, one of the more senior judges, a grandfather many times over. A crowd had already gathered outside his courtroom on the eighth floor, which indicated to Jack that all public seating in the gallery was taken.

The judge's bailiff stopped Jack and Zahra the moment they stepped out of the elevator. "Judge Carlton would like to see the lawyers in his chambers," she said.

Jack was there for a pretrial conference, which judges normally held in the courtroom, open to the public. Jack wondered if it was his opposing counsel who had requested that this one take place behind closed doors. He and Zahra followed the bailiff around the corner to the secure entrance to Judge Carlton's chambers. The bailiff entered the security code on the keypad, unlocked the heavy door, and led Jack and Zahra inside. Zahra was directed to a small office near the library and told to wait there. The bailiff led Jack to the larger office at the end of the hallway, where Judge Carlton was seated behind his desk. He was wearing his black judicial robe, and the court reporter was present, even though they were not in the courtroom.

"Come in, Mr. Swyteck," said the judge.

Jack's opposing counsel was standing before the judge's desk but slightly to the right of center. Heather Beech was one of the top family lawyers in Miami, a woman who'd made a name for herself defending only men in divorce proceedings. Even in heels, she was barely five feet tall, but she'd slain many a giant in her spectacular career.

Jack approached the judge's desk and stood slightly to the left, leaving a comfortable distance between himself and Beech.

"Most federal judges have no experience in family law," said Judge Carlton. "I, on the other hand, was in the family division for five years as a state court judge. One thing I learned right off the bat is that some things are better addressed to the lawyers, without the husband and wife clawing at each other. Make sense?"

The lawyers agreed.

"I also don't like to admonish lawyers in front of their clients." He was looking at Jack, which required a response of some kind.

"Admonish for what, Your Honor?" asked Jack.

"I am directing my remarks to both sides," the judge said—but still he was looking only at Jack. "If you or your client alerted the media and encouraged demonstrations outside the courthouse in hopes that anti-Iranian government sentiment would sway the outcome of this proceeding under the Hague Convention, you've made a bad mistake. And it will backfire."

Jack waited for the admonition to go both ways, but that seemed to be the end of it.

"Your Honor, it is my firm commitment to try this case in your courtroom, not in the court of public opinion."

"Mm-hmm," the judge responded.

Smelling blood, Farid's counsel was quick to take advantage of the judge's obvious displeasure with Jack.

"Judge, I didn't want to start this proceeding by attacking my opposing counsel, but there is something I feel compelled to bring to the court's attention."

"Yes, what is it?"

"I understand that Mr. Swyteck has hired an ex-con by the name of Theo Knight to act as his client's bodyguard."

It was a cheap shot, and Jack resented it. "Judge, Mr. Knight is not an 'ex-con.' He spent four years on death row for a crime he didn't commit."

"I'm not here to split hairs," said Beech. "Over the weekend, Mr. Knight had an improper confrontation with my client, during which he physically threatened Mr. Bazzi."

Jack shot his opposing counsel a look of incredulity. "What?"

The judge's gaze fixed on Jack. "Is it true that this Mr. Theo Knight is acting as your client's bodyguard?"

"Yes, Your Honor. And with good reason. I was assaulted outside my office ten minutes after my first meeting with my client, and I feared my client might be next."

"Assaulted? Did you report this to the police?" asked the judge.

"No, Your Honor. My client didn't want to escalate matters and asked me not to."

Beech chuckled. "Judge, even if this unreported 'assault' on Mr. Swyteck actually happened, that doesn't justify hiring a thug like Theo Knight to retaliate against my client."

The judge threw up his hands. "All right, both of you. I don't take allegations of physical assault against lawyers or litigants lightly. But it only reinforces my original point. This proceeding will be resolved on the merits, not driven by sensational headlines and public demonstrations. Am I understood?"

"Yes," the lawyers said in unison, but Jack sensed that he was the principal target of the judge's ire. Beech apparently had the same impression, and she acted on it.

"Your Honor, my fear is that the longer this case drags on, the worse these external distractions will become. I would like to propose a way to streamline matters."

"I'm listening," said the judge.

"We all agree that a mother accused of abducting her child has a limited number of defenses under the Hague Convention," said Beech.

"Yes, agreed," said Jack. "And we intend to prove them."

"Not so fast," said Beech. "I think we can also agree that none of those defenses applies if Zahra Bazzi was never the lawful wife of Farid Bazzi."

"Judge, my client has a certified copy of the marriage certificate," said Jack.

"That certificate is worthless," said Beech. "We can prove that Mr. Bazzi was induced to marry Zahra Bazzi under false and fraudulent pretenses, which renders the marriage void."

"What pretenses?" asked the judge.

"We will prove that Ms. Bazzi planned this abduction from the very beginning. She married Mr. Bazzi as part of a premeditated plan to become his wife, to become Yasmin's adoptive mother with rights of custody, and then to flee the country with Mr. Bazzi's daughter. This was all a fraud."

"How do you intend to prove it?" the judge asked.

"That's the beauty of my proposal, Judge. If the court proceeds in the usual fashion, we will surely hear days and days of testimony about Ms. Bazzi's supposed defenses under the Hague Convention. It will be a tsunami of baseless accusations of physical and psychological abuse. Or, the court can accept my proposal and wrap this up in one day with one witness who has agreed to appear by videoconference from Iran."

"Who is your one witness?"

She glanced at Jack smugly, then back at the judge. "The imam who performed the wedding ceremony."

"Judge, we object," said Jack.

"On what ground?"

"For one, any communications Ms. Bazzi may have had with her imam are protected by the ecclesiastical privilege. That privilege is well established in the Judeo-Christian tradition, but it is no less applicable to communications between Muslims and their imams."

"Judge, the imam's testimony will not be based on confidential communications. It will be based on indisputable facts."

"We still object," said Jack. "My client has the right to put up evidence in support of her defense and create a record."

"I'm aware of everyone's rights," the judge said. "But I remind you that this court has great flexibility in deciding how to conduct proceedings under the Hague Convention. This is not a traditional trial governed by rules of evidence and procedure."

"These are ambush tactics," said Jack. "Even if the ecclesiastical privilege does not apply, my objection is grounded in simple fairness."

"There's nothing inherently unfair about streamlining this proceeding so that each side can address a single issue that is dispositive of the case," the judge said.

Jack did not back down. "Ms. Beech has raised a new issue that was not included in Mr. Bazzi's petition, and it involves a new witness. I need adequate time to prepare."

"I'll allow everyone adequate time," said the judge. "Ms. Beech, how soon can you be ready to proceed?"

"We're ready to start today, Judge."

"Judge—"

"Don't get excited, Mr. Swyteck. We're not starting today."

"Thank you," said Jack.

"My ruling is as follows," the judge said, as if speaking from the bench. "Day one of testimony and evidence will be limited to a single issue: whether Zahra Bazzi induced Farid Bazzi to marry under false pretenses and solely for the purpose of establishing custody rights as Yasmin's adoptive parent. Mr. Swyteck, how much time do you need to prepare?"

"I'd like a week, Your Honor."

"You can have a day. I will see you all in my courtroom tomorrow morning at nine a.m."

"Tomorrow?" said Jack.

"Better than today, Mr. Swyteck."

There was no bang of the gavel, but it was clear enough that the session had ended.

"Thank you, Your Honor," said Beech.

Jack said nothing. The judicial assistant opened the door, and Jack was the first to leave the room. He wasn't angry. He was simply in a rush to speak with his client.

And then with Theo.

CHAPTER 7

Jack went straight from the courthouse to Theo's club in the heart of Coconut Grove. Cy's Place didn't open until noon, but Theo was already at work behind the bar, preparing for the lunch hour. Jack took a seat on a cushioned barstool.

"What're you drinking?" asked Theo, wiping down the bar top.

Even when empty, Cy's Place oozed that certain vibe of a jazz-loving crowd. Creaky wood floors, redbrick walls, and high ceilings were the perfect bones for Theo's club. Art nouveau chandeliers cast just the right mood lighting. Crowded café tables fronted a small stage for live music.

Cy's Place was special for Jack, and not just because it was the club Theo had told his lawyer he would own someday, if ever he got off death row. At the grand opening, on a pair of barstools that drew closer together as the night wore on, sparks had begun to fly for Jack and FBI agent Andie Henning. They'd talked and laughed till 2:00 a.m., listening to Theo's Uncle Cy give them a taste of Miami's old Overtown Village through his saxophone. A few months later, beneath a banner announcing THE SECOND ANNIVERSARY OF JACK'S 39TH BIRTHDAY, Jack had popped the question.

It seemed like yesterday; it seemed like so long ago.

"Just water," said Jack.

Theo reached for a water glass, and Jack popped a question of a different sort.

"Dude, did you forget to tell me about a little encounter you had with Zahra's ex-husband this weekend?"

Theo placed the water glass on a coaster and smiled thinly. "I don't think Farid will be bothering you anymore."

"Damn it," Jack said, groaning. "Your little stunt blew up in front of the judge this morning. Please tell me you didn't hunt this guy down."

"Nope. He came by the club last night. Sat right where you are and drank a glass of mango juice, neat."

"Came here why? And how'd you even know it was him?"

"He introduced himself. And obviously he didn't come for the mango juice."

Jack drank his water. "What did he say?"

"He said he knew someone jumped you outside your office, and he knew I was Zahra's bodyguard. How he knew all those things I don't know."

Jack had told no one but the State Department, which sent his mind racing. But he brought himself back to Theo.

"Why would he tell you that?"

Theo shrugged. "I assumed it was his way of saying he knows everything. His way of intimidating Zahra and making her feel like she'll never be safe—he can always find her. I just kept the whole thing to myself so she didn't get all freaked out."

"Are you saying that was the end of the matter?"

"Well, not exactly. When he got up and went to the men's room, I followed him."

"Into the men's room?"

"Yeah. I kinda locked the door."

"Oh boy," said Jack. "Do I want to hear this?"

"I set him straight."

"Theo, what did you do?"

"Didn't have to do nothin'. He was scared shitless."

"What'd you say to him?"

"I told him there's two things I hate more than anything in this world: men who abuse their wives and kids, and men who show up at my best friend's law office and threaten him. Then he just started blabbering."

"Blabbering what?"

"He said he didn't come into my club to intimidate Zahra or anybody else. Said he never abused Ava, Zahra, or his daughter. He even denied he roughed you up outside your office."

"Of course he denied it," said Jack. "Abusers always do."

"That was my reaction too. At first."

"Do you have some other impression now?"

"I've seen a lotta punks so scared they'll say anything. You grow up on the street, you kinda develop a knack for telling when they're feeding you bullshit and when they're not."

"What's your take?" asked Jack.

Theo's expression turned very serious. "I'm not sure Farid's lying."

Andie walked down the hall to the kitchen for coffee, but she found cake. It was the tenth anniversary of the opening of the FBI's state-of-the-art field office, which of course called for sheet cake with red, white, and blue icing. One sheet cake for one thousand employees in a 330,000-square-foot facility situated on twenty acres. First come, first served. Andie had never known the old field office, so she only grabbed coffee and left the cake for the more deserving agents and staff who'd endured the month-long move from North Miami Beach.

"Henning, I need you," her ASAC said. He'd come to the kitchen for cake and found Andie. She followed him out.

Todd Tidwell was the newest assistant agent in charge, one of three in south Florida, having transferred from the Chicago office, which had reportedly celebrated with *two* sheet cakes upon his departure. Andie was doing her best to get used to his style, which included annoying little things like walking ahead of Andie, not with her, to his office, as if he were King Charles and she were Camilla.

Tidwell closed the door and told her to pull up a chair for a video-conference. A man and a woman appeared on the forty-inch LCD screen on the wall. Tidwell introduced Andie to division directors Comstock and

Davis from the State Department. Davis, director for the Eastern Hemisphere, did the talking.

"Agent Henning, we had a videoconference with your husband yesterday."

Andie was taken aback. It would have been nice to have a heads-up from her ASAC that this was about Jack, but she rolled with it. "Oh? Jack didn't mention it."

"How much do you know about his case under the Hague Convention for Zahra Bazzi?"

She assumed the division chief had no idea that the question of what Andie knew or should know about Jack's cases had landed them in marriage counseling. "I know very generally that Jack is trying to stop an abusive husband from using the US court system to take a little girl away from her mother."

"Two years ago," said Davis, "Zahra's sister, Ava Bazzi, disappeared after Iran's morality police arrested her at a hijab protest. The Iranian government says she escaped and is still alive."

"Others say she was murdered by the morality police," said Andie. "I do follow the news."

"As we explained to your husband, Ava Bazzi's disappearance is a very sensitive issue right now in US-Iranian diplomatic relations. It would be most unfortunate if Zahra Bazzi's Hague proceeding turned into a political football about Ava Bazzi."

"What did Jack say?"

"He hung up on us."

Andie's heart sank. "Maybe you got disconnected."

"No. He told us that our opinions don't matter, and he hung up."

Andie's gaze was fixed on the LCD screen, but she could almost feel the look of disapproval from her ASAC. She suddenly felt the need for damage control.

"Director Davis, all I can tell you is that Jack is a good lawyer. He wouldn't inject Ava Bazzi into Zahra's case just to make trouble or grab headlines."

"It's already an issue. There were protests outside the federal courthouse this morning. The Iranian government's fear is that Ava Bazzi is becoming a launchpad to revive international outrage over thousands of other arrests that, for whatever reason, the world simply stopped talking about. Media coverage so far indicates that the demonstrators' strategy is working."

"I'm having a hard time seeing how international awareness of government oppression is a bad thing," said Andie.

"It's not. You're missing the point. Every movement needs a face. If your husband's case makes Ava Bazzi that face, the Iranians are going to hold us accountable. Our negotiations with the Iranians will be dead in the water."

"I'm sure your negotiations are very important," said Andie. "But it might help me understand things better if you could tell me something about them."

There was complete silence, which left Andie feeling less than convinced.

"Look," said Andie, "just because the demonstrators and the media are making Ava Bazzi the face of a new wave of opposition to the Iranian regime doesn't mean Jack will make his case about Ava Bazzi."

"It's unavoidable," said Davis. "The State Department has been in communication with lawyers for both sides. Farid Bazzi's lawyer has a silver bullet argument that Zahra has no rights under the Hague Convention because her marriage to Farid was a fraud. It could end the case on day one. But if the judge doesn't buy the argument, or if he defers ruling on it and the case moves forward, Farid's lawyer has made it crystal clear that Farid intends to prove that Ava Bazzi is alive."

"Why would he do that?" asked Andie.

"Perhaps to curry sympathy with the judge by showing that Ava Bazzi abandoned her husband and their daughter. Perhaps to curry the support of the Iranian government by taking a position that is consistent with the official position of the Iranian regime."

"Or maybe the Iranian government is forcing Farid to take that position," said Andie. "Especially in light of today's protests."

"Whatever the reason, this case is on a fast track to becoming a flashpoint in US-Iranian relations," said Davis.

Andie could see where the conversation was leading, and she wasn't comfortable with it. "Have you made that clear to Jack?"

"Yes. To no avail. We thought it would help if he heard it from you."

The response caught in Andie's throat. "I can't tell Jack how to handle his case."

"We understand," said Davis. "And this is not an order. We simply ask that you communicate a message to your husband."

"What message?" she asked with trepidation.

"One, no one will *ever* be able to prove that Tehran's morality police murdered Ava Bazzi. Two, by trying to prove the unprovable, he's only hindering the US government's ability to negotiate."

"Again, I have to ask: Negotiate for what?"

Tidwell spoke up. "Henning, you're not even close to having the level of clearance needed to hear the answer to that question."

The State Department officials seemed put off by the ASAC's ham-handed approach. Davis rephrased it. "Agent Henning, we can assure you of this much: for the sake of your country, it is critically important that you communicate our message to your husband."

Never in her tenure with the bureau had the US government asked Andie to communicate with Jack about an active case. But if it was true that Jack had actually hung up on the State Department, telling them that now was not a particularly good time wasn't going to help matters.

"I'll give it serious consideration," she said, committing to nothing.

I t was after 10:00 p.m., and Jack was still in his office with Zahra.

The mini trial on the threshold issue in the case—the legitimacy of Zahra's marriage to Farid—was less than twelve hours away. They were short on time to prepare. Jack was even shorter on time to provide Zahra with the needed assurance that the American system of justice wasn't stacked in favor of men—at least not to the extent of the Iranian system.

"Do you think the judge will let the imam testify about things I told him in private?" she asked.

"He shouldn't," said Jack. "I made it clear this morning that we will assert the ecclesiastical privilege."

"I didn't ask if he *should* protect my confidences. I'm asking if you think he *will*."

It was a fair question—whether a cranky old federal judge who'd never set foot in a mosque might decide that confidences were somehow entitled to less protection because the religion was something other than his own.

"My expectation is that Judge Carlton will do the right thing," said Jack. "But in case I'm wrong, let me ask you this: Is there anything you told the imam that worries you?"

Zahra took a moment. The moment turned into a minute. The minute dragged on.

"Not that I can think of," she said finally.

Jack arched an eyebrow. "Are you sure?"

There was another pause. "Yes."

"When I was at your house the other night, you indicated that you married Farid to protect Yasmin."

"Is that what you heard me say?" asked Zahra. "You may have misunderstood."

"I'm pretty sure I didn't," said Jack, absolutely certain that he hadn't.

"Whatever you may have heard, all I meant is that I married Farid because a little girl needs a mother. Is that fraud? Is that a marriage under false pretenses? I don't think so. Do you?"

Jack knew spin when he heard it. "Zahra, it's late, so let's take the shine off the penny. Between lawyer and client: If I asked you whether you made the decision to abduct Yasmin and leave Iran before you even married Farid, what would your answer be?"

She dug her car keys from her purse and rose from the chair. "My answer would be, 'Don't ask me that question.'"

Their eyes locked a moment—nothing confrontational, just an understanding between the two of them. Jack laid his notepad aside, choosing not to write anything down.

"Fair enough," he said, rising. "I'll walk you out to your car."

CHAPTER 8

Jack got home very late Monday night. He opened the front door quietly, praying not to set off the alarm and wake Andie, Righley, and the entire neighborhood. The living room was dark, save for the amber glow of the streetlight through the picture window. Their vintage 1950s house had its share of creaky old floorboards, but Jack knew the exact location of each one. Slowly, like a soldier through a minefield, he started across the room, careful not to step on the wrong plank.

"Jack?"

The unexpected voice in the darkness nearly stopped Jack's heart. "Andie?"

She was a silhouette on the couch, wearing her robe and slippers. Their golden retriever was asleep at her feet, too old now to run to the door and greet him the way he used to, back in the day when poor Max must have thought that every time Jack walked out the door he was planning never to return. Jack wasn't sure why Andie had waited up, but her next words were the four most ominous in any relationship.

"We need to talk," she said.

Jack caught his breath and took a seat beside her on the couch. "Now?"

"No, I waited up to tell you we need to talk tomorrow."

"Good point."

She repositioned herself on the couch, putting enough distance between them to face Jack as she spoke. "We agreed that you would cut back on your criminal caseload."

"If this is about Zahra Bazzi, that's not a criminal case."

Andie sighed. "Yes, which is like saying oral sex is not sex. I was called into a videoconference this morning with the State Department."

"About my case?"

"About your case and Zahra's sister, Ava. They told me they had the same meeting with you, so don't play dumb."

Jack connected the dots. "They want you to make sure I don't make my case about the disappearance of Ava Bazzi. Is that it?"

"Okay, before you get up on your 'This is America' soapbox, just calm down and listen to me. I'm not going to tell you how to try your case. I would never do that, any more than you would tell me how to conduct an FBI investigation."

Jack was feeling a little better. "Thank you." He reached for her hand, but she pulled away.

"I'm not finished."

"I'm listening," said Jack.

"A marriage between an FBI agent and a criminal defense lawyer isn't easy."

"No marriage is easy."

"Right. But we agreed in our last session with Dr. Stanger that living our professional lives in information silos, unable to talk to one another about our jobs like a normal husband and wife, wasn't good for our marriage."

"Which is why we agreed to relax the Rule."

"We also agreed that you would shift more toward civil cases, away from criminal. But then right out of the starting block, you take on a high-profile civil case that puts you opposite the US State Department."

"Like I said, this is not a criminal case."

"It's worse. Unlike any criminal case you've ever had, it puts me right in the middle, between you and the US government."

"Are you asking me to drop the case?"

With that question, Jack could see that he'd put his finger on the source of Andie's angst. She couldn't possibly make that ask.

"Without a good lawyer, a six-year-old girl will never see her mother again," said Andie. "Yasmin goes back to Iran to live in the sole custody of an abusive father. What tune would I be whistling if we were talking about Righley, instead of Yasmin?"

"So, you're actually happy I have this case."

She chuckled with exasperation. "No, I'm not *happy*."

"I'm totally confused," said Jack.

"Look at this from my perspective. The rub, as I have always seen it, is that your criminal defense work always put you adverse to law enforcement, adverse to the FBI—to the people I see at work every day. I asked you to cut back on your criminal work. You agreed. And I was so grateful for that. I *thought* I had come up with the solution to our problem."

"It will take time. I can't just drop all my criminal cases."

"Don't drop anything. There's no point."

"Now I'm beyond totally confused."

"This new case proves that my proposed solution accomplishes nothing."

"That's a little hasty, don't you think?"

"No, it's obvious. Getting ambushed by the State Department was the realization of my worst nightmare. Don't you see what that tells us, Jack?"

"It tells us that your solution didn't work in this case. But the verdict is still out. It could still be a good solution."

"No, Jack," she said, breathing out the words. "It tells us there is no solution."

Jack felt chills. "What are you saying, Andie?"

Her eyes glistened, and even in the dim lighting, Jack could see that she was on the verge of tears.

"That makes me so sad, Jack. Really sad—for us."

Jack struggled to sound positive. "Hey, come on now. This is us. We can work this out."

"I've tried so hard."

"Let's talk about this."

"I'm exhausted."

"Let's talk it out with Dr. Laura," he said, alluding to the radio talk show host.

She tried to smile. "Dr. Stanger."

"Yes. Dr. Stanger. I'll even make the appointment."

"Let me sleep on it." She rose and started across the room, but she wasn't headed toward the master bedroom. She stopped at the entrance to the kitchen, then turned.

"Good night, Jack."

Jack heard the scuff of her slippers on the floor as she continued down the hall to Righley's room. Max finally woke and immediately looked for Andie.

"Et tu, Brute?" asked Jack.

Max just wagged his tail, as if everything he did was an act of love, then followed Andie's trail into the bedroom.

And the door closed.

CHAPTER 9

At 9:00 a.m., Jack and his client were in Judge Carlton's courtroom, as ready as they could be for the promised witness: the presiding imam from Zahra and Farid's wedding ceremony.

The courtroom was packed, and the scene outside the courthouse had confirmed exactly what Zahra told Jack about activists using Ava as a launching pad for broad opposition to the Iranian regime. A few demonstrators held signs asking, WHERE IS AVA BAZZI? But there were many others. FREE NILOUFAR HAMEDI, referring to the woman journalist who was sentenced to six years in prison for writing about the funeral of a hijab protester. REMEMBER ARMITA GERVAND, for a teenage girl beaten to death by the morality police on the subway for not wearing a head covering. DEATH TO THE DICTATOR. The crowds were not just for Ava. Nor was the media coverage. Inside the courtroom, more than a dozen journalists filled the first two rows of public seating. Behind them sat many of the same demonstrators Jack had seen outside the courthouse, their voices silenced not by the Iranian regime they denounced but by courtroom etiquette. A large LCD screen was off to one side, positioned so that the judge, lawyers, and spectators had a clear view of the witness's virtual appearance. The screen was black.

Farid's counsel rose. "Your Honor, I have some unfortunate news," said Beech. "We've just been informed that the witness is unavailable at this time."

"When will he be available?"

"We're not sure."

"What's the reason for his sudden unavailability?"

"I don't have that information."

The judge was openly annoyed. "Ms. Beech, your client is the petitioner in this proceeding. Leading off with the imam was *your* idea, so you have a binary choice to make. Call your first witness, whoever that may be. Or dismiss your case."

"Your Honor, we have a replacement witness who is available to testify via videoconference."

Jack smelled a rat. "Your Honor, Ms. Beech is trying to pull the courtroom equivalent of a bait and switch. We scrambled on short notice to prepare for the testimony of the imam, and now the petitioner wants to call a surprise witness."

"It appears that my esteemed opposing counsel hasn't handled many Hague proceedings." Beech's tone was condescending. "Surprise witnesses are the norm. They appear live in court, by videoconference, by telephone, by videotaped deposition, by written affidavits, by handwritten letters to the judge, and in every other conceivable manner."

Jack was reminded of his earliest court appearances, right out of law school, when prosecutors seemed to think there was some tactical advantage to calling him out as a newbie to death penalty cases. It always backfired.

"Judge, I fully understand that this is not a trial governed by the federal rules. But unless Ms. Beech is representing herself as having learned of the imam's unavailability literally fifteen seconds ago, the simple courtesy of a heads-up would have been nice."

"Let's move on," said the judge. "Mr. Swyteck, make whatever objections you deem necessary. Ms. Beech, call your witness."

"The petitioner calls Sasan Sherif, MD."

Jack checked with his client, but she had no idea who Sherif was.

An English/Farsi translator took a seat in the witness stand. The screen flickered, and the image of the witness appeared. The blurred background gave no clue as to Dr. Sherif's actual location, but he was wearing a white doctor's coat, which led Jack to guess either a hospital or other medical facility. His hair was jet-black, but his beard was a more natural-looking salt-and-pepper mix. The oath was through the translator, as were the questions and answers, beginning with his occupation, which explained the white coat.

"I am the head medical examiner for Tehran Province, which includes the city of Tehran."

"How long have you held that position?"

"Five years, approximately."

The witness described his duties, which were like those of any medical examiner in a major metropolis.

"Dr. Sherif," said Beech, "under what circumstances does the medical examiner's office receive a body for examination?"

"When unnatural or suspicious circumstances surround the cause of death, or if the deceased is the victim of a crime or accident."

"Do your duties as medical examiner include the issuance of death certificates?"

"Yes."

"Has your office ever issued a certificate of death for Ava Bazzi, whose next of kin include a husband, Mr. Farid Bazzi, and a daughter, Yasmin Bazzi?"

Jack jumped to his feet. Farid and his counsel had apparently moved past their initial strategy of proving that Zahra had no rights under the Hague Convention because her marriage to Farid was a fraud. The separate question of whether Ava was alive or dead was irrelevant to the fraud argument. For whatever reason, Farid's new witness would utter in a court of law the very same position the Iranian government had asserted in the court of public opinion: that Ava Bazzi was still alive.

"Objection, Your Honor. Ava Bazzi has nothing to do with this proceeding."

"Judge, the relevance will become quickly apparent," said Beech.

"Make it very quick," said the judge. "The witness may answer."

The translator delivered the response. "No, the Tehran medical examiner's office has never issued a death certificate for Ava Bazzi."

"Am I correct that your medical office is located in the same province as the Tehran prison, where Ms. Ava Bazzi was jailed?"

A demonstrator shouted something in Farsi from the back of the courtroom, which drew the crack of the judge's gavel and a stern warning.

"Order! Any further outbursts will result in immediate removal from this courtroom. Ms. Beech, I'll give you two more questions to wrap this up."

"I need only one. Dr. Sherif, at any time, was the body of Ava Bazzi brought to your office for examination, from the Tehran prison or from anywhere else?"

"No. Never."

"I have no further questions," said Beech.

"Mr. Swyteck, do you have any cross-examination?"

"No, Your Honor. I move to strike this witness's testimony as completely irrelevant to this proceeding."

The judge seemed to agree. "Ms. Beech, you promised that the relevance would be quickly apparent. I must be missing something."

"Judge, even if we assume the marriage was valid, Zahra Bazzi became a stepmother. As stepmother, she has no rights of custody over Farid's daughter, Yasmin. That's the law of Iran. It's even the law of Florida. If she has no custody rights, she has no right to assert any defenses to child abduction under the Hague Convention. The case is over."

Jack was fully prepared on that point of law. "Your Honor, we concede that my client is not the biological mother. But in the eyes of the law, she is more than a stepmother. She formally and legally *adopted* Yasmin. An adoptive mother has the full legal rights of a biological mother."

The judge grimaced. "I still don't see how any of this makes the testimony of an Iranian coroner relevant to this proceeding."

"Nor do I," said Jack.

"It's really quite simple," said Beech. "Under Iranian law, if both biological parents are still alive, a stepparent's adoption of a stepchild is not valid unless *both* biological parents consent. As the medical examiner just testified, there is no evidence that Ava is dead. In the eyes of the law, Ava is a living biological parent of Yasmin who never consented to Zahra's adoption of Yasmin. Without Ava's consent, it is irrelevant whether Farid consented to the adoption or if his consent was obtained by Zahra's fraud. By itself, Ava's lack of consent renders the adoption invalid, which means that Zahra has no custody rights to Yasmin. As between Farid and Zahra, the court must order Yasmin's return to Farid."

The judge seemed impressed. "Ms. Beech, I give you points for creativity. Mr. Swyteck, what's your response?"

Jack wasn't aching to turn a courtroom battle into all-out war against the Iranian government, not to mention the US State Department. But Farid's "creative" new strategy made the nuclear option his only option.

"Your Honor, if this court allows the testimony of this witness to stand, you will have opened Pandora's box. I will have no choice but to present any and all evidence I can find to prove one point: Ava Bazzi is dead. More specifically, she was murdered by the Iranian government."

The courtroom erupted with cheers and applause from the demonstrators, which the judge immediately gaveled down.

"Final warning!" he bellowed. "If there is one more outburst, I will close this entire courtroom to the public."

The courtroom fell silent—so silent that the judge's deep sigh was picked up by the microphone, audible to all.

"Mr. Swyteck, I take your point. I'm not eager to expand the scope of this proceeding."

Beech interjected. "Judge, you are not expanding the proceeding. You are streamlining it. In the absence of any evidence—*any* evidence—that Ava Bazzi is dead, Zahra Bazzi is not a lawful adoptive parent. This case is over."

The judge paused, thinking, then spoke. "This is an important issue. My recollection under Florida law is that the consent of both biological parents is required, if they are both alive. But I'm no expert in Iranian law."

"Judge, it's the same under Iranian law," said Beech.

"You may say so, Counsel. But I don't know that for a fact. So, here's what we're going to do. I will give each side until five p.m. to deliver an affidavit from an expert in Iranian law who can answer this question. I will issue a ruling tonight. We are adjourned until nine o'clock tomorrow morning," he said, and the proceeding ended with a bang of his gavel.

"All rise!" called the bailiff.

The courtroom was silent until the judge disappeared through the side door to his chambers. Members of the media rushed to the rail, shouting questions at both the petitioner and the respondent. Jack led his client away from the commotion to the far side of the empty jury box, well away from the public seating, out of earshot of the media.

"How did this become all about Ava?" asked Zahra. "Does this mean I will lose?"

"I won't lie to you," said Jack. "It makes the case harder."

"Because of the politics?"

Proving Ava's death was something Jack was hoping to keep out of the Hague Convention proceeding, and not because he was trying to accommodate the State Department's concerns—or Andie's.

"Not just politics," he said. "Under the law, it's not easy to prove that a missing person is dead. In fact, until a person has been missing for seven years, the legal presumption is that she is *not* dead."

"So this actually helps Farid's case," she said, thinking aloud. "He's not trying to prove that Ava is alive just to make the Iranian government happy."

"Maybe a little of both."

"What do we do?" Zahra asked.

"We prove that your sister was murdered by the Iranian government."

"With or without the help of the US government?"

"Yes," said Jack.

She blinked, confused. "No, I'm asking: Will the US government help us prove that my sister is dead, or will they not?"

"And I'm giving you the best answer I can," said Jack, his gaze drifting toward the crowd on the other side of the rail. "We will prove it. With the US government's help. Or without it."

"Thank you," she said.

"You're welcome," said Jack, knowing that either way, he wouldn't make any friends in Washington.

Or at home.

CHAPTER 10

A ndie was chopping carrots at the kitchen counter, preparing beef stew for dinner, when a news alert lit up her cell phone. She normally ignored breaking news, as it rarely even qualified as "news," let alone "breaking." But this one caught her eye: CHILD CUSTODY BATTLE IN MIAMI COURTROOM REIGNITES US-IRAN TENSION OVER MISSING MOTHER.

Jack was still at work, so it was truly breaking news for Andie. She laid her cutting knife aside and opened the app.

"What's wrong, Mommy?"

Righley was at the other end of the kitchen counter, doing homework. It hadn't been Andie's intention to telegraph her reaction, but Righley was getting to the age at which daughters read something into a mother's every facial expression.

"It's nothing," said Andie, but she read on, skimming to glean the essential facts. The medical examiner's testimony about no death certificate. Judge Carlton's 5:00 p.m. ruling that adoption requires the consent of both biological parents, if living. Jack's statement to the media outside the courthouse, which played on a video loop without any prompting from Andie: "*Sadly, in order to keep her daughter from being taken away from her, my client must now prove that her sister Ava is deceased—murdered at the hands of the Iranian morality police, like so many other innocent victims of this oppressive regime.*"

"That's Daddy!" said Righley. "Is he on the news?"

"Apparently so."

"Is that why he's working late again?"

Andie scraped the chopped carrots into the bowl with the other veggies. "He's very busy."

"Do you miss him?"

The question took Andie by surprise. "What?"

"When he doesn't come home for dinner and stuff—does that make you sad?"

Andie remembered a time, early in their marriage, when dinner together was a priority, something to look forward to. They could talk about things as big as their future together or as small as their day at work. That was before they invoked the Rule, and their marriage became more like a Wall Street law firm or an investment bank, the bounds of their conversations constrained by information barriers and walls of confidentiality.

"All right, missy. Are you a third grader or a psychiatrist? Finish your homework."

Andie heard a car pull up in front of the house. She went to the living room, switched on the porch light, and checked through the window, but it wasn't Jack. A taxi had stopped in front of the neighbor's house across the street. She walked back to the kitchen and served dinner, monopolizing the conversation to make sure there were no more questions about her "sad" marriage. The usual battle over shower time ensued, with the usual outcome. On the way to Righley's bedroom to get her pajamas, Andie noticed, through the window, that the taxi was still parked across the street. In the darkness, it was hard to discern any distinguishing details other than that, like most taxis, it was yellow. But Andie was pretty sure it was the same one as before. The headlights were on. The driver was at the wheel, with a passenger in the back seat. Andie stayed at the window for a minute to see if the passenger got out, or if the cab pulled away. Nothing. They just sat there, waiting.

Strange.

Andie dialed Jack's cell phone, but it went to his voicemail. She left a message.

"Jack, are you expecting anyone to come by the house tonight? Call me."

She shot one more suspicious glance out the window, then returned to the bathroom to get Righley ready for bed.

"Are you and Daddy having a fight?" Righley asked.

Andie slipped the nightgown over Righley's head, then tried to deflect the question with a smile. "What's with all these questions tonight?"

"Cassandra's parents used to fight a lot. Even when I was over there. Now they don't live together anymore."

Cassandra was a friend from school. Andie supposed that "divorce without war" was theoretically possible, but Cassandra's parents had gone down the path of divorce with no survivors.

"That was a sad situation," said Andie, and then she hugged her daughter tightly. "Come on. Bedtime."

"Carry me."

"You carry me."

Righley groaned, trying. Andie snatched her up and carried her down the hallway to her bedroom, where Righley chose a book from her shelf. Andie tucked her into bed and got in beside her, but as she cracked the book open, her cell phone vibrated in her pocket. It was a text from Jack.

Missed your call. Crazy day. Not expecting anyone at the house. Why?

Andie put her phone away and climbed out of the bed.

"What's wrong?" asked Righley.

Andie went to the window and separated the blinds just enough to see across the street. The taxi was still there with headlights on, both the driver and passenger still waiting.

"Go ahead and start without me," said Andie.

"Aw, Mommy. This one has big words."

"I'll be right back. I have to check on something."

Andie closed the door on the way out and went to the master bedroom. Her Sig Sauer was locked in the safe. She collected both her sidearm and her FBI shield, loaded the pistol with ammunition, and tucked it away in her holster. She walked to the living room, opened the front door, and stepped out to the porch.

The taxi was still there.

Andie started across the lawn toward the street, stopping at the curb. It was dark inside the cab, but there was enough light from the streetlamp at the corner for Andie to see the passenger lean forward, perhaps to say something to the driver. Then the rear door opened. Andie didn't draw her weapon, but she was at the ready. A woman stepped out of the taxi, closed the door, and walked toward Andie.

"Can I help you?" asked Andie.

The woman didn't appear to be a threat. She was well dressed, conservatively so, perhaps in her fifties. "Are you FBI Agent Henning?" she asked. Her voice was soft, and Andie detected a hint of a southern accent—not unheard of in Miami, but given the taxi, she probably wasn't a local.

"Yes."

The woman stopped a few steps away from Andie. "I was hoping to speak to you and your husband, Mr. Swyteck."

"He's not home."

"I know. I didn't see his car, so I waited."

"What are you, a reporter?" asked Andie.

"No. It's nothing like that. I know that both you and your husband have been in conversation with the State Department."

Andie didn't confirm or deny. "Who are you?"

"A wife who hasn't seen or heard from her husband in years."

Andie noticed she was still wearing a wedding ring. "Who is your husband?"

"My husband is an ordinary American who was in the wrong place at the wrong time."

"What does that mean?"

"He's in jail. He's a political prisoner in Tehran. The Iranian government convicted him on bogus charges of espionage."

The response could not have been further from what Andie had expected. "I'm very sorry."

"The State Department is my lifeline, of course. It's all about political backchanneling between governments, which the family can't control. I'm told we were close to negotiating his release last year, but it didn't work out. My life is an emotional roller coaster."

"That must be very difficult."

"It's unbearable. Which brings me here tonight."

"I don't understand."

"Like I said, I'm aware that the State Department met with both you and your husband."

Andy felt like the woman deserved at least some response. "If you're asking whether the State Department said anything to me about an American hostage in Tehran, they didn't."

"Yes, they did."

"Excuse me?"

"They told you that now is not the time to resurrect Ava Bazzi and the diplomatic crisis caused by the hijab protests. They told you that, right this minute, the US government is engaged in sensitive negotiations with the Iranians."

"They didn't tell me what those negotiations are about."

"That's because those negotiations are not directly under the control of the State Department. The National Security Council is involved. The negotiation is for my husband's release."

Andie felt a chill. The image of a woman alone at the dinner table, night after night, flashed in her mind, and Righley's voice was suddenly in her head. *Do you miss him?*

"I'm begging you. Please do not let your husband try to prove that Ava Bazzi was murdered by the morality police. If he embarrasses the regime, my husband will never come home. That's all I came to say."

The woman turned and started across the street. Andie called to her, and she stopped.

"What's your name?" asked Andie.

She didn't answer. She climbed into the back seat, the door closed, and the taxi drove away.

CHAPTER 11

Jack came home from the office to a quiet house.

He'd spent the evening with his client, learning more about Ava Bazzi and other women and girls who fell victim to the morality police during the hijab demonstrations. Zahra found news clips on the internet and translated them for him. The story of a sixteen-year-old girl weighed on Jack's mind all the way to Key Biscayne.

Nika Shakarami went missing in Tehran on a Tuesday, after telling a friend she was being chased by police. On Wednesday night, a state TV report showed her aunt, Atash, saying, "Nika was killed falling from a building." Her uncle was also seen on TV. He was denouncing the demonstrations and all those who participated, but only after someone off camera spoke in a harsh whisper to him in words that Zahra translated: "Say it, you scumbag!"

Jack entered quietly through the front door. It occurred to him that his own daughter was only eight years younger than Nika, and it made him shudder to think how quickly the last eight years had gone. He stopped by Righley's room, stepped around Max the sleepy guard dog, and gently planted a kiss on Righley's forehead without waking her.

The master bedroom was dark, but he didn't switch on the lamp. He navigated his way in the darkness, getting ready for bed, so as not to wake Andie. Then he quietly slid beneath the covers. She propped herself up on one elbow, staying on her side of the mattress.

"I have something important to tell you," she said.

Jack was exhausted, but her tone made it clear that this couldn't wait. He listened as Andie told him about the unexpected visitor, saying nothing until she was finished.

"I didn't see that coming," said Jack.

"I hope it makes a difference."

"To my case, you mean?"

"Yes," said Andie. "I know it's not my place to tell you how to try your case. But I'm asking—just asking—for you to consider what this woman said to me. Will you do that?"

"I will, but . . ."

"But what?"

"I don't necessarily agree that keeping the Iranians happy in a negotiation to release an American prisoner is more important than keeping a six-year-old girl safe and with her mother."

"Jack, I'm a mother, and I get where you're coming from. But you have to look at the big picture."

"Meaning what?"

"This is not just about *an* American or *a* negotiation. Do you realize that three Americans are kidnapped or wrongfully imprisoned somewhere in the world *every day*? That's a thousand American families a year whose world is turned upside down. Hostage negotiators on both sides have long institutional memories. If something is promised and not delivered, they don't forget it when the next negotiation starts. Undermining the US government's negotiating power in one case undermines it everywhere."

"Okay, fair point. Of course, you're assuming that this woman is on the level and telling you the truth."

"Why should I question that?"

"Did she give you her name?"

"No."

"Did she tell you her husband's name?"

"No. But, Jack, even without names, she is probably breaking every rule in the book just by telling me that the US government is in active negotiations for her husband's release."

"Or . . ."

"Or what?"

Jack sighed, not sure he should say what he was about to say. "Andie, look at the pattern here. First, a thug jumped me outside my office and told me I better not make this case about what happened to Ava Bazzi."

"A thug named Farid."

"Maybe. Maybe not. Then tonight, out of nowhere, a woman shows up and tells you that her husband's life depends on my courtroom strategy. Who is this woman? Who is her husband? How do we know she's really the person she claims to be? How do we know she's any more reliable than the so-called medical examiner who testified in court today? That guy was a puppet of the Iranian government."

"This woman is not a puppet of the Iranian government."

"I agree. But how do we know she's not a puppet of her own government?"

"Have you been binge-watching *Jack Ryan* on Prime again?" she asked, scoffing. "That's ridiculous."

"Is it? First, the State Department asked me not to prove that Ava Bazzi was murdered. When that failed, they recruited you to change my mind. When that failed, a woman shows up at our house and tells you her husband's life is in my hands, depending on what strategy I adopt in court."

There was just enough light in the room for Jack to see the incredulity on Andie's face.

"I can't believe what I'm hearing," she said. "It's exactly like Dr. Stanger said in counseling. We have mirror image syndrome."

"What?"

"We look at the same set of facts. I see a woman in desperate need of help to save her husband. You see a devious scheme by the US government to support its own diplomatic position."

"I didn't say it *is* a scheme. I said I have questions."

Andie fell into her pillow. "You make me furious."

"You're not even listening to my side of it."

"I've been listening to your side of it for nine years." She rolled onto her side and showed Jack the back of her head. "I'm tired of the aggravation, Jack. This is fucked up."

Jack lay in the darkness, staring up at shadows on the ceiling, afraid to ask if by "this" she meant the Ava Bazzi predicament. Or their entire marriage.

CHAPTER 12

The hearing resumed at 9:00 a.m. in courtroom 9, Judge Carlton presiding.

Jack hoped the next witness would shift the focus away from Ava Bazzi and bring the hearing more in line with a traditional Hague proceeding, where a petitioner like Farid would focus on his own rights to the return of his child. But Jack had no more control over the strategy of his opposing counsel than the State Department had over his.

"The petitioner calls Nouri Asmoun," Beech announced in the crowded courtroom.

It was another appearance by videoconference from Iran. As the witness came into focus on the LCD, Jack discreetly checked with his client.

"No idea who he is," Zahra whispered, but his opening testimony fleshed out the details. He was fluent in English, so there was no translator.

Asmoun was a thirty-year-old banker who had lived in Tehran all his life. He was a handsome man who was mindful of his appearance. His hair was neatly trimmed, as if he'd just come from the stylist, and his suit was worthy of a *GQ* magazine cover. His hands were folded and resting on the tabletop, fingers interlaced. Jack couldn't be certain by video, but it appeared that his nails were buffed and manicured.

"Mr. Asmoun, did you know Ava Bazzi while she was married to my client, Farid Bazzi?"

So much for Jack's hope that the hearing would move past Ava.

"I did," he said.

"Did you know Farid Bazzi?"

"No. I never met him."

"How did you know Ava Bazzi?"

He hesitated, then answered, a hint of shame in his voice. "We were . . . romantically involved."

The courtroom rumbled. Jack jumped to his feet and objected, but the judge was one step ahead of him.

"Ms. Beech, yesterday this court agreed with you that Mr. Swyteck's client has no legal right to custody as an adoptive parent if Ava Bazzi was still alive at the time of the adoption. My ruling was clear and narrow: evidence relating to Ava Bazzi is relevant to this proceeding only if it shows that she is alive or dead."

"Understood, Your Honor," said Beech. "Ava Bazzi's extramarital affair with Mr. Asmoun shows that, as the Iranian government has said for the past two years, Ava had every reason to flee the country, did in fact flee, and is alive and well in hiding."

Jack doubled down on his objection. "Judge, this is a smear tactic against a woman who is unable to defend herself because, sadly, she is no longer on this earth."

"I understand your position, Mr. Swyteck," said the judge. "Ms. Beech, how does an extramarital affair tend to prove Ava Bazzi is still alive?"

"Adultery is a criminal offense in Iran," said Beech. "Technically, it's a capital offense. Even though no woman has been executed in quite some time, it is still a serious enough crime to cause a married woman like Ava to flee the country. As this court ruled yesterday, if Ava Bazzi fled the country and is still alive, Zahra Bazzi's adoption of Yasmin is a nullity, and this court must order Yasmin's immediate return to her father."

It was obvious that Farid and his lawyer were pandering to the Iranian government, parroting the regime's position on Ava Bazzi's disappearance. Jack was reluctant to inject the US-Iranian diplomatic crisis directly into the hearing, but he was no less forceful in his objection.

"Judge, the only thing the petitioner proves by calling Mr. Asmoun as a witness is that, in death as in life, Ava Bazzi continues to be an abused woman. This is malicious victim shaming."

Beech laid her hand on Farid's shoulder, responding with complete in-dignation. "Let's be clear about who the victim is here, Your Honor. My client's first wife cheated on him and fled the country, bringing shame to him and their daughter in their abandonment. Then his sister-in-law defrauded him into marriage and immediately ran off with his daughter."

"Enough argument," said the judge. "I will overrule the objection. However, there will be no lurid details. Ms. Beech, you can establish how long the affair lasted, and that will be the end of the matter."

Farid's lawyer thanked the judge and addressed the witness. "Mr. Asmoun, when did your affair with Ava Bazzi end?"

"When she was arrested."

"How long did it last?"

"Six months."

"Did you see each other regularly during that six-month period?"

"At least once a week."

The judge interjected. "Wrap it up, Ms. Beech."

Beech was a smart enough lawyer to take her win without angering the judge. "No further questions," she said, and she returned to her seat at the table beside her client.

The judge invited cross-examination, and Jack rose. Since it was a video-conference, he could have asked his questions from a seated position at the table beside his client. But he wanted a better view of Farid—the alleged "victim."

"I have a brief cross-examination," said Jack. He turned to face the witness on the LCD screen, but his gaze landed on Farid. The "victim" of the Bazzi sisters was staring at the man who claimed to have had sex with his wife Ava every week for six months. Yet Jack saw no sign that Farid was angry with Asmoun. Maybe Farid didn't care. Or maybe he didn't believe it.

"Good morning, Mr. Asmoun," said Jack as he buttoned his suit jacket.

"Good afternoon," said the witness, referencing the time difference.

Jack had one hand tied behind his back, knowing virtually nothing about this witness. For Andie's sake, and the sake of his marriage, he would have preferred not to inject the Iranian government directly into the hearing. But seeing the witness on the screen triggered the research Jack had done in his office the night before—in particular, the video of Nika Shakarami's uncle on state television to condemn the hijab protests after his sixteen-year-old niece was murdered by the morality police. The very idea of someone off camera, threatening Nika's uncle, informed Jack's first line of cross-examination.

"Mr. Asmoun, where are you right now?"

"I'm in a conference room. At my work."

"Are you alone?"

"No."

"Who is in the room with you?"

"The videographer."

"Anyone else?"

"No."

It wasn't the answer Jack had wanted, but he forged ahead. "Have you had any conversations with anyone from the Iranian government about your testimony today?"

"No."

"Did anyone—including Farid Bazzi and his lawyer—tell you that your testimony here today would be looked on favorably by the Iranian government?"

"No."

Farid's lawyer rose. "Your Honor, for the record, neither I nor my client has *ever* spoken to Mr. Asmoun outside of today's testimony."

Jack didn't think Beech would lie in open court to a federal judge, which could only mean one thing. Someone had told her to call Asmoun as witness with the promise that his testimony would be helpful to Farid's case. It was no coincidence that it was also helpful to the Iranian government's position on Ava Bazzi. But he wouldn't score points by arguing with the witness. He moved on.

"Mr. Asmoun, you heard Ms. Beech tell the judge that adultery is a crime in Iran. Were you aware of that?"

"Yes."

"So you are here, under oath, admitting that you committed the crime of adultery. Do I have that right?"

The question gave Asmoun pause. "I'm not proud of it."

"Not proud. But you didn't flee the country, did you?"

"I don't understand your question."

"Let me clarify," said Jack. "Based on your testimony, Mr. Bazzi's lawyer is arguing that Ava Bazzi fled the country because she committed the crime of adultery. You're every bit as much of a criminal, but you didn't flee, did you, sir?"

Again, Asmoun seemed uncomfortable with the question. "Well, it's different for a man."

That drew a rumble of disapproval from the courtroom, and it was loud enough to be heard by videoconference. The witness immediately back-pedaled.

"I can explain," said Asmoun. "Even under the strictest and oldest interpretations of Islamic law, the penalty of death applies only to an adulterer who is married. Ava was married to Farid. I'm not married. The punishment for an unmarried adulterer is far less severe."

Jack was not letting him off the hook so easily. "But you said earlier that 'it's different for a man.' Tell us how that makes a difference."

"That's not what I meant. My English is not perfect."

Zahra signaled for Jack to come over, and with the judge's permission, they had a brief exchange of whispers. Jack then returned to his place to question the witness, armed with a few useful pieces of ammunition Zahra had shared.

"Mr. Asmoun, when you said 'It's different for a man—'"

"My English not good," he said, suddenly struggling with the language. "Not what I meant."

"Please let Mr. Swyteck finish his question," said the judge.

The witness apologized, and Jack continued.

"When you said that adultery 'is different for a man,' you were simply referring to historical reality, were you not, sir?"

"I don't know what you mean."

"Dating back centuries, married and unmarried women were stoned to death or otherwise punished for adultery. Men, on the other hand, often went completely unpunished, whether they were married or unmarried. You're aware of that fact, are you not?"

"Not really."

The witness was losing credibility with every answer, which was Jack's only objective.

"Let's speak of more recent events. You are aware that Ava Bazzi disappeared at a turbulent time in Iran, correct?"

"Turbulent for some."

"For some, and especially for women. Ava Bazzi disappeared at the height of a crackdown by the morality police *against women* who were openly violating Islamic modesty laws. Isn't that a fact?"

"I don't know that as a fact."

Asmoun's credibility was shot. Jack used it to make one final point. "Mr. Asmoun, you're afraid to say anything in this courtroom that will make the Iranian regime unhappy. Isn't that true, sir?"

Farid's counsel rose. "Objection."

"Overruled. If there is some external influence on this witness's testimony, this court wants to know about it. The witness may answer."

"That's not true," he said.

"Mr. Asmoun, you're so afraid that you won't even admit, as a matter of historical fact, that women of *any* faith, not just Islam, have faced more severe judgment for adultery than men."

"I'm not a historian."

"You're so afraid, you won't even admit that women were unjustly arrested, imprisoned, and even killed during the hijab protests."

"Some men were executed too," Asmoun said, then he quickly realized that he was helping Jack's case, not his own. "But I don't know what for."

Jack could have stopped, but this was his only opportunity to completely discredit Asmoun's testimony.

"Mr. Asmoun, you said you were unmarried. But do you have other family in Iran?"

"Yes. My parents. And my younger sister."

"Are you a close-knit family?"

"Yes, very much so."

"Fair to say that you would do whatever you could to prevent any harm from coming to your family?"

Farid's lawyer was on her feet. "Judge, I object. The insinuation that this witness is being strong-armed by the Iranian government has gone on long enough."

"Sustained. Mr. Swyteck, I believe you've made your point."

"Yes. I believe I have. Thank you, Your Honor. No further questions."

CHAPTER 13

Judge Carlton adjourned the hearing for a long lunch break, so Jack and Zahra returned to his office to prepare for the afternoon session. Jack's longtime assistant met him at the door and followed him to his desk. Bonnie was affectionately known as "the Roadrunner" for the way she kicked into high gear in times of crisis, and she was in full crisis mode.

"Jack, I'm so sorry I let you head off to court unprepared for today's witness. I didn't pull a single exhibit for you to use."

"Bonnie, there's no one better than you. But not even Clarence Darrow could have anticipated that a witness we've never heard of would appear by videoconference from Iran and claim to be Ava Bazzi's lover."

"Maybe so," she said as she laid a folder on his desk. "But I pulled together a witness file on Mr. Asmoun. The whole timeline is here with supporting documents, starting with the date Ava and Farid got married, the day Yasmin was born, the date they moved to London. I was even able to track down the exact date of their return flight to Tehran: two months before Ava was arrested. It's everything you'll need—just in case you have to cross-examine Mr. Asmoun again."

Jack wasn't sure why Bonnie thought all that information was relevant to Mr. Asmoun, but it was beside the point.

"Thank you, Bonnie. But there's zero chance Mr. Asmoun will reappear as a witness."

She was openly disappointed, as if truly wishing to redeem herself for something that wasn't the least bit her fault.

"I'll keep this file at my desk," she said, "if you need it. Lunch is in the kitchen. Zahra's waiting for you."

Jack thanked her and went to the kitchen. He took a seat at the table, across from his client, and unwrapped his sandwich. Zahra didn't touch her kale salad. She was too nervous to eat.

"You certainly made that witness look like a liar," said Zahra. "I hope you know it *is* all a lie. Ava would never have cheated on Farid."

"She loved him?"

"No. She would have been terrified to cheat on him."

It was an interesting point, and it made Jack realize that his opposing counsel was indeed clever. Beech wasn't just pandering to the Iranian government by painting Ava as an adulteress. She was preempting Zahra's testimony that Farid was an abuser. *Your Honor, if Farid really was violent, wouldn't his first wife have been too afraid to cheat on him?*

"Do you think that witness truly is being threatened by the regime?" asked Zahra.

"It's the most logical explanation until we hear another one," said Jack. "He did say he had a younger sister. She could be in some kind of trouble over the protests, and this is his chance to make things good for her."

Zahra poked at her salad, but she didn't eat. "Have we heard the last about Ava?" she asked.

"If it were up to Farid's lawyer, I would say yes."

"Do you really think Farid's legal strategy is controlled by the regime?"

"Not controlled. Beech wouldn't risk her law license over this. But clearly Beech is advancing the Iranian government's propaganda about Ava. There's a quid pro quo that we don't know about. The regime could be paying Farid's legal bills or promising him some kind of help down the road if the judge rules against him."

The kitchen suddenly shook with the sound of crashing glass in the other room. Zahra screamed. Jack instinctively searched for some form of protection, but the only thing readily available was his prized autographed Carl Yastrzemski baseball bat.

"Sorry, Yaz," he said as he grabbed it from the display shelf. He told Zahra to stay put and ran into the reception area. His assistant was coming down the stairs, having heard the crash from the second floor.

"Stay right there, Bonnie!" said Jack.

She froze. Jack stood in the doorway and assessed the damage. The lobby area had once been a living room, and the huge picture window overlooking the front porch was shattered. What remained of the tempered glass was in pellet-sized pieces, strewn across the Persian rug and surrounding wood floor, glistening like diamonds in the streaming sunlight. Lying on the rug in the middle of the room was a metal pipe about the size of a relay race baton.

"Somebody threw a pipe?" said Bonnie, utter disbelief in her voice.

"Did you see anything from upstairs?" Jack asked.

"No," she said, her voice quaking. "I just heard an awful crash."

Jack stepped carefully across the room, the glass pellets crackling beneath the leather soles of his shoes. He noticed handwriting along the side of the pipe. It was in black marker or maybe black paint pen, and it ran from one end of the pipe to the other along the smooth cylinder, framed by the piping thread at each end. Jack lowered himself into a squat and read the message:

"Final warning," the top line read, and then on the next line: "Stop trying to prove Ava is dead."

The message continued onto a third line. Jack took a pen from his pocket and rolled the pipe a half turn so he could read the rest. It was a signature of sorts:

Someone Who Knows.

Jack inserted the same pen into the opening on the right and stood the pipe on end. Stuffed inside was a clear plastic baggie that had been compressed to about the size of a golf ball for a tight fit. Using the pen, Jack dragged the baggie from inside the pipe. With the release of compression, it blossomed on its own inertia, and as the clear plastic unfolded, the baggie revealed its contents.

"Bonnie, call the police," said Jack.

Zahra entered the room from the kitchen. "What is it, Jack?" she asked.

"Someone's wedding ring," he said.

Bonnie raced back up the stairs and dialed the police.

Jack stayed where he was, afraid to even guess who that "someone" might be.

The afternoon session began at 2:00 p.m., but not in the courtroom. Counsel and their clients were in Judge Carlton's chambers.

Jack had notified the judge and his opposing counsel within minutes of the arrival of the police at his office. The Miami-Dade Crime Scene Investigation Unit collected the pipe, the message, and the plastic baggie in sealed evidence bags. The judge summoned counsel and both parties to his chambers for a session that was closed to the public. Detective Charlene O'Hara from the CSI Unit was with them. The pipe and plastic baggie, each marked by an evidence tag, rested on a felt pad on Judge Carlton's desktop. Beside them, also tagged, was the ring.

Judge Carlton started the session with the necessary legal formalities.

"Ms. Beech, for the record, I understand that your client has consented to make an identification of the ring."

"Yes, Your Honor."

"Very well," said the judge. "Mr. Bazzi, please step forward."

Farid rose from his chair, stopped before the judge's desk, and looked down at the evidence on display.

"Mr. Bazzi, do you recognize the ring in front of you?" the judge asked.

"Yes, Your Honor."

It was the first time Jack had heard Farid's voice—unless it was Farid who had jumped him outside his office. His voice here, compared to the muffled mouth full of cotton, didn't move the needle on that question.

"How do you recognize this ring?" asked the judge.

Farid stared at the ring for what, to Jack, seemed like a very long time. Finally, he spoke in a solemn voice. "It belongs to my wife. It is her wedding ring."

"By 'wife,' do you mean Zahra Bazzi or Ava Bazzi?" the judge asked.

"Ava," said Farid. "Our rings matched. White-gold rope band. They were heirlooms from my grandparents. This is Ava's ring."

The judge directed Farid back to his seat. Then he addressed the lawyers.

"Counsel, I understand that each of you believes this ring is relevant to the question of whether Ava Bazzi is dead or alive, but you have polar-opposite views as to how it may be relevant. Mr. Swyteck, what is your position?"

"The ring needs to be considered together with the message on the pipe," said Jack. "It's all one threat, and the point is to stop us from proving the tragic truth. This threat came from 'someone who knows' Ava Bazzi is dead."

"The exact opposite is true," said Beech. "The ring and the message came from someone who knows she's alive. The obvious point is to stop Mr. Swyteck from perpetrating a complete fraud on this court."

"May I respond?" asked Jack.

"No," the judge said. "The bottom line is that none of us knows who came into possession of Ava Bazzi's ring after she disappeared, who wrote the message on the pipe, or who threw the pipe through Mr. Swyteck's window."

Jack tried another angle. "Judge, I would submit that, more likely than not, the ring came from whoever is responsible for Ava Bazzi's death."

"I can't agree," said the judge. "A woman who abandoned her family and fled the country has no more need for her wedding ring than a deceased woman. My ruling is that the ring has no probative value as to whether Ava Bazzi is alive or dead. I will not consider it as evidence in this proceeding."

Neither lawyer showed any reaction other than to accept the ruling.

"At this time, I'd like to have a word with just counsel," said the judge. "I would ask petitioner and respondent to wait outside my office with my judicial assistant."

Jack noted the fear in his client's eyes. "Judge, as we will prove later in this hearing, my client is in grave danger of physical and psychological harm. I would therefore request that she be allowed her own space in a separate room."

"That's fine," said the judge.

The judicial assistant entered, and as she led Zahra and Farid out to their respective waiting rooms, Beech whispered so only Jack could hear:

"Well played, Swyteck."

It spoke volumes about his opposition, who seemed to think this was all a game, and it made Jack's skin crawl. The door closed, and the lawyers were alone with the judge.

"Counsel, we are all in agreement that if Ava Bazzi is alive, Zahra Bazzi's adoption of Yasmin was invalid and the case is over. But, Ms. Beech, how many more witnesses do you intend to call to prove that Ava Bazzi is alive?"

"One, at most, Your Honor."

"I'm going to hold you to that. We need to move this along. Am I clear?"

Beech looked unhappy, but her tone was respectful. "Yes, Judge."

"I have one more thing to say," said the judge. "Based on what I've heard so far, it's impossible to know if that pipe was thrown through Mr. Swyteck's window by 'someone who knows' Ava Bazzi is alive, 'someone who knows' she's dead but wants the rest of the world to think she's alive, or some nutjob who doesn't know anything and simply wants his fifteen minutes of fame. I'm expressing no view on the matter. But I offer this advice to both of you."

Judge Carlton paused to look at each of them as individuals, not as opposing counsel, his expression one of concern. "For the sake of your own families, please, be careful. Both of you."

"Yes, Your Honor," they said in unison.

"The hearing will resume at three o'clock," said the judge. "I'll see you in my courtroom then."

Jack nodded with appreciation, and the lawyers stepped out to catch up with their clients.

CHAPTER 14

The courtroom came to order at 3:00 p.m., and Judge Carlton directed Farid's lawyer to call her next witness.

"The petitioner calls Imam Hassan Reza," she said.

Jack rose, addressing the court, though his question was for opposing counsel. "Your Honor, for the sake of clarity: Is this the same imam who was unavailable yesterday?"

"Judge, the answer to Mr. Swyteck's question is yes," said Beech. "Fortunately, the imam is available now via videoconference."

Jack found it interesting that only after their second witness blew up in Farid's face was the "unavailable" imam suddenly available.

The imam's image appeared on the LCD screen, and the witness was sworn. The imam was dressed in the traditional black camel-hair robe with a blue jacket underneath. His crown-style turban was the same type made popular by the hardline lawmaker Mahmoud Nabavian. The imam was a calm, poised witness, answering Beech's questions in English, though his accent was thick.

"Imam Reza, do you know the petitioner, Farid Bazzi?"

"Yes, very well."

"Did you play any role in connection with his marriage to Zahra Bazzi?"

"Yes. I presided at their wedding ceremony."

"When was that?"

"It will be two years this coming January. The fifteenth of January."

"Did you play any role in his divorce from either Ava Bazzi or Zahra Bazzi?"

"Yes. I served as a witness on Farid's behalf in his divorce both from his first wife, Ava, and his second wife, Zahra."

"Explain to the court how the divorce process works, please."

"Under Islamic law, a man can divorce his wife by so stating, verbally, in the presence of two 'just men' as witnesses. I was one of those 'just men' to bear witness to Farid's pronouncement of divorce as to both of his wives, first for Ava and then later for Zahra."

"When was Farid's divorce from his first wife, Ava?"

"She was arrested in mid-October. The divorce was approximately six weeks later, the first day of December."

"In his divorce from Ava, did Farid state a reason for the divorce?"

Jack rose. "Your Honor, I would ask the court to direct the witness to answer that question with either a 'yes' or 'no' answer."

"Point taken," said the judge. "The witness shall give a one-word response."

"Yes," the imam said.

"As to Ava Bazzi, what did Farid state as the reason for the divorce?"

Jack was back on his feet. "Objection. Hearsay."

"You're technically right, Mr. Swyteck. But the rules regarding hearsay do not apply in Hague proceedings. Ms. Beech, what's your response?"

"What you just said," she quipped. "Plus, Farid made the statement to Allah in the presence of an imam, and the imam is testifying under an oath to God."

"The statement does seem trustworthy," the judge said. "The witness may answer."

The imam paused, making sure the back-and-forth between lawyers was over, then answered. "Farid stated that the reason for his divorce from Ava was abandonment."

Bomb number one had just hit its mark. Testimony from a holy man that supported the Iranian regime's position: Ava Bazzi was alive and well, having fled the country after abandoning her husband and daughter. As for the Hague proceeding, Zahra's adoption of Yasmin was a nullity.

The carpet-bombing campaign continued. "Imam Reza, let me ask you now about the second divorce. What grounds did Farid state in support of his divorce from Zahra?"

The imam looked directly at the camera, his dark eyes clouded with cataracts. "Divorce was warranted because the marriage was never consummated."

Bomb number two: Zahra's marriage to Farid was a fraud, all part of her premeditated plan to adopt and then abduct his daughter. Whether Ava was dead or alive, Zahra's adoption of Yasmin was void. Jack had to find a way to continue the fight.

"Judge, I move to strike the response."

"On what grounds?" the judge asked.

Zahra tugged at her lawyer's elbow. Jack asked the judge for a moment to confer, and Zahra whispered into his ear. "Don't object," she said. "It's true. Farid and I never . . ."

Jack glanced across the courtroom at Farid. He was staring down at the table, embarrassed—as any man would have been—by the truth.

Jack rose slowly to address the court. He would have been a fool to stand on his objection, only to have Zahra confirm the imam's testimony later in the case, when she took the stand.

"Your Honor, I withdraw my objection."

"Very well," the judge said. "The testimony is admitted as evidence."

Beech appeared satisfied. "I have no further questions."

"Cross-examination, Mr. Swyteck?"

Lack of consummation didn't conclusively establish that the marriage was a fraud, but the imam had done serious damage to Zahra's defense, and Jack had to repair it.

"Yes, Your Honor," said Jack, and then he turned to the witness on the screen.

"Imam Reza, I'm told by my client that some members of your mosque refer to you not as imam but as mullah. Is that true?"

"Some do, yes."

"In Tehran, the term *mullah* is sometimes used to describe clerics who adhere to a literal interpretation of Islamic law. Isn't that true?"

"That is generally true," he said.

"Is it fair to say that *you* adhere to a literal interpretation of Islamic law?"

"I would not deny that statement."

"Under Islamic law, a divorced man or a widower is allowed to remarry, correct?"

"Yes, of course."

"Is it also true that, in the case of divorce, Islamic law has very specific rules on how long a divorced man must wait before he can remarry?"

"I believe you are referring to what Islamic law refers to as *iddah*. That is a three-month waiting period. Normally, this waiting period applies only to a divorced woman, not to a divorced man."

"Under what circumstances does the waiting period apply to a divorced man?" asked Jack.

"Only if the man intends to marry the sister of the divorced wife. In such a case, he will need to wait for the *iddah* to expire because a man is not allowed to be married to two sisters at the same time under the principles of Islam and sharia."

Jack was out of his depth on the nuances of Islamic law, but so far, so good.

"Let me make sure I understand," said Jack. "In a situation where a divorced man seeks to marry the sister of the divorced wife, at least three months would have to pass before you would perform the wedding ceremony. Correct?"

"That's correct," he said.

"Let's look at the timeline for Farid Bazzi's situation, specifically. Farid's wife Ava was arrested two years ago this month. The seventeenth of October. Will you accept that representation?"

"Yes. That sounds right. I will accept that date."

"And as the story goes, Ava Bazzi fled the country soon after that date, abandoning her husband and her daughter."

"That's correct."

"As you testified earlier, Farid Bazzi then sought divorce on grounds of abandonment, correct?"

"Yes."

"You also testified that Mr. Bazzi's divorce from Ava was final on the first of December. So how long would he have to wait before marrying Ava's sister, Zahra?"

"Three months. The first of March."

"But you performed the wedding for Zahra and Farid on the fifteenth of January, did you not?"

The imam froze, the wheels clearly spinning in his head. But Jack had put him in a tight spot: he couldn't deny the marriage date with both Zahra and Farid in the courtroom. "Yes. It was the fifteenth of January."

Jack paused, then made his point. "It appears that one of two things is true, Imam Reza. One possibility is that you performed a wedding ceremony in violation of Islamic law. That's not something you would do lightly, is it?"

"No, of course not."

"The other possibility is that your actions were completely appropriate under Islamic law."

"My goal is that all my actions are appropriate under Islamic law."

"Naturally," said Jack. "Even though *iddah*—the waiting period—ran until the first day of March, you acted in accordance with Islamic law in performing the wedding ceremony on the fifteenth of January, correct?"

"I hope so. If not, I would ask for forgiveness."

"No forgiveness is needed," said Jack. "Your actions were in accordance with Islamic law, because you knew Farid was not subject to the *iddah* waiting period. Is that correct?"

"I don't understand your question."

"When you performed the wedding ceremony in January, you knew Farid was not a divorced man."

"I was the witness at his divorce."

"You performed his wedding ceremony in January because you knew Farid was a *widower*. A widower is not subject to the waiting period of *iddah*, correct? Imam Reza, when you performed that wedding ceremony in January, you *knew* Ava Bazzi was dead, *didn't you?*"

"Objection!" Beech shouted.

"Grounds?" asked the judge.

Beech struggled for an answer, and she seemed to be reaching into the same bag of tricks that Jack had explored minutes earlier, only to come up with the same last-ditch defense. "It's . . . prejudicial, Your Honor."

"I suppose that's true," said the judge. "I can't imagine that Mr. Swyteck is trying to *help* your case. Overruled."

Jack checked his notes, but there was no more work to do. The Iranian government could spin the political story however it liked. Farid Bazzi and his lawyer could spin the evidence however they liked. But Jack's questioning had put the mullah in a box. And in that figurative box lay the truth, as Jack saw it: Ava Bazzi was dead.

"No further questions, Your Honor," said Jack, and he returned to his seat.

CHAPTER 15

Wednesday night was bingo night at the Palace skilled nursing facility. Jack's *abuela* said he brought her good luck, so he tried to go as often as he could. This time he brought Righley with him. Laying eyes on her great-granddaughter always put a smile on Abuela's face.

"Ay, mi vida," said Abuela as Jack and Righley entered her room. *My life.* It was her way of expressing how important family was to her.

Abuela had been born in Bejucal, a small town near Havana, a city best known to Americans as the birthplace of Hollywood star Andy Garcia. Her only daughter—Jack's mother—fled Castro's Cuba with only her mother's blessing and the shared hope that her mother would be among the next wave of asylum seekers to land in Miami. It took decades. Jack's mother was long dead, having fallen to eclampsia after giving birth to Jack, and Jack was a grown man when Abuela finally made it. By then, the damage was done. Jack could barely speak a word of Spanish, had never eaten an empanada in his life, and wouldn't have known the smell of a good cigar from a smoldering rope. Upon her first visit to her daughter's grave, Abuela committed herself to giving her gringo grandson a crash course in all things Cuban. He topped out at about a C-minus.

"She talks funny," Righley whispered into Jack's ear. She was no stranger to her great-grandmother's Spanish, but lately she'd become somewhat of a linguistic critic. Her third-grade Spanish teacher was Castilian. Cuban Spanish was to Castilians as a Brooklyn accent was to British royalty.

"Be sweet," said Jack.

Abuela called for the nurse and insisted on a change of clothes before bingo. She looked just fine, and she would miss the start of bingo, but there was no changing her mind. With each passing month Jack found her a little more stubborn and difficult to reason with. Her memory was fading too. She was having trouble with the timeline of her important life events. When she got married. When her daughter was born. When her husband died. Like many Cuban immigrants in their eighties and nineties, she recalled things, if at all, as either "before Castro" or "after Castro."

"We'll wait in the lobby," Jack told the nurse.

Jack and Righley walked hand-in-hand down the hallway. He was impressed that she'd remembered that it wasn't polite to look inside the rooms, even if the door was wide open.

"She's your mommy's mother, right?" asked Righley.

"That's right," said Jack.

"How old was your mommy?"

"You mean when she died?"

"No, I'm asking how old she was when she was born," Righley said with sarcasm. "Duh."

Righley was unquestionably her mother's daughter. "She died when I was very young. A baby."

"Not you. How old was she?"

It made Jack sad to say it. "She was twenty-three."

"How old is Abuela?"

"Eighty-nine."

Righley stopped cold in the hallway. "That's so unfair. Why did your mommy die so young, and her mother is still alive?"

Jack took a knee and looked her straight in the eye. "I can't answer that, honey. I don't think anyone can."

"Mommy says that's what your new trial is about. A mother who died too young."

"Your mother told you that?"

"Mm-hmm."

"When did the two of you talk about my case?"

"We saw you on the news. I asked, and she told me it's about a mommy who died young and her daughter who misses her. That's why it's so important to you, and why you've been working so late every night."

Jack found it interesting that Andie thought the case was more about Ava and Yasmin than Zahra and Yasmin. "That's really what Mommy said?"

Righley covered her mouth. "Oh. Was I not supposed to tell you that?"

"It's okay. I'm glad you told me."

"Is Mommy right?"

Even though it hadn't occurred to Jack that this case might be personal to him, he couldn't say Andie was wrong. Maybe that was what his father had meant, too, when he'd told Jack that the stakes in this civil case were higher than any criminal case he'd ever handled.

He rose from his knee and took Righley by the hand. "Come on," he said. "Let's go save Abuela a seat at the bingo table."

I t was after seven, and Andie was still at the Miami field office, knowing that Jack and Righley were visiting Abuela. Wednesday was supposed to be "Mom's night off," the one evening each week that she didn't have to cook dinner for the family, help Righley with her homework, make her lunch for the next school day, and get her ready for bed.

Somehow, Mommy's night off had turned into Mommy's night to work late at the office. Seven was the soonest the division chiefs from the State Department's Office of Children's Issues could videoconference with her. She was alone in her office, and their images were on her desktop LCD screen: Chief Comstock, overseeing Europe, and Chief Davis, covering the Eastern Hemisphere.

"I'm sorry," said Comstock. "The State Department can neither confirm nor deny what you've told us, Agent Henning."

Andie had laid out in detail the visit from the woman who had taxied to Key Biscayne and told her that the US government was negotiating with the Iranians for her husband's release from a political prison.

"Let's break this down a little," said Andie. "When this woman told me that the United States and the Iranian regime are currently engaged in sensitive negotiations, that was true, correct?"

"Chief Davis and I told you that much in our last meeting," said Comstock. "We are in active negotiations of some form."

"And she was also in sync with the State Department when she told me that Jack is putting those negotiations at risk by resurrecting the sensitive issue of whether or not Ava Bazzi was murdered by the Tehran morality police."

"Yes. We are in sync," said Comstock.

"And you're not denying that those negotiations are being led by the National Security Council, not the State Department—because the NSC is negotiating for the release of her husband."

"We are neither confirming nor denying."

"What if I told you that, if you do confirm, I might be willing to help you."

"Speaking to you in your capacity as a federal agent, I find that statement troubling," said Comstock.

"I agree," said Davis.

"Troubling? How?"

"As a federal agent, it's your duty and responsibility to convince your husband to back away from the Ava Bazzi controversy," said Comstock.

"I'm also a wife. The State Department is asking me to ignore the fact that I'm married to Jack Swyteck. You're essentially asking me to do undercover work inside my own marriage."

Chief Comstock paused, then said, "That's a fair characterization of our request. What's your answer, Agent Henning?"

Andie hadn't expected such a straight answer. "My answer is that I would need to lay out some ground rules."

"Such as?"

"Before I would even consider such an assignment, I would need to know that someone's life is at stake. In other words, I certainly would not provide any assistance to the State Department vis-à-vis Jack if the only thing at stake is some nebulous and ultimately meaningless matter of international diplomacy that the president and his administration would tout in the short term as a political feather in their cap."

"The State Department does not negotiate for reasons of political expedience," said Comstock.

"My point is that I won't help you for anything less than a matter of life and death. I want to see with my own eyes and hear with my own ears, firsthand, that the hostage negotiations this woman described to me are real."

"We can't do that," said Comstock. "We can't make you privy to the negotiations."

"Then we don't have a deal," said Andie.

Davis, whose division included Iran, spoke up. "Let's try a slightly different approach. What if we showed you proof—actual evidence—that Jack's argument in court is completely wrongheaded?"

"Are you saying that the State Department has proof that the Iranian morality police did *not* murder Ava Bazzi?"

"Yes," said Davis. "And we will show you that proof in your capacity as a federal agent. All we are asking you to do is tell your husband the truth. Tell him that you have seen a classified dossier confirming that Ava Bazzi was not murdered by the morality police."

Andie was naturally skeptical. "Why don't you just tell Jack yourself?"

"That should be obvious, Agent Henning."

"Indulge me," said Andie.

"If we share the contents of a confidential dossier with your husband, he would be free to share that information with the court, the press, or anyone he desired. It's not a crime for your husband to disclose confidential information that the State Department voluntarily shares with him."

"But the same thing applies if *I* tell him there's a confidential State Department dossier showing that Ava Bazzi is still alive."

"It's a little different," said Davis.

"How is it different?"

"If Jack Swyteck publicly reveals that his wife told him about a confidential dossier about Ava Bazzi, *you* would go to prison."

Andie understood the implicit threat: if Jack were to go public with anything Andie told him about the dossier, the State Department would

flatly deny ever having authorized her, much less directed her, to disclose
the contents of the classified dossier to her husband. But that was not her
chief concern.

"Let me make sure I understand," says Andie. "You're asking me to share
classified information with my husband to get him to completely reverse
his position on Ava Bazzi. Is that right?"

"Yes."

"And you expect me to bet that Jack would say nothing about the reason
for his about-face? He'd offer no explanation to his client, to the judge,
or to the media—solely to keep me from going to prison for revealing a
confidential dossier?"

Her question seemed to surprise both division chiefs. Comstock spoke
this time. "Is that not a safe bet?" she asked Andie.

Andie wanted to say that was a safe bet. That Jack would put her above
his duty to his client. But in light of all that was happening between them,
she honestly didn't know the answer—which troubled her in ways that she
couldn't possibly share with the State Department.

"As safe as it would be in any marriage, I suppose," she said.

"Good," said Comstock. "Because these negotiations are as sensitive as
they come. They are truly a matter of life and death."

A matter of life and death. Their use of her own words was as close to
confirmation as she would get. The division chiefs would never admit
explicitly that the life of an imprisoned American was hanging in the
balance, but all signs indicated that the woman who visited her had been
for real, that her husband was on the verge of a negotiated release or perhaps
even a prisoner swap, and that Jack was putting those negotiations in
jeopardy by reopening the issue of Ava Bazzi and taking the position that
Ava was murdered by the morality police.

"Okay," Andie said. "Show me the proof."

CHAPTER 16

The hearing entered its third day on Thursday morning. It was the first day of live testimony from a witness in the courtroom.

"The petitioner calls Zahra Bazzi," said Farid's lawyer.

Zahra grabbed Jack's arm so firmly that he felt her fingernails through his suit. In a proceeding under the Hague Convention, the petitioner has the right to call the abducting spouse to the witness stand. Jack had done his best to prepare Zahra for this moment, but sometimes a lawyer's best wasn't quite good enough.

"I can't do this," she whispered.

It wasn't Jack's style to watch from the sideline as his client fought for survival on the witness stand. He did what he could to stop Farid's lawyer in her tracks.

"Your Honor, I presume Ms. Beech is calling my client as a witness to establish that she brought Yasmin to Miami without Mr. Bazzi's consent. If it would streamline matters, we are willing to stipulate to those facts."

The judge seemed open to the idea. "Ms. Beech, are you willing to accept Mr. Swyteck's stipulation and forgo your examination of the witness?"

"Absolutely not, Your Honor. I have a right to question Zahra Bazzi on my own terms."

"Nice try, Mr. Swyteck," the judge said. "Ms. Bazzi, please come forward."

With a subtle show of encouragement from Jack, Zahra rose from her seat beside him, stepped slowly to the other side of the courtroom, and stopped before the bailiff. It took only a moment to swear the familiar oath and settle into the proverbial chair that no one ever found comfortable. Zahra seemed particularly nervous, sitting up a bit too straight, her hands clenched tightly in her lap. The bailiff adjusted the gooseneck microphone to her level and stepped away, leaving nothing between her and Farid's counsel.

"Good morning, Ms. Bazzi," Beech began.

"Good morning," Zahra replied, and that was the end of the pleasantries.

Beech worked quickly, getting Zahra to agree to basic facts that could not be disputed. Zahra and Farid were married in January. Zahra adopted Yasmin soon after. In July, the family traveled to London on visas. Those opening questions would serve as the foundation for the lawyer's attack.

"I'd like to ask you more about that trip to London," said Beech.

Her tone changed. The questions became sharper, more like accusations, which made it easier for Jack to discern her strategy. Beech had rejected his proposed stipulation because she wasn't really interested in gathering information per se. Her aim was to expose Zahra as an unworthy mother skilled in the ways of fraud and deception.

"Ms. Bazzi, about six months after your marriage, you and Farid took your daughter Yasmin on a flight from Khomeini Airport in Tehran to Heathrow in London. Do I have that right?"

"That was in July, yes."

"To be exact, your flight landed in London on the twenty-second of July."

"That's correct."

"The three of you checked into a hotel in Kensington, correct?"

"Yes. The Adria."

"You had to be there by the twenty-second because Farid had an all-day business meeting scheduled for the twenty-third of July. Isn't that right?"

"Farid had a meeting. I don't know if it was all day."

"You knew about that meeting before you left Tehran, did you not, Ms. Bazzi?"

"I may have."

"Ms. Bazzi, isn't it true that Farid's business meeting was the primary purpose of the trip to London?"

"He was thinking about reviving his hotel business in the UK. So, yes, business was the reason for the trip. But it was also to see if I liked London. My sister Ava loved it there, and Farid wanted to make sure I did too."

"That was very thoughtful of him," said Beech.

"Or controlling," said Jack, rising.

"Mr. Swyteck, if that was an objection, it is overruled. I would advise both of you to keep your opinions to yourselves."

The lawyers apologized.

"Ms. Bazzi," Beech continued, "you don't dispute that Farid left the hotel early on the morning of July twenty-third for that business meeting, do you?"

"That's my recollection."

"Isn't it a fact, ma'am, that as soon as he left, you took Yasmin from your hotel in Kensington, got in a taxi, and returned to Heathrow Airport?"

She glanced in Jack's direction, but he couldn't change the facts. "Maybe not right after Farid left. But yes, we went back to Heathrow that same morning."

"You didn't tell Farid you and Yasmin were going back to the airport, did you, Ms. Bazzi."

"I didn't tell him. No."

"In fact, you kept it all a secret from him, didn't you?"

"Like I said, I didn't tell him."

"You knew that the only place you could take Yasmin without your husband's permission was back to Iran, didn't you, Ms. Bazzi?"

"I believe so."

"You more than 'believed' it, Ms. Bazzi. You came up with a plan to get around those travel restrictions."

"Objection, argumentative," said Jack.

"I'll rephrase," said Beech. "When you and Yasmin reached Heathrow Airport, you presented an affidavit to the customs agents, did you not?"

"Yes."

"That affidavit purported to grant Farid's written permission for you to travel alone with Yasmin, correct?"

She paused, but she had to answer. "That's true."

"You told the customs agent that the signature on that affidavit belonged to Farid, didn't you?"

"I don't recall. I don't think he ever asked."

"Let's be candid with the court, Ms. Bazzi: the signature on that affidavit was forged, was it not?"

"It was not Farid's signature."

"You forged his signature, didn't you, Ms. Bazzi?"

"I—I signed it for him."

"Without his permission, correct?"

Again she glanced at Jack, but there was no objection he could make.

"Yes. Without his permission."

"In fact, you traveled to the UK with that forged document in your possession, didn't you?"

"Yes."

"Before you even boarded the plane in Tehran on the twenty-second of July, you *knew* that you were going to use that forged document to abduct Yasmin the very next day. *Didn't you*, Ms. Bazzi?"

She didn't answer. The judge looked down from the bench. "The witness shall answer," he said.

She drew a breath, then answered. "Yes."

"That was all part of your premeditated plan, wasn't it?"

"I don't know what you mean by 'plan.'"

"It was your plan to abduct Yasmin and take her to Miami, so that Farid would never see her again. Isn't that true, Ms. Bazzi?"

"Objection," said Jack.

"Overruled," said the judge. "The witness will answer."

"It took some planning, I suppose."

"Yes. I'll bet it did," said Beech. "No further questions, Your Honor."

Farid's lawyer stepped away from the lectern, and Jack's gaze followed her to her seat beside her client. Both looked satisfied. In fact, it was the most content Jack had seen Farid since the start of the hearing.

Judge Carlton looked at Jack. "Mr. Swyteck, do you have any questions for Ms. Bazzi at this time?"

Jack was entitled to question his own client so that Zahra could explain *why* she abducted Yasmin, but it was up to him to decide when to ask those questions.

"Your Honor, as I stated earlier, we do not dispute the fact that my client took Yasmin Bazzi to Miami without her husband's consent. Our defense is under the Hague Convention: that returning Yasmin to her father would put her in grave danger of physical or psychological harm. My preference is not to put on evidence in support of that defense until the petitioner has presented his case in full and this court rules that a defense is necessary."

"Very well," the judge said. "We will proceed with the petitioner's case to its conclusion, at which time the respondent may retake the stand to present her defense, if necessary."

"Thank you, Judge," said Jack.

"Ms. Bazzi, you are excused."

Zahra stepped down from the witness stand and returned to her seat beside Jack. Her hands were shaking, and her eyes sought Jack's approval, or at least his reassurance that things hadn't gone that badly.

"Are we going to be okay?" she asked in a hushed voice.

Jack rested his hand atop hers to stop the shaking. "We'll be fine," he said, though he didn't want to mislead her. "But we have a lot of work to do."

Andie flew into Reagan National Airport and arrived at the State Department midafternoon Thursday. The confidential dossier on Ava Bazzi was viewable only in person, which made the trip necessary, though Andie imagined it would take a team of bureaucrats to sort out whether the cost of the plane ticket should come out of the FBI's budget or the State Department's.

A middle-aged man met Andie in the fourth-floor lobby of the Office of Children's Issues. He introduced himself only by his last name, Westbrook, and led her down the hallway to a small conference room. The room had no windows. The only furniture was a small rectangular table with a chair on each side. A dossier folder was on the tabletop.

"It's not the full dossier on Ava Bazzi, of course," said Westbrook. "Some portions of the dossier are classified as Top Secret. Obviously, those are not here for you. The rest of the dossier is classified as Secret, but most of the Secret information is irrelevant for your purposes."

"Then what do you intend to show me?" asked Andie.

"Frankly, as little as possible—just enough to satisfy you that Ava Bazzi is alive."

Westbrook unsealed the dossier, speaking into a Dictaphone to make a record of the exact time of each step of the process—opening the dossier, removing six sheets of paper marked SECRET, and finally placing the documents before Agent Henning.

"What is this?" asked Andie.

"We got it from the Department of Homeland Security. It's a law enforcement certification in support of a U visa. A U visa is—"

"I know what a U visa is," said Andie.

A U visa allows noncitizens to stay in the United States if they are the victim of a crime and are providing assistance to a law enforcement investigation. Andie had seen U visas issued to victims of crimes ranging from blackmail to sex trafficking.

Andie flipped through the pages. "Are you saying that the US government issued a U visa to Ava Bazzi?"

"No. Ava Bazzi requested a U visa. It was denied."

"When did she apply?"

"The date is on the application. Next to her signature."

Andie flipped to the last page and checked the date. "February of this year," she said aloud. "Eight months ago."

"Put another way, sixteen months after your husband claims Ava Bazzi was murdered by the Tehran morality police."

"What crime did Ava offer to help law enforcement investigate?"

"Torture by the Tehran morality police. Obviously, no US law enforcement agency has jurisdiction over that crime. That's why the application was denied."

Andie studied the application for a moment. "This form could have been filled out by anyone. How do I know it was the real Ava Bazzi?"

"Are you accusing the State Department of defrauding you?"

"I'm just being thorough," she said. *And asking the questions my husband would ask*, she decided not to say.

"Applications for U visas are processed in two stages. First, the application is reviewed. If everything is in order, then the applicant appears in person at the nearest consulate or embassy to be fingerprinted. This application never made it to step two."

"There was no fingerprinting?" asked Andie.

"Not in the normal way fingerprints are collected. But turn to the last two pages of the dossier," said Westbrook.

Andie did. The penultimate page was an FBI report describing the collection of latent fingerprints found on the U visa application and setting forth two very clear prints from a thumb and an index finger. Attached to it was an Interpol fingerprint specimen for Ava Bazzi. Most people are unaware that Iran was a founding member of the International Criminal Police Organization, but Andie knew.

"I presume Ava Bazzi's prints became part of the Interpol database when she was arrested in Tehran."

"Correct. The FBI examiner's conclusion is on the last page."

Andie checked the examiner's name. Leslie T. Cahill. It wasn't anyone she recognized, but every FBI examiner was part of an elite group.

"Based on a comparison of the latent prints on the application to those in the Interpol database, it is this examiner's opinion that Ava Bazzi is the source of the latent prints to a reasonable degree of scientific certainty," said Andie, reading aloud from the report.

"Proving that Ava Bazzi had her hands on the application," said Westbrook.

Andie laid the dossier aside. "Why is this document classified?"

"It's a sensitive piece of information that bears on active negotiations between the United States and Iran."

"How so?"

"It supports the position of the Iranian government that Ava Bazzi is still alive. But it also supports the allegation that she was tortured, which the Iranian government vehemently denies."

"So, it's classified because it cuts both ways?"

Westbrook considered her words before responding. "It's classified because the State Department finds it useful in the current negotiations with the Iranian government."

"Do you plan to share this document with the Iranians?"

"That depends."

"On what?"

"Whether the Iranians give us what we want."

Andie was thinking only of a woman so desperate that she'd traveled all the way to Key Biscayne and begged an FBI agent to help save her husband's life.

"You mean whether they give you *who* you want," said Andie.

"If you say so," said Westbrook.

"I do," said Andie. "Otherwise, I wouldn't be here."

CHAPTER 17

Farid's lawyer called her final witness to the stand. Farid Bazzi raised his right hand, and the bailiff administered a slightly revised oath.

"Do you swear by Allah to tell the truth, the whole truth, and nothing but the truth?"

A Muslim witness was not required to swear "by Allah," any more than Christians, Jews, or atheists were required to say "so help me God." It was enough to affirm to tell the truth.

"I do," said Farid.

Jack leaned closer to his client and whispered, "Is Farid a believer?"

"He would tell you he is," said Zahra.

To a believer in Islam, there was no more powerful incentive to telling the truth than swearing an oath by Allah. Jack had once represented a Muslim on death row who wouldn't have sworn by Allah to save his own life, so fearful was he of the temptation to lie and the eternal consequences of lying under oath. It made Jack wonder if Farid also took his oath that seriously—or if swearing by Allah was part of the courtroom theater choreographed by his lawyer to enhance his credibility.

"Good morning, Mr. Bazzi," his lawyer began.

Direct examination of your client is one of the most difficult tasks for a trial lawyer. Leading questions were not allowed, so the only way to control the witness was to have the client's complete trust before he took the stand. In a case where the Iranian government had such a vested interest, Jack wondered if Farid trusted his lawyer enough to stick to their script—or if there might be surprises.

"Good morning," said Farid.

"Let's begin by telling Judge Carlton a little bit about yourself."

As if on cue, Farid turned, looked at the judge, and started talking. Farid was a good conversationalist, and wisely, his lawyer was taking advantage of that skill to help him build a rapport with the judge. Jack took a few notes. One year of college at the University of Tehran. Dated Zahra. Broke up. Went abroad and earned a degree in entrepreneurship from the London School of Economics. Returned to Tehran and focused on the hotel and hospitality business sector.

"When did you meet Ava Bazzi?"

"I first met her while dating her older sister, Zahra. Ava was just a sixteen-year-old girl at the time. But when I came back to Tehran from London, she was a grown woman."

"How would you describe the moment when you met Ava as a grown woman?"

Farid paused, and Jack watched his expression carefully. It was an interesting question to ask a man who'd sat through the testimony of his wife's lover—assuming Asmoun had been truthful.

"I had never looked at her this way," he said, almost wistfully. "It was like seeing her for the first time. In a way, it was like . . . love at first sight."

Zahra coughed into her fist, and it sounded more like a scoff.

"Did the two of you start dating?" asked Beech.

"Yes," said Farid, and then he looked in Zahra's direction for the first time. "With her sister's blessing."

"*Warning*, not blessing," Zahra whispered to Jack.

"How soon were you married after you started dating?" Beech asked.

"Things moved quickly. Six months."

"You and Ava had a child?"

Farid smiled warmly. "Yes. Our daughter Yasmin is now six years old."

"Let's talk more about your daughter," said Beech. "What role did you play in raising Yasmin?"

"A very active role."

"Did you ever change her diapers as a baby?"

"Yes."

"Feed her?"

"Yes."

"Bathe her?"

"Yes, I did all those things. To some people in my country, it is shameful for a man to care for an infant. Ava was an excellent mother, but we agreed that both of us should be involved."

"As Yasmin grew older, did you continue to be active in her upbringing?"

"Absolutely. I read to her every night. I was her first soccer coach. I taught her to ice-skate and ride a bicycle."

For Jack, it was like listening to himself talk about Righley. It went on for another ten minutes. Farid taught her to pray and love Allah. Farid taught her to play piano. Farid knew the names of all Yasmin's friends, her favorite color, her favorite TV shows. At his lawyer's request, he sang to Judge Carlton the English translation of Yasmin's favorite children's song:

You are the sky's great moon,
And I'll become a star and go around you.

Jack had to do something before the judge nominated Farid for father of the year.

"Your Honor, I object. This is all very heartwarming, but this is not a custody trial. It is a Hague proceeding in which the issue is whether my client wrongfully removed Yasmin from her habitual place of residence in violation of Farid's rights of custody."

"Judge, that's a very disingenuous objection," said Beech. "The mud-slinging will start the minute I rest my case, as Mr. Swyteck tries to prove that Yasmin will be in grave danger if she is returned to her father. Mr. Bazzi's testimony will put those allegations in the proper light."

"I will overrule the objection," said the judge. "But, Ms. Beech, please do tie your questions more closely to the issue this court must ultimately decide: whether Mr. Bazzi presents a risk of physical or psychological harm to his daughter."

"Happy to, Your Honor," said Beech, and then she addressed her client. "Mr. Bazzi, did you ever strike, beat, hit, slap, push, shove, or spank Yasmin?"

"Never."

"Did you subject Yasmin to physical abuse of any kind?"

"Never."

"Did you ever threaten Yasmin with any kind of physical abuse?"

"Never."

"Did you ever threaten her in any way?"

"No, I would never do that."

"Did you use words or gestures to make Yasmin afraid of you?"

"No. I wanted my daughter's love, not her fear."

"Did you ever say anything to embarrass or humiliate her in front of others?"

"No. Yasmin was not perfect. No child is. But Ava and I corrected her privately, not in public. We were in complete agreement on that."

Farid's lawyer paused and flipped to the next page of her notepad. Chapter 1, Farid the good father, had been written. On to chapter 2, Jack presumed: Farid the victim.

"Let's talk now about your two marriages, starting with the most recent one. We've already heard testimony that you dated Zahra some years ago, before you dated Ava. Tell us how Zahra came back into your life."

"After Ava disappeared—"

"You mean, fled the country and abandoned you?" said Beech.

"Objection," said Jack. "Counsel is putting words in her client's mouth."

"Sustained. This court has not yet decided whether Ava Bazzi is alive or dead. 'Disappeared' seems like an appropriate word. The witness may continue."

Farid started over. "After Ava disappeared, I did my best to raise Yasmin alone. But I quickly realized she needed a mother. Zahra stepped in and helped. At first, she visited as the good aunt providing support for Yasmin."

"Did that change over time?"

"Yes. I'd say it evolved to include not just caring for Yasmin but also companionship for me."

"Were you courting?"

"I would say *she* was courting *me*."

Zahra grabbed Jack by the wrist. "That's such a lie," she said in a coarse whisper.

"I don't want lurid details," said Beech. "But in a general sense, what do you mean when you say Zahra was courting you?"

"I wasn't ready to start touching another woman. Zahra exploited the fact that we had once dated to make me feel comfortable about those things. It was Zahra who suggested we try being a couple again."

"Who first raised the idea of marriage?"

"Zahra."

"Who first raised the idea of Zahra adopting Yasmin?"

"Zahra. It wasn't required under Iranian or Islamic law that Zahra adopt Yasmin, but she insisted on it."

"Soon after the adoption was final, the three of you went to London, correct?"

"Yes. Zahra persuaded me to reapply for the UK Entrepreneur visa, take one more shot at expanding my hotel and restaurant business outside Iran. She said it would be a fresh start to return to London as a new family."

"Zahra fled with Yasmin the day after you landed at Heathrow, correct?"

It was an ugly fact, but Jack couldn't object simply on the grounds that the truth was ugly.

"Yes, that's correct," said Farid.

"Did you feel deceived?"

"Absolutely. I felt like a fool."

Beech adjusted her tone to be more understanding. To Jack, she sounded like a radio-show psychiatrist.

"Mr. Bazzi, what has your life been like since the day that Zahra took your daughter?"

"Hell on earth."

"What have you done since then?"

"I stayed in the UK. I spent thousands of hours trying to locate my daughter and have her returned to me. When I wasn't doing that, I was building my hotel business under the Entrepreneur visa program. That has been my life for more than a year."

"If this court returns Yasmin to you, what is your plan?"

"We will settle in London. My first hotel and restaurant are already a success. In two months' time, we can apply for British citizenship."

If Farid had been his client, Jack would have ended right there, keeping Farid above the controversial debate as to whether Ava was alive or dead. But Farid was not his client.

"Finally, Mr. Bazzi, we've heard a lot about your first wife, Ava, in this proceeding. I want to ask you briefly about that relationship."

"Okay."

"Would you describe your marriage to Ava as a happy one?"

"Yes. Especially when we lived in London."

"Did you love Ava?"

"Yes. With all my heart."

"Did there come a time when you stopped loving her?"

Farid hesitated. Jack sensed this might be the moment that all trial lawyers dreaded—when the client's answer is off script, something other than what his lawyer expected, something different from what they'd rehearsed.

"I don't think so," he said.

Beech did her best not to appear surprised, but Jack could read her body language. She continued. "Let me be more precise with my question. Did you stop loving Ava after she abandoned you and your daughter?"

"Objection," said Jack, rising. "The record does not show that Ava Bazzi abandoned anyone. Only that she is dead."

"Actually, Mr. Swyteck, the record is inconclusive either way. Nonetheless, your objection is sustained."

"I'll rephrase," said Beech. "Did you stop loving Ava after the Iranian government informed you that she fled the country, abandoning you and Yasmin?"

Farid paused, seeming to struggle for a response. "I—it's hard to say how I felt."

Again, Jack was reading body language, this time both the lawyer's and the client's. Without a doubt, Farid was off script. Beech continued, doing her best to get him back on track. "Surely you stopped loving her after her affair with Mr. Asmoun."

Farid blinked slowly, and then cleared his throat. "If Ava cheated on me, as Mr. Asmoun testified, I was the last to know. In fact, I didn't know anything about it until I found out that Mr. Asmoun was going to be a witness in this proceeding. My feelings for Ava—"

"That'll do," said Beech, cutting off her own client.

Jack rose. The response had clearly taken Farid's lawyer by surprise, and Jack wanted to hear the rest of it. "Your Honor, I don't think the witness has finished his answer."

"Judge, Mr. Bazzi answered my question," said Beech.

The judge looked down from the bench. "Mr. Bazzi, did you finish your response?"

Farid's eyes welled. Jack noticed. The judge noticed. His lawyer glared at him, a stern warning not to say anything to lose the case. He looked down at his hands and spoke in a sad, quiet voice.

"My feelings for Ava are complicated."

"Thank you," said Beech, quick to shut things down.

"Crocodile tears," Zahra whispered to Jack.

"One last question," said Beech.

The final question was always well rehearsed, and despite the surprises along the way, Beech was not to be denied the power of those final words.

"Mr. Bazzi, why did you bring this action under the Hague Convention?"

He took a deep breath, then let it out. "I'm not out for revenge. I don't have hard feelings toward Zahra or Ava. My daughter was taken from me. I just want her back."

"Thank you," said Beech. "I have no further questions."

Beech closed her notebook and returned to the table. Jack rose for cross-examination, but the judge stopped him.

"We are coming up on four thirty. Let's call it a day and resume tomorrow morning at nine with cross-examination. The witness may step down. We are adjourned." He brought down the gavel.

"All rise!" said the bailiff.

Jack and his client got quickly to their feet. Behind them, rows of spectators followed suit, their thumps and thuds in the wooden bench seats echoing in an otherwise silenced courtroom. Zahra looked at Jack, as if asking for his immediate assessment of how much damage Farid had done. Farid had done his job. Jack might even say he was a perfect witness. But that wasn't what his client wanted to hear.

"The judge did us a favor," he said quietly. "I have the whole night to prepare my cross-examination."

As Judge Carlton exited through the side door to his chambers, the rumbling of a hundred different conversations broke the courtroom silence. The clock was ticking on Jack's night of preparation.

CHAPTER 18

It was a ten-minute walk from the State Department to the nearest Metro station. A transfer to the Yellow Line would have taken Andie to Reagan National Airport in time to catch her flight to Miami. But the review of the classified dossier on Ava Bazzi was only part of the reason for her trip. Andie took the Red Line to Maryland.

"Next stop, Takoma Station."

Andie rose with the robotic-sounding announcement. The metallic screech of steel wheels on steel rails brought her train to a stop, and she exited to the platform.

Andie had been planning this side trip since the night the woman showed up in a taxi outside her house in Key Biscayne. After the woman refused to tell Andie her name, Andie had jotted down her cab's license plate number. A follow-up call to the driver gave her the name of the hotel where he'd dropped his passenger. A call to the hotel manager got her the name the woman had used at check-in, which was as phony as Jane Doe. She'd been careful enough to pay the cab and the hotel in cash, leaving no credit card trail. But there had been an outgoing phone call from the hotel room. The number was on the billing statement. It was to a landline, and belonged to a seventy-seven-year-old woman in Takoma Park, Maryland. Her name was Irene Guthrie. Irene's address was Andie's destination.

And people said *cell phones* were the end of personal privacy.

The walk from the Metro station to Irene's house was one of the crunchiest Andie had ever taken. Takoma Park was known for its tree-lined streets, and autumn had come late, leaving sidewalks covered in fallen leaves, with still more falling as Andie passed through the quiet neighborhood. The wood-frame houses dated to before World War II but were well maintained. They all started to look the same to Andie, distinguished only by the color of the latest coat of paint on the clapboard siding. Andie stopped outside a yellow house and checked the street number. She was in the right place. She walked up the sidewalk—*crunch, crunch, crunch*—and knocked on the front door. To Andie's surprise, Irene didn't even ask who it was before opening the door.

We're not in Miami anymore, Toto.

"Irene Guthrie?" asked Andie.

"Yes, can I help you?"

It wasn't kosher for an FBI agent to flash a badge on a personal matter, and it was a close call as to whether this visit was FBI business. Andie had played it conservatively and not used her FBI status when talking to the cabdriver and hotel manager. Years of undercover work had trained her to open doors without a badge. She played this visit the same way.

"Hi, my name is Andie. You don't know me, but we have a mutual friend. Frankly I'm a little worried about her, and I was hoping you could help."

Irene's eyes clouded with concern. "Who are you talking about?"

Andie pulled a photograph from her purse. It was an image captured by video surveillance at the hotel. The hotel manager had been more than cooperative, though Andie doubted that she would have gotten the surveillance video if she'd been wearing her wedding ring at the time.

"This is a photo of her in Miami," she said.

Irene took the photo and looked at it. "That is definitely Margaret."

Margaret. That was a start. "Did you know she was in Miami?"

"Yes, we spoke on the telephone while she was there. We speak almost every day. She's the only family I've got, since, you know—my son went missing."

It wasn't quite the jackpot, but it was close.

"Did Margaret tell you why she was going to Miami?"

"I don't remember, specifically. I seem to have the idea in my head that it was to see someone. A friend."

That worked for Andie. "That's what I wanted to talk to you about. Margaret came to Miami to see me. She said some things that worried me. Things about . . ."

Andie let the question dangle and held her breath.

"About Brian?"

Jackpot, assuming Brian and his mother had the same surname. "Yes, about Brian." *Brian Guthrie.*

"Would you like to come inside, Andie? I could make some tea."

Andie smiled on the inside. "Yes, I'd like that very much," she said, and another door opened.

J ack invited Zahra back to his office for the end-of-day download on things going well, going wrong, or going nowhere, but Zahra wanted a place where she could relax. It was Jack's first visit to a hookah lounge.

"I honestly didn't know Miami had hookah lounges," he said.

"Not authentic ones," said Zahra. "Most of them are trendy variations on a nightclub that use hookah as a gimmick. A real hookah lounge would be more respectful of customers who don't drink for religious reasons. They might serve alcohol, but not to the point where people are openly drunk and prying their way into each other's pants."

The lounge was dimly lit, with comfortable sitting areas for small groups to relax and converse. Jack and Zahra were seated on a couch with the hookah resting on the low table in front of them. Zahra chose the apple-flavored tobacco, and their server loaded it. It was a typical hookah, standing about two feet tall, consisting of a bulbous glass base, a bowl for the tobacco, a hose, and a hose handle. Zahra explained that charcoal heated the flavored tobacco in the bowl, and the smoke was drawn through the water in the glass base and into the hose, where the smoker inhaled it. For Jack it brought back memories of his college roommate, who before his expulsion taught everyone in the dorm to smoke pot through a bong.

The server brought a pitcher of water and two glasses.

"No ice for me," said Zahra.

The server poured accordingly and left them alone.

"Is that an official hookah thing, no ice?" asked Jack.

"No. It's a Zahra thing. Sensitive teeth. Persians were making cold drinks with ice thousands of years before there were freezers. Big clay cooling systems right in the middle of the desert. They were called *yakhchāl*s."

"Ancient slushies," said Jack. "A culture ahead of its time in so many ways."

Zahra drank to that, then said, "And in other ways, not so much."

Zahra took the hookah hose, brought the nozzle to her lips, and inhaled. The smoke curled up to the lights as she exhaled.

"The hookah lounge is my safe place," said Zahra. "Part of my culture. Birthdays. Graduations. Crying over the cute boy who didn't like you back. Amazing your friends with your smoke-ring skills. You don't do it alone. Always in a group."

"Was this something you and Ava did together?"

"Ava," she said, rolling her eyes. "I tried to take her for her sixteenth birthday, but she wouldn't come."

"Too young?"

"Hah! No. It didn't fit her image."

"Her image?"

"Ava was the 'perfect daughter,'" she said, making air quotes. "She *pretended* to listen when our mother said it was *haram* and *aib*—forbidden and shameful—for girls to smoke. Meanwhile, she was smoking hookah every weekend with her friends. You could smell it on her clothes. Did that make a difference to our mother? No. Ava was the good girl. Zahra was the bad girl."

"Second child privilege," said Jack. "Firstborn has to obey all the rules. The rest get away with murder."

Zahra passed the hose to Jack. "Funny thing is, had Mother left out the guilt and just told me that hookah causes cancer, like all other tobacco, I probably would have listened."

Jack coughed on the inhale. She laughed, and Jack smiled back. Then he turned to business. "Let's start by managing expectations for tomorrow."

Zahra smiled thinly. "I can't wait to see Farid squirm on the witness stand."

"That's what I meant by 'managing expectations.' There are a few points I can score tomorrow, but we are not going to win the case on cross-examination."

She looked at him with confusion. "But . . . that's your job."

"Zahra, this is not a trial. This is a hearing under the Hague Convention. There's been no discovery."

"What do you mean by 'discovery'?"

"I have no ammunition. No phone calls to the Iranian equivalent of nine-one-one. No medical records showing bruises or injuries from abuse. No photographs of kicked-down doors or broken dishes thrown across the apartment. In a trial, I would have those things and confront Farid with them on cross-examination. Without them, we can't expect him to just break down on the witness stand, cry like a baby, and admit he's an abusive parent."

It was like watching the air escape from a balloon; Zahra seemed to deflate before his eyes. "Are you saying we can't win the case?"

"Not at all. I'm saying we can't win the case *tomorrow*. To win, we have to present strong evidence next week as part of our case."

"Okay. What kind of evidence?"

"That depends. If we want to show that Farid was an abusive husband, your testimony will be enough. But if we want to prove that Farid was an abusive *father*, we may need another witness."

"Who?"

Jack hesitated to say it, but there would never be a good time. "We may have to put Yasmin on the stand."

"No," she said firmly.

"Farid's testimony today made a big impression on Judge Carlton."

"No," she said, even more firmly.

"Legally, it's our burden to prove that returning Yasmin to her father puts her in grave danger of physical or psychological harm. And we have to prove it by clear and convincing evidence. A battle of he-said, she-said is not going to win this case."

"I said *no*! Yasmin is not testifying. She's *six*."

It was the reaction Jack had expected, but it was his job to raise it. "I understand," he said. "I really do."

"I don't care if you understand or not, Jack. I care about winning this case. How do you plan to do that?"

"There is one other angle."

"Tell me."

"Under the Hague Convention, the abuse doesn't have to be directed at the child. There's a strong argument that a child suffers psychological harm by witnessing the abuse of her mother."

Zahra inhaled from the hookah, thinking, then exhaled. "So it's not enough to prove that Farid was abusive to Ava and me. We need to prove he did it in front of Yasmin."

"That's right," said Jack.

Zahra swallowed hard, looked off somewhere to the middle distance, and then brought her gaze back to Jack. "We'll prove what we have to prove," she said.

"I'm going to need details."

"Not here," she said quietly. "Let's not spoil my safe place."

CHAPTER 19

Andie took the Metro back into the district and reached the J. Edgar Hoover Building just after dark. She had several friends at FBI headquarters, none better than her very first supervisory agent in the Seattle field office.

Isaac Underwood had gone out on a limb for an agent just two years out of the Academy, entrusting Andie with an undercover assignment that would change the trajectory of her career. Her infiltration of a cult in Washington's Yakima Valley led to the apprehension of a serial killer, earning her accolades throughout the bureau. Leaving Isaac had been the hardest part about her transfer to Miami. Soon after, Isaac was bound for headquarters, though some said he would never have left Seattle if Andie hadn't transferred. Rumors. In any event, it had worked out well for him. He became section chief in the international operations division, overseeing operational units covering Africa, Asia, and the Middle East. Several promotions followed, most recently to assistant director of the counterterrorism division.

Andie didn't consider her visit official FBI business, so they met at a bar across the street and found a booth in the back where they could talk in private. It was after hours, so Isaac ordered a draft beer. Andie had a glass of chardonnay.

"So, you're a big shot now," said Andie. "Assistant director."

"You make it sound like there's only one assistant director."

"Not all assistant directors are created equal. What side of the building is your office on?"

"West."

"Wow, Isaac. A view of Judiciary Square."

"Meh. It's not Puget Sound or Mount Rainier, but I can't complain."

Andie recalled their "definitely not a date" goodbye dinner for her at Restaurant San Michele in Pike Place Market, when the other agents on their team were a no-show. It ended up just Andie and Isaac on the terrace, enjoying steamed mussels and a breathtaking sunset view of Puget Sound with the Olympic Mountains in the distance. Andie still wondered if it was a no-show by design.

"How's Jack?" Isaac asked.

"Jack's good."

"How are you and Jack?"

"Jack's good," she said, not sure why she'd repeated herself.

"Oh? Trouble in paradise?"

"Nothing we can't handle. It's not easy being an FBI agent married to a criminal lawyer."

Criminal defense lawyer, she could almost hear Jack saying.

"Well, if you ever need someone to talk to, I'm around."

"Thank you."

"So," he said, shifting gears. "You didn't come all the way to Washington to talk about old times. You said you've hit a brick wall with the State Department?"

Andie had called Isaac after tea with Irene Guthrie in Takoma Park. She'd been purposely vague.

"I need some advice. From someone I trust." She leveled her gaze. "From someone who would never acknowledge that this conversation ever happened, let alone what was said."

"I'm sure I owe you one of those."

Jack's representation of Zahra Bazzi and the Ava Bazzi angle were public knowledge. The only part she needed to fill in was the woman in the taxi on Key Biscayne and her talk with Brian Guthrie's mother in Takoma Park. Isaac listened as Andie talked, and then he had a few questions.

"Has the State Department told you that the US government is negotiating for the release of a political prisoner?" he asked.

"No."

"But his wife and mother told you that's the case?"

"Yes. His name is Brian Guthrie. But here's the rub. I've checked everywhere. I can't find any record or mention of an American prisoner in Iran named Brian Guthrie."

"That's not unusual, Andie. Remember the last time the United States and Iran swapped prisoners?"

"The six-billion-dollar ransom that was not a ransom?"

"And that was never paid," said Isaac. "Those funds were frozen in Qatar after Hamas murdered twelve hundred Israelis and kidnapped two hundred more with Iran's support. But it took a promise of six billion dollars to get five Americans released from Evin Prison in Tehran. And the point I'm making here is that the names of two of those hostages were never revealed, even after they came home."

"Sounds like I was lucky to find out what little I did about Brian Guthrie."

"Yeah. What do you know about him?"

"Only what his mother told me. He was an art broker who specialized in antiquities. It was his job to chase down promising artifacts and bring them to auction houses like Sotheby's and Christie's. He was scouting in Iran when the police arrested him."

"The art trade in antiquities can be a sketchy business," said Isaac. "Plenty of the objects that end up in penthouses in New York or London were looted. One of the most respected trustees at the Met got into hot water over that not too long ago."

"I read about that. But I don't think the State Department would prioritize the negotiation of his release from prison if Mr. Guthrie was an actual criminal."

"No, but if he has less than a squeaky-clean record in a controversial line of business, that could be the reason the State Department is keeping his name under the radar. Especially if he's become a pawn in a bigger diplomatic negotiation with the Iranian government."

Andie had been thinking the same thing, but it was reassuring to hear it from Isaac.

"I'd be curious to know what the FBI databases would tell me about him," she said.

Isaac's expression turned serious. "Don't do it, Andie. Margaret Guthrie contacted you because you're Jack's wife, not because you're an FBI agent. This is not official FBI business. Accessing that database for a personal matter could cost you your job. You could even end up in jail."

"I understand," said Andie.

"Good," said Isaac. "Pinkie swear?"

She smiled, and they locked fingers. "Pinkie swear. Goofball."

A man hurried past their booth on the way to the bathroom and then stopped abruptly.

"Andie?" he asked.

It took a minute in the dim lighting, but the name came to her. "Dennis? How are you?"

He smiled at Andie, then looked at Isaac, then glanced at their drinks, and then smiled again at Andie—awkwardly.

"Um . . . ," he said, flustered. He was clearly under the impression that he'd stumbled upon something he wasn't supposed to see.

Andie reacted quickly. "Dennis, this is my former supervisory agent, Isaac Underwood."

The men shook hands.

"Well, great to see you again, Andie. See you around." He hurried off.

"That was awkward," said Isaac. "Who was that guy?"

"Dennis Devoe. He was Jack's roommate all through law school. He works in the Justice Department. I've seen him maybe once or twice since our wedding, but he and Jack do a golf weekend once a year."

"Does he think that you and I—"

"Yeah, Dennis would think that way. His ex-wife cheated on him for five years before he finally figured out what was going on."

"Do you want me to follow him into the men's room and straighten him out?"

"No. That's way too defensive. I'll call Jack and let him know I had a drink with my old boss after work. No big deal."

"I hope this isn't going to create a problem."

"The only way it would create a problem is if Jack heard it from Dennis."

"You sure?"

"Yes," she said, hoping. "I'm sure."

Jack left his office just before nine o'clock. Righley was already asleep, and the babysitter was booked until ten, so he stopped at Cy's Place to see Theo. He found an open stool at the bend in the long U-shaped bar.

Theo sniffed the air like a bloodhound. "What the hell, dude? You spill applesauce on yourself while reaching for your bottle of Ensure?"

Jack took a whiff of his shirt sleeve. "That's apple-flavored tobacco you're smelling. Zahra took me to a hookah lounge."

Jack and Zahra had gone back to his office for the download on Farid. Two hours and two boxes of tissues later, Jack had what he needed.

"What're you drinking?" asked Theo.

"Club soda. Big day in court tomorrow."

"Who's on the menu?"

"Farid."

Theo filled Jack's glass from the fountain. "You got the goods to prove he's an abuser?"

"I have only what Zahra has told me."

"You believe her?"

Jack shrugged. "Is there some reason I shouldn't?"

"I suppose not."

Jack sensed his friend was holding back. "If you have something to say, spit it out."

Theo wiped down the bar top and placed Jack's glass on a napkin. "You ever see that old movie where Jimmy Stewart plays the criminal defense lawyer?"

"*Anatomy of a Murder*? Every trial lawyer has seen it. When did you watch it?"

"We had about five DVDs to watch when I was on death row. This was one of them. You know the story. Jimmy Stewart defends a man accused of murdering the guy who raped his wife. His client admits he killed him. Stewart tells him there's only one defense. It's the famous scene where he lays out the legal elements of a temporary insanity defense."

Jack knew the plot. "And then the client suddenly starts saying all the things he needs to say for his lawyer to build a temporary insanity defense. But what's your point here?"

"Dude, your client admits she abducted Farid's daughter. You laid out a road map with only one path that leads to keeping her daughter. Zahra has to prove that Farid is an abuser."

"Are you saying I put ideas in my client's head? I'm Jimmy Stewart?"

Theo answered in his Jimmy Stewart voice. "Well, uh. You know, Jack. There's, uh, worse people that you can be, uh . . . than Jimmy Stewart."

"Don't gloss this over with a joke."

"Don't get all defensive on me. I'm not saying for sure that Zahra is lying. There's just a few things that make me wonder."

"A *few* things? What else you got?"

"Well, since you asked. You offered my services as her bodyguard. She's never taken me up on it. Seems like she would have jumped on your offer if she was afraid of Farid. I've stopped checking in on her."

"Maybe she doesn't want to impose on you," said Jack.

"I would definitely say you're right . . . if I hadn't talked to Farid myself. The guy was shittin' his pants when I cornered him in the men's room and called him a fucking coward for beating his wives and then threatening you outside your office. He still denied everything. I told you what I thought."

Jack remembered: *I'm not sure he's lying.*

"It's all such a blur," said Jack. "These Hague proceedings move so fast. Too little time to verify the facts."

"All you can do is go with what your gut tells you."

"I suppose," Jack said in a voice that faded.

Theo rested his forearms on the bar and looked at Jack. "Somethin' else is eatin' you. I can tell. What's up?"

Jack looked away, then back. "Andie called me from DC. She was at a bar having a drink with her old supervisory agent from Seattle. Isaac is his name."

"So?"

"So, what if she's thinking about taking a job at headquarters?"

"And do what? Commute home on the weekends? She wouldn't leave you and Righley like that."

"No," said Jack. "But she might leave just me."

Theo's jaw dropped. "Dude, Andie is crazy about you. This case is making you paranoid. Your wife is not going to take your daughter and run off."

Jack turned very serious. "Ten minutes after Andie called me, I got a call from my old law school roommate. He happened to be in the same bar. He saw them alone in a booth on his way to the bathroom."

"Stop acting like a middle-schooler. Just because a woman goes into a bar with a man doesn't mean she's playing footsie with his balls under the table."

"He said they were holding hands."

"What? Come on. Maybe your friend didn't see what he thought he saw."

"Maybe."

"What're you gonna do about it?"

"Talk to Andie when she gets home. What else can I do?"

"Study for the DC bar exam?"

Jack didn't laugh.

"Sorry, bad joke," said Theo. He opened a bottle of beer and set it before Jack. "On the house."

Jack watched a drop of condensation work its way down the bottleneck. When it finally reached the label, he took a drink.

"I don't feel like ripping into Farid tomorrow," said Jack.

"Get over it, dude."

"Yeah. You know I will."

CHAPTER 20

Jack approached the witness, shrouded in courtroom silence.

"This court reminds the witness that he is under oath," said Judge Carlton. "Mr. Swyteck, proceed."

As a young lawyer, Jack had learned the hard way that the key to effective cross-examination was to control the witness, and the key to control was a full command of the facts. That morning, as he stared down Farid, Jack had only his client's version of the facts. As Farid stared back, sizing up the lawyer, he seemed to know Jack's limitations. With only one side of the story, Jack wasn't playing a game of control. It was more like a game of blackjack—a dealer's game, but the wrong card might still turn up.

"Mr. Bazzi, I want to ask a few questions about my client's adoption of your daughter, Yasmin."

Opposing counsel was quickly on her feet. "Objection, Your Honor. Without Ava Bazzi's consent, there was no adoption. Which is why this is an open-and-shut case."

"Overruled. Ms. Beech, knock off the speaking objections, please."

Jack continued. "Let me follow up on your lawyer's point, Mr. Bazzi. Your position is that Ava Bazzi's consent was required because she is still alive, correct?"

"Well, she couldn't very well give consent if she was dead, could she, Mr. Swyteck?"

A few snickers from the audience only added to Farid's smugness.

"More to the point," said Jack, "the adoption is valid if Ava is dead, correct?"

"Objection."

The judge groaned. "Ms. Beech, I'm fairly certain you've conceded that point. The respondent has parental rights and her abduction of the child is defensible under the Hague Convention if the biological mother was deceased at the time of the adoption."

"Yes, Judge," she said, settling back into her seat.

Jack continued. "Sir, you haven't seen Ava Bazzi since she was arrested by Tehran's morality police, am I right?"

"No, I haven't."

"You've had no communication with her since her arrest. Right?"

"That's right."

"The only basis for your belief that Ava Bazzi is still alive is that the Iranian government told you so. Isn't that right, sir?"

"Objection. Judge, the medical examiner testified that Ava Bazzi's body was never shipped to the morgue, and there is no death certificate."

"The witness can answer," the judge said.

Farid looked at Jack. "That's what the Iranian officials told me, yes—that Ava is alive."

"Now, here's where I get confused," said Jack. "In response to Ms. Beech's questions yesterday, you said you would describe your marriage to Ava as a happy one. Especially when you lived in London."

"That's right."

"And when Ms. Beech asked if you loved Ava, you said . . ." Jack checked his notes, then read aloud. "'With all my heart.'"

"Yes."

"Sadly, the woman you loved with all your heart was arrested and taken to jail."

"Yes."

"And the Iranian government told you she was still alive."

"Yes."

"I listened very carefully yesterday." Jack took a step closer, his eyes narrowing. "I didn't hear you say a single thing you did to try and find her—this woman you loved with all your heart and who is still alive."

Farid was silent.

"You didn't look for your wife, did you, Mr. Bazzi?"

The question clearly made him uncomfortable. "Well—she was unfaithful."

"No, hold on right there," said Jack. "You made it very clear yesterday that the first time you heard about the alleged affair was when you found out Mr. Asmoun was going to testify in this proceeding. Isn't that right, sir?"

He swallowed the lump in his throat. "That's right."

"So, let me ask you this: Were you lying when you said you loved Ava with all your heart? Or were you and the Iranian government lying when you said she's still alive?"

"Objection. Argumentative."

"Sustained."

Jack paused. His point had been made, and it probably wasn't necessary to twist the knife. But something inside was propelling him forward. It wasn't just his gut telling him that he could get more from this witness. It was his sense that Farid was more than willing to give it to him.

"Mr. Bazzi, you don't believe Ava Bazzi is still alive, do you?"

The question, so direct, seemed to catch the witness off guard. And his lawyer.

"Objection," said Beech.

"Grounds?" the judge asked.

"Umm . . . Calls for an opinion."

"Mr. Bazzi's opinion is pertinent," said Jack.

"Overruled," the judge said. "The witness shall answer."

Farid sat up straight, refocusing. He seemed more flustered than confused. "I'm sorry, what was the question?" he asked.

Jack put the question again, even more firmly. "You don't believe that Ava Bazzi is alive. Do you, sir?"

Long silence. Jack waited. The judge waited. Jack imagined that the State Department and the Iranian government were waiting too. The judge peered out over the top of his spectacles.

"Mr. Bazzi, did you hear the question?"

"I'm . . . having trouble with it."

The judge's gaze landed on Jack. "Mr. Swyteck, one more time."

Jack took a half step closer. *Control.*

"Mr. Bazzi," he said, his voice a little louder than before. "The *story* that Ava Bazzi is alive: You don't believe it, do you?"

Farid's dark eyes glowed like embers. But if there was anger in his glare, it didn't seem to be directed at Jack. At least not *only* at Jack. He lowered his head.

"I don't know what to believe anymore," he said, his voice weak.

It was a bigger score than Jack could have hoped for. The argument that Ava was alive and Zahra had no parental rights was Farid's silver bullet. And the bullet was a blank. The judge would have no choice but to let Zahra put on all her evidence. To explain *why* she abducted Yasmin.

"Your Honor, may I have thirty seconds to confer with my client?" Jack asked.

"You may."

Jack went to the table and took a seat beside Zahra, speaking softly. "I'm going to leave it right there."

"But what about all the things I told you last night?"

"Zahra, I could spend the next hour leveling accusations of abuse. Farid will only deny them. Worse, his denials could come across as credible."

"Credible? How can you say that?"

Twice Jack had been warned by his best friend. Confronted by Theo at his badass scariest, Farid had denied all accusations of abuse. And Theo's takeaway? *I'm not sure he's lying.*

"Trust me on this, Zahra. It's better to put you on the witness stand and let you make the accusations. If I put it to Farid now, we're just giving his lawyer a preview of what's coming, and she'll have all weekend to prepare her cross-examination."

Zahra didn't seem persuaded, but she didn't push back. "Fine."

Jack rose and rebuttoned his suit coat. "No further questions, Your Honor."

"Very well," the judge said. "Ms. Beech, do you have any additional witnesses?"

"No, Your Honor. The petitioner rests his case. At this time, I would ask the court to enter judgment in favor of Mr. Bazzi as a matter of law. We have proven that Zahra Bazzi's marriage to Mr. Bazzi was a fraud, and that the alleged adoption of his daughter Yasmin was without Ava Bazzi's consent. As such, the respondent has no rights under the Hague Convention, and any defense she may have to the abduction of Mr. Bazzi's daughter is irrelevant."

"Judge, if I may respond," said Jack.

"No need, Mr. Swyteck. The petitioner's motion is denied."

The ruling wasn't totally unexpected, but it still came as a relief to Jack.

The judge continued. "I have an emergency hearing in a criminal matter that I must deal with today. This proceeding will therefore adjourn early today and resume Monday at nine a.m. Mr. Swyteck, as I understand it, your client is asserting a defense to the abduction under Article Thirteen of the Hague Convention."

"Yes, Your Honor. We intend to prove that the court's return of Yasmin to Farid Bazzi would put her in grave danger of physical and psychological harm."

"I'll set aside three days for your presentation. Be prepared to call your first witness on Monday morning. We are adjourned," the judge said, ending it with the bang of his gavel.

CHAPTER 21

Jack left the courthouse but didn't go back to the office. With the afternoon off, he drove to Miami International Airport to pick up Andie. She was standing on the sidewalk outside arrivals. Jack knifed his way through the traffic jam and pulled up to the curb.

"Move along," a traffic cop said as he approached Jack's vehicle.

Jack rolled down his window. "I've been here ten seconds."

"You want a ticket, bud?"

Jack had almost forgotten how much fun it was doing pickup at MIA.

Andie quickly threw her carry-on in the back seat and climbed into the passenger seat. Jack pulled away from the curb and merged into the far-left lane, the so-called fast lane, which was slower than walking.

"It was a pinkie swear," said Andie.

Jack had no idea what she was talking about. "What?"

"I was not holding hands with Isaac. Your friend Dennis saw us doing a pinkie swear."

She was starting to make sense, but it still didn't quite compute for Jack. "How did you even know I talked to Dennis?"

"Because Dennis's wife cheated on him, and misery loves company."

Jack stopped for the line of suitcase-toting pedestrians on the zebra crossing.

"I'm still confused."

"Jack, the last time you picked me up at the airport was before we were married. I knew you wanted to talk, I knew Dennis would call you, and I knew what he was going to say."

"But how? It's like you have ESP or something."

"It's not ESP. Dennis pulled Isaac aside on our way out of the bar. He said he saw us holding hands, and that Isaac was lucky he's FBI or he'd punch him in the mouth."

Jack knew she wasn't lying, since he could easily verify it with Dennis. The traffic started to move, and their car crept forward.

"Did you think it was even possible I would cheat on you?" Andie asked.

"Not really."

"Not really, as in no way? Or not really, but maybe?"

"No maybe about it."

But Jack wasn't sure she believed him. He wasn't sure he believed himself. "Okay, so I admit it. The fact that it was Isaac made what Dennis said a little more believable."

"Isaac is just a friend. A good friend."

"Pinkie swear?" He offered up his finger.

Andie rolled her eyes.

Jack didn't drop it. "What is that, the new FBI motto? Fidelity. Bravery. Integrity. Pinkie swear."

"You're a riot, Jack."

"Seriously, what were you and Isaac pinkie-swearing about?"

"I can't tell you without breaking the Rule."

"You mean our rule?"

"Yes, our rule. The Rule. The stupid fucking rule that keeps us from talking to each other about the most important thing in our lives outside our family. The rule that has landed us in marriage counseling."

Jack followed the road signs and steered onto the busy east-west expressway. "Then break it."

"Fine. But if I'm going to break the Rule, I'll break it big-time."

"What does that mean?"

"Forget about the stupid pinkie swear. I'm going to tell you how I know Ava Bazzi is alive."

"I pretty much proved that false in court today."

"Oh, believe me, I heard all about it."

"More pressure from the State Department?"

"Jack, you are jeopardizing negotiations to release an American citizen who is being held in an Iranian prison."

"I'm helping my client keep her adopted daughter safe."

"By proving something that isn't true? Is that your idea of help?"

"Not even Farid believes Ava Bazzi is still alive."

"Then Farid is wrong. And you're wrong."

"And you know this because . . ."

"Because I've seen the State Department's confidential dossier on Ava Bazzi."

Jack drove in silence.

"There," Andie added, "I said it."

Jack was holding the speed limit, thinking, as traffic heading to the cruise ships or hotels on Miami Beach sped past him.

"Are you going to tell me what's in the dossier?"

Andie looked out the passenger side window. "An immigration document was filed under Ava Bazzi's name eight months ago."

"That could be a fake."

"The application has Ava Bazzi's fingerprints on it."

"Those could be fake too."

"The FBI verified them."

"Maybe the FBI faked them."

Jack sensed the weight of Andie's glare. A quick glance in her direction confirmed it, and then his eyes returned to the road.

"What?" he asked.

"I just shared the contents of a classified dossier with you, and your only response is that it's a fake? Not just that it's fake, but that both the State Department and the FBI are in on it."

"I'm not saying you're part of it."

"Oh, well, that's a relief," she said with a heavy dose of sarcasm.

"You're being used, but you're not in on it."

Her jaw dropped. "That is the meanest thing you've ever said to me. How could you think I would let myself be used like that?"

"That's not—I'm not saying you're *letting* it happen."

"I'm too stupid to *even know* I'm being used? Is that it?"

"No! You're totally not hearing me."

Jack was struggling, and he was intimately familiar with "the first rule of holes," when digging yourself into one: *Stop digging!* But he couldn't stop.

"Andie, here's a true story. In the middle of my videoconference with the State Department, a thought popped into my head: I see a federal conspiracy under every rock. That's my flaw. But you have the opposite problem. You refuse to accept that not everyone in the federal government is made of the same material you are."

"Can we just stop talking about this, please?"

"Why?"

"It's not healthy. You sound more like a nutjob conspiracy theorist than you realize. I'm starting to think we were better off under the Rule."

"No. This *is* healthy."

"Jack, just stop talking and drive."

They rode in silence. Jack steered onto the Rickenbacker Causeway toward Key Biscayne. He could see the blue-green waters of the bay, the speedboats skimming along in the shadows of the signature Miami skyline, the windsurfers gliding just off the sandy beaches. He loved living on the Key. It never failed to work its magic on his state of mind, making everything chill. It seemed to be working on Andie, too.

"By the way," she said, "I would never cheat on you."

"Good to know."

"I might kill you. But I would never cheat on you."

Jack tried a bad Jimmy Stewart imitation. "Well, lucky for you, I, uh, happen to know a good country lawyer who, uh, could get you off on a defense of, uh, temporary insanity."

"That is the worst Tom Hanks imitation I've ever heard."

Jack didn't bother correcting her. "I'll work on it," he said.

CHAPTER 22

Righley's Saturday-morning soccer game was a family event. Jack watched with pride, but unlike some parents, he accepted that he probably wasn't witnessing the next Mia Hamm or Abby Wambach. Andie wasn't an official team coach, but seeing her daughter on the field seemed to bring out the old Junior Olympian in her, and she couldn't help weighing in from the sidelines.

"Righley, run to open space!"

It was Andie's answer to youth soccer's perennial problem: two teams surrounding the ball and kicking each other in the shins as an amoeba-like glob of children inched across the field. All it took was one kid to break from the pack—"Run to open space!"—and a teammate with the presence of mind to pass her the ball, and it was an easy goal. It struck Jack as a metaphor for life.

Somehow, the ball found the back of the net. The fact that it was the *wrong* net didn't preclude the usual reaction.

"*Goooooooooooooal!*"

The game was over before nine o'clock, followed by a visit to Righley's favorite pancake house. A weekend off would have been nice, but phase two of Zahra's case—the dispositive phase—was less than forty-eight hours away. Jack had an 11:00 a.m. meeting with a child psychiatrist at his office.

Dr. Margot Vestry arrived right on time. She was about fifteen years older than the headshot on her website, having reached the age where many women tire of their long hair and opt for a more practical shoulder-length cut. The kitchen felt less like a workplace on a Saturday, and it got the best natural light in the morning, so their meeting began at the table over coffee.

"Have you worked with a psychiatrist before?" the doctor asked.

"Well, my wife and I are seeing a marriage counselor who's a psychiatrist."

"I meant, have you ever engaged a psychiatrist as an expert witness in your past cases?"

Jack chuckled with embarrassment. *Andie on your mind much, Swyteck?*

"Yes, many times," he said. "Mostly in the sentencing phase of capital cases. Being the victim of child abuse or other trauma is irrelevant to guilt or innocence, but a jury might consider it when deciding whether to recommend the death penalty."

"So you've actually worked with *child* psychiatrists?"

"Yes."

"Well, that comes as a relief," she said. "When you told me this was your first proceeding under the Hague Convention, I thought—"

"God help us?"

She smiled. "I wouldn't go that far. Luckily, this is not my first rodeo."

Not by a long shot. Harvard Medical School, residency at Johns Hopkins Hospital, and postgraduate fellowship in child and adolescent psychiatry at Boston Children's Hospital made for an impressive résumé. But her experience in international child abduction cases was the reason Jack had selected her—and the reason Myra Weiss's Washington law firm had agreed to pay for her.

"Our job isn't going to be easy," said Jack. "You should assume that we won't be able to prove that Farid directed any physical or verbal abuse at Yasmin. Our theory of the case is that Yasmin witnessed the abuse of her biological mother, Ava, and then her adoptive mother, Zahra. If the judge returns Yasmin to her father, it will be more of the same."

"Abusers rarely change their ways, and if they do, it's a long-term process. Farid's pattern will likely continue in future relationships."

"That's our argument," said Jack. "My plan is to put you on the stand to render an expert opinion as to whether witnessing abuse can cause psychological harm to a child."

"It certainly can," she said. "I've published a number of peer-reviewed articles on that topic and seen it countless times in my practice. Children exposed to violence can develop everything from ADHD to Tourette's syndrome."

"That's what I need you to explain to the judge."

"And that's fine, but it only goes so far. I would be a much more compelling witness if I could take it to the next step."

"Which would be?"

"I would need to conduct my own forensic psychological examination of Yasmin. I would then render a professional opinion as to whether she is already exhibiting symptoms of having witnessed Farid's abuse of her mothers."

"I agree that would be ideal. But here's the problem. If you examine Yasmin, Farid's lawyer will hire another psychiatrist to examine her. Before we know it, Yasmin is *the* key witness in the hearing, which Zahra wants to avoid at all costs."

"I understand. But does she want to win the case or not?"

Jack had hired quite a practical-minded psychiatrist. "Fair question," he said. "Ultimately, it's Zahra's decision."

"May I speak to her about it?"

"Not without me in the room."

"That would be fine," she said. "Is she coming this morning?"

The doorbell rang, a speak-of-the-devil moment. Jack excused himself, went to the lobby, and let Zahra in.

"Sorry I'm late," she said. "Babysitter problems."

"No problem. I was just having a nice talk with Dr. Vestry. She has some questions for you."

"What kind of questions?"

"Basic stuff. Nothing to be worried about." Jack stopped outside the door to the kitchen and lowered his voice so that Dr. Vestry couldn't possibly overhear. "Before we go in, there's something I want to talk to you about."

"Jack, I've slept on it, and I'm not going to change my mind about putting Yasmin on the witness stand."

"It's not that," said Jack. "It's about Ava."

"What about her?"

Jack didn't have a ton of information from Andie about the confidential dossier on Ava, but he was hoping that Zahra could fill in the blanks.

"Eight months ago, an immigration form was filed with the US government in the name of Ava Bazzi."

"Yes, a U visa application."

"You know about that?" he asked.

"Of course. I filed it."

"Under Ava's name?"

"Yes, Jack. The whole time I was living in the United States, I was living under Ava's name. You knew that. I *told* you that."

"That you did," said Jack, no quibble there. "There's just one thing that doesn't add up."

"What?"

"Do you have any idea how Ava's fingerprints got on the application?"

Zahra's mouth opened, but the words seemed to be on a few-second delay. "Ava's fingerprints?"

"The FBI says they're on the immigration form that was filed eight months ago."

"I don't see how that's possible."

"I hope that's true," said Jack. "Or is there something going on here I should know about?"

"Like what?"

"Sisters. The bond between them can be very strong."

"What are you suggesting?"

"Call me crazy, but some thoughts have crossed my mind."

"Such as?"

"Little sister Ava is alive and in hiding, separated from her daughter. Big sister Zahra is working to unite Ava with her little girl?"

"That would mean the Iranian government is speaking the truth, and Ava is alive."

"Yes, it would." Jack's tone was matter-of-fact.

Zahra seemed taken aback. "Are you asking if I'm conning you, Jack?"

"Are you?"

"No. That's not what's going on."

Jack gave her an assessing look. She looked back with equal intensity and never blinked.

"If you're being less than a hundred percent honest with me, you're only hurting yourself," Jack said.

"Do I look like a masochist to you?"

"And Yasmin."

"I would *never* hurt Yasmin."

Jack had absolutely no evidence to doubt that statement. "Let's go talk to Dr. Vestry."

Andie drove alone to Miami International Airport, but she wasn't flying anywhere. Isaac Underwood had a two-hour layover on his flight from Washington, DC, to Freeport, where he was scheduled to meet with Bahamian officials about the funding of suspected terrorist activities through offshore bank accounts. He'd called Andie from the lounge.

"I have something for you," he'd said. "It's about Brian Guthrie."

Thirty minutes later TSA cleared Andie through security, and she met Isaac in the Admirals Club. They sat away from the crowd in a pair of club chairs that faced the window, overlooking a long line of delayed departures on the busy runway. A plate of tortilla chips with guacamole rested on the table between them. Isaac loaded up a chip and made it disappear in one bite.

"Fresh guac for frequent flyers," he said with a smile of satisfaction. "The only good thing left about flying."

Andie couldn't argue the point. "You said you had something for me?"

Isaac put the chips aside, opened his briefcase, and removed a small manila envelope. "This contains a memo written by the FBI's legal attaché in Kuwait."

"About Guthrie?"

"Yes."

"Can I see it?"

He put it away and closed his briefcase. "No."

"Why?"

"Iran is one of just four countries designated as a state sponsor of terrorism. A report like this is certainly within the purview of the FBI's assistant director of the counterterrorism division. For someone like you? Better to be able to say you've never seen it."

Andie blinked, confused. "Then why did you ask me to come out here?"

"Because I wanted you to know that what I'm about to tell you isn't just hearsay. It's part of an official FBI record. And because I need your personal assurance that this is just between us."

Andie sighed, thinking of her last conversation with Jack about Isaac. "Please don't make me pinkie-swear again."

He laughed, then turned serious. "Just be aware that there are things in this report I can't share with you."

"Got it," she said. "What can you tell me?"

"According to the attaché's report, Mr. Guthrie was driving to Kuwait when he was stopped in the southwest province of Khuzestan and was arrested."

"Does it say why he was arrested?"

"Yes. Smuggling."

"That makes some sense," said Andie. "His mother told me he was a broker in ancient art and antiquities."

"That's also in the report. But there's no mention of any art that was confiscated."

"Just because it's not in the FBI report doesn't mean it's not in the local police report."

"True," said Isaac. "There's one other interesting thing in this report I can share with you: the timing of Guthrie's arrest."

"When was it?"

"October twenty-ninth."

"Twelve days after Ava Bazzi's arrest."

"More important, the day after the Iranian government claims Ava Bazzi escaped from prison and fled the country."

"Hmm," said Andie, thinking.

"Yeah," said Isaac. "Raises a question in one's mind, doesn't it? Was Brian Guthrie an art smuggler—"

"Or a human smuggler?" said Andie, finishing his question.

"Or neither," said Isaac. "Just some poor guy in the wrong place at the wrong time."

"Is the answer in that report?"

"No. Which means my work on Mr. Guthrie is done, and yours is just beginning. You're on your own from here on out, kiddo."

"Understood."

Isaac's phone chimed with an alert. "My plane is boarding," he said, picking up his carry-on bag. "Anyway, I thought this would give you something to think about."

"Thank you," said Andie, her gaze drifting toward the runway. "Plenty to think about."

CHAPTER 23

Monday morning came too soon. The courtroom was full, and by 9:00 a.m. Jack's first witness was sworn and seated.

"Could you please state your name for the record?" Jack asked.

Over the weekend, hours of preparation and rehearsal had gone into Zahra's direct examination. By Sunday afternoon, she'd finally felt comfortable telling her story in her own words without sounding like a B-rate actress reciting a lawyer's script. A flawless rehearsal, however, was like the perfect speech delivered to the bedroom mirror. It was no guarantee of performance when it mattered.

"My name is Ava Bazzi," she said.

The slip didn't totally shock Jack, given that Zahra had been using her sister's identity for over a year, but Judge Carlton did a double take from the bench.

"You mean Zahra Bazzi, right?" said the judge.

A look of horror came over her face. "Yes. Zahra Bazzi. I'm so sorry. I'm a little nervous."

If Zahra was "a little nervous," D-Day was "a disagreement." But Jack understood. *Any* woman called to testify about an abusive husband would be a nervous witness, especially with the accused abuser sitting in the courtroom, staring her down. Jack started with easy background questions to calm her nerves, which went reasonably well, and then gently moved into questions of substance.

"How did you hear about your sister Ava's arrest by the morality police?"

"Farid called me," said Zahra. "He said Ava was one of the women rounded up at the protests on Keshavarz Boulevard."

"What else did he say?"

Zahra took a deep breath, paused, and let it out. They had only just begun to touch on matters important to the case, and her nervousness was creeping back with a vengeance.

"I—I don't remember everything he said."

"Tell me what you can remember about the conversation," said Jack.

There was another long pause. She glanced quickly in Farid's direction and then looked away. It was Jack's impression that she was reluctant to put words in Farid's mouth, even if Jack's question was framed as benignly as her recollection of a phone conversation.

"I can't really remember what else Farid said. But I offered to come by and help with Yasmin."

"Did he accept your offer?"

"Yes."

"Did you stay overnight in the apartment with Yasmin and Farid?"

"Not at first. I would go over for a few hours, and then go back to my apartment. But then we lost contact with Ava. That's when I essentially moved in and started spending all my time with Yasmin."

"And Farid?"

"Farid was there, of course. But I was there for Yasmin, as her aunt, and I slept in Yasmin's room."

"What did you mean when you said you 'lost contact' with Ava?"

"The authorities would no longer deliver our letters to her in prison. They told us nothing about her. Even our lawyer had no information."

"At some point, did you get any information about Ava?"

"Yes. From the mullah."

"Imam Reza, who testified earlier in this proceeding?"

"Yes."

"What did the imam tell you?"

"He gave us the story that the whole world has now heard—that Ava escaped, fled the country to pursue her wanton ways, and was never coming back to her country or her family."

"How did you react to that news?"

"I didn't believe it."

"How did Farid react?"

"He—he did not react well."

"Was he angry?"

She didn't answer. Jack pressed, but gently. "Zahra. Was Farid angry when he heard the news from Imam Reza?"

There was no verbal response, just an almost imperceptible nod of her head.

The judge spoke up. "Ms. Bazzi, you must answer in a voice that can be heard."

She leaned closer to the microphone, her voice barely above a whisper. "Yes."

"What, specifically, did Farid do that makes you say the news made him 'angry'?"

Zahra stared back at Jack, her eyes conveying a mix of confusion and reluctance. "I'm not sure I understand what you're asking."

"Rephrase your question, Counselor," the judge said.

"Yes, Your Honor," said Jack, and then he addressed the witness. "Ms. Bazzi, did you, personally, see or hear Farid express any kind of anger after hearing the news about Ava?"

"Yes."

"What did you see?"

"I—I can't remember."

"What did you hear?"

"I don't recall, exactly."

Jack gave her a moment. Dr. Vestry had warned Jack that survivors of abuse do not always make effective witnesses. Even in the privacy of a psychiatrist's office, it is difficult or even impossible for them to describe what has happened to them. A courtroom setting is even more difficult.

"Did you see or hear Farid direct any kind of anger toward Yasmin?"

"Toward Yasmin? No."

Not a helpful answer, but not unexpected.

"Did you see or hear Farid direct any kind of anger toward you?"

"Yes."

"Can you provide any details?" asked Jack.

She paused, as if searching her mind. "I don't remember," she said, then she caught herself. "I can't recall at this time."

In their prep session, Jack had reminded her to say that she couldn't remember "at this time." It left an opening to come back to the question later if her mind went blank on the witness stand.

"That's all right," said Jack. "We'll come back to this later."

Jack took a moment to collect his thoughts. Despite the disturbing tale of Farid's abuse that she had shared with Jack in his office, Zahra seemed unwilling—or afraid—to say in open court that Farid had abused her. Jack could only hope that Farid's abuse of Ava would be within her comfort zone—that talking about Farid's abuse of someone else would somehow be easier for her.

"Was Farid ever abusive in any way toward your sister Ava?"

"Yes," said Zahra.

"Verbally or physically?"

"Verbally. He would . . . berate her."

Can you give us any examples?" asked Jack.

"Farid said she was a terrible cook. That she was a messy housekeeper. Basically, he would say that she could not do any of the things a wife is expected to do around the house. That she had no business being a homemaker—which is a very hurtful thing to say to a mother."

"Did Farid merely complain, or did he actually try to do something about it?"

"He . . . he forced her to improve."

"Forced her? How, exactly?"

Zahra didn't respond right away. Jack prodded.

"Zahra, please tell us how Farid forced her."

"I can think of one thing."

"Share it with us, please."

She swallowed hard, then continued. "In Iran, a wife cannot get a passport or other legal documents to travel to another country without her husband's consent. When Farid's Entrepreneur visa was approved by the United Kingdom, Ava assumed she would be going with him. He told her that he would consent only if she improved her domestic skills."

"Did Farid, in fact, withhold his consent and travel to the UK without Ava?"

"For a time."

"How long?"

"He went to London by himself and gave Ava one month to improve. He told her if she did not improve by the time he came back, he would divorce her. But if things were to his satisfaction in one month, he would grant his consent and allow her to come with him to London."

"What happened?"

"He returned, as promised. He literally walked around the apartment with a white glove to test for cleanliness. Ava prepared a meal and served it to him."

"Were things to his liking?"

"Apparently. He granted his consent."

Jack was pleased; she seemed to have regained her confidence. It was worth a shot at eliciting some of the other things she'd shared about Farid in their prep.

"Can you tell us any other ways in which Farid berated or abused Ava?"

She paused, seeming to consider his question. "No, not at this time."

Jack could have backed away, but he tried again. "Can you recall any other examples of psychological or emotional abuse? Any at all?"

"Not at this time."

Jack had hit a wall, but he needed one more thing.

"You mentioned earlier that Farid berated Ava as a homemaker. Did any of these instances of verbal abuse occur in front of Yasmin?"

Farid's lawyer rose. "Objection to counsel's characterization of these instances of constructive criticism as 'abuse,' Your Honor."

"That one is definitely overruled, Ms. Beech. The witness may answer."

"Yes," said Zahra. "It happened in front of Yasmin."

It was the most important point, and Jack was tempted to inquire further. But he couldn't risk the possibility that Zahra would back away from her answer. He shifted to a line of questioning that had proven to be within Zahra's comfort zone.

"Let's talk a bit more about Ava's arrest and incarceration," said Jack. "You're aware, of course, that your sister Ava was one of many women swept up by the morality police during the demonstrations on Keshavarz Boulevard."

"Yes."

"Are you aware of any protesters who were released from prison, unharmed?"

"Yes. Dozens."

"Did you ever discuss this with Farid?"

"Yes, in a way we did."

"Tell me about that," said Jack.

"Every day we got news of more prisoners being released, only to find out Ava was not among them. It was a very worrisome time. We were alone in the apartment one night. I said something like, 'Why Ava? With everyone else released and gone home, why was she kept locked up in prison?'"

"Did Farid respond?"

"Yes. I wasn't really asking him the question. But yes. He responded."

"What did he say?"

"Farid told me that he was responsible."

Jack paused to let the answer linger. Then he continued.

"To be clear," said Jack. "Farid admitted to you that *he* was the reason the military police kept Ava locked up in prison, even after other demonstrators were released. Do I have that right?"

"Yes."

Jack was tempted to end his direct examination on that high note. But in their prep session, Zahra had filled Jack's ear with examples of the ways in which Farid had abused her. He needed to give her one more chance to make it part of the record.

"Now, let's go back to the question I asked earlier," said Jack. "I know this is difficult, but can you please tell the court whether Farid was ever abusive toward you?"

There was a long silence. Zahra appeared frozen on the witness stand. Jack tried some verbal encouragement.

"Either before or after your marriage, Zahra: Was Farid ever abusive toward you?"

More silence. Zahra seemed to have gone almost catatonic.

Jack continued. "Zahra, all we need from you is a one-word answer. Was Farid ever abusive toward you?"

Her voice was barely audible, but the answer was clear enough: "Yes."

Progress. "Can you give any examples of his abuse toward you?"

Zahra fell silent. Finally, she answered. "I don't remember."

Jack was at a loss. At some point, the court would force him to live with her answer. *I don't remember.* It proved nothing.

"Your Honor, could I have a short recess?" asked Jack.

Farid's lawyer sprang from her seat. "Judge, taking a break so that the lawyer can coach his witness and put words in her mouth is not proper grounds for a recess. If Mr. Swyteck is not getting the answers he wants, then it's time to pass the witness to me for cross-examination."

The judge addresses the witness. "Ms. Bazzi, do you want a recess?"

Zahra looked up at the judge. "Not really."

"Then, Mr. Swyteck, let's wrap this up."

Jack had taken the direct examination as far as he could. If being in the courtroom with Farid was so traumatizing that Zahra suppressed all memories of abuse, things could only get worse if he pushed her for more. Any holes left in the case would have to be filled by other witnesses.

"I have nothing further at this time," said Jack.

"Very well," said the judge. "The witness may not need a break, but I do. We are in recess for five minutes and will then proceed with cross-examination."

Farid's lawyer rose. "Judge, I request that the witness be ordered not to speak to her counsel between direct and cross-examination."

"My client has a right to speak to her lawyer," said Jack.

"The witness testified several times that she couldn't recall certain details," said Beech. "If Mr. Swyteck intends to refresh her recollection, it should be done in open court, not during the break."

Judge Carlton grumbled. "My bladder has no patience for these last-minute motions. But seeing how this is not a criminal case with a constitutional right to counsel, it is so ordered. Ms. Bazzi, please stay right there on the witness stand. I'll be back in five."

All rose on the crack of the gavel and the bailiff's command. As Judge Carlton stepped down from the bench, Jack's eyes met his client's. She appeared frightened and confused, but she seemed to get the gist of it:

She was firmly in the hands of Farid's lawyer.

CHAPTER 24

Zahra felt the weight of all eyes upon her. The final words of wisdom from Jack prior to her direct testimony had proven all too true in the five-minute break before cross-examination: the witness stand was the loneliest seat in the courtroom.

Farid was with his lawyer at the table near the empty jury box, looking straight at Zahra. Jack was at the other table, close enough to talk to her, had the judge not forbidden it. It had been relatively easy for Zahra to ignore the crowd of onlookers while seated beside her lawyer with her back to the public gallery, but there was no escape from those probing stares on the witness stand. Spectators were constantly exchanging whispers, cutting glances in Zahra's direction, clearly talking about her. Everything was on hold until Judge Carlton's return.

Zahra checked her wristwatch. Little more than a minute had passed since Judge Carlton had announced the break. She needed to get her nerves under control. The five-minute recess was starting to feel like five hours.

Breathe, she reminded herself.

Zahra was certain that her testimony had surprised Jack. Her answers were replaying in her mind. She wondered how Farid's lawyer might challenge her testimony, and she worried how she would hold up. She hadn't mentioned the story about the white-glove test to Jack in their prep session. She wasn't sure why it had suddenly popped into her mind on the witness stand. She wondered if it had come across as made up, or at least exaggerated. Zahra imagined that Farid had already slipped his lawyer a handwritten note with a message in all caps, LIES, LIES, LIES! To be sure, the story was out of step with a modern Muslim marriage, though Zahra and her sister had grown up in a home where the husband did no housework and the wife never complained. The oft-debated verse 4:34 of the Quran, "righteous women are obedient," was open to different interpretations.

Zahra checked her watch again. Three more minutes. She wanted to get up and walk around, but the judge had ordered her to sit and wait, so she didn't move.

Obedient.

Her mind drifted back to the testimony she'd just given, but she couldn't hold her focus on the evidence, the hearing, or even the last year she'd spent in Miami. She was sifting through more distant memories, her thoughts racing back in time until, finally, she landed on the day she married Farid.

Zahra was at the mosque, alone in the bride's room, waiting. The Nikah ceremony was less than an hour away, and not all was right.

For Yasmin's benefit, things had moved fast with Farid, leaving Zahra less than two weeks to plan her Sofreh Aghd, the traditional ceremonial floor spread for a Persian wedding. The florist had delivered beautiful red roses and white orchids, but she'd forgotten the wisteria. Zahra's mother had stepped out to fix the problem. Ava would have been a mess if this screwup had happened at her wedding. Zahra had bigger things to worry about.

There was a knock on the door, and the imam's voice followed. "I would like to speak with you, Zahra."

She let him in, and the imam closed the door.

"Sit," he told her.

Zahra took a seat on the leather ottoman, careful not to crease her gown. The expression on the imam's face concerned her.

"Is something wrong?" she asked.

"It's about your vows," he said. "Traditionally, there is no exchange of vows at the Nikah ceremony."

"I understand. Farid wanted to include vows."

"That's fine," said the imam. "There is no rule against them. But if the Nikah ceremony is at the mosque, they must be approved by the imam."

"Is there something wrong with these vows?"

"Farid's vows are fine," he said, and then he read from the script. 'I, Farid, pledge, in honesty and sincerity, to be for you a faithful and helpful husband.'"

"My vow is the same," said Zahra, "'to be a faithful and helpful wife.'"

"That's the problem."

"I don't see the problem," said Zahra.

"As I said, vows are not required. But if they are to be exchanged in the mosque, I must grant my consent. I will grant my consent only if the vows are in accord with Islamic law. *Strictly* in accord."

"What are you proposing?"

He handed her a slip of paper, and Zahra read aloud.

"'I, Zahra, offer you myself in marriage in accordance with the instructions of the Holy Quran and the Holy Prophet, peace and blessing be upon him. I pledge, in honesty and with sincerity, to be for you an obedient and faithful wife.'"

She lifted her gaze from the paper and looked the imam in the eye. "'Obedient?' You want me to invoke the Holy Quran and the Holy Prophet and pledge obedience?"

"If you want my consent."

Zahra tried to be respectful. "The vows Farid and I chose are the same vows he exchanged with Ava: 'faithful and *helpful*.' Not '*obedient*.'"

"Yes," said the imam. "And we know how that turned out."

A ll rise!" the bailiff announced, stirring Zahra from her memories.

Judge Carlton entered through the side door and ascended to the bench. The courtroom settled into silence, and Zahra lowered herself into her chair.

"Counsel, you may proceed with cross-examination," the judge said.

"Thank you, Your Honor."

Farid's lawyer was looking straight at Zahra as she approached. Zahra tried not to show any sign of fear or intimidation, but there was no fooling herself. It was worse than Jack had warned her. Worse than she'd ever imagined.

CHAPTER 25

Jack watched from his seat at the table. Farid's lawyer was standing between him and his client—literally and figuratively.

It was unrealistic to think that a skilled trial lawyer wouldn't land a single punch on cross-examination. The only question was how many blows the witness could take and how hard they would land. Jack had come to know Zahra well enough to realize that she was probably more nervous than she looked—and she looked plenty nervous. Farid's lawyer seemed poised to take full advantage.

"Ms. Bazzi, you testified earlier that your sister was held in jail even after other demonstrators were released. Is that correct?"

"Yes."

"And Farid told you that he felt 'responsible' for the way the police were treating her. Was that your testimony?"

"Farid said he *was* responsible. Not that he *felt* responsible."

Jack had covered that distinction in the prep. He was pleased to see his client sticking to her guns. But Farid's lawyer only turned up the heat, speaking sharply.

"I want to get a better understanding of how, exactly, Farid was 'responsible.' Isn't it true, Ms. Bazzi, that you and Farid had a conversation with Imam Reza after Ava was arrested?"

It was a new detail for Jack. Zahra hadn't mentioned a conversation with the imam in their prep.

"We may have. I don't recall specifically."

The lawyer took a step closer, showing zero tolerance for evasiveness. "Ms. Bazzi, your sister's arrest was the most important thing going on in your life at this time, was it not?"

"Yes, I would say so."

"Farid and you had an important conversation with Imam Reza about your sister's arrest, and you're telling us now—*under oath*—that you have no memory of it?"

"Objection, harassing," said Jack.

"Overruled. The witness shall answer."

Zahra hesitated, then capitulated. "The imam came to the apartment. I was there, but the conversation was really between Farid and Imam Reza."

"The imam wanted to know if Ava cut her hair short in London before the family returned to Tehran. Correct?"

"Yes, that sounds right."

"Farid answered the imam's question truthfully: no, Ava, did not wear her hair short in London. She cut her hair sometime after the family returned to Tehran."

Zahra paused before answering, seeming to know that the lawyer was setting a trap. "Yes," she said, her voice quaking. "I believe that's true."

Beech returned to the lectern and retrieved a document. "Your Honor, several weeks ago, I submitted a request under the Freedom of Information Act, asking the State Department for a copy of the arrest report for Ava Bazzi. Today I received this certified copy, together with an English translation."

Jack smelled a rat. "Judge, if the plan is to question the witness about this document, I object. I've never seen it."

"The timing of the State Department's response to my request is beyond my control," said Beech.

Jack held his tongue. The State Department had not been his ally in this proceeding, but accusing the department of dirty tricks wasn't going to advance his position in the courtroom or at home.

"Let me see the document," the judge said.

Beech handed it up. Judge Carlton read it, then laid it aside.

"The certification of authenticity from the State Department seems to be in order," said the judge. "I won't prohibit counsel from using the document. Mr. Swyteck, I will consider your objections on a question-by-question basis."

Beech thanked the judge, handed the witness a copy, and then returned to her place before the witness. "Ms. Bazzi, I direct your attention to page one of the translated report, paragraph three. Could you please read it aloud for us?"

The report shook in Zahra's hand as she read. "'At the time of her arrest, the subject denied that she cut her hair in protest of the hijab laws. Subject stated that her hair was short because she wore it that way in London with her husband's permission.'"

"Thank you," said Beech. "Until just now, when you read it in the police report, you didn't know that Ava had lied to the morality police, did you?"

"Objection," said Jack. "Just because it's in the report doesn't mean Ava actually said it."

"Overruled."

"I had no idea what Ava told the police."

"Precisely," said Beech. "Neither did Farid, did he?"

Jack objected, but the judge directed Zahra to answer "if she knows."

"I don't see how Farid would have known about any statement to the police," said Zahra. "The police gave us no information."

Farid's lawyer went for the jugular, her cadence quickening. "When Farid told you that 'he was responsible' for the way the police were treating Ava, he didn't say that he reported her to the morality police for violation of the hijab laws, did he, Ms. Bazzi?"

"No, of course not."

"He didn't say that he *told* the police to keep his wife in jail, did he?"

"No."

"All he did was tell the truth in response to the imam's questions, correct?"

"I'm not sure I understand."

"Farid regretted telling the imam the truth because it was the exact opposite of what Ava had told the morality police, which made things even worse for Ava."

"I—I don't know."

"Your sister Ava was kept in prison after other protesters were released because she lied to the morality police about cutting her hair. Isn't that right, Ms. Bazzi?"

"Objection."

"Overruled."

Zahra was in obvious distress. "Possibly. Maybe. I don't know."

Counsel's voice grew louder. "Farid's *only* 'responsibility' for what happened to Ava is that he told the truth to Imam Reza. Isn't that correct, Ms. Bazzi?"

"Objection!"

"Overruled."

"I . . . I don't know how to answer. I suppose so."

The line of questioning wasn't entirely fair, but it was plain to see that Farid's admission of "responsibility" for Ava's trouble with the police was a far cry from what Zahra had described to Jack at the prep sessions in his office. Zahra had been caught exaggerating, and Farid's lawyer seemed to smell blood in the water. The pointed questions continued.

"Ms. Bazzi, earlier, when your lawyer was asking you questions, you did your best to answer, didn't you?"

"Yes, of course."

"Yet you couldn't remember a single time when Farid was abusive toward you, could you."

"My mind is . . . I'm having trouble focusing."

"Let's be honest, Ms. Bazzi. It's not that you can't remember. It simply never happened. Isn't that right?"

"Objection," said Jack. "Argumentative, harassing."

The judge sustained the objection, mercifully. Regardless, the record was devoid of any testimony that Farid had ever abused Zahra, which was contrary to what she had told Jack.

Beech paused, ostensibly to flip through the pages of her legal pad, but also to let the witness stew in uncomfortable silence. "I'm checking my notes," she said.

Jack, too, did a mental check. Nerves were to be expected on the witness stand, but the disconnect between Zahra's testimony and her private conversations with her lawyer was beginning to trouble him.

"Ah, yes, here it is," said Beech. "Ms. Bazzi, you were quite clear that Farid never abused Yasmin or any other child. True?"

"Not to my knowledge."

Beech flipped to the next page of her pad. "And when asked about Farid's abuse of Ava, you said that he 'berated' her?"

"Yes."

"Your testimony was that Farid 'literally' used a white glove to check her housecleaning. Now, 'literally' is one of those words that is often misused, so let me ask you this: You don't mean that Farid was actually wearing a white glove, do you?"

"I—I don't know if he was or not. My testimony was based on what Ava told me."

For Jack, it was another unexpected retreat by his client. For Farid's lawyer, it was manna from heaven.

"To be clear," said Beech, "you weren't actually there to see whether Farid was wearing a white glove or not?"

"No."

"So, when you testified that Farid abused Ava, what you really meant is that Ava told you he abused her."

"We're sisters. Of course she told me."

Counsel's tone sharpened. "You don't know if what she told you is true or not, do you?"

"Well, your question implies that Ava would lie."

"Like the way she lied to the police about cutting her hair?"

"Objection," said Jack.

"Sustained."

"Let me ask it this way," said Beech. "If Farid ever berated or abused Ava, you never actually saw it or heard it firsthand, did you, Ms. Bazzi?"

Zahra paused, seeming to recognize the importance of her response. "Ava told me it happened many, many times. It went on for years."

"My point is, you never actually saw it with your own eyes or heard it with your own ears, did you, Ms. Bazzi?"

"Not that I can recall," she said quietly.

"Not the kind of thing you're likely to forget, if you'd actually witnessed it, is it?"

"Objection," said Jack.

"I'll withdraw the question, Your Honor."

Beech tapped her notepad with a flick of her finger. She seemed beyond satisfied. "I have no further questions," she said, and returned to her seat beside her client.

"Mr. Swyteck, do you have redirect examination?" the judge asked.

Redirect was the lawyer's chance to rehabilitate his own witness and repair some of the damage done on cross. But twice already, Zahra had stated under oath that she could not recall specifics about Farid's abuse. Her third bite at the apple would likely not be any different, and if she finally did change her testimony, it would only raise further doubts about her credibility. Jack needed a better strategy.

"Your Honor, it's obvious from today's testimony that the witness is psychologically and emotionally unable to provide specifics about the abuse she and her sister have suffered. It's not uncommon for victims of abuse to experience this chilling effect in a public courtroom while on a witness stand just a few feet away from their abuser."

"*Accused* abuser," said Beech, rising. "And if Mr. Swyteck is about to ask for a do-over, this is not a game of sandlot baseball."

"Ms. Beech, let's hear what counsel is proposing. Go on, Mr. Swyteck."

It was an unorthodox move, but Jack saw no alternative. Either Zahra had lied to him in private about Farid's abuse, in which case she didn't deserve to win, or she was too terrified to tell the truth in public, in which case she was currently poised to lose.

"Judge, I would request a recess in this proceeding so that Ms. Bazzi can be evaluated by a forensic psychiatrist."

"For what purpose?" the judge asked.

"She has suffered several traumatic events. Her sister lost her life in mass arrests that were condemned worldwide as a violation of human rights, and the fact that the petitioner denies the death of Ava Bazzi only adds to that trauma. It is clear that my client sincerely believes her sister was murdered by the Iranian morality police, and she feels threatened by the Iranian regime, a foreign government that is on the State Department's list of terrorist states. On top of all that, she has suffered emotional abuse by her husband, which she is unable to articulate in a courtroom."

"Are you claiming that Ms. Bazzi suffers from post-traumatic stress disorder, Mr. Swyteck?"

"I'm asking that a qualified psychiatrist render an expert opinion as to whether she is exhibiting signs of PTSD or other injury that is either causing her to suppress her memories of domestic abuse or making it impossible for her to testify about that abuse in open court."

Farid's lawyer could not contain herself. "Judge, this is a Hail Mary by a child abductor who has completely failed to prove any danger of physical or psychological harm to Yasmin if she is returned to her father."

"Ms. Bazzi does bear the burden of proof on her defense to the abduction," said the judge. "This is an important case, and I want to give everyone a fair shake."

"Fairness cuts both ways," said Beech. "We will need our own expert evaluation. My client has a right to present a rebuttal expert."

"It's not my intention to turn this into a battle of the experts," the judge said. "We will use one independent forensic psychiatrist appointed by the court. That psychiatrist will perform a comprehensive evaluation of Ms. Bazzi. Both sides will have the opportunity to cross-examine the expert after the report is issued. Any questions?"

"How long will this process take?" asked Jack.

"I will let the psychiatrist set a reasonable timetable based on professional needs. But obviously time is of the essence. Anything else?" the judge asked.

Jack glanced across the courtroom at his client, who was still on the witness stand. She seemed to understand they were in a difficult spot and that Jack was looking for any way possible to keep her case alive.

"Nothing more from the respondent, Your Honor," said Jack.

"Nothing," said Beech.

"We are adjourned," said the judge, ending the day with a crack of his gavel.

CHAPTER 26

Zahra went straight from the courthouse to the mosque for Jumu'ah.

Friday is not technically the Muslim sabbath, so Zahra was not prohibited from appearing in court, but it is the holiest day of the week in the Islamic tradition, believed to be filled with blessings and mercy for all. Zahra's favorite hadith as a schoolgirl was "The best day on which the sun rises is Friday." Her father would from time to time remind her that "the Prophet, peace be upon him, has noted that the day of judgment will occur on Friday." The irony was not lost on her that she'd never felt more judged in her life, and it was indeed a Friday.

Pickup time at Yasmin's elementary school was 3:30 p.m. Zahra arrived at 3:00, parked in the visitor lot, and walked to the public playground across the street. She had an appointment. Theo Knight was waiting at the picnic table next to the monkey bars.

"You came," she said, a little surprised.

"All you ever had to do was ask."

Zahra took his remark as a reference to the fact that she'd never taken up Theo's offer to be a bodyguard. She took a seat across from him at the picnic table. It was a warm afternoon for late October. Zahra removed her head covering, which she was still wearing from Jumu'ah.

"I just came from the mosque," she said. "It's not mandatory for women to attend Friday-afternoon prayer, especially mothers whose lives are filled with family responsibilities. But I like to go."

"That's cool," said Theo.

"Muslims believe there are extra-special times when our *dua*s have a very high chance of being accepted. At the Friday service there is a special time set aside for *dua*."

"What is 'dua'?"

"It's very different from the five daily prayers. *Dua* is a chance to worship Allah and call upon him for whatever it is we need. It could be anything. Salt for your food. Wisdom to raise your adopted daughter. Strength to handle the death of a younger sister."

"Is that your *dua*?"

"I go light on the salt."

Theo smiled a little, and Zahra continued.

"I'm afraid your friend Jack no longer believes me."

"About what, specifically?"

"Ava, for one. He went so far as to ask me if I was playing him—if Ava is still alive."

"The important thing is whether the judge believes you."

"True. But it is becoming a bad pattern with Jack. His . . . skepticism. I'm not sure he even believes me when I say Farid is an abuser."

"That's between you and Jack."

"No, not entirely. I think he is hearing it from you."

"Hearing what from me?"

"I know you confronted Farid when he visited your club. You must have given Jack your take on whether Farid is a good man or the awful person I've described to Jack."

"What I said to Jack was, like, 'Take it for what it's worth.'"

Zahra glanced at the school building across the street. Dismissal was underway at the circular drive at the main entrance. Teachers were organizing students into somewhat straight lines for pickup.

"My daughter is six years old," said Zahra. "I don't want to put her on the witness stand."

"I understand."

"You're forcing me to do it."

"Me? How?"

"I might not be able to win this case without her testimony."

"How is that my fault?"

"Something has changed about Jack. I know he and his wife are having some kind of difficulties. Maybe he is worried about losing his own daughter and is sympathizing with Farid."

"That's not Jack," said Theo.

"I agree. Which leaves only one other possibility, as I see it. He actually believes Farid."

"I can't help you with that."

"You are Jack's best friend. He trusts what you say."

"I'm not sure what you're asking me to do."

"It's simple. I want my lawyer back. My fighter. Whatever you've told him about Farid, tell him you were wrong. Because you are wrong. Dead wrong."

Zahra met his gaze and held it for a moment.

"Yasmin's waiting for me. Good day, Mr. Knight."

She rose from the table and started toward the school.

Andie spent most of the afternoon at the federal courthouse, waiting in the lobby outside courtroom 4. Testifying in criminal prosecutions was one of the things she liked least about being a law enforcement officer, but it was an important part of her job.

This latest case had grown out of an undercover assignment. The defendant claimed that Andie had entrapped him by befriending him over drinks. "A drink" was as far as it had gone, but the defendant's attorney would probably accuse her of everything from performing oral sex to promising him a threesome with Margot Robbie. No disrespect to Jack, but sometimes the term *criminal lawyer* fit.

The double entrance doors to the courtroom opened, and the prosecutor stepped into the lobby. Andie had known Daniela Diaz almost ten years and testified in her cases at least a half dozen times. Daniela had never failed to get a conviction.

Andie rose from her seat on the bench as Daniela approached.

"How much longer do I have to wait?" asked Andie.

"Hopefully not too much," said Daniela.

"That's what you said two hours ago."

The prosecutor just shrugged, as if to say there was nothing she could do. Andie didn't fault her. The hearing was in a brief recess, and they'd already talked ad nauseam about Andie's testimony. Small talk was in order.

"I see your husband is in the news again," said Daniela. "Ava Bazzi: Dead or Alive?"

"Yeah, the media seems to be all over it."

"I like Jack. He's a good guy."

"I agree. Most of the time."

"For what it's worth, I think he's on the right side of this one."

Andie did a double take. "You think Ava Bazzi is dead?"

"Yeah. Don't you?"

There was no reason a Miami prosecutor in the US Attorney's Office would know anything about the State Department's confidential dossier on Ava Bazzi.

"I don't know," said Andie. "But I'm curious to know why you think she's dead."

"I have my reasons," she said coyly.

"You mind telling me?"

"Just between us overworked and underpaid warriors?" asked Daniela.

"Of course."

Daniela lowered her voice. "About eight months ago, Homeland Security referred a case to the Miami office for criminal prosecution. It involved an application for a U visa. It was supposedly submitted by Ava Bazzi."

The fact that Daniela was willing to say even that much only confirmed that she knew nothing about the confidential dossier or the latent fingerprints found on the U visa application. Andie played dumb.

"Homeland Security asked you to prosecute Ava Bazzi?"

"Not Ava. Zahra Bazzi. For submitting a fraudulent U visa application under her sister's name."

The State Department had told Andie nothing about the referral for criminal prosecution. She wondered if Jack was aware.

"Was it Homeland Security's position that Ava Bazzi had no connection to the application?"

"No connection?" she said, seemingly amused. "That's an interesting choice of words."

"What do you mean?"

"To put a finer point on it, Homeland Security told us that the application was a fraud because Ava Bazzi is dead."

Andie froze, the words echoing in her mind. *Ava Bazzi is dead.*

"What happened to Homeland's referral for criminal prosecution?" asked Andie.

"It just shut down. Hard stop. No explanation."

The courtroom doors opened. A junior prosecutor stepped out and hurried toward Daniela. "The judge is back," he said.

"Gotta go," she told Andie. "Hang tight. This may be your turn."

"Sure," said Andie.

Daniela hurried back into the courtroom.

Slowly Andie returned to her seat on the bench, her testimony the farthest thing from her mind. Instead she was reeling from the pivot from "Ava is dead" to "Ava is alive." It was like a dust storm of confusion, but as it settled, she was able to break things down to a couple of key questions.

Had they pivoted from "Ava is dead" to "Ava is alive" because they found the latent fingerprints on the application? Or had they "found" the latent fingerprints because—for some other reason—they had already pivoted from "Ava is dead" to "Ava is alive?"

Andie didn't know the answer. But she knew what Jack would say.

It was after sunset, and an unseasonably hot day in Miami had transformed into a pleasant evening. The noisy blast of her car's air conditioner was no longer needed to keep cool. Zahra turned off the engine and rolled down the driver's-side window. She was parked in a metered space on the street outside the hotel. Farid's hotel.

She'd been there nearly forty-five minutes, debating whether to act on her impulse and go inside the hotel or just put the car in gear and go home.

Her meeting at the playground had left her with little hope that Theo would do anything to persuade Jack that she, not Farid, was telling the truth. It was going to take more drastic measures to regain her courtroom warrior. If she couldn't convince Jack, she had no hope of winning over the judge.

Unless she could get through to Farid, directly.

It was definitely a long shot. But if Farid knew she was willing to do whatever it took to win the case, it might make a difference. If he knew—or at least *believed*—Zahra was willing to put Yasmin on the witness stand, maybe he would back down. Maybe. She had to try.

Zahra put on her headscarf and checked herself in the rearview mirror. Not as pretty as Ava. Not as young as Ava. But stronger than Ava.

She opened the door, climbed out of the car, and walked toward the hotel entrance.

CHAPTER 27

Jack hated Monday morning surprises. He was on his way to the criminal courthouse for the arraignment of a new client when Judge Carlton's assistant reached him on his cell phone. As Jack's *abuela* might have said, it was one heck of a *chiste mal de lunes*, a bad Monday joke.

"Judge Carlton has just issued a digital order directing both parties and their counsel to appear in his chambers at noon today," she said.

It didn't sound optional. "My client and I will be there."

"The attendance of Yasmin Bazzi is also required."

As of Friday, the judge's order on a forensic psychiatric evaluation had extended only to Zahra. "Can I ask why Yasmin has to be there?"

"That's all the information I have, Mr. Swyteck."

Jack thanked her, and the call ended.

At noon, as ordered, Jack, Zahra, and Yasmin appeared outside the electronically secured door to Judge Carlton's chambers. Jack had gone to Zahra's town house first, and they'd kept the conversation light since picking up Yasmin from school. He'd explained what a courtroom is, what judges do, and why they wear black robes. The "field trip" continued all the way to Judge Carlton's chambers.

"Yasmin, this is where the very nice judge and his helpers do their work when they're not in the courtroom."

"What if he's not nice?" asked Yasmin.

"Oh, he'll be very nice to you, Yasmin." Jack couldn't say the same for the lawyers.

The door opened, and the three of them entered the reception area. A young woman introduced herself as Judge Carlton's law clerk and took Zahra and Yasmin to the conference room. The judge's assistant escorted

Jack down the hall to the judge's private chambers. Farid's lawyer was waiting in one of the wing chairs. Jack sat in the open chair. Judge Carlton entered from the robing room and took a seat behind his desk, facing the lawyers. He greeted them and then delivered the news.

"Counsel, I've summoned you here because I have changed my mind about moving forward with a forensic psychiatric examination of Zahra Bazzi."

Jack thought his opposing counsel might jump up and dance a jig. He saw little chance of winning the case without an independent expert's opinion that Zahra's inability to testify about Farid's abuse was due to PTSD.

"Bottom line is that the process takes too long," the judge continued. "We could be looking at weeks, not days."

"Judge, in the scheme of things, a few weeks is not an unreasonable delay," said Jack.

"My client has been separated from his daughter for over a year," said Beech. "A few weeks is an eternity."

"There's a better solution," the judge said. "But it will require the cooperation of both parties."

The lawyers listened as the judge described a technique used to great effect by the Honorable Denny Chin, a highly respected federal district judge in New York who had since taken senior status on the court of appeals.

"Judge Chin was a pioneer and an innovator in abduction cases under the Hague Convention," the judge said. "He also graduated magna cum laude with a BA in psychology from Princeton University, so it's fair to say he knew his way around the block."

Jack had read about Chin in preparing for Zahra's case, which gave him a hint as to where Judge Carlton was heading.

"Judge Chin recognized that the rules in a Hague proceeding are relaxed for good reason—namely, the child's well-being. He understood long ago that sometimes the best interest of the child calls for an unconventional approach.

"So, with a tip of the hat to Judge Chin, here's what I propose. I want to sit down with Yasmin here in my chambers. Just the two of us, one on one. No lawyers, no parents. A court-appointed forensic psychiatrist will be in the room with us, but only to observe. I will not be wearing my scary black robe. It'll be more like a visit with my grandchildren. We'll watch the Disney channel, color, play cards—whatever it takes for her to feel comfortable. I want to talk to her. I want to observe her."

"Will there be a court reporter, or is this off the record?" asked Jack.

"No court reporter."

"What about the lawyers?" asked Beech. "Can we observe and listen too?"

The judge considered it. "I don't want you in the room with me, but I think I can make it work."

"How?" asked Jack.

"For better or worse, after the attack on the Capitol on January the sixth, I had security cameras installed. Technically, they're only for an emergency—in case some lunatic wearing buffalo horns on his head comes charging in here to kidnap me and my law clerks at spearpoint. But I could have the marshals activate the cameras."

"What about audio?" asked Jack.

"I have a mic I use for judicial conferences. We can put it right there on the coffee table."

"I like the approach," said Jack. "But I'll have to confirm with my client."

"Of course," the judge said. "Ms. Beech? Thoughts?"

"What if my client chooses not to consent?" she asked.

The judge leaned forward in his chair, resting his forearms atop the desk. "Well, Ms. Beech, that would be very disappointing."

It wasn't technically coercion, but even a rookie lawyer with the most basic ability to read judicial tea leaves would have gotten the message.

"I anticipate no objection," said Beech.

"Good," said the judge. "We'll begin at one o'clock, barring the unexpected."

The lawyers were dismissed.

Jack rose and started toward the door, well aware that, in this case, "unexpected" had a meaning all its own.

A ndie stared at her computer screen, confused.

She couldn't count the number of times, over the span of her career, that she'd accessed the FBI's Integrated Automated Fingerprint Identification

System (IAFIS), Interstate Identification Index, and other data systems administered by the FBI's Criminal Justice Information Services Division. The system was designed to provide a binary response: "No record found," or a "hit." Her search for the name Brian Guthrie had produced a response she'd never seen before.

"What the hell?" she asked, though no one was there to hear.

She retyped Guthrie's name and was about to run it through the database a second time—but something made her pause. Technically, an FBI agent's use of the system was limited to "official business." She was not one to break rules, at least not without good reason. Curiosity was not a good enough reason, but her need to know was way beyond mere curiosity. If someone wanted to make the case that Guthrie was not her "official business," so be it.

She hit ENTER. In seconds, the same message reappeared on her screen.

LOCKED.

Andie considered the range of possibilities. It didn't necessarily mean that Brian Guthrie had a criminal record. His fingerprints could have been collected for noncriminal reasons, like a background check for employment. The only thing for certain was that he was in "the system," and anyone in the system stayed there at least until age ninety-nine if there was a criminal record, age seventy-five if there was none. Yet Guthrie was "locked." Andie supposed it could have had something to do with negotiations for his release from an Iranian prison, but she wanted to know for certain. She could think of only one person to call. She dialed his cell, and he picked up. He sounded happy to hear from her—until she mentioned Guthrie, her search of the FBI database, and the confusing result. He stopped her in mid-sentence.

"Andie, what the heck were you thinking when you made this call?"

"I'm just asking you a generic question about the system."

"You're asking me about Brian Guthrie."

"I'm asking about information in the database, which is not classified."

"It is if it's *locked*," he said, his voice rising.

It wasn't the harshest tone Isaac had ever used with her, but it was up there with the time she'd rushed in to make an arrest without waiting for backup from the rest of the Seattle bank robbery squad.

"I'm not trying to put you in an awkward position," said Andie.

"You never should have run Guthrie's name through the system. Just because a hundred thousand searches a day go through the system doesn't mean no one is watching."

"Watching? Are you saying I'm being *watched*?"

A tense silence followed, and then, finally, he answered.

"Andie, what was the last thing I told you when we talked at the airport?"

She wasn't sure what he meant by "the last thing," but she remembered the most important: "You said Guthrie was arrested the day after the Iranian government claims Ava Bazzi escaped from prison."

"No, the last thing. What did I say right after that?"

His last words didn't come to mind. Isaac filled in the blank.

"I told you that you're on your own from here on out," said Isaac. "Remember?"

"Understood. I won't call you again."

"I didn't say don't call me."

"You said I'm on my own."

"Which means that—"

"Which means that if there's any fallout from this, it's on me, not you."

"Shit, Andie. Makes me feel pretty small to hear a friend say it out loud, but I'm afraid that's the way it is."

"I understand. You're doing the best you can."

"Thank you."

"But I'll give you another chance to do better."

It was a light ending, but she hoped he knew she was serious.

"I know you will," said Isaac, and the call ended without another word.

CHAPTER 28

'm a terrible mother."

Jack and Zahra were alone in the conference room. It was the third time Zahra had proclaimed herself the world's worst mother since the court-appointed psychiatrist had come for Yasmin and taken her down the hallway to see Judge Carlton.

"It's the right decision," said Jack.

"Yasmin turns seven today. We're doing this on her birthday."

"I wish you had told me that," said Jack.

"Oh, I'm sure that would have made a huge difference," she said with heavy sarcasm. "As if the judge has been showing every willingness to accommodate our personal lives."

There was a quick knock on the door, and the judge's assistant entered.

"It's time," she said.

Under Judge Carlton's instruction, the lawyers were to wait with their clients while the judge and Yasmin got acquainted. He'd borrowed his granddaughter's dolls, Lego kit, and other age-appropriate toys to put her at ease. When the psychiatrist decided that Yasmin was ready to talk about matters pertinent to the case, the lawyers alone—allegations of abuse made it unwise to put ex-spouses in the same room—could move to the security center to listen and observe by surveillance camera.

A US Marshal met Jack and Farid's counsel outside the judge's chambers and led them down one flight of stairs to the courthouse's security control center. It was a rectangular room with no windows. Long tables lined three of the four walls in a U shape. A row of flat-panel monitors rested on the tabletops. Another row of smaller monitors was suspended from the ceiling. Each monitor displayed a different view of the inside and outside of the courthouse. The marshal directed the lawyers' attention to the view of Judge Carlton's chambers on one of the larger monitors.

"There's no mic in here," said the marshal. "You can hear, but the judge won't hear you."

Jack turned his full attention to the monitor.

The judge, as promised, was not wearing his robe. He'd even removed his necktie, opting for a casual open collar. They were away from his desk in the sitting area of his private chambers. An assortment of toys covered the coffee table. Yasmin was on her knees, paying full attention to what Jack recognized, thanks to Righley, as an American Girl doll. Samantha, if he was not mistaken. Yasmin seemed quite comfortable and content, as far as Jack could tell. The judge was nearby, seated in the armchair. It was Jack's understanding that the court-appointed psychiatrist was in the room to observe, but she was off camera,

"When my daughter comes to visit, she likes to draw pictures," the judge said.

Yasmin's focus remained on the doll.

"Do you like to draw pictures, Yasmin?"

She didn't look at him, but she nodded shyly.

The judge rose and stepped off camera for a moment. He returned with several sheets of blank paper and a box of crayons, which he placed on the coffee table. They immediately caught Yasmin's attention.

"Go right ahead," said the judge. "Draw anything you like."

Yasmin laid the doll aside. She opened the box of crayons, selected a handful of colors, and started drawing.

Jack leaned a little closer to the monitor for a better look, and so did his opposing counsel. But he couldn't tell what Yasmin was drawing.

Yasmin drew in silence for several minutes, choosing more colors as the work progressed. The judge didn't interrupt, speaking only when it was clear that she was finished.

"Can I see it?" the judge asked.

She nodded and handed it up to him.

The judge examined it and smiled. "This is *really* good, Yasmin."

"Thank you," she said, though her voice was barely audible over the speaker.

"Is this your school?" the judge asked.

"Yes."

"And that's the American flag, right?"

"Uh-huh."

"Who are these people by the flagpole?"

"My friends."

"Do you like school, Yasmin?"

"Yes."

"Do you feel safe at your school?"

She nodded.

The judge laid the drawing aside, then sat forward on his chair, getting a little closer. "Could you do me a favor, Yasmin?"

"Okay."

"Can you draw me a picture of your family?"

Jack presumed that the psychiatrist had scripted that question.

Yasmin nodded. She took another piece of paper and chose another set of crayons. The judge waited patiently as she drew, again saying nothing to steer or influence her art. Jack watched the monitor, still unable to see what she was drawing. Several minutes passed. When finished, she handed her drawing to the judge. Judge Carlton examined it. Jack tried to read his expression, but it revealed nothing.

"Another splendid drawing," the judge said.

"Thank you."

"I'm going to step away for just a minute," the judge said. "You can stay right here and keep drawing."

"What should I draw?"

"Draw whatever you like," he said, rising. "I'll be right back."

Yasmin helped herself to a blank sheet of paper. The judge stepped away, but the camera did not follow him. The image on the monitor was Yasmin alone at the coffee table, drawing. A moment later, the marshal directed the lawyers' attention to another screen. Judge Carlton was in a different room with the forensic psychiatrist. The judge faced the camera and spoke to the lawyers.

"Counsel, I am going to share Yasmin's drawing with the forensic psychiatrist. You may observe, but please do not comment or interrupt."

Jack understood the rules. He watched as the psychiatrist examined the drawing of Yasmin's "family." Finally, the psychiatrist shared her thoughts.

"For the benefit of counsel, I note that Yasmin's drawing of her family contains only two people. A girl, whom she labeled 'me,' and a woman, who is labeled 'Mommy.'"

Jack took that as a positive development. A drawing of a "family" without Mommy would have been devastating to Zahra's case.

The psychiatrist continued. "I find it noteworthy that the mommy in this drawing has short hair. Zahra Bazzi has long hair, so I must assume that the mommy with short hair is Ava Bazzi."

"What do you make of that, Doctor?" the judge asked.

"Even if we assume that Ava had short hair for only a few days after she cut it in protest of the hijab laws, that was obviously a traumatic episode for her daughter. The image of Ava with short hair is burned into Yasmin's memory of her mother, even though she is very young. The upshot is that Yasmin still thinks of Ava as 'mommy,' even though she has been with Zahra for nearly a year."

Jack would have preferred a drawing with Zahra as "Mommy," but it certainly wasn't helpful to Farid's case that there was no father in the family—which was precisely the judge's next question.

"Is it significant that Farid Bazzi is not in the picture?"

The psychiatrist paused, then responded. "It is understandable that a girl of Yasmin's age would not include her father in the drawing of her family. Farid has been out of her life completely since she was five years old. While Zahra may have shared photographs or other items to remind Yasmin that Ava was her 'mommy,' it seems doubtful under the circumstances that Zahra would have shared anything with Yasmin to remind her that Farid is her father."

It seemed to Jack that the psychiatrist went further than necessary to explain Farid's absence from the drawing, but there was nothing he could do to challenge her opinion under the judge's rules in this informal setting.

"All right," said the judge. "I don't want to leave Yasmin alone too long. I'm returning to my chambers now."

Jack and his opposing counsel turned their attention back to the other monitor. Yasmin was busy drawing. Just as the judge reappeared on camera, she pulled the drawing from the table and tried to hide it in her lap. The judge noticed.

"What you got there, Yasmin?" the judge asked.

"Nothing."

"Come on," he said, smiling. "You can show me."

"No."

Jack's interest was piqued, and he was not alone.

"Yasmin, it's okay," the judge said. "You can show me anything. No one ever gets in trouble here."

Jack knew that was a lie, but it did the trick. Slowly, and with obvious reluctance, Yasmin handed the judge her drawing.

Jack couldn't see the drawing. But he could read the expression on Judge Carlton's face. It conveyed nothing short of alarm.

"Yasmin, I'll be right back," the judge said, and he stepped out of view, taking Yasmin's drawing with him.

Yasmin was alone on the monitor for less than a minute, until the judge returned with the psychiatrist. The audio didn't pick up the conversation for Jack to hear, but Yasmin left the room with the psychiatrist. The judge then turned to the camera and spoke to the lawyers, presumably out of earshot from Yasmin.

"Counsel, I have shared Yasmin's third drawing with the forensic psychiatrist. It is my view that this informal, off-the-record conversation with Yasmin is not the appropriate way in which to explore the meaning and possible trauma behind this drawing."

The judge paused, and Jack, too, felt the need to catch his breath. The judge continued.

"I therefore ask that the lawyers and their clients gather in my court-room. I will then show you the drawing and make a formal determination of how to proceed. That is all for now."

The marshal switched off the monitor, and the screen went black. Jack and his opposing counsel exchanged a quick glance.

"Interesting," said Beech. "Hard to tell if this is going to be bad for your client or mine."

Jack didn't answer. His thoughts were with Yasmin, and what terrible image had come from her innocent mind.

CHAPTER 29

The lawyers and their clients returned to the main courtroom and seated themselves at their respective tables. A spontaneous hearing allowed for no advance public notice, so the entire gallery, even the media section, was empty. The only other people in the courtroom were the bailiff, the stenographer, and the clerk.

"Where is Yasmin?" Zahra whispered.

"Let's see what the judge has to tell us," said Jack.

Jack had told his client exactly what Judge Carlton had said about Yasmin's third drawing. Beyond that, the only clue as to the judge's plan was the flat manila envelope on the mahogany tabletop before them. It was marked SEALED—DO NOT OPEN. Farid and his lawyer had an identical envelope.

Judge Carlton entered from the side door to his chambers. The lawyers and their clients rose on the bailiff's command.

"You may take your seats," the judge said from the bench. "Here's what I've decided to do, in consultation with the court-appointed child psychiatrist. In a few moments, I will direct each side to open the envelope in front of you. It contains the drawing at issue. The drawing will not leave this courtroom. Each side will have ten minutes to review and discuss it. Yasmin Bazzi will then be brought into the courtroom and sworn as a witness."

Jack could hear his client gasp, which drew a reaction from the bench.

"Mr. Swyteck, is there a problem?" the judge asked.

"No, Your Honor," said Jack, and he gave his client a reassuring touch on her wrist.

"As I was saying," the judge continued, "Mr. Swyteck will question the witness first. Ms. Beech, you may cross-examine if you wish. I admonish both sides to bear in mind that the witness is a six-year-old child."

Beech rose. "Not to quibble, Judge, but today is actually Yasmin's seventh birthday."

The judge's expression soured. "We're doing this *on her birthday?*"

"Not that Mr. Swyteck's client cares," said Beech.

"Really?" said Jack. "Judge, I object."

"Ms. Beech, enough with the cheap shots. Whether she's six or seven, my point is that we are dealing with a child of tender age. Mind yourselves accordingly. Are there any questions?"

Jack spoke. "Judge, would it be possible to speak with Yasmin before questioning her?"

"Absolutely not," the judge said. "As I stated, I made this decision in consultation with the child psychiatrist. I am adopting this procedure to avoid any possibility of witness coaching by either side. Yasmin created this drawing while she was completely alone, influenced by no one. I don't want anyone—stepmother, father, lawyer, judge, or psychiatrist—putting ideas in her head about what her drawing means. Yasmin's testimony will be completely untainted."

"Understood," said Jack.

"Any other questions?" the judge asked.

There were none.

"All right, Counsel. You may open the envelopes."

Andie spent the sunny afternoon in Bayfront Park, taking a walk along the seawall with a confidential informant.

Loco Lenny was a member of Miami Murda, a violent street gang in the Liberty City area. Andie wasn't officially assigned to the Gang and Criminal Organization Unit, but years of experience as an undercover agent made her the go-to liaison between the Miami safe-streets task force and nervous informants. Lenny was having second thoughts about wearing a wire to his next meeting with a local rapper named Piss-Tahl, the lead suspect in the execution-style murder of two spring-breakers who stiffed the wrong drug dealer and ended up on the wrong end of Piss-Tahl's pistol.

"Piss-Tahl gonna shoot me in the head, and then light me on fire."

Or he might light Lenny on fire and *then* shoot him in the head. But Andie didn't go there. All she could do was reassure him and, when that didn't work, give him a hard dose of reality.

"If you back out now, Lenny, we can't protect you. You'll be on your own."

It was the recurring theme of her pep talk. By the hour's end, Lenny was solid. Andie left him at the bronze statue of Christopher Columbus and walked alone to the park exit on Biscayne Boulevard, Miami's main north-south thoroughfare. Four lanes of bumper-to-bumper traffic flowed in each direction, divided by the elevated tram platform and a mile-long row of fifty-foot palm trees. Andie was in the long shadow of office towers across the street, waiting at the crosswalk for the green light, when a man wearing a suit and dark sunglasses stopped beside her.

"Agent Henning?" he asked.

She didn't recognize him. "Do I know you?"

"I came to discuss your application to the international corruption squad."

Miami was the fourth field office—joining New York, Los Angeles, and Washington, DC—to have an entire squad of senior agents and forensic accountants dedicated to combating foreign bribery, kleptocracy, and other complex investigations into transnational corruption with a US connection. The required coordination with foreign law enforcement and FBI legal attaché offices made it Andie's dream assignment, and she'd been waiting almost six months for a promotion. But not many people knew that she'd even applied.

"Who are you?" she asked.

"Someone who is concerned for you. The application seems to have hit a wall."

"What are you talking about?"

"Walk with me," he said.

He started up the sidewalk. Andie hesitated for a moment, then walked with him, the park to their right and northbound traffic to their left.

"It has come to our attention that you ran a Brian Guthrie through the FBI database."

One more thing that was known to very few—Andie, Isaac, and the geeks who conducted the occasional IT audits of the system. But Andie wasn't about to confirm or deny anything until this guy identified himself.

"Are you with headquarters?"

He ignored her question. "Have you figured out what 'locked' means, Agent Henning?"

She didn't respond; they continued walking.

"It means Mr. Guthrie is one of us."

"Us?"

He stopped, and so did Andie. He flashed his badge. His name—Hartfield—meant nothing to her. But she recognized the agency.

"You're CIA?" she said. "Guthrie is *CIA*?"

"One of us," he said, driving the point home.

"Well, you're late to the game," said Andie. "The State Department made it crystal clear that my husband is jeopardizing the negotiations for Mr.—*Agent* Guthrie's release. They already asked me to get him to back away from the 'Ava is dead' theory."

"We play harder than the State Department," he said.

"Meaning?"

"We're not asking. We're telling you."

"I get it. Do as I'm told or kiss my promotion goodbye. Is that it?"

"Promotion?" he said with an extortionist's chuckle. Then he turned serious. "Unauthorized use of the FBI database is no small thing. You'll be lucky to keep your current job."

Andie was speechless.

"Have a good day, Agent Henning."

Andie watched him walk away, suddenly feeling as though she had fewer options than Loco Lenny.

CHAPTER 30

A stony silence filled the near-empty courtroom. Jack could only imagine what was going through Yasmin's mind, as she stared out from her seat on the witness stand. Her hands were in her lap, clenching the doll from the judge's chambers, her eyes wide with fear.

"Mr. Swyteck, you may proceed," Judge Carlton said.

Jack chose not to rise. He would question the witness from his chair, seated right beside her mother. His aim was to be as nonthreatening as possible.

"Thank you, Your Honor. And hi, Yasmin."

"Hello," she said softly.

Jack had examined child witnesses before in other cases. It was never easy. The image depicted in Yasmin's drawing made it even more difficult in this case. Jack was still trying to wrap his mind around it.

"Can you hear me okay, Yasmin?"

"Uh-huh."

"Not too loud or too soft?"

"No."

"Good. So, it's just right. You're Goldilocks today, Yasmin. Everything should be just right. You let me know if it's not, okay?"

She gave him a little smile, but it was a nervous one.

Jack eased into things, first getting her to talk about the visit to Judge Carlton's chambers. His questions were purely conversational, intended only to reduce her stress, eliciting nothing that he didn't already know from having watched by camera. Then he turned to the matter at hand.

"I want to talk about the drawings you made for Judge Carlton," said Jack.

"Okay."

"The first one was a drawing of your friends at school, right?"

"Yes."

"The judge tells me that was a really good drawing."

"Thank you."

"The one we're here to talk about is the third one," said Jack. "The one you drew all by yourself, when no one was around."

Yasmin averted her eyes. Jack gave her a moment, and the judge interjected.

"We'll mark this as exhibit 1," the judge said, and then he addressed the court-appointed psychiatrist, who was seated to the side. "Dr. Emanuel, could you please come forward and provide the witness with a copy?"

The psychiatrist complied. Yasmin took the drawing and looked at it, saying nothing. Jack placed his copy flat on the table in front of him.

"Did you make that drawing, Yasmin?"

"Yes."

"Why did you make this drawing?"

"I dunno. I just did."

"That's fine," said Jack, and he was suddenly thinking about Righley, and not just because of the way she said "I dunno." Righley had an art teacher who liked to teach her class how to look at art. "IAI," she'd say; "Identify, analyze, interpret." Jack started with the "I."

"First, I just want you to tell me what's in the picture. I see three people, is that right?"

"Yes."

"The person in the middle is a grown-up, right?"

"Mm-hmm."

"You labeled her 'Mommy.' Is that your mommy?"

"Yes."

"Next to her is another grown-up, right?"

"Yes."

"You labeled that one 'Him.' Is 'Him' a man?"

"Yes."

"Who is the person you labeled 'Him'?"

Yasmin glanced in Farid's direction, then looked away quickly. She didn't answer verbally, but it was answer enough.

"Is 'Him' in the courtroom now?"

"Yes."

"Okay, we will leave it at that, for now. I see a third person in the drawing. A smaller person. You labeled that one 'Me.' Is 'Me' you, Yasmin?"

"Yes."

Jack paused. Step two of the IAI method: analyze. His focus shifted to the lines and techniques the artist used to convey the intended image.

"It looks to me like Mommy and Him are right next to each other, right?"

"Yes."

"But 'Me' is off to the side. Is that you standing off to the side, Yasmin?"

"Uh-huh."

"Why are you off to the side?"

"Afraid."

"Afraid of what?"

"Him."

"Why are you afraid of him?"

Yasmin didn't answer. Jack tried another approach.

"Your mommy has short hair in this drawing. Is the mommy in this picture sitting in this courtroom now?"

"No."

"The mommy sitting in this courtroom has long hair, right?"

"Yes."

"Who is the mommy with short hair in your picture?"

"Mommy before."

"Did the 'mommy before' always have short hair?"

"No."

"How did she get short hair?"

"She cut it."

"With what?"

Yasmin shifted nervously in the chair. "The scissors."

"With the scissors you drew in your picture?"

"Uh-huh."

Jack knew the next few questions were critical—and that they would be most difficult for his witness. "Yasmin, why is the man labeled 'Him' holding the scissors?"

Farid's lawyer rose. "Judge, I have to object."

Jack had expected as much. He was moving to the final step of the IAI method, from "identify" and "analyze" to "interpret."

"Let's hear the answer," said the judge. "Yasmin, the question is, 'Why is the man labeled 'Him' holding the scissors?"

Yasmin hesitated. She almost froze.

Jack asked again, more gently. "Can you tell us why, Yasmin?"

Yasmin struggled, clearly digging deep for the answer. "Because he doesn't like her hair."

"Is the man mad in your picture?"

"Objection, leading."

"Overruled. Yes, it's leading, counsel. But again, the witness is a child. Let's keep the objections to a minimum, please. Continue, Mr. Swyteck."

"Is the man in your picture mad?" Jack asked again.

"Uh-huh."

"Is he mad at Mommy?"

She nodded.

Jack continued. "Is the man saying anything?"

She nodded again.

"Is his voice soft?" Jack asked. "Or is it loud?"

Yasmin's voice tightened. "Loud. Real loud."

"When I take a good look at the figure you labeled 'Me,' it looks like she has her hands over her ears. Am I right?"

"Uh-huh."

"Why?"

"Because it's so loud."

"Were you afraid?" Jack asked.

"Yeah."

"Afraid of what?"

She didn't answer, but again she glanced nervously in Farid's direction. Jack was concerned that she might shut down if he pushed too hard for an answer. But there was one more important point to make.

"In your drawing, the man is holding the scissors. He's holding them high in the air, right?"

She nodded.

"Above Mommy's head," said Jack.

She didn't answer.

"What is he doing with the scissors?"

She started to tremble.

"Did you see what he did with the scissors, Yasmin?"

She was trembling, but she managed a little nod.

"Yasmin, what did he do with the scissors?"

Her eyes welled, and a sudden scream filled the courtroom. "*Mommy!*"

Farid launched from his chair. "This *never* happened!" he shouted.

It was the first and only time Farid had displayed a temper in these proceedings, and Yasmin cowered on the witness stand. Farid's lawyer tried to reel him in, almost forcing him back into his seat, but she addressed the court with equal anger.

"Judge, this is outrageous! This child has obviously been coached!"

Jack remained seated, so as not to overwhelm Yasmin, but he spoke forcefully. "Judge, there has been no coaching. That was the whole point of the process you adopted here. Yasmin drew the picture alone in your chambers, and she was immediately put on the witness stand to answer questions about it, having spent no time alone with me or my client to prepare."

"I demand the right to cross-examine," said Beech.

The psychiatrist rose—to protect Yasmin from further trauma, Jack presumed—but the judge was one step ahead of everyone else.

"We're not going to do that," the judge said.

"But you said I would have the right to question the witness," said Beech.

"Obviously, the circumstances have changed," the judge said, and then he put on his grandfatherly face to address the witness.

"You're a brave girl, Yasmin. Dr. Emanuel is going to take you back to my chambers, and you'll be safe there."

The doctor followed the judge's directive. She and Yasmin disappeared through the side door to the chambers. Judge Carlton continued.

"To be clear, I am not going to make a finding on the record that Farid Bazzi murdered Ava Bazzi, his first wife. I won't even go so far as to find that Mr. Bazzi stabbed or otherwise physically harmed her. But it is clear enough from the testimony today that Mr. Bazzi threatened or otherwise 'abused' Ava for cutting her hair in protest of the hijab laws. The key point is that the abuse—whatever form it took—was done in the presence of the child. Witnessing the abuse of the mother constitutes grave danger of psychological harm to a child within the meaning of the Hague Convention—which is a complete defense against a father's claim of unlawful abduction."

Zahra's grip on Jack's arm tightened. She could read the tea leaves as well as he could.

"This court finds that returning the child, Yasmin Bazzi, to her father, Farid Bazzi, would put the child at grave risk of physical or psychological harm. I therefore rule in favor of the respondent, Zahra Bazzi. We are adjourned," he said, ending with a crack of his gavel.

The bailiff gave the command to rise, but both sides were already standing.

"It's over?" Zahra asked, breathless.

"It's over," Jack whispered.

His client shrieked so loudly that Jack's ears started ringing.

"Order, please," the judge said.

Jack got his client under control. The judge stepped down from the bench and exited to his chambers. Before Zahra could say "Thank you," Farid's lawyer crossed quickly to Jack's side of the courtroom for a lawyer-to-lawyer moment.

"This is far from over, Swyteck."

"Yeah, good luck with your appeal," said Jack.

"Appeal? Right," she said with a smirk. "You really don't know how this game is played, do you?"

She turned and walked back to her client.

"What did she mean by that?" Zahra asked.

Jack had his own ideas, but none that he was ready to share. "Nothing," he said. "Sore loser."

CHAPTER 31

Andie went straight from the park to the gym.

Chasing bad guys required a certain level of stamina, so physical strength and endurance was certainly part of the FBI's continuing fitness requirement. But it was also about stress reduction. For Andie, forty-five minutes on the treadmill was pure mental therapy, a time to turn off her brain and clear her head. Unfortunately, she'd made the mistake of turning on the TV app. The cable news headline was impossible to ignore:

MIAMI JUDGE RULES FOR IRANIAN MOTHER IN CONTROVERSIAL CHILD ABDUCTION CASE.

Andie kept running but turned up the volume to listen through her earbuds.

Judge Carlton's ruling was breaking news in every media outlet, so Andie switched from one network to another to get the total picture. The consensus among talking heads was that while the judge did not expressly find that Farid Bazzi murdered his wife for defying Iran's hijab laws, that was one reasonable interpretation of Yasmin's testimony. Another reasonable interpretation was that he tried to kill or at least hurt her—reason enough for Ava to have fled the country.

Andie's cell rang. Isaac was calling. She hit pause on the treadmill, wiped the sweat from her face, and answered.

"Hey, kiddo. Congratulations."

He sounded like his old self again, but Andie had no idea what he was talking about.

"For what?"

"Your application to the international corruption squad was approved."

Andie caught her breath. "What?"

"You haven't heard?"

Andie didn't want to jump to conclusions, especially with Isaac. But he'd undergone a serious attitude adjustment since their last phone conversation, and it was too soon after her "pep talk" from the CIA to be a coincidence.

"I haven't heard a thing," she said, deciding not to mention her walking companion.

"I guess word travels faster here at headquarters. I'm so proud of you. Well deserved."

"Um, that's great news."

"What's with the 'um'? You've earned this. Let yourself be happy about it."

"I am happy," she said. "Also a little confused."

"What about?"

If Isaac knew about the pressure from the CIA, he would deny it, so Andie didn't bring it up. But he was fully aware of the pressure from the State Department.

"Apparently the United States government is just as happy with Jack trying to prove that Ava Bazzi was murdered by her husband as it is with the Iranian government's claim that Ava Bazzi fled the country and is still alive."

"I'm not sure I follow your concern," said Isaac.

"You must be aware of the judge's ruling in Jack's case."

"Yes. A good day for both of you."

"Jack wins. I get a promotion. What a coincidence."

"Coincidences do happen."

"Isaac, cut the bullshit. One thing has come clear today. The *only* public narrative the US government has a problem with is that the Iranian government killed Ava."

"You knew that long before today."

"But today puts things in the proper context. Isn't it a bit odd that the only version of Ava's disappearance that was *not* supported by Yasmin's testimony is the theory that Jack originally advanced in Zahra's case: that Ava was murdered by the morality police in an Iranian prison?"

"Jack was wrong. You should feel vindicated."

"I don't."

"What's your problem now?"

"For all the times that Jack has taken a position in the courtroom that embarrassed or even infuriated me, he has *never* been so dead wrong."

"There's a first time for everything."

"Do you really expect me to believe that?"

Isaac's tone changed again, more like that guy on their previous call. "Andie, be smart. Leave this alone."

"Thanks for the advice," she said, and ended the call.

There was a double celebration at Zahra's town house. At his client's insistence, Jack was there to raise a nonalcoholic toast to the courtroom victory and to fend off any unwanted journalists. Righley and a dozen other girls had come to wish Yasmin a happy seventh birthday. Andie drove her straight from after-school dance classes.

"Tavallod-et mobaarak, Yasmin!" said Righley—literally, "May your birthday be blessed."

"Ah, you speak Farsi?" said Zahra.

"No. My mom googled it."

Zahra laughed and took both girls by the hand. "Come on, Yasmin. Let's introduce Righley to your friends."

They headed into the family room, leaving Jack and Andie alone near the long line of shoes the guests had taken off near the front door. Jack and Andie removed theirs and then moved into the living room, stopping at the stack of colorfully wrapped birthday gifts on the coffee table.

"I guess congratulations are in order," said Andie.

"Yeah. I guess."

"Oh, come on. Don't act like it was just another day at the courthouse. This was big."

"Definitely big," said Jack. "But I have to say I'm a bit ambivalent about the way it went down."

"Ambivalent in what way?"

"Maybe it's the criminal defense lawyer in me. I understand better than anyone that this was not a trial by jury, and that Farid wasn't entitled to all the rights afforded to a criminal defendant. But it just doesn't sit well when a man gets accused of murder, and the judge doesn't give his lawyer the chance to cross-examine the only witness against him."

"That witness just turned seven today, Jack."

"I get it. I really do. The rules are different in a Hague proceeding."

"And the reason they're different, I assume, is to protect children like Yasmin."

"That's totally true. But still, things need to be . . . fair."

"Are you saying Farid didn't get a fair shake?"

Jack took a breath. "Don't get me wrong. I'm happy Zahra and Yasmin are together. It was the right result. It's the way we got there that makes me uncomfortable."

"I'm sure everyone in the courtroom was uncomfortable. From what I heard on the news, it must have been shocking."

"I can deal with 'shocking.' What makes me uncomfortable is that someone could look at this objectively and say it played straight to the worst stereotypes of 'the abusive Muslim man.'"

"The key witness against Farid was his own daughter, Jack. I hardly think Yasmin is Islamophobic."

"I'm talking about the way the judge reacted. Arguably, *over*reacted. Shutting things down immediately and ruling from the bench."

"You think the judge is Islamophobic?"

"I don't know. You don't have to be an outright bigot to have prejudices. He wouldn't be the first."

Andie walked over to the coffee table and added the gift from Righley to Yasmin's stack.

"I hope you're wrong," she said. "But if it's any consolation, there's someone else in the room who has every reason to celebrate but doesn't feel like it."

She was clearly talking about herself, but Jack was still confused. "Celebrate what?"

"I applied to the international corruption squad here in Miami. I got it."

Jack was familiar with the squad, which had put one of his former clients in federal prison. "Well, that's great news. But now I feel like a schmuck of a husband."

"Why?"

"I should have been supporting you all this time. But honestly, I guess I just forgot you'd even applied."

"You didn't forget. I didn't tell you."

Jack didn't quite comprehend. "You didn't tell me? Andie, this is a huge step. It means moving on from your undercover work."

"That's kind of why I didn't tell you."

"I don't understand."

She stepped a little closer, lowering her voice. "This was when things were pretty shaky between us. I spoke to the marriage counselor about it, and she agreed. Undercover work requires time away from family for extended periods. That's not the best gig for a single mother."

Jack took a moment, but there was no way to read a happy Jack-and-Andie ending into her words. "But she would still have me, and we would be equal parents."

"But what if we weren't in the same city? Would you want her pulled out of school for weeks at a time?"

Jack was still trying to comprehend. "Let's get out of the weeds and go back to the beginning. So, you went into marriage counseling thinking you were going to come out a single mother?"

"Jack, please. I wasn't being pessimistic. I was being . . ."

"Realistic?"

"I was going to say 'practical.' Jack, like I said, things were at a low point then. We're better now."

"I guess I didn't know how bad things were."

"But we're better now, right?"

"Uh, yeah," he said without heart. "Better."

Zahra's doorbell rang. Jack was standing just a few feet away from the front door. Zahra was in the family room trying to fasten birthday hats on a dozen overexcited girls who appeared to be incapable of standing still.

"Jack, could you get that, please?" Zahra called from across the room.

Jack answered the door. The man on the porch was dressed in street clothes but flashed a badge with his photograph on it. He had court papers with him.

"Are you a process server?" Jack asked.

"Yes. I'm here to serve Zahra Bazzi."

On another day, Jack might have slammed the door on him. He didn't see the point, especially with an FBI agent as witness.

"I'm her attorney. I'll accept service."

The man made a notation on his return-of-service form and handed Jack the papers. Jack closed the door, asked Andie to get Zahra, and stepped away from the party to a quiet place in the dining room. He was just finishing a quick first read through the papers as Zahra entered.

"What is it, Jack?"

"Farid has filed another lawsuit against you."

All signs of happiness drained from her expression. "But we just won our lawsuit."

"That was in federal court under the Hague Convention. This lawsuit is in state court."

She stepped farther into the room. "What kind of a justice system is that? Farid loses before one judge, and he can just file another lawsuit in front of another one?"

"The Hague Convention is a treaty with a very specific focus," said Jack. "It deals only with the question of whether one parent wrongfully abducted the child and took her to another country."

"And we won that case. It's over."

"There's a catch," said Jack.

"A catch?"

"A Hague proceeding is not a custody case. Judge Carlton ruled that your defense to child abduction was valid. But he didn't enter a child custody order. He didn't rule that you have sole custody of Yasmin. Custody decisions are made in state court."

She seemed to grasp the legal distinction. "So, this new case. It's a lawsuit to decide who should have legal custody over Yasmin?"

"It's a little different," said Jack.

"Different how?"

"Farid alleges in his complaint that he already has an order from a court awarding him full custody over Yasmin."

"From what court?"

"Family court. In Iran."

Her confusion turned to horror. "Is that valid?"

"We'll find out. He's not asking the Florida state court to decide custody. He's asking the court to enforce the order already entered by the Iranian court—which gives him custody."

She lowered herself slowly into the chair, stunned. "That's what Farid's lawyer meant when she came up to us and said 'This isn't over.'"

"I presume so."

She looked at him with fire in her eyes. "We have to fight this, Jack."

"Yes," said Jack. "We will."

CHAPTER 32

A classic rock radio station was playing in the elevator as Andie rode to the fourth floor of the Miami Field Office on Tuesday morning. The receptionist flagged her the moment the chrome doors parted. Andie was slammed with work, and the last thing she needed was an unscheduled visitor, but as the elevator music had just reminded her, you can't always get what you want, and when Murphy's law collides with the wisdom of the Rolling Stones, you just might find, you get *more than* you need.

"Agent Henning, there's a Mr. Farid Bazzi here to see you."

Andie stopped. She had yet to take her morning coffee, so the message didn't quite compute.

"Seriously? The Farid Bazzi from my husband's case?"

"Unless you know another one. He's waiting in the lobby."

Andie stepped around the front desk and glanced through the bullet-proof glass that separated the employee entrance from the visitors' lobby. Only one person was waiting, and he looked like the Farid Bazzi she'd seen on the news.

"Would you like me to tell him you're not available?" the receptionist asked.

Andie had faced danger of every stripe in her career, but the sage advice of an instructor from her training at the Academy in Quantico came to mind: "There's no situation more dangerous than a domestic dispute."

"He's been through the metal detector, right?" asked Andie.

"Yes, of course."

"It's fine. I'll see him. This should be interesting."

The receptionist buzzed her through the locked security door, and Andie entered the lobby. Farid rose and politely introduced himself.

"How can I help you, Mr. Bazzi?"

"I would like to speak with you," he said. "It's about my daughter, Yasmin."

Andie could see in his eyes that he probably hadn't slept all night.

"You do understand that my husband is Jack Swyteck, Zahra's lawyer?"

"Yes, of course. That's half the reason I'm here."

"And the other half?"

"The fact that you're an FBI agent. A mother. And I presume a very intelligent woman. Can we go somewhere and talk, please?"

So far, not so threatening. "Here is fine," she said.

Farid returned to his seat. Andie took the chair across from him, near an engraved bronze plaque honoring the two Miami field agents killed in a 1986 shootout that left five other agents wounded. They were alone in the lobby, save for the indistinct murmuring of a Weather Channel reporter on the flat-screen television in the corner.

"I know you are busy, Agent Henning. So pardon my directness. Your husband seems convinced that Ava is dead. Do you believe she is dead?"

"My, we are being direct. That's not for me to say, Mr. Bazzi."

"The Iranian government says Ava fled the country and is still alive. The US State Department has never contradicted that statement."

"I can't speak for the State Department," she said.

Farid paused, then looked Andie in the eye. "I didn't kill my wife."

"I didn't say you did."

"Everyone thinks it."

"Not everyone," said Andie. "Some people think you tried to kill her, or that you abused her so badly that she fled the country and went into hiding."

"What do you believe?" he asked.

Andie couldn't tell him about the confidential dossier, which contained the visa application with Ava's fingerprints on it—the State Department's "proof" that Ava was still alive. "It doesn't matter what I think, Mr. Bazzi."

"It does matter," he said, his voice taking on urgency. Then he took a breath, as if to slow himself down, maybe even take a step back. "Agent Henning, you have a daughter. She's a little older than Yasmin, no?"

"I do."

"Imagine that you are married to an abuser. Would you *ever* run away and leave your daughter behind to live alone with a monster? What mother would do that to her daughter, no matter how much she feared for herself?"

Andie didn't want to judge any woman in that situation, but she understood Farid's point. Fleeing an abuser and leaving your own daughter behind was almost unimaginable.

"I understand what you're saying, Mr. Bazzi. But I don't see where your hypothetical leads us."

He leveled his gaze, again looking Andie straight in the eye. "I know why Ava ran away," he said in a very serious voice.

Andie was beginning to wonder if she needed a witness to this conversation, but Farid had come to see *her*, and she didn't want to shut down the flow of information. "Go on, please," she said.

"Before she was arrested, Ava was part of a . . . how should I call it? Not an organization. A group of women."

"Women in Tehran?"

"From all over Iran. Women who wanted change and who specifically opposed enforcement of the hijab laws."

"Women who participated in the street demonstrations, you mean?"

"No. To the contrary. Most of them did not show their faces. They were too afraid. Or they had children and there was too much to lose."

"Then how did this group operate?"

"Mahsa Amini's death changed everything in Iran. You know of Mahsa?"

"Yes. The young woman killed by morality police for disrespecting the Islamic Republic's dress code."

"The police said she was being 'educated' on hijab rules and suffered a heart attack—happens all the time to twenty-two-year-old women in Iran. But yes, after Mahsa's death, the demonstrations exploded. The government shut down the internet so that protesters couldn't organize. Information was hard to come by. This group of women—Ava included—became a network of information."

"A network?"

"They shared text messages on their cell phones. 'Street protests in Rasht.' 'Nine-year-old boy shot and killed in Izeh.' 'Dress code crackdown at Anushiravan Dadgar High School in Tehran.' The idea was to keep the information flowing. A woman sees something, and she texts her friends, who text their friends, and it goes on and on."

"I imagine it would be very dangerous if those messages were detected," said Andie.

"Yes. Definitely. That was the reason for 'the rule.'"

The rule. It made her think of Jack and the nonsensical rule that had caused so many problems in their marriage, but she killed that thought. "What was 'the rule'?"

"Pass on the message to another woman in the network and then immediately delete both the incoming and outgoing text message. That way there would be no record of the substance of the communication if the morality police confiscated a woman's cell phone."

"Brilliant," said Andie. "Not even the tech geniuses at the FBI can retrieve the substance of deleted text messages. We can only confirm the sender, recipient, and time of transmission."

"Ah, but you are assuming the rule was followed."

"Ava broke the rule?"

"Partly. She deleted the messages from her phone, but she saved them to a flash drive."

"She told you this?"

"No. I found the flash drive in our home computer at our apartment. She left it there by accident. I knew nothing about the network until then."

Andie showed no reaction, but she'd read about Yasmin's testimony about the scissors. She was certain that Farid's version of "what happened next" would be very different.

"Did you ask her about it?"

"Yes, of course."

"What did she tell you?"

"She cried at first. It was such an emotional release for her to unload her secret."

"What secret?"

"Ava was different from the other women. What I mean by that is that she played a different role in the information network. A special role."

"Meaning?"

"Ava didn't just pass along information to other women in Iran. She was on the front line of gathering information about what was happening in Iran and getting it to the outside world."

Andie hesitated. Farid's story was going in a direction she hadn't anticipated. "Tell me how that worked."

"She was saving all the text messages to a thumb drive and passing it along to her contact in Tehran. Her contact than passed it along to whatever channels were available."

"Who was her contact?"

"I have no idea. I'm not sure even Ava knew. She told me she did blind drops. Never met her contact. Could have been a Western journalist. Maybe Amnesty International or some other human rights organization."

Andie's imagination led to other possibilities, especially on the heels of a visit from the CIA.

"I should have told her to stop what she was doing," said Farid. "It was too dangerous. But I didn't. I was actually . . . proud of her."

Andie studied his expression closely. She wasn't sure if Farid was being truthful or deserving of an Academy Award.

"You said you knew why Ava fled the country."

"Well, I don't *know*. I have my own idea."

"Tell me."

"When Ava was arrested, the morality police took her to Evin Prison."

"I've heard of it," said Andie.

Evin was for political prisoners. It held so many students and intellectuals that an entire wing was nicknamed "Evin University." Reports of human rights violations in Evin were legion.

"Evin is notorious for its methods of interrogation," said Farid. "They would have beaten every bit of information out of Ava if she had not escaped. The names of every woman in her text-messaging network. Hundreds of them. They all would have been arrested—or worse."

"So, you believe Ava fled to—"

"To protect those women."

"That's your theory?"

"It's more than a theory. Can you imagine how difficult that must have been for Ava? She left her daughter behind. But she left knowing that Yasmin would be safe with me."

"So, naturally, you divorced her and married her sister," she said with a healthy dose of skepticism. "I'm not buying it, Farid."

"I was given no choice," he said, a hint of desperation in his voice. "Divorcing Ava fit with the government's story that Ava was an unholy woman who abandoned Yasmin and me."

"The regime forced you to divorce Ava. Is that what you're saying?"

"Yes, exactly. After your wife is hauled off to Evin and you are left to raise a daughter on your own, it is the regime that holds all the cards."

"But the regime didn't force you to marry Zahra."

"That's true."

"Then why did you?"

He was about to answer, it seemed, but he stopped himself.

"There is a simple answer," Farid said. "But so far, the information has flowed only one way in this conversation. I've opened myself up, and you won't even tell me if you think Ava is alive or dead."

"Like I told you: what I think doesn't matter."

"It matters to *me*," said Farid.

"Why?"

"Until I heard the evidence in court, I was certain that Ava was still alive."

He was plainly tired of her taking without giving, but Andie had to ask the obvious follow-up question—gently. "You're not so certain anymore?"

"Your husband's cross-examination of Imam Reza made me wonder. It may seem like a technicality to a non-Muslim, but Mr. Swyteck was right. The imam would never have married me to Zahra so soon unless he believed Ava was dead."

"Still, that's not direct and incontrovertible proof of her death."

"That's why I've come to you. Your husband seems so certain that Ava is dead. Is he getting that information from you?"

"From me?"

"Does the US government know something I should know? Do they know Ava is dead?"

Andie couldn't answer that question. The State Department dossier with Ava's fingerprints on a visa application was classified.

"I can't speak to you on behalf of the entire United States government."

"I'm not asking you to be a spokesperson. I want to know how your husband has gotten the idea so firmly in his head that my wife is dead."

Andie noted that he still referred to Ava as "my wife," but she still hadn't decided if it was about love or ownership.

"I'm sorry," she said. "I can't help you. Your lawyer will have to speak to Jack about that."

"I was hoping to get around the lawyers," he said, rising. "But so be it."

Andie rose too. "Thank you for coming, Mr. Bazzi."

"You don't believe a word I said, do you?"

Andie chose not to say. "Again, thank you for coming."

Farid headed for the exit, opened the door, and then stopped.

"Persian women have the most beautiful hair," he said. "In our culture, hair is one of the most recurring metaphors in poetry. It's almost spiritual, the essence of a person's soul. Ava had such beautiful hair. She sacrificed that beauty to keep her dignity. I don't judge her for making that choice."

Andie didn't respond, but their gaze held for a moment. It wasn't that Andie didn't believe he was speaking the truth. She just wasn't proud—let alone prepared to *admit*—that in her world, there could be more than one "truth."

Farid stepped out, and the door closed with a click of the electronic lock.

CHAPTER 33

Jack and Zahra were back in court on Wednesday, but not before Judge Carlton. This time, it was Florida state court, family law division.

The Lawson E. Thomas Courthouse was just a few blocks from the federal courthouse, but in every other respect, it was worlds away. Federal judges had the lifetime presidential appointment and all the prestige that came with it, but family division judges were in the trenches every day dealing with family matters—dissolutions of marriage, child custody and support, adoptions, paternity, and domestic violence. Jack had never appeared before a judge in the family division. It gave him a sinking feeling in the pit of his stomach to think that, had things gone differently in counseling, Jack's first appearance before Judge Lauren Carpenter could have been as a party, not a lawyer.

Jack shook off that thought. Zahra was his only concern. He'd heard good things about Judge Carpenter. She had more than a decade of experience, though Jack doubted that she'd ever presided over a case quite like this one.

"Counsel, I've handled a number of cases involving the enforcement of custody orders issued by courts in another country," she said from the bench. "Canada. Mexico. Brazil. I think I even had one from Australia. But I must admit, this is the first one from Iran."

Jack rose. "Your Honor, I would point out another 'first.' It is probably the first time any judge in this division has been asked to enforce a foreign custody order after a federal judge has ruled that returning the child to the father would put that child at grave risk of serious physical or psychological harm."

"Yes, I was going to ask Ms. Beech about that. Counsel?"

"Judge, an action under the Hague Convention has a narrow focus: Was the child improperly abducted from her habitual place of residence? The Hague Convention, however, does not override the authority of the child's home country to determine custody. Under the Uniform Child Custody Jurisdiction and Enforcement Act—which has been enacted by every state in the United States, including Florida—a state court must enforce a custody order issued by the home country."

"Excuse me," said Jack. "Ms. Beech left off an important limitation. The state court must enforce the order *unless* the child custody law of that foreign country violates fundamental principles of human rights."

The judge raised an eyebrow. "Is that what you intend to prove, Mr. Swyteck?"

"If we have to, Your Honor."

"Well, I must say, I admire your determination. Last week you tried to prove that the Iranian regime was lying to the world about the death of Ava Bazzi. This week, you intend to prove that the entire family law system of Iran violates human rights."

His opposing counsel could barely contain her laughter.

"With all due respect, it's simpler than that," said Jack. "It violates basic common sense and all principles of decency to return Yasmin Bazzi to her father after a federal judge has decided that doing so would put her in grave danger."

"That's not the issue," said Beech.

"All right, enough," the judge said. "I have nine dissolutions of marriage, five name changes, and three motions to modify child support—and that's all before lunch. I don't have time for this now. But I will put this on a fast track. A slot just opened on my calendar this Friday. Ms. Beech, you can present your case to enforce the custody order then. Mr. Swyteck, be prepared to present any challenge at that time. We're adjourned. Next case."

"*Cruz v. Cruz*," the clerk announced, and a new set of lawyers elbowed Jack and his opposing counsel out of the way and took their seats at the table.

Jack and Zahra made their way to the rear exit.

"Why did she put our case on a fast track?" Zahra asked.

Jack had the same question. Compared to the hallowed halls of the federal courthouse, the state court family division was a legal meat grinder. Thousands upon thousands of cases worked through the overtaxed system, from simple uncontested divorces to hotly contested domestic violence cases and emergency restraining orders. Many cases got bogged down in the glut for years.

"She didn't say why," said Jack. "But it does seem odd that an entire day this week suddenly became available on her calendar. Family division judges in Miami are some of the busiest judges in America."

"Then what's going on here? What's the rush?"

The gallery was filled with lawyers and clients waiting for their turn before the judge. Jack waited until he and Zahra were out the door and in the lobby before responding.

"For some reason, Judge Carpenter has given your case priority status."

"*Why*, Jack? If you can explain this to me, I have a right to know."

Jack's knowledge of the US government's negotiations with the Iranians was limited to what Andie told him. But whatever they were negotiating, it seemed to Jack that the State Department was being forced to make one concession after another. For the Iranians, it apparently wasn't enough that the State Department tried to shut down Jack's efforts to prove in federal court that Ava Bazzi was murdered by the Tehran morality police. It wasn't enough that the State Department created a classified dossier with documented support for the Iranian government's claim that Ava fled Tehran and was still alive. Even after all that, the Iranian government wanted Ava's child removed from the United States and returned to the father in Iran—as quickly as possible. Jack could think of only one reason. He didn't know for sure, but he suspected that someone was making another concession to the Iranian government.

"It could have something to do with the State Department," he said.

"You think the State Department got to the judge?"

"I'm not saying that."

"But you're thinking it."

Jack pushed the call button for the elevator. "All I'm saying is that our opposition extends beyond these courthouse walls."

Andie stopped by the Cuban coffee shop for a 2:00 p.m. jolt of espresso. She was deep in thought, coffee in hand, when she turned away from the cashier to find the man behind her right in her face.

"Whoa!" she said, startled.

"Did I scare you?"

She'd nearly spilled her coffee, but she quickly recognized him as the CIA agent—Hartfield—who had tracked her down outside Bayfront Park.

"Yes, you did," said Andie. "I fully appreciate who you work for, okay? But do you really have to make these sudden appearances out of nowhere like the ghost of King Hamlet?"

"Please, sit with me," he said.

He was polite enough, but Andie knew it was more of a direction than an invitation. She followed him to an open table by the window, where they sat opposite one another.

"I see your husband is at it again," Hartfield said.

"At what again?"

"Doing his best to sour relations between the US and Iran at a tender moment in our negotiations."

"I really don't know what you're talking about."

"My intelligence from this morning's court hearing is that now he intends to prove that the entire family law system in Iran is a violation of basic human rights."

"I'm sure that's an overstatement."

"The *judge* said it."

Andie drank from her demitasse. "This doesn't concern me."

"Well, that's where you're wrong, Agent Henning. That was quite a stroke of genius you and your husband came up with in the Hague proceeding."

Andie was truly confused. "I really don't know what you're referring to."

"Jack needed to prove that Ava Bazzi is dead. I told you our concerns about trying to prove that she was murdered by the morality police. On a dime, Jack pivots: Farid did it."

Hartfield was only confirming her suspicions. "And voilà, my promotion came through."

He smiled wryly. "I have no comment on that. Except to say that as the newest member of the FBI's international corruption squad, you will of course be interacting with various agencies that have international reach, including mine. Jack's latest position seriously undermines my confidence in your ability to do that."

"Are you threatening to rescind my promotion if he doesn't change his position?"

"No, of course not. I'm merely pointing out that in every squad, there are career-advancing assignments, and there are dead-end assignments. I want you to have a rewarding experience."

Andie quelled her anger. "Your concern is noted. But this conversation is over."

"I'm trying to help you," he said.

"I don't want your help. I want what Jack wants."

"Which is what?"

"The truth."

Hartfield chuckled. "That's cute."

"Not one bit of the story about Ava that was presented through Yasmin in the courtroom was in the classified dossier that the State Department shared with me. There was nothing in the dossier about Ava having fled domestic violence. And there was nothing about her role in a secret 'network' of messengers, which I just heard about from Farid."

"No dossier tells the complete story. Especially one that isn't designated Top Secret."

"All I know is this. The dossier doesn't line up with what Judge Carlton has determined are the real facts, or what Farid now claims are the real facts. It makes me wonder."

"Wonder what?"

"Whether the things that you and the State Department have told me about the hostage negotiations—and the hostage—line up with the real facts."

Andie rose and started away from the table, but Hartfield stopped her.

"Be smart about this, Agent Henning."

"I'm a lot of things. But stupid is not one of them."

Andie grabbed her cup and headed for the door.

CHAPTER 34

J ack entered the courtroom on Friday with his client at his side.

Zahra was more nervous than Jack had ever seen her. The possibility of Farid snatching away her hard-fought victory was more than she could bear.

"I would rather have lost before Judge Carlton than lose Yasmin this way," she'd told Jack before the hearing, seeming to expect the worst. Jack completely understood. She'd not merely tasted victory; she'd lived it, if only for a few hours.

Judge Carpenter's announcement at the outset of the hearing only heightened the concern.

"Counsel, I had originally set aside the entire day for this matter. Unfortunately, that is no longer possible. I can give you one hour. Adjust your presentations accordingly."

Zahra leaned closer and whispered, "She's already made up her mind, hasn't she?"

"Then we'll have to change it," he whispered back.

"Ms. Beech, please proceed," the judge said.

Farid's lawyer rose and stepped to the podium. "Judge, we have no problem with the abbreviated schedule. In fact, we could do this in one minute, much less one hour."

Her assistant brought up an image on the courtroom's LCD screen.

"Your Honor, on the left side of the screen is an order entered by the Iranian family court. On the right is a certified translation. Mr. Bazzi seeks enforcement of this order. The pertinent language, highlighted in yellow, states that Farid Bazzi 'shall have full and sole custody of Yasmin Bazzi upon her seventh birthday.'"

The judge peered out over the top of her reading glasses. "Is Yasmin seven years of age?"

"Yes, Your Honor. Her seventh birthday was on Monday."

"Is there any dispute as to the child's age, Mr. Swyteck?"

Jack didn't like stipulating to facts without understanding the legal significance, but he was in no position to quibble, having attended the party.

"No dispute," said Jack.

"Next slide," Beech told her assistant, and a new image appeared.

"Judge, it is important to understand that this order is consistent with mandatory provisions in the Iranian civil code, which I have put on the screen for the court's convenience. The code explicitly provides that a daughter 'will remain under the custody of the mother till seven years' and 'after the lapse of this period *custody will devolve on the father*.' Under Iranian law, the period of custody for Zahra Bazzi as mother has ended. The father's custody must begin. Under US law, this court must enforce the order. Case closed."

Beech returned to her seat.

"Counsel, thank you for your brevity," the judge said. "Mr. Swyteck, what's your position?"

Jack rose. "Your Honor, I wish I could tell you that—suddenly and out of nowhere—an order from an Iranian court has appeared and my client has been granted sole custody. But I can't. I wish I could point to provisions of the Iranian family code—which, by the way, is stacked against women. But I can't. All I can say is this.

"Any requirement under Iranian law that custody of a daughter automatically transfers to the father at age seven can't possibly apply where a US federal judge has just decided that returning her to her father would put her in grave danger of physical and psychological abuse. Any argument otherwise should shock the conscience of this court."

"Mr. Swyteck, I understand your argument," the judge said. "And it certainly has some weight. But I've also read the cases cited in Ms. Beech's brief. It would appear that the law is not on your side."

Farid's lawyer interjected. "That's exactly right, Judge. The leading case on this point involved a family from Turkey. The mother won the Hague proceeding based on allegations of abuse by the father. The father filed suit in state court in New Hampshire to enforce a custody order from the Turkish court awarding *him* sole custody. The supreme court said that the custody order entered by the Turkish court must be enforced. It's exactly the situation here."

"It's not the same," Jack fired back. "In the Turkey case, the Turkish court considered and rejected the mother's allegations of abuse. Here, no Iranian court has even considered Zahra's allegations, much less rejected them. The only court to consider the issue was Judge Carlton, who found that returning Yasmin to her father presents a grave danger of physical or psychological harm."

"Judge, what Mr. Swyteck is telling you is flatly incorrect. An Iranian court *did* consider Zahra's allegations of abuse."

That was news to Jack.

"When did the Iranian court consider this issue?" the judge asked.

"Farid filed a custody action in Iran. Zahra's lawyer appeared at the hearing in Tehran and presented evidence on her behalf. The Iranian court ruled in favor of Farid and granted custody to Farid, effective upon Yasmin's seventh birthday. It was all part of the proceeding that resulted in the order we seek to enforce."

Jack was completely blindsided. He needed to regroup.

"Your Honor, could I have a few minutes to confer in private with my client?"

"I'm sorry, Mr. Swyteck. I have enough work for three judges today. As soon as we adjourn here, I'm moving on to the next hot mess. Mute your microphone and sort it out here. I'll give you two minutes."

"Yes, Judge," he said, and he muted the mic.

"This is a sham," said Zahra. Her voice was a whisper, but it was filled with urgency.

"Do you know anything about a hearing in Iran?"

"No!" she said in the same urgent whisper. "And I never hired an Iranian lawyer. This so-called order is completely bogus. You have to do something!"

Jack rose and addressed the court.

"Your Honor, I appreciate that the court's time is limited today. But we need time to investigate the circumstances surrounding the entry of this custody order. My client has reason to believe that it is a complete fabrication. We would ask that the court schedule this matter for a full evidentiary hearing to make sure that a fraud is not being perpetrated."

Farid's lawyer fired back, filled with indignation. "Oh, we're making accusations of fraud now, are we? Judge, I would point out that the order Mr. Swyteck characterizes as a 'fraud' has been legalized for use in the United States in accordance with all requirements of the Office of Authentications of the US Department of State. It is valid and authentic on its face."

Jack was reluctant to pick another fight with the State Department, but mention of the formal process of "legalization" only confirmed his suspicions.

"Your Honor, Ms. Beech's explanation underscores the need for a full hearing. I've gone through the process of legalizing orders by foreign courts so that they can be enforced in the United States. It can take months, even when the US has diplomatic relations with the country in question. Here, we're talking about a court order from Iran, where the United States doesn't even have an embassy. Yet the entire process—including the final certificate of legalization issued by the State Department—was completed in less than three weeks."

The judge narrowed her eyes, apparently less than receptive to Jack's point. "Mr. Swyteck, are you suggesting that the State Department is part of a fraud on the court?"

Jack didn't shrink under her stare, but it was plain to see that it wouldn't help matters for him to say, *Yes, Judge, that's exactly what I'm saying.*

"Your Honor, I'm merely suggesting that we need time to look into this matter."

"Time?" said Beech. "Judge, they've had enough time. What about the time my client has spent waiting to be with his daughter again?"

Jack was about to respond, but the judge shut it down.

"I'm prepared to rule," she said. "Counsel, please be seated."

Jack lowered himself into his chair. It was tempting to say that the fix was in before he and Zahra had entered the courthouse—that the US government had been forced to make yet another concession to the Iranians in the ongoing negotiations. But Jack held his tongue.

"In the matter of Bazzi versus Bazzi," the judge said, speaking slowly enough for the court reporter to get every word, "it is hereby ordered that the petitioner's request to enforce the order of custody issued by the Family Court of the Islamic Republic of Iran is granted. Counsel and their clients are directed to complete an orderly exchange of the child, Yasmin Bazzi, within twenty-four hours. We are adjourned."

The pistol-shot crack of the gavel ended the matter, and Zahra's reaction completed the metaphor. It was as if the judge had drawn a pistol from beneath her robe and shot her dead from the bench. Just that quickly, and with the blessing of the US Department of State, Zahra had gone from winner to loser.

Farid's lawyer approached the respondents' table, just as she had at the conclusion of the Hague proceeding. But this time the message was different.

"Now *this* is justice," she said.

Jack watched as she and Farid headed for the exit. "I'm so sorry, Zahra," was all he could say.

CHAPTER 35

Zahra picked up her daughter from school at the usual time. At the usual place. And asked the usual question.

"What did you learn today, sweetie?"

Yasmin was in the back seat in her booster, looking out the window, as their car inched forward in the long line to the campus exit.

"Did you know the longest one-syllable word in the English language is 'strengthed'?"

Zahra caught her daughter's eye in the rearview mirror. "That doesn't even sound like an actual word. Can you use it in a sentence?"

"I just did."

Zahra thought about it, and then they shared a laugh. Laughing almost made her want to cry. "You're such a clever little girl."

The drive home was neither the time nor the place to break the bad news to Yasmin. Zahra tried her best to act as if nothing was wrong, which was impossible.

Her immediate reaction to the judge's ruling had been shock and disbelief. Her mind and body had gone completely numb. Only in the last couple of hours had she become functional enough to process actual thoughts, none of which were pretty. She was angry at Farid, but even angrier at herself for losing to him. She was angry at the so-called justice system, but mostly angry at herself for having put her faith in it. She was angry at Iran, at the US State Department, at the judge, at Jack—but it all came back to angry at herself. The result was a car ride in complete silence and rumination, which was anything but normal.

"Are you okay, Mommy?"

"Uh—yes, sweetheart. I just have a lot on my mind."

Zahra parked in the driveway. They went inside and dropped their shoes near the door. In a hurry to get out of her school clothes, Yasmin ran to her bedroom. Zahra went to the kitchen. It was Friday, which meant Jumu'ah, but attendance at the mosque was optional for women, especially for mothers with childcare obligations. Zahra assumed that went double for a mother planning her last meal ever with her daughter.

"Yasmin, what do you want for dinner tonight?" she asked in a voice loud enough to be heard upstairs. The patter of footsteps preceded Yasmin's quick entry to the kitchen.

"*Toot*," she said as she climbed onto the stool at the counter.

Toot was a popular Iranian sweet made with almond powder and sugar, then shaped into colorful bite-size pieces that resembled mulberries. Yasmin had once declared it "better than cookie dough."

"Okay, we have dessert covered. What do you want for dinner?"

"What are my choices?"

"You can have anything you want."

"Really? Anything?"

"Yes."

"More *toot*!"

Zahra smiled, but it pained her to think how much she was going to miss Yasmin. She sent her to the pantry to gather the ingredients while she cleared their workspace on the counter. Yasmin returned with almost everything.

"You forgot the rosewater," said Zahra.

Yasmin crinkled her nose. "Rosewater doesn't taste like roses."

"How do roses taste?"

"They should definitely taste like chocolate."

Zahra loaded the slivered almonds into the food processor. "Yes, they should. We'll just use a little rosewater, for fragrance."

Zahra loved cooking with Yasmin, and Yasmin loved being her helper. Zahra wasn't ready to let go. She didn't know how she would ever let go.

They worked side by side, getting the dough just right, enough for two dozen mulberry-shaped sweets, more than enough for dinner and dessert. Yasmin was adding the final touch, a sliver of almond that was the "stem" for each mulberry, when Zahra's cell phone rang. The caller ID read, "Dr. Vestry." Jack had told her to expect the call. Zahra wiped her hands clean of sugary dough, told Yasmin to carry on, and stepped outside to take the call, closing the sliding glass door behind her.

"Do you have a moment to talk?" Dr. Vestry asked.

Zahra glanced through the glass door at Yasmin in the kitchen. "A minute," she said.

Zahra had met Dr. Vestry only once before, at Jack's office. Dr. Vestry had laid out the pros and cons of having Yasmin testify. She'd warned Zahra that even if they decided not to put Yasmin on the witness stand, Judge Carlton might take her into his chambers and interview the child himself, using the same techniques that Dr. Vestry would use to prepare a child to testify in court—drawing pictures of her family, playing with dolls, and so on. The doctor had proven quite prophetic.

"I understand that this is a very difficult time for you," said Dr. Vestry. "I'm sorry for that."

Difficult didn't begin to describe it. "Thank you."

"Jack told me that the exchange is scheduled to take place tomorrow at his office."

It bothered Zahra the way everyone kept calling it an "exchange." She was the only one giving. There was nothing in return.

"Yes. Two o'clock."

"Jack suggested that I meet with you and Yasmin before that happens, if you would like."

"That would probably be helpful," said Zahra.

"After the exchange, I would like to make myself available to meet with you. Probably a series of visits."

"You mean therapy?"

"Don't worry about the cost. Jack feels terrible about what has happened, and he is covering it."

"It's not really the cost. What kind of therapy?"

"All situations are different, but I've had many patients in your situation—mothers who have lost custody of a child. I've found that the most effective form of psychotherapy combines elements of mindfulness practices and cognitive behavioral therapy. Specifically, ACT. Acceptance and commitment therapy."

The word *acceptance* hit Zahra like a punch to the gut. "Wait. What is the goal of this therapy?"

"Generally, ACT involves learning to accept unpleasant thoughts, emotions, or experiences without viewing them as problems."

"How is losing my daughter not a problem?"

"It's a terrible problem, of course. The idea is to gain some detachment from the pain without trying to hide from it or pretend that it's not there. ACT will help you accept certain aspects of your life without judgment. It's about accepting realities, especially painful ones."

Acceptance. Detachment. Those were the farthest things from Zahra's mind.

"Can we talk about this later?" she asked.

"Of course. But as for tomorrow, would noon in Jack's office be a good time to meet with you and Yasmin?"

"Yes. That's fine."

The call ended, but Zahra's emotions continued to roil. The anger was returning, but it felt different. It was more like rage, and it was no longer directed at herself. She stepped farther away from the closed sliding glass door, putting more distance between herself and Yasmin in the kitchen, and dialed Jack's cell. It went straight to his voicemail, and at the beep, her words just flowed.

"Acceptance?" she said into the phone, hissing with anger. "Is that what you and Dr. Vestry want from me? Well, let me tell you something, Mr. Swyteck. I'm not *accepting* this. I'm not a bad mother. I'm a good mother who hired a bad lawyer! You're the one to blame, not me! I'm going to sue you for malpractice!"

She ended the call. It was her first release of steam since the judge's ruling, and it left her breathless. She took a minute to gather her composure and then went back inside.

"Look!" Yasmin said.

The *toot* was finished. Yasmin practically had her nose in the serving platter, inhaling the fragrance.

"I changed my mind," said Yasmin. "I like rosewater. It smells good. We should put it everywhere. It makes everything better."

It took all of Zahra's strength to stop the tears from flowing. "Yes," she said. "Almost everything."

Jack put Righley to bed at eight o'clock. Andie was in the master bath, getting ready to go out. The babysitter was in the family room watching television. Jack closed the door to Righley's bedroom and stared down the hall. Only then did he notice that he had a voicemail message. It was from Zahra.

He put the phone to his ear and listened. It stopped him in his tracks.

Jack couldn't count the number of chilling messages he'd received from clients. Many of them had come from death row. None had hit him the way Zahra's had. But he didn't feel an urge to respond. Far from it.

He turned, walked back to Righley's room, and went inside. The lamp was off, but the Barbie nightlight was glowing. Righley was under the covers. Jack walked toward the bed and sat on the edge of the mattress. Righley stirred a bit, not quite asleep, but drifting off. Jack lay beside her. She scooted over a few inches, and Jack rolled onto his side, slipping one arm beneath her and the other over her shoulder.

"Too tight," Righley groaned. "You're smooshing me."

Her little voice touched his heart like never before.

He went right on smooshing her.

CHAPTER 36

Jack woke early Saturday morning and took Max for a walk.

His beloved golden retriever was getting on in years, his gentle face a shade of white gold. Their long runs through Crandon Park were a thing of the past, but the air felt different that morning. Even Max seemed invigorated. Halloween had been the usual sweat festival, with dinosaurs and superheroes melting faster than their chocolate kisses and peanut butter cups. But every year, come November, the summerlike heat and humidity vanished like the flip of a light switch. Jack picked up their pace from geriatric waddle to senior stroll.

"Come on, boy. Like old times."

It was certain to be the high point of a day Jack was dreading.

The transfer of custody to Farid was scheduled for two p.m., and Zahra's meeting with the child psychiatrist was at noon. Jack and Dr. Vestry arrived at his office on time. Zahra did not. Jack and the doctor waited at the kitchen table over coffee. He told her about the voicemail message.

"Have you spoken to Zahra today?" Dr. Vestry asked.

"I sent a text asking her to call me, but I haven't heard back."

"I'm not surprised she lashed out. Anger provides an outlet for the powerlessness a mother feels after losing custody. Even though you're her lawyer, she may see you as part of the system that stole her child away from her."

"Maybe I am part of that system."

"That kind of self-flagellation will land you on my couch."

Jack wasn't entirely sure she was joking, but he smiled anyway, and their wait continued. Dr. Vestry further explained the feelings Zahra was likely to experience. Anger. Despair. Grief. Dissociation. Self-blame. More anger. When their coffee cups were empty, Jack checked the time. Zahra was seriously late. He dialed her number, but it went straight to voicemail. Jack left a message.

"Zahra, I'm in my office with Dr. Vestry. Hope you're on the way. If you're not, please call me." He put his phone aside. "It's not like Zahra to be late."

"Not like Zahra to leave you angry voicemail messages either, I presume."

"Are you saying I should or shouldn't be worried?"

"*Are* you worried?" she asked.

Psychiatrists weren't mind readers, but Jack wasn't trying to hide his concern. "I've had clients leave me at the altar before. No-shows for arraignment or sentencing. Zahra is giving me that same vibe."

"The system failed her. It wouldn't shock me if she went to see Farid and made one last effort to reason with him, negotiate with him, or . . ."

She'd left it unsaid, but Jack filled in the blank. "Threaten him?"

"Confront him. Give him a piece of her mind. Whatever she might be up to, those 'final' interactions never end well."

Jack felt the need to take action. "Would you mind waiting here in case she shows up? I'm going to drive over and check on her."

"That's a good idea," she said.

Jack grabbed his car keys and hurried out the door. The drive to Zahra's town house was less than twenty minutes in traffic, even quicker on the weekend, and quicker still when ignoring the speed limit. Jack's cell phone was connected to his Bluetooth, and he kept hoping for a call from Zahra—*On my way, see you soon*—but it didn't come.

Jack rounded the corner on Zahra's street, and the scene outside her town house made his heart sink. A Miami-Dade squad car was in the driveway. A pair of uniformed officers was at the front door, which was closed. A handful of curious neighbors had gathered near the mailbox. Jack parked across the street and jumped out of the car. He went straight to the officers on the front step and told them who he was.

"We need to speak to your client," the officer said. "Is she home?"

"I don't know where she is," said Jack.

Farid's lawyer was suddenly coming up the walkway. "She's long gone," said Beech, joining the conversation.

"What are you talking about?" asked Jack.

"She left before sunrise," said Beech. "She took Yasmin with her."

"How do you know that?" asked Jack.

"Farid got a tip twenty minutes ago. I called the police immediately."

Jack glanced at the car in the driveway. "They can't be far away. Her car is still here."

"She used another one, obviously," said Beech. "Smart. No vehicle to list in the AMBER Alert."

Child abductions by strangers were the primary mission of AMBER Alerts, but about forty percent were family abductions. Either way, a vehicle to track was a critical part of the alert.

Jack looked at the officer. "Are you planning to issue an AMBER Alert?"

"We have a tip that she left with the child in the middle of the night," he said. "She's not answering the door or our calls to her cell phone. This is not the behavior of a parent who intends to comply with the transfer of child custody. If you can't tell us where your client is, it seems prudent to issue an alert."

"Who was the tipster?" asked Jack.

"That's confidential," said the officer.

That old feeling—client turned fleeing fugitive—hit Jack like a punch to the gut.

"Okay, but let's not jump to conclusions," said Jack. "The time to transfer custody is still an hour away."

"By then, she and Yasmin could be in the Bahamas," said Beech.

"I'm just saying that, as of now, no crime has been committed."

"There doesn't have to be a crime for an AMBER Alert," said Beech. "Just reasonable suspicion of a child in danger."

"Zahra would never hurt Yasmin," said Jack.

"Neither would Farid," said Beech, "but that didn't stop you from trying to take Yasmin away from him."

The officer silenced the lawyers and leveled his gaze at Jack. "Mr. Swyteck, can you guarantee that your client is going to show up by the two-o'clock deadline and transfer custody to Mr. Bazzi?"

Jack couldn't, so he offered the best he could. "I'm trying to reach her."

"Well, you keep on trying," Beech said in a condescending tone. "The AMBER Alert should be issued now. If your client doesn't show, I'm going to ask the state attorney to get an arrest warrant."

She turned and walked back toward her car.

Jack couldn't argue with her position. In a situation like this, the principal concern of everyone—Jack included—was Yasmin's safety. He stepped away and dialed Zahra's number on his cell phone. Again, it went to voicemail.

"Zahra, the police are at your town house," he said into his cell. "If you've done something stupid, it won't work. You have until two p.m. to be in my office, or in the eyes of the law, you're a child abductor. Call me right now. I mean it. *Right now.*"

CHAPTER 37

t was 2:00 p.m. Nothing from Zahra.

Jack was in his car across the street from her town house. The MDPD squad cars were still parked in the driveway. Until Jack heard from his client, the police were his best source of information. He would stay there as long as they did. Dr. Vestry was waiting at his office in case a miracle happened. He called her a few minutes after two.

"No news?" Jack said into the phone.

"Zahra is officially a no-show," she said. "Any update on your end?"

Jack glanced toward the squad cars. "The AMBER Alert went out around one thirty. Cops have been sitting in their cars for almost an hour now. Just waiting for an arrest warrant to issue, I presume."

"How soon will that happen?"

"Farid's lawyer wants her arrested for child abduction. A bench warrant for contempt of court would be quicker. Zahra's in flagrant violation of the judge's order to transfer custody."

"I'm so sorry it's come to this," she said.

A white sedan pulled to the driveway and stopped behind the squad cars. Jack recognized a "bucar" when he saw one—a term he'd heard Andie use for a bureau-issued vehicle. A van pulled up right behind the bucar.

"The FBI is here," said Jack.

"For violation of a state court custody order?" asked Dr. Vestry. "Even if Zahra was there, it doesn't make sense for the feds to be involved."

"No, it doesn't," said Jack. "Except in this case, it does. I gotta go."

A team of FBI agents climbed out of the van and started toward the town house. The MDPD officers exited their vehicles and met the lead agent at the edge of the driveway. Jack approached and introduced himself as Zahra's attorney.

"Special Agent Logan, FBI," the man responded. "We have a search warrant."

Jack had been expecting an arrest, not a search. "Searching for what?"

"A seven-year-old girl, for starters," the agent said.

Jack's heart skipped a beat. A warrant to search for a person was unusual. Unless the "person" was a body.

"You don't think Yasmin is—"

"We're going in," Agent Logan said.

There was a loud knock on the front door, followed by the announcement: "FBI! We have a warrant to search the premises. Open the door!"

No one was home, but it was Fourth Amendment protocol: knock and announce.

"I'd like to see the warrant," Jack asked, "as her lawyer."

Agent Logan showed it to him, and the front door was breached with a loud thud as Jack read. The search team entered. Jack continued up the front steps but stopped in the doorway.

"You can observe, but stand to the side," said Agent Logan.

Thoughts of the worst kind raced through Jack's mind. A mother so desperate as to decide that her daughter would be better off dead was almost inconceivable. A mother-daughter homicide-suicide wasn't possible. But it occurred to Jack that he didn't really *know* Zahra. Two weeks wasn't long enough to know anyone.

Anything is possible.

Then Jack noticed something: no shoes by the door. He knew from previous visits that Zahra and Yasmin observed the Muslim custom of removing their shoes upon entering the home, and the absence of even a single pair at the door gave rise to a logical inference.

"They're not here," Jack said to Agent Logan.

Another agent emerged from the kitchen. "Hardly any food in the place," he said to Agent Logan.

"Because they're gone," Jack said, answering for Logan. "They took their shoes, their food, and whatever else they needed."

"Are you admitting that your client took flight?" asked Logan.

"I'm merely pointing out that the search warrant has been executed, and you didn't find the one thing—the *only* thing—the FBI is authorized to look for. You can leave now."

"I'll decide when it's time to leave," said Logan.

Jack heard a commotion in the bedroom. He started down the hallway.

"Swyteck, stop right there!" said Logan.

Jack complied, but he'd walked far enough to see inside the bedroom, which was a mess. The mattress had been overturned. Clothes were on the floor. Agents were rifling through dresser drawers, spilling the contents onto the rug.

"You're not going to find a seven-year-old girl in a dresser drawer," Jack said. "What is the FBI looking for, Logan?"

"We're executing the warrant," said Logan.

"The warrant is a pretext," said Jack. "What are you *really* looking for?"

The agent didn't answer.

"This is an illegal search," said Jack. "My client does not consent to the search for anything not listed on the warrant."

"Noted," said Logan.

Another agent came halfway down the stairway and stopped. "Nothing in the upstairs bedrooms," he said to Logan.

"Check again," said Logan.

The agent headed back up the stairs.

Jack locked eyes with Logan. "This is about Ava Bazzi, isn't it," said Jack.

"Excuse me?"

"You're not here looking for a child," said Jack. "The FBI is looking for evidence of what happened to her mother. Her *biological* mother."

Logan said nothing, but Jack had his answer. He excused himself, headed for the door, and dialed Andie on his cell phone. She picked up.

"Andie, we gotta talk," he said. "But not on a cell phone."

"What's this about?"

He was no longer sure his cell phone was secure. "It's important. Can you meet at home?"

"Jack, what is this about?"

"Andie, please. Can you meet me?"

She hesitated, and Jack realized he probably sounded paranoid or crazy. But she gave him the benefit of the doubt.

"I'm at Sir Pizza with Righley's soccer team. They finally won a game, but the celebration's almost over. I can be there in half an hour."

"I'll see you then," he said, and the call ended.

CHAPTER 38

Zahra's drive ended on a barrier island. Jupiter Island.

"Are we on another planet?" Yasmin asked from the back seat, smiling.

They'd left the house before dawn, Zahra having told her daughter that their destination was "a surprise." That was kind of true—at least not as blatantly false as telling her that they were borrowing a friend's car because Zahra's was broken, or that she was wearing no headscarf because she'd forgotten it. The idea was to avoid detection by state troopers or anyone else who might see an AMBER Alert for a Muslim mother leaving Miami with her seven-year-old daughter. Not until they'd exited the interstate and driven as far east as possible did Zahra begin to relax. South Beach Road was a quiet residential street abutted by nature preserves and pristine dunes that, along with the sea turtles, made Jupiter Island a unique ecological haven.

"We're still in Florida," said Zahra. "I have no idea why they call it Jupiter."

"It's where the boys go," said Yasmin.

"What?"

"Boys go to Jupiter to get more stupider. Girls go to college to get more knowledge."

The singsong cadence suggested a rhyme that Yasmin had picked up at school, but it sure was a bad one.

"Well, if you want to go to college, you'll need to stop saying things like 'more stupider.'"

Zahra couldn't remember the exact street number, but she had a clear memory of a distinctive mailbox forged from an old ship anchor. It marked the narrow entrance to a private road, and it held true to its purpose. She made the turn and followed the two lines of sand and gravel away from the dunes and up a slight incline to higher ground. The sea oats and mangroves gave way to sprawling oaks, towering palm trees, and thick undergrowth. Deep in the tropical forest, at the highest point, was a six-bedroom estate. Behind it was a guest cottage. Zahra knew every inch of the well-concealed compound. She'd come to the US without a work visa and, through a friend of a friend, got a job as a housekeeper. The owner of the house, a Shiite Muslim who'd escaped tyranny, emigrated to the United States, and worked his way up from dishwasher to billionaire, had sympathized with her plight. Zahra parked in front of the guesthouse and turned off the engine.

"Like it?" asked Zahra.

Yasmin's mouth was agape. Guest cottages on Jupiter Island were hardly "cottages." This one was two stories tall and bigger than their town house.

"Are we staying here?" asked Yasmin.

"Yup."

"Cool! Can we go to the beach?"

"Maybe tomorrow," said Zahra.

Zahra had once heard that Jupiter Island was, per capita, the wealthiest town in America, home to the likes of Tiger Woods and Celine Dion. If that was true, it was also the world's least ostentatious collection of billionaires, at least in Zahra's experience. In Miami, it seemed, people were always dropping names or flashing money, whether they had it or were just pretending to have it. Jupiter Island was the kind of place where a dinner guest might insist on clearing his own plate, speaking to the housekeeper as if she were actually a human being, never once mentioning that he used to be the CEO of NASDAQ and that his wife was the retired board chair of a Fortune 100 company.

The island was also the perfect place for Zahra to disappear. For most of the nine hundred residents, Jupiter Island was strictly a winter haven that didn't fully come to life until after Thanksgiving. Zahra knew that this particular estate would be vacant at least until December. She still had her housekeeper's key to gain entry.

"Let's go inside," said Zahra.

They climbed out of the car and went to the front door. Her key worked, but the alarm began to chirp. She had thirty seconds to input the code from memory. She prayed the property manager hadn't changed it. Nerves made her mess up on the first try. The second time was the charm. The chirping stopped.

"I get the biggest room!" said Yasmin.

She started off, but Zahra stopped her. "Shoes off, missy," she said.

Yasmin complied and raced up the stairs. "*Now* I get the biggest room!"

Zahra smiled to herself, knowing that, come nightfall, Yasmin wouldn't last sixty seconds in separate rooms in a strange house.

Their car needed to be unloaded. Zahra brought in the coolers and put the perishables in the refrigerator, but the rest of the food and luggage could wait. She hadn't slept since Thursday night. Exhausted, she relaxed on the couch in the Florida room while Yasmin explored upstairs.

Zahra wasn't sure how long they would stay on the island. At least until the AMBER Alert was no longer flashing on the overhead signs up and down I-95. She hadn't seen an alert on the drive up, but surely Farid and his pit-bull lawyer would get the word out in every way possible. Zahra the child abductor. Zahra the horrible mother. Zahra the terrible person. And, in one final twist of the ironic knife: Zahra, the grave risk of physical and psychological harm.

It was a cozy room, and her gaze drifted toward the assortment of framed photographs on the coffee table. Seasons of life in three generations of a wealthy Muslim family. The patriarch and his wife on camelback at the pyramids. Grandchildren building sandcastles on what Zahra guessed was Dubai's famous Jumeirah Beach. A beautiful bride dancing with her new husband as flower petals rained down upon them. Persian weddings had many traditions, but there was no better photo op than the *gol baron*—literally, "raining flowers"—where guests tossed flower petals on the newlyweds as they danced and kissed. Zahra's gaze held on to that photo. It was the *aroosi*—the celebration after the wedding ceremony—she'd dreamed about as a little girl. The celebration she'd planned with Farid as a teenager, before Ava came of age. Completely unlike the celebration she got as Farid's second wife.

More disappointing than the wedding was the wedding night.

The fault was not Zahra's. She'd spent many hours and a small fortune on body hair removal, which was a bride-to-be ritual in Iran. There had been no sexual relations between Zahra and Farid in their second round of dating—not even a kiss, with Yasmin in the picture. But intimacy short of intercourse had been part of their relationship before Farid started dating Ava. Zahra knew what Farid liked. And on that night alone in the hotel room, sharing a bed for the first time in years, she approached him accordingly.

D on't, please," said Farid, pulling away.

Zahra withdrew. "What's wrong?"

He rolled onto his side and propped himself up on one elbow, as if he wanted to explain. But no words came. Zahra couldn't read his mind, and in the darkness his face was little more than a silhouette. But she knew what was in his heart.

"It's Ava, isn't it?"

Farid sighed audibly. "No."

"You're not being truthful. But let me be truthful with you: Ava is never coming back."

"She . . . I loved her."

Zahra pulled away in anger, climbed out of the bed, and covered herself with a silk robe. "You're hopeless," she said, and she started toward the bathroom.

"Zahra, please," he said.

She stopped short of the bathroom door.

"Ava was my wife," he said, his voice cracking. "I—I loved her."

It took all her strength just to turn around and face him, her eyes lowering with anger that pierced the darkness. "No, Farid. You are still *in love* with her."

He looked away. But Zahra heard no denial.

Mom, I saw the ocean from upstairs!" shouted Yasmin, stirring Zahra from her memories.

Zahra popped up from the couch, and Yasmin came to her.

"Can we go to the beach? Please, please, *please*?"

"Maybe tomorrow."

"Aww. Why can't we go now?"

"Let's bake some cookies," said Zahra, a surefire change of subject.

"Yay!"

"I just put a package of Toll House dough in the refrigerator. I'll bet there's a cookie sheet somewhere in that kitchen."

"I'll find it!" Yasmin said, and dashed from the room.

Zahra let her go. She needed a minute to make a quick phone call. She couldn't tell anyone where she was, but she was in a borrowed car, and she'd promised to let the owner know she'd arrived safely, wherever she was headed. She owed him that much, and so much more. Meeting him had been the best thing to happen to her after leaving London and landing in Miami. He was her emotional support. Her financial support. Her rock.

Zahra's cell phone was in her purse, but it was wrapped in aluminum foil to prevent the police or anyone else from tracking her GPS coordinates. Another tip from her rock. There was a landline telephone on the credenza. She checked it, got a dial tone, and dialed the number from memory. Her rock answered.

"It's me," she said.

"Hi, baby. How are you?"

"Okay," she said wistfully. "I miss you already."

"We can fix that."

Zahra smiled. "Maybe. I'll call you tomorrow."

CHAPTER 39

Jack was in his car, halfway home from Zahra's town house, when Andie called.

"Jack, um. Change of plans."

He stopped at the red light. The "um" gave him pause. Andie was not one for filler words. Self-assuredness was one of the things he found so attractive about her.

"You're not going to the house?"

"No. Um . . ."

There it was again. "Andie, what's going on?"

"I got called in to the field office. It's better if you come here. You need to speak to Agent Logan, not me."

A metallic blue sports car pulled up beside him at the red light. The music was so loud that Jack's head started pounding. "Andie, I asked to meet at home because I need to talk to my wife in absolute privacy. Your response is that I should meet with the FBI?"

"Except you're not reaching out to me as *your wife*. Agent Logan told me what happened at Zahra's town house. You think the FBI is up to something sneaky, and you're putting me in the middle. Just because we ditched the rule against talking about our work, that doesn't mean you can use me to your strategic advantage against the FBI. That's not fair, Jack."

"That's not what I'm doing," he said, but she wasn't totally off the mark. "I'm sorry. I understand how you could see it that way."

"So, you'll come downtown?"

"Yes. You're off the hook. Tell Logan I'm on my way."

The call ended. The sports car beside Jack made a right on red, and a sedan pulled forward in the lane. Jack did a double take. It was Farid. He signaled for Jack to roll down the passenger-side window, which he did.

"Talk?" he asked, pointing to the coffee shop across the street.

Apparently, Jack wasn't the only one who had been sitting in his car outside Zahra's town house to watch law enforcement's next move.

"Sure," Jack shouted back, and when the light changed, he followed Farid into the parking lot. They climbed out of their cars, but Jack had to make something clear before they entered the coffee shop.

"We're in a gray area," said Jack. "If you and Zahra were still in litigation, the rules of professional conduct would prohibit me from speaking directly to the adverse party without his counsel. My position is that the case is over."

"Over or not, I have no lawyer," said Farid.

"I just spoke to her," said Jack. "She was talking to the police on your behalf."

"I fired Ms. Beech. Not that it matters. You might say I never had a lawyer."

"I don't understand."

"Come," he said as he opened the door. "I'm buying."

Jack followed him inside. They ordered two cups at the counter and took a table away from other customers, where they could talk in private.

"Ms. Beech and I had many disagreements," said Farid. "Mostly about case strategy. I think she felt free to ignore my views because I wasn't paying her legal bills."

Jack couldn't hide his surprise. "She did all that work without getting paid?"

"No, I said I didn't pay her. She got paid top dollar—by the Iranian government."

"Just so you know, it's not unusual in this country for a lawyer to represent a client whose legal bills are paid by a third party. It could be a parent. An employer. An insurance company. I once represented a college

professor whose students raised money for her defense. But even where
someone else pays the bills, the client makes the decisions. Not the person
paying the bills."

"That's nice in theory," said Farid. "But in this case, I wasn't the one calling the shots. I would never have told my lawyer to present a fake custody
order to the family-court judge."

Jack was in the middle of a sip and nearly coughed through his nose. Zahra
had told Jack the order was a fake. And now Farid had confirmed it.

"What?"

"You heard me."

Jack cleared his throat. "You understand that anything you tell me, I can
use against you. I could go to the judge, tell her what you just told me, and
ask her to vacate her judgment enforcing the Iranian order."

"I won't repeat any of this publicly," said Farid. "If you go to the court
with this information, I will have to deny this conversation ever happened.
And how far will you get with the judge when even the US State Department says the Iranian order is authentic?"

Jack couldn't argue with Farid on that point. But it was still a lot to
swallow. "Did Heather Beech know the Iranian order was a fake? A lawyer
should never knowingly put on false evidence."

"*You* did," said Farid. "When you painted me as an abuser. None of that
happened."

Jack looked him straight in the eye from across the table. He feared
Farid could be playing him, setting him up for a complaint to the Florida
Bar—or worse.

"Is that your angle here, Farid? Are you trying to get me to say something
that sounds like an admission that the evidence against you was false? Are
you recording this conversation on your cell phone and planning to make
strategic edits before you send it to the FBI or the State Department?"

"You are a very suspicious man, Mr. Swyteck."

"Why did you come to me, Farid?"

"I tried to get through to you before. I went to your friend's bar. I spoke
to your wife."

Jack knew about the visit to Cy's Place, where Farid had denied all allegations of abuse, and Theo had come away "not sure he's lying." He didn't know about the meeting with Andie—but that was between him and his wife, along with so many other things.

"You have my ear now," said Jack. "Talk to me."

Farid looked off to the middle distance for a moment, then back at Jack. "If I take Yasmin back to Iran, it is not my daughter who is in grave danger of physical harm. It's me."

"Excuse me?"

"The regime was very unhappy with me when I filed this petition under the Hague Convention. You know why."

Jack did, but he said it anyway. "Because it would reopen questions about Ava's disappearance."

"Yes, obviously. That is why they hired a new lawyer for me. Ms. Beech hijacked the case."

"Well, hold on," said Jack. "I'd hardly say she was trying to lose the case for you. She almost won the Hague proceeding. And she *did* win the custody case."

"True. But make no mistake: job one was to prove that Ava Bazzi is still alive. Proving the Iranian government right was the most important thing. Yasmin and I were secondary."

"That's a very serious accusation for a client to make against his lawyer."

"Do you have any idea the sums of money the Iranian government must have paid her? Ms. Beech is not the first lawyer in America to serve two masters and answer to the bigger bank account."

More than a few examples came to Jack's mind. "To be honest, I did wonder how much control you had over the case when Nouri Asmoun took the stand."

"Exactly," said Farid. "I would never have called a witness to lie about an affair he claims he had with Ava."

"How do you know he was lying?"

Farid exhaled sharply. "I didn't flag you down on the street to talk about that nonsense."

"Then what is this about?" asked Jack.

"I've run out of people I can bargain with."

"Bargain for what?"

Farid paused, which only added import to his words. "Ava wanted Yasmin to grow up in the West. I would like to honor her wish."

Jack's first instinct was to laugh out loud, but Farid's expression was deadly serious. He was either still in love with Ava or a manipulative and sociopathic abuser.

"Then leave Yasmin here in the United States with Zahra."

"No. Not with Zahra."

"I'm sorry, Farid. I can't put your wishes ahead of my own client's best interests."

Farid took a deep breath, then let it out. It did nothing to quell his anger.

"I'm beyond disappointed," said Farid. "But now I understand how you and Agent Henning stay married. You two deserve each other. I shouldn't have wasted my time on either one of you."

He rose and walked away, leaving Jack alone at the table. Jack didn't go after him. His mind was awhirl. If Farid was telling the truth, Jack had been right all along: the Iranian government, not Farid, was calling the shots, and the US government was spreading the same narrative for diplomatic reasons. But being "right" led to the wrong result: there was no defense under the Hague Convention for what Zahra had done.

Jack didn't appreciate Farid's take on his marriage—that he and Andie "deserved each other." But maybe they could help each other. And help Yasmin.

He grabbed his phone and texted Andie. "Slight delay. On my way now."

CHAPTER 40

Jack made it downtown to the Miami field office in less than fifteen minutes. Andie met him in the main lobby and took him up in the elevator. It was just the two of them.

"Have you tried reaching out to Zahra?" asked Andie.

"I thought you didn't want to be in the middle of this."

"I don't. But I'm worried sick about that little girl."

"Me too," said Jack.

The elevator doors opened, and they stepped out. The building wasn't officially open on weekends, but the basic job description for FBI special agents was fifty-hour weeks, minimum, so the entire floor was active. Andie led him to the conference room but didn't join the meeting. Jack took a seat at the table with Agent Logan and Andie's boss, Todd Tidwell, the assistant special agent in charge. Tidwell began the meeting.

"Your client is a fugitive, Mr. Swyteck. We hope we will have your cooperation."

"I'm as concerned as anyone about Yasmin," said Jack. "But my client violated a state court order to transfer custody. That's not the kind of abduction case that triggers FBI involvement. So I'll ask you the same question I asked Agent Logan at the town house: What's this really about, and why is the FBI all over it?"

"It's a federal case," said Tidwell. "We have reason to believe the child has been transferred across state lines."

"They haven't been gone long enough to even reach the Georgia border," said Jack, stopping short of calling it *bullshit*.

Neither agent responded. Jack leaned closer, tightening his gaze across the table. "Look me in the eye and tell me this has nothing to do with Ava Bazzi."

Again, there was no response, at least not immediately. When Tidwell finally did speak, his tone changed to the voice of reason.

"This is a dangerous situation, Jack. I'm looking for a path forward. One option is for you to make accusations about Ava Bazzi, in which case we can all sit here and listen to the A/C whistling through the overhead vents. Or we can make this productive and keep a child out of harm's way."

The common ground was compelling. "What do you have in mind?" asked Jack.

"Child abduction is a crime. A heinous crime."

"Agreed."

"As I'm sure you're aware, a lawyer can be disbarred—or worse—for counseling or assisting a client in conduct that is criminal."

"As I'm sure *you're* aware, this lawyer doesn't need to be threatened to do the right thing." Jack didn't overdo the sarcasm, but Tidwell deserved it, having made a remark like that after his offer of an olive branch.

"I'll accept that," said Tidwell. "So far, our tech agents have been unable to detect a signal from Zahra Bazzi's cell phone, much less pick up calls or texts. At some point she'll have to contact someone. We believe it will likely be her lawyer."

"I've heard nothing from her."

"But when she does call, we want to be in a position to spring into action."

Jack could read between the lines. "Are you asking me to consent to a wiretap?"

"Only until she calls you."

"Which could be days or weeks," said Jack. "The answer is no. I'm a criminal defense lawyer. Zahra Bazzi is not my only client."

The ASAC sighed. "That's what Andie said you would say."

"Wait. You talked to my wife about a wiretap?"

"She does work here."

"I'm aware," said Jack. *All too.*

"We were hoping you would prove her wrong."

"Let's put a pin in this conversation," said Jack. "I need to speak to Andie."

"What about?"

"I don't need your permission to talk to my wife."

The ASAC couldn't argue, and Agent Logan followed him out of the room. Jack struggled to find the right approach as he waited. He flashed to Andie's confession of her plans to become a single mother, and thought of how far they had come in trying to navigate the difficult terrain of their marriage. But as much as Jack tried to give her the benefit of the doubt, it sure looked like his wife had lured him downtown to a meeting with the FBI without the full story.

A minute later, Andie entered. She stood with her back to the door, choosing not to join Jack at the table. He spoke first, trying to keep the accusation out of his voice.

"You said you couldn't meet me at home because I was putting you in the middle."

"And you agreed with me."

"Yeah. But you didn't tell me you were *already* in the middle."

"It was sort of implied, don't you think?"

"You could have at least given me a heads-up that the FBI wants to tap my phone."

"That's something for you and Tidwell to work out, not the two of us."

"Tidwell said he discussed it with you before I got here, and you told him I would say no."

"I told him *any* criminal lawyer would say no. It was hardly a 'discussion.'"

"And I'm hardly just *any* criminal defense lawyer."

"I realize that."

"Do you? Tidwell also schooled me on the ethical rules that prohibit a lawyer from counseling a client on how to evade capture by police. Did you also discuss that with him, Andie? Did you think *I* needed to be reminded of *that*?"

Her back was against the door, and her body language seemed to say, *Guilty as charged.*

"It's not that I don't trust you to do the right thing, Jack. With all this talk of wiretaps on your phone, I was afraid you might say something that could be pulled out of context and come back to hurt you."

Jack wanted to accept that explanation, but he needed a moment.

Andie exhaled sharply. "Remember when you first raised the idea that the State Department's dossier on Ava Bazzi could be fake?"

"What does that have to do with—"

"Please, just listen. You said the State Department was using me to convince you that Ava Bazzi is alive. Remember how mad I got at you?"

"Oh, yes. I remember."

She swallowed hard. "You told me you were sorry."

For a moment, Jack thought she was looking for another apology, but she was suddenly contrite—genuinely so.

"I'm sorry now. Very sorry. Can we call it even?"

Keeping score was what had killed Jack's first marriage, but he supposed that "even" was better than "game, set, match."

"Apology accepted. Let's call it even."

"Thank you."

An awkward silence followed, as Jack wrestled with the question of whether it was okay to hug an FBI agent on government property.

"Should I tell my ASAC to come back?" she asked.

"Not yet," said Jack. "Here's the deal. I think Tidwell is right about one thing: at some point Zahra will probably call me. I won't agree to a wiretap on my phone. But I will do everything I can to encourage her to turn herself in or, short of that, tell me where she is."

"That sounds reasonable."

"In exchange, you're going to tell me what the US government is negotiating for, and why it's so damn important for the FBI to control the story of whether Ava Bazzi is alive or dead."

"I can't do that," she said with a pained expression.

"Yes, you can, Andie. Because you care about this little girl as much as I do."

Their eyes met and held. For another minute, maybe longer, Andie stood at the door, silent. Finally, she took a seat at the table across from Jack.

And they talked.

CHAPTER 41

Andie was alone in her office. Jack had gone home ahead of her. Andie had more work to do.

Her talk with Jack had been a long time coming. She couldn't say that she'd held back nothing, but she'd shared everything he'd earned the right to know. The name of the American hostage—Brian Guthrie—was still secret. But it was important for Jack to understand why the State Department had put so much pressure on him not to upset the negotiation with Iran. And it was important to Andie that he understand the pressure that the FBI, the State Department, and the CIA had put on her. She told him that the US was negotiating with Iran for the release of a CIA agent.

"You should have told me sooner," Jack had said.

"Rules, rules, rules," she'd said, though it was really just one rule—"The Rule"—that had made their marriage so difficult.

"All set, Agent Henning?"

A young man from office services was standing in the doorway. Andie's desktop was wiped clean, and the bookshelves were empty. She loaded the contents of her credenza into a banker's box and placed it on the moving dolly with the other boxes. She was officially leaving the third floor. Monday would be her first day in her new office, one floor above, with the international corruption squad. As the newbie, she'd share an office area with two other agents. The bureau had a strange notion of "promotion."

"All set," said Andie.

The young man pushed the cart out the door, but Andie didn't follow. She settled into her desk chair one last time. Even with bare shelves on the walls, memories abounded. But there was no reminiscing. Her talk with Jack was still top of mind.

The confidential nature of the State Department's dossier on Ava Bazzi had not precluded Andie from telling Jack what *wasn't* in it. Not a word about fleeing domestic violence. Nothing about Ava's role in a secret network of messengers. The holes had only fueled Jack's suspicions that the State Department was feeding Andie fake evidence that Ava Bazzi was alive. Her talk with Farid was also weighing on her mind. Even he seemed to have come around to the view that Ava was dead.

Yet Andie couldn't deny what she *had* seen in the dossier: an FBI examiner's certification that the fingerprints on an eight-month-old U visa application belonged to Ava Bazzi. Andie had noticed the examiner's name on the report, and with a little brain strain, it came back to her.

It was worth checking out.

She picked up the phone and put in a call to the Criminal Justice Information Services Division, the FBI's high-tech hub in the hills of West Virginia. She gave her ID number to the operator, who transferred her to the fingerprint identification division.

"I'm trying to reach an examiner named Leslie T. Cahill," said Andie.

"One moment, please."

Andie waited.

"Can I put you on hold?"

Andie waited another minute.

"Agent Henning, can you spell the name, please?"

Andie did. More waiting, and then the answer came.

"We have no examiner by that name."

"Could she possibly be at another location?"

"I checked the global database. Not here. Not anywhere."

"The report I have is eight months old," said Andie. "Maybe she's no longer there."

"Eight months? No. Retired, deceased, terminated—she'd still be in the database. We purge after two years. You must have wrong information."

"Okay, thanks for checking."

Andie ended the call. She could follow up with Human Resources on Monday, but she didn't see the point. There was no Leslie T. Cahill. There were no fingerprints from Ava Bazzi on the visa application that the State Department had shared with Andie.

Jack, it seemed, had been right. Ava Bazzi was dead. And for some reason, the US government didn't want Jack, Andie, or the rest of the world to know it.

She dialed Jack's cell, and he picked up from his car.

"Hey, it's me," she said. "There's one more thing you should know."

CHAPTER 42

Jack's call from Andie didn't last long. When it ended, he made a U-turn at the traffic light, picked up Theo from Cy's Place, and drove to Zahra's town house.

"How we getting in?" asked Theo.

"Zahra told us she keeps the spare key in the bird feeder on the back patio. Remember?"

"Dude, she was being a smart-ass about Farid and the Republican Guard taking her hostage. There's no spare key."

"We'll find out," said Jack.

They climbed out of the car and followed the sidewalk around the building to the back of the town house.

"Did you tell Andie we're doing this?"

"Nope."

"Is that because this is technically breaking and entering?"

"It's not B&E. The FBI conducted an illegal search of my client's home, and we're going back inside to document and photograph the invasion of her Fourth Amendment rights."

"B&E *with attitude*," said Theo. "Cool. What was illegal about the search?"

Jack opened the gate to Zahra's fenced-in patio.

"Right off the bat, I knew a warrant to search for Yasmin was a pretext. My suspicion was that the FBI came to confiscate any evidence Zahra might have that Ava is dead."

"Part of the whole Ava Bazzi, US-Iran, you-scratch-my-back-we'll-release-the-hostage cover-up?"

"You got it. After talking to Andie, I'm certain that's what this was about."

Jack went to the bird feeder, poked around, and found the spare key.

"I'll be damned," said Theo, eating crow.

Jack slid the key into the lock, the tumblers fell into place, and the dead-bolt gave up the sweet sound of success, like the shuck of a shotgun.

"We're in." Jack pushed the door open and switched on the light. Theo followed him inside.

"Shoes off," said Jack.

"Seriously? The place is a mess."

Theo was right. The FBI had emptied virtually every drawer and cabinet and turned furniture upside down, ostensibly in search of a seven-year-old girl who they apparently thought might be hiding next to the loose change in the sofa cushions. The shoeprints left by the search team seemed especially intrusive in a home where shoes were left at the door. Jack snapped photographs of the overturned love seat in the living room, the open kitchen cabinets, the upturned mattress in the bedroom, and articles of clothing scattered across the laundry-room floor. Then he started up the stairs to the second floor.

"What do you want me to do?" asked Theo.

"Stand right there and look intimidating in case a neighbor or somebody comes by to see what we're doing."

"Nice to be needed. What'd you bring me for? Break down the door if there was no key in the bird feeder?"

Jack just smiled and went upstairs. The hallway was short, and a door was open to the first bedroom. Jack reached around the doorjamb and flipped the light switch.

The room practically screamed "Yasmin." Just enough pink accents to appease a child's demand for bubblegum-pink everything. White linen curtains with pom-pom fringes and a brushed-gold rod. A reading corner with a bookcase, a comfy barrel chair, and a floor lamp that was low enough for anyone to reach the switch, even if you were too short to ride Thunder Mountain. It reminded Jack of his own daughter, and it broke his heart to think of a child having to endure all that Yasmin had in her young life, only to end up on the run with her stepmother.

He took another step inside. Compared to the rest of the town house, Yasmin's room had been largely spared by the search team. No mess on the floor from hastily emptied dresser drawers. The bed was unmade, but it looked no worse than Righley's bed in the morning, probably more Yasmin's doing than the FBI's. The closet door had been left open, but not much was left inside. Jack doubted the FBI had taken Yasmin's clothing. Wherever Zahra had taken her, it wasn't an overnight trip.

Jack's gaze was drawn to the wastebasket beside Yasmin's drawing table. And then to the box of crayons on the tabletop. Then back to the papers in the wastebasket. Judge Carlton's voice was suddenly in his head:

Do you like to draw pictures, Yasmin?

Jack crossed the room and picked up the wastebasket. It was filled with crayon drawings on looseleaf paper. Some were intact, others torn in half. A few were crumpled into paper balls. Jack selected one at random, looked at it, and stopped cold.

Jack would never forget the drawing he'd questioned Yasmin about in Judge Carlton's courtroom. The details were burned into his memory. The crayon colors Yasmin had chosen. The placement of her mother and father. The little girl off to the side. The crisscross of the blades over Ava's head that made them, unmistakably, scissors.

It was the drawing he was staring at now.

Jack pulled another page from the trash. Same colors. Same figures. Same scissors. Jack uncrumpled one of the paper balls. The colors and figures were the same. The scissors were a little messy, more like bent sticks. He checked one of the drawings that was torn in half, then matched it with the other half. It was like the others, except there were no scissors at all. Jack dug through page after page, uncrumpled one ball of paper after another. It was the same discovery over and over again. Based on his mental comparison of Yasmin's drawing in Judge Carlton's chambers to these discarded drawings in her bedroom, the conclusion was inescapable.

It was as if Yasmin had *practiced* her drawing.

Except for one—and it chilled him. The drawing at the bottom of the wastebasket definitely bore a resemblance to the drawing that Yasmin made for Judge Carlton. But it was not *exactly* like Yasmin's drawings. This one was more precise, drawn with more skill. The scissors were especially well defined. It didn't look like a child's artwork.

It looked more like a drawing by an adult.

A template.

Jack laid the drawing on the desktop and reached for his cell phone. He needed the input of a professional. Dr. Vestry took his call.

"Sorry to call on a Saturday, but this is important," said Jack.

"No problem."

"I have a memory of you telling Zahra that Judge Carlton might ask Yasmin to draw pictures for him, even before the judge brought it up. Am I remembering correctly?"

"Yes. It came up when we were weighing the pros and cons of making Yasmin a witness. I told both of you that even if we decided against calling her to the stand, the judge could invite her into his chambers and interview her informally, maybe ask her to draw pictures of her family or play-act with dolls. With a child of Yasmin's age, that's not unheard of in a Hague proceeding."

"And you also said the judge would be very alert to make sure there was no coaching of Yasmin. You had a name for it."

"PAS," she said. "Parental alienation syndrome. It's basically a constellation of symptoms caused by one parent brainwashing the child, resulting in the child's subsequent vilification of the target parent. What's this all about, Jack?"

"Would you be able to meet me in the next hour or so?"

"If it's important."

Jack glanced again at the drawing—the one that definitely was *not* Yasmin's.

"It's very important," said Jack. "There's something I need to show you."

CHAPTER 43

Zahra turned on the Disney Channel for Yasmin, locked the cottage door on her way out, and took a walk around the compound. She needed time to clear her head and take stock. And make sure they were alone.

She'd brought enough food for a week, so there was no need to make a run across the bridge to the convenience store on the mainland. That was a good thing. Thousands of Floridians had surely seen her photograph on the local news, and she needed to make sure no one recognized her. She supposed it helped that most people were "on the lookout" for an "Iranian mother with a child." Unless she dressed up Yasmin in a Princess Jasmine costume, covered herself in a full-body chador, and started ululating in the public square, the typical Martin County resident probably wouldn't spot them.

The compound was well maintained, but Zahra and Yasmin were indeed alone. Zahra tried to recall the off-season maintenance schedule so that she could prepare for possible visitors to the property. Swimming pool cleaner on Mondays. Landscaping team and insecticide sprayer on Tuesdays. Some guy with a small tractor came to roll the clay tennis court every other week. None of them had reason to come knocking on the door to the guest cottage, even if there was a car in the driveway. They did their job and left.

Zahra walked to the east side of the property and followed a woodchip pathway up the incline through the tropical garden. She spotted banana shrubs, angel's trumpet, bird of paradise, and other gems of the subtropics, all presented in their natural beauty, without the overly manicured look that seemed to dominate south Florida residences. At the top of the hill, just high enough for her to see over the tops of palm trees to the Atlantic Ocean, was an open space. It had easily the most beautiful vista on the grounds. And it was the one place that made the property distinctly Muslim.

Zahra stepped to the center of the clearing, where a square deck with a thatched roof was supported by four posts. Except for two locations—a cemetery and a bathroom—Muslims could offer the five daily prayers virtually anywhere. The owner had chosen this spot, facing northeast, though it looked more like a tennis hut than a *musalla*, probably because the local building code was more accommodating to the former than to a private place of worship.

Zahra found a prayer mat in a storage chest and placed it on the deck. When away from home, she normally used a prayer app to find *qibla*—the direction facing Mecca—but her cell phone was wrapped in aluminum foil to prevent tracking by police, so she trusted that the owner had positioned his prayer space properly. She had no Quran, but there was a *tawla*, a foldable X-shaped bookrest, before her, engraved with a familiar Islamic verse, which she read aloud to herself. Translated, it read:

VERILY, WITH EVERY HARDSHIP COMES EASE.

It was a popular verse, and billions of people around the globe found comfort in it. Zahra, too, found the words comforting on a spiritual level. But under these circumstances—on the run with Yasmin—it was a bit unsettling to find this particular verse on display in her chosen hideaway. The fact that the owner had selected it for his prayer space wasn't surprising: Quran 94:5 was one of those verses that could be found framed and hanging on the wall in millions of Muslim homes. Zahra's problem with it was personal: she'd seen the same verse, framed and on display, when visiting Imam Reza in Tehran.

That meeting had been well after the wedding ceremony. In fact, it was the last time Zahra had seen the imam before his testimony by video-conference in the Hague proceeding. She'd gone to him seeking guidance after Ava's arrest and imprisonment.

W hat troubles you, Zahra?" Imam Reza asked.

Zahra was seated in the chair facing his desk. She spoke in a soft, respectful tone. "My sister, Ava. I went to visit her today at Evin."

The imam's eyes clouded with concern. "You need to be very careful about that. Your sister is in serious trouble."

"I'm afraid she has only made things worse."

"How?"

"She lied to the morality police."

His concern deepened. "Lied? How?"

Zahra collected herself, then continued. "She said she wears her hair short with Farid's permission. She told them that she cut her hair while she and Farid were living in London."

"And that was a lie?"

"Yes," Zahra said with urgency.

"What is the truth? You must tell me, Zahra."

She answered quietly. "She cut it last week at a protest against the hijab laws."

The imam drew a deep breath, then offered words of praise. "You have done the right thing by sharing this information with me, Zahra."

He picked up the phone that was on his desk.

"Who are you calling?" asked Zahra.

"You can go now," he said. "This is in my hands."

"Who are you calling?"

The imam gave her a stern look, a warning. "You can go, woman."

A cockatoo cawed from somewhere in the garden, bringing Zahra back to her more immediate problem. She placed the prayer mat back in the storage bin and walked back to the cottage. The front door was locked, just as she'd left it, and she used her key. The door opened a few inches but then stopped, having caught on the chain, which gave her concern. She hadn't told Yasmin to fasten the chain lock, though she knew how to use the one at home, albeit with the help of a stool to reach it.

Zahra spoke loudly through the opening. "Yasmin, it's me. Open the door."

She waited, but there was no response.

"Yasmin," she said, louder this time. "I'm not fooling around. Open the door, please."

Zahra could hear the television playing in the other room, which did nothing to ease her concern. She listened more intently, blocking out the noise of the TV show, straining to hear any other sound. She thought she heard Yasmin's voice.

"Yasmin!" she shouted. "Who are you talking to? Open the door!"

She heard footfalls on the other side of the door. Someone was coming.

"Just a minute, Mommy."

Zahra felt a moment of relief, then anger. "No, not 'just a minute.' Open the door. Now!"

She could hear Yasmin climbing up on the chair in the foyer. Zahra pulled the door shut, and the chain rattled off the slide on the other side. She pushed the door open quickly but carefully, so as not to knock Yasmin off the chair. Zahra hugged Yasmin, then looked her squarely in the eye and shared some tough love.

"What were you doing?"

"When?"

"Don't give me 'when.' Who told you to put the chain on the door?"

"Nobody."

"Were you talking to someone?"

"When?"

"Yasmin, stop asking me when! I heard you talking."

"I was on the phone."

Zahra's heart skipped a beat. "*My* phone?"

"Yeah, I wanted to play a game. I found your phone in the bedroom."

"The phone that was wrapped in aluminum foil?"

"Yeah. It was like a present."

"It's not a *present*. You weren't supposed to use it!"

"I just used it to play a game."

"So, you were talking *to* the phone? Is that part of the game?"

"No, I was *on* the phone. It rang, so I answered it."

"Yasmin, no! Who called?"

Her shoulders slumped. "You're going to be mad at me."

"No, I won't be mad—mad*der*. Who were you talking to?"

Yasmin hesitated. "Mr. Swyteck."

Zahra kept control. Better Jack than the police. "What did you tell him?"

"Nothing," Zahra said quietly.

"Did you tell him where we are?"

"Planet Jupiter," she said, quieter still.

"Oh, my goodness, Yasmin," she said, breathing out her words.

"Are you mad at me, Mommy?"

"No. It's not your fault. But I need you to listen to me, okay? I want you to go get your suitcase and pack up everything you brought inside. I'm going to do the same."

"But we just got here. We didn't get to go to the beach yet. Are we leaving before we even go in the ocean?"

"I don't know. Mommy has to figure something out. Just pack your bag. And be quick about it."

"So we are leaving?"

"I don't know, honey. I *really* don't know what we're going to do now."

CHAPTER 44

Jack's phone conversation with Yasmin ended abruptly. He laid his cell phone on the bar top.

He was at the Area 31 restaurant on the sixteenth floor of the Epic Hotel in downtown Miami, seated at the bar with Dr. Vestry. The annual gala for the Miami Children's Hospital was in the hotel's grand ballroom, and the doctor had agreed to break away and meet Jack in the lounge. He was underdressed for the Saturday-evening crowd, but Dr. Vestry more than made up for his fashion shortcomings. Her sequined gown, Judith Leiber handbag, and diamond earrings glittered more than the panoramic view of Biscayne Bay at twilight.

"Planet Jupiter?" said Dr. Vestry. "Children have quite the imagination, but that's rich."

It was at the doctor's urging that Jack had dialed Zahra's cell one more time. The theme for the hospital's fundraising gala was "Vegas Night," and evidently, she was feeling lucky. Jack hadn't expected anyone to answer, much less Yasmin.

"She could have meant the town of Jupiter in Palm Beach County," said Jack. "Or a little farther north there's Jupiter Island. Both are straight up I-95."

"You should call again."

"Give it a minute," said Jack. "Yasmin said her mommy was at the door."

"Zahra is not going to call you, Jack."

"Let's see."

"Jack, who is the psychiatrist here? I'm telling you, in my professional opinion, there is no way Zahra is going to—"

Jack's cell vibrated. The caller ID was not a number he recognized, which probably meant that the warranty on his car was about to expire. Or . . .

Jack answered, and the voice on the line was Zahra's.

"It's me," she said.

"Zahra, where are you calling from?"

"A landline."

"No, I mean where are you?"

"I'm with Yasmin, and we're safe."

Jack stepped away from the noisy bar area and found a quieter place outside on the terrace, away from the crowd. He was standing at the rail, cell phone in hand, overlooking the Miami River below and the parade of yachts and sailboats coming in from the bay.

"As your lawyer, my advice is to turn yourself in."

"As Yasmin's mother, I say your advice stinks."

There was no smooth segue to the drawings—the reason for his meeting with Dr. Vestry in the first place—so Jack just said it. "I went to your town house. I saw Yasmin's practice drawings in the wastebasket. And your drawing as well."

There was silence on the line.

"You coached her, didn't you?"

"No."

"Dr. Vestry told you that Judge Carlson might invite Yasmin into his chambers and ask her to draw pictures of her family, and you coached her."

"I didn't tell her what to draw."

"It sure looked that way to me."

"No. You're wrong. I showed Yasmin *how* to draw it, Jack. Her memories are *her* memories. There was no one telling her *what* to draw."

Jack understood the distinction. It was valid—but only if it was true.

"This won't end well, Zahra. Going on the run never does."

"And the alternative is what? Give up on Yasmin? Is that what you're asking me to do?"

"Not give up on Yasmin. Give up on *this plan*. A voluntary surrender at least leaves you in a position to fight another day."

"We lost, Jack. Fight how?"

"The courts don't always have the last word. Maybe we can still work something out."

"Work *what* out, Jack?"

Jack feared that if he brought up his conversation with Farid—*Ava always wanted Yasmin to live in the West*—she might hang up on him.

"Let's take this one step at a time. The most important thing I can do for you right now is help you avoid criminal charges for child abduction and keep you out of jail. I don't know exactly where we go from there, but I'm certain I can come up with a better plan than turning you into a fleeing felon."

She paused, seeming to consider it.

"If I do this . . ."

Jack waited for more, but she was clearly struggling.

"Yes?" he asked, encouraging her.

"If I do as you ask, I don't want Yasmin to see me handcuffed and hauled away by the police in a squad car."

"I understand."

"I want you here when it happens. I need my lawyer with me."

The last time he'd heard those words, he was speaking to a man on death row. Zahra's plea affected him even more deeply. There was an innocent child involved.

"Of course. Just tell me where you are."

"But if you betray me," she said, her voice quaking. "If you just take what I'm about to tell you and hand the address over to the police—"

"I would never do that," Jack said. "Never."

Her deep sigh crackled over the landline. "Okay."

"Just tell me the address," said Jack.

There was a moment of hesitation, and then she told him.

Jack entered the address into his navigational app. The mystery of Yasmin's planetary reference was solved.

"I'm on my way," he said.

Jack hurried back into the lounge, said good night to Dr. Vestry on his way past the bar, and caught the hotel elevator to the ground floor.

He was cutting through the lobby when his phone rang again. It wasn't Zahra.

"Andie, what's up?"

"You know what's up. Our tech agents have been monitoring Zahra's cell phone. They picked up a call from your number to hers."

"Please don't tell me the FBI is monitoring *my* phone."

"Did you not hear me the first time? I just said they got it from Zahra's phone."

Jack wanted to believe his own wife simply because she was his wife. But the fact that she made no mention of the call from Zahra on the landline was welcome corroboration. She would have known about the second call if the FBI was monitoring *his* phone, too.

"Did your techies calculate the location of Zahra's phone?"

"No. Your call didn't last long enough. Triangulation takes time."

Jack had cross-examined enough tech witnesses to know that cell tower triangulation worked only if the cell phone signal was picked up by at least three cell towers, which allowed law enforcement to calculate the point of intersection of the three signals and, thus, the coordinates of the cell phone. Remote places like Jupiter Island didn't always interface with three towers.

"So, you *don't* know where she is?"

"No. But you told me that if you spoke to Zahra, you would do your best to get her to give up her location."

"Right. And that I would try to convince her to surrender. Which I did."

"Great. Where is she?"

Jack continued out of the hotel lobby to the valet stand at the motor court. "You'll know soon enough," he said into his phone.

"Do you know where she is?"

"Yes."

"Then don't play games, Jack. You need to tell me."

"If I do, the FBI will send in SWAT before I get there. That's the worst thing that could possibly happen."

"There will be no SWAT. I promise you."

"I wish—"

Jack stopped himself, but they both knew he was about to say, *I wish I could believe you.* It gave them both a moment to reflect on the state of their marriage, but this wasn't the time to discuss it.

"Yasmin has been through enough trauma," said Jack. "I'll call you when I get there, and we can have a quiet and peaceful surrender."

"Jack, your client is a child abductor. You can't help her."

"My other client is a seven-year-old girl," said Jack. "I intend to do everything I possibly can to help *her.*"

"Jack, you're putting me in a terrible spot. *Again.*"

"It's not on you. It's on me. Tell your ASAC I got involved in this case to protect Yasmin from grave danger of physical and psychological harm. I'm not going to be the one who inflicts it. Or let anyone else inflict it."

He heard Andie's sigh over the line.

"Please be careful," she said.

"I will."

He ended the call before Andie had a chance to change her mind—and his.

The valet attendant approached. "Can I have your ticket, sir?"

Jack reached into his pocket, then stopped. He didn't want the police riding his bumper all the way to Jupiter Island.

"Actually, I need a taxi."

CHAPTER 45

The taxi left Jack at the end of the private road, and the taillights faded into darkness. Jack could hear the ocean, even feel the salt in the air. Urban light pollution was nonexistent on Jupiter Island, and the thick tropical canopy blanketed the stars, making it impossible to see beyond the glow of the cottage porch lights. Jack went to the front door and rang the bell.

Zahra answered and invited him inside. "Yasmin tried so hard to wait up for you, but she fell asleep."

"I'm sure she's exhausted," said Jack. "Better that we talk out your surrender in private anyway."

"About that," she said as they entered the kitchen.

Jack stopped and did a double take: they were not alone. Even though Jack recognized the man seated on the stool at the granite-top island, he wasn't sure he believed his eyes.

"You remember Nouri," said Zahra.

Jack had cross-examined Nouri Asmoun about his alleged affair with Ava Bazzi. "Of course I remember him. What's he doing here?"

"Nouri is a friend," said Zahra.

"A friend *of yours?*"

"I think it would be helpful for the three of us to talk," she said.

Jack hesitated, his mind still processing what his client had sprung on him. Zahra walked around to the other side of the kitchen island and sat on the stool next to Nouri. He took her hand, and their fingers interlaced.

Jack blinked hard. "You two are—"

"Friends," said Zahra, interrupting.

"Good friends," said Nouri.

Jack took a seat on the barstool opposite them. "Mr. Asmoun—"

"Please," he said cordially. "Nouri."

"Nouri," said Jack, not sure where to start—where the lies began. "I'm guessing you're not an investment banker from Tehran."

"I am a banker," said Nouri, "though I'm not strictly 'from Tehran.' I have dual citizenship with the UK, which makes travel easier. I'm in the US quite often."

"When did you get your UK passport?"

"About a year ago."

"That's when we met in Miami," said Zahra. "Nouri *found* me in Miami, I should say."

"Why was he looking for you?"

With the exchange of a quick glance, Zahra and Nouri seemed to agree that the explanation should come from him.

"What happened to Ava was very upsetting to me," Nouri said.

"Upsetting to you as what? Her once-a-fortnight lover?"

"I knew Ava very well," said Nouri.

Jack studied his expression, drawing on his years of experience as a trial lawyer to discern what "very well" meant.

"There are those who say you're lying about that affair," he said, but he otherwise kept his conversation with Farid to himself.

"How I knew Ava is not important," said Nouri. "I felt terrible about what happened to her. And to Yasmin. When I heard that Zahra left Farid and took Yasmin with her, I wanted to help them. I owed Ava that much."

"How did you help?"

"It started with money," said Nouri. "When I found her in Miami, Zahra had no work visa."

"It's tough cleaning houses and getting paid under the table," said Zahra.

They were no longer holding hands, but Zahra was still sitting quite close to him.

"Obviously, it grew beyond financial support," said Jack.

Zahra blushed, and Nouri smiled a little.

"Yes. Obviously."

Jack looked at his client, conveying a mixture of anger and disappointment. "You've been nothing but deceitful, Zahra. I believed in you."

"And I believed in you, Jack. But I don't believe in your system of 'justice.' Look where it got me."

Jack was in no frame of mind to defend the Western system of justice. He wanted only answers. "If the two of you are so close, how did Nouri end up being a witness for Farid at the hearing?"

"Our plan backfired," said Nouri.

"What plan?" asked Jack.

"When Farid filed his lawsuit against Zahra, I was in Tehran. We agreed that I should go to Farid and try to talk him into dropping the case."

"How did you plan to make him do that?"

"Farid is a proud man," said Nouri. "Ava's infidelity is not something he would want to be made public."

"At least we thought he wouldn't," Zahra added.

Jack was already confused. "But Farid had already divorced Ava for abandoning him and Yasmin and fleeing the country. Why would he care if you called her an adulteress?"

"The Iranian government needed to explain Ava's sudden disappearance," said Nouri. "It's one thing when the government speaks in its own self-interest and tells you that your wife fled the country. It's another thing when a man looks you in the eye and says he slept with your wife."

"But Farid didn't drop the lawsuit," said Jack.

"No. Clearly, he wasn't moved by our threat to embarrass him over Ava."

"Well, it's worse than that," said Jack. "He actually took your threat, turned it against you, and used your testimony to help prove his case at the hearing. His lawyer argued that Ava's adultery was one more reason for her to abandon her family and flee the country in shame."

"True, Farid's lawyer made that argument," said Nouri. "But we do not believe it was at Farid's behest."

Jack fully understood the implication of Nouri's words, which only confirmed what Farid had told him. The Iranian government wasn't just paying Farid's legal bills. It was calling the shots.

"This is all very interesting," said Jack. "But you're lying."

"Excuse me?" said Zahra.

"Nouri, as I recall your testimony from the hearing, your affair started six months before Ava disappeared."

"Yes. I'm not proud of it. But this was not a onetime indiscretion."

"Shame on me as well," Jack said cryptically.

"For what?" asked Nouri.

"I don't often miss the opportunity to hammer a lying witness, but I missed this one."

"Meaning what?" asked Nouri.

"You claim it was a six-month affair," said Jack. "Ava, Yasmin, and Farid didn't move back from London to Tehran until *two* months before she disappeared."

Jack was relying on the flight information in the detailed timeline Bonnie "the Roadrunner" had created for him *after* Nouri's testimony by videoconference—"*Just in case you have to cross-examine Mr. Asmoun again.*"

The color drained from Nouri's face, but he quickly recovered. "Well, the affair started in London. I just told you: I have dual citizenship."

"Yes, and you also said you got your UK passport about a year ago, right about the time you came to Miami and found Zahra. Long after Ava disappeared."

There was only silence.

Jack's eyes narrowed. "You're lying," he said. "Both of you."

"We're not lying," said Zahra. "Nouri is confused. There are a few . . . inaccuracies. Let me explain."

"No, let *me*," said Jack, as matters were coming clear to him. "Nouri went to Farid and threatened to tell the world he was sleeping with Ava unless Farid dropped his lawsuit. I believe that much: you threatened him. But the basis for that threat was a lie. You never slept with her, did you, Nouri?"

It was more of an accusation than a question, and Nouri seemed to accept the fact that Jack had left him no wiggle room.

"No," said Nouri. "I didn't have an affair with Ava."

Jack's glare shifted to his client. "Zahra, I understand that you desperately wanted to keep Yasmin. But Ava was your sister. After all she went through, the best plan you could come up with was to paint her as an adulteress? What kind of person does that?"

Zahra inhaled sharply. "What kind of person? You really want to ask that question?"

"After I trusted you, I think it's a fair question."

Zahra's eyes lit up like burning embers. "Let me ask you this: What kind of mother would cut off her hair at a public protest and risk being arrested and taken away from her daughter? What kind of person is *that*?"

"I'm not here to judge your sister."

"No! Of course you aren't. *No one* judges Ava. No one questions her actions. It's always, 'What's wrong with *you*, Zahra?' 'What kind of person are *you*, Zahra?' 'Why can't *you* be a better role model so your perfect sister can be even more perfect?' Well, let me tell you this. Ava was not perfect!"

"Zahra, that's enough," said Nouri.

"She was anything *but* perfect," said Zahra, her voice rising. "Do you want to know what she was, Jack?"

"Enough," said Nouri.

"She was evil!"

"Zahra!"

"I'm telling you, my sister was an evil woman!"

There was a small voice from the hallway, just outside the kitchen. "Mommy, why are you yelling?"

Jack and Zahra were locked in a stare-down. Jack had seen her crack once before, and had attributed it to the stress of the case. This was different.

"Mommy?"

Jack had more to say, but not in front of a seven-year-old girl. Zahra climbed down quickly from the stool and went to Yasmin. Jack and Nouri stayed at the island, seated in silence as Zahra led Yasmin back to the bedroom, their voices fading in the hallway.

Jack had plenty of questions for Nouri. He asked the most obvious one.

"What are you doing here, Nouri?"

"I could ask the same of you."

"I'm here to tell Zahra she needs to surrender to the authorities."

"And I'm here to tell you she's not going to do that."

"That's a problem," said Jack. "With me here, the FBI is going to expect Zahra's cooperation."

"We can deal with the FBI," Nouri said with confidence.

Jack had heard enough. "There is no 'we,' Nouri. As soon as Zahra comes back, she and I are going to have a conversation—without you. Then, one of two things is going to happen. Either Zahra walks out that door with me and surrenders to the FBI. Or I walk out that door with Yasmin, and the two of you can hide out in the dunes with the sea turtles and the beach mice and deal with the shitstorm you seem determined to create. Got it?"

Nouri answered in a flat, even tone. "Sure, Jack. Whatever you say."

The words said one thing, but Nouri's cockiness said quite another. Jack stared back at him coldly. It was a look he'd perfected over years of representing incarcerated clients who had nothing more to lose and bullied everyone, even their lawyers, just for the fun of it.

"You're not going to screw this up, Nouri. Not on my watch."

Jack let the warning hang in the air for a moment, then pushed away from the counter and went to see his client.

CHAPTER 46

Andie and her longtime partner, special agent Grace Kennedy, were in Blowing Rocks Preserve, a seventy-three-acre nature conservancy on Jupiter Island. They left the car in the parking lot, found a couchlike formation of limestone rock just a stone's throw from the Atlantic Ocean, and sat beneath the stars, facing the waves. More important, they were less than a mile from Jack's location, according to the GPS coordinates they'd picked up from his cell phone.

"You think Jack will be mad when he finds out?" asked Grace.

"That I tracked him?"

"Tracked him *without telling him*."

The FBI had no legal basis to surveil Jack's electronic devices, but Andie had the same app that millions of other mothers had on their cell phones. It allowed her to track Jack, Righley, Abuela, Jack's father, their dog Max—the whole family.

"He'll thank me one day," said Andie. "Maybe. In another life."

The spray of the ocean soaked the dunes around them like a car wash. The southern tip of Jupiter Island has the largest exposed bluff of Anastasia limestone on the entire East Coast of the United States, and the chimney-like formations could funnel plumes of seawater fifty feet in the air at high tide.

Andie zipped up her jacket; the night was turning cool. A minute later her cell phone chimed with a text message. It was from Jack:

> With Zahra and Yasmin now. Both fine. All under control. Will
> ping you a location for surrender when ready. No SWAT.

Andie shared it with her partner.

"Sounds positive," said Grace. "But you've given him enough time."

"What would you do?"

"I understand you promised to let Jack work out the surrender with his client before taking this up the chain of command," said Grace. "But there's a child at risk."

"I asked, what would you do?"

"I wouldn't call in SWAT to bust down the door. But I'd call in the location and put hostage rescue on alert. If it was anyone but Jack, you'd do the same. Right?"

The question answered itself. "You're right," said Andie.

"You want me to call it in?" asked Grace.

Another plume of ocean spray shot into the air and washed the limestone at their feet.

"No. I'll do it," said Andie.

Jack took Zahra outside to speak privately on the patio. It was a crisp night, and Zahra lit the gas firepit. The outdoor furniture was in storage for the off-season, so the only place to sit was a curved, built-in bench that faced the circular pit. They spoke in the warm glow of the flickering flames.

"I want you to send Nouri away," said Jack.

"Why?"

"I came here because you agreed to surrender. Nouri came here to talk you out of it, didn't he?"

"He came because I asked him to come."

"Why would you do that?"

"He's my friend. I trust him."

"I don't," said Jack.

"You should," said Zahra. "Nouri makes good sense. You want me to surrender unconditionally. Nouri says I shouldn't surrender without some guarantees."

"Trying to negotiate concessions from law enforcement while you're on the run with Yasmin in violation of a court order is a terrible mistake. It turns you into a hostage taker."

"She's not a hostage. I'm her *mother*."

"If you have any sympathies left as a mother, you'd be throwing them away by using Yasmin as leverage to get your way."

Flames flickered in Zahra's eyes, a fitting reflection from the firepit.

"Get *my* way? Really, Jack? The only ones getting their way are the Iranian government and the US State Department."

The patio door slid open, and Nouri stepped out from the kitchen. He joined them near the firepit but didn't take a seat.

"We're losing valuable time," he said.

"Jack won't negotiate," said Zahra. "He still says I should just give up and put myself at the mercy of the FBI."

"Lawyers are such terrible negotiators," Nouri said with disapproval. "But that's fine. We don't need Jack to negotiate for us."

"Yes, we do! I can't do this by myself, Nouri. And if you do it, they'll know you're here with me."

"Trust me, they already know Nouri is here," said Jack, bluffing.

"No, they don't," said Nouri. "If they thought Yasmin was with anyone other than her mother and her highly respected lawyer preparing to surrender, they would have sent in SWAT already. Actually, let me put a finer point on it: if the FBI knew Zahra and Yasmin were here with a *Muslim man*, they would have sent in SWAT already."

Whether Nouri was right or wrong, Jack knew he had no chance of changing his view.

"You know I'm right," said Nouri. "We're talking about a mother who violated a family court order to transfer custody of her daughter. This happens twice a minute in this country. But somehow this one is a federal case, and the FBI is all over it."

Jack saw no advantage in explaining the US government's negotiations with Iran. "This case is different because of Ava Bazzi, not because you're Muslim."

"Two things can be true at once," said Nouri.

Jack didn't debate it. "I'm not your negotiator," he said.

"Agreed," said Nouri. "Your only job is to present Zahra's demand to the FBI as her lawyer. No negotiation."

Jack rose. "I don't take orders from you, and no one is making any demands. This is a surrender, not a negotiation."

"Yes, you made your position clear," said Nouri. "If Zahra won't surrender, you're walking out of here. And you're taking Yasmin with you."

Zahra's mouth was agape. "Is that the reason you came here, Jack? To take Yasmin away from me?"

Jack looked straight at Zahra—his client—but he wasn't thinking like a lawyer. "I'll do what I have to do."

"You can't!" said Zahra.

"Zahra's right," said Nouri. "We can't let you do that."

Jack's gaze swung back to Nouri, and in the glow of the firepit, he saw the business end of a Beretta pistol.

"Nouri, no!" said Zahra.

"He leaves us no choice, Zahra."

Jack tried to keep calm. "Put the gun away, Nouri."

"We're no longer asking for your help," said Nouri. "You'll do as you're told. Give Zahra your cell phone."

"Zahra, don't be part of this," said Jack.

"Give it to her!" said Nouri.

Zahra held out her hand. Jack slid his phone from his pocket and gave it to her.

Nouri continued. "Here's the drill. You're going to call your wife and present Zahra's demand."

"Leave my wife out of this," said Jack.

"She's been right in the middle from the very beginning."

"Not by choice," said Jack.

"Maybe not," said Nouri. "But that's the way your government operates. It uses people. Puts them in a position where they can't say no, ruins their lives, and then leaves them to fend for themselves."

Nouri was clearly talking about someone other than Andie—something personal. Jack guessed it had to do with the circumstances under which he'd become a witness in the Hague proceeding. He made one more appeal to reason.

"Zahra, this has gone too far. If Nouri has his own score to settle, don't make yourself part of it."

Zahra was silent.

"Listen to me closely," said Nouri. "Zahra's demand has two parts."

"Zahra, you're putting Yasmin in danger," Jack said.

Nouri kept talking. "One, Zahra will not be charged with kidnapping or any other crime; she goes free. Two, Zahra gets to keep Yasmin."

"This is pointless," said Jack. "Zahra, I'm being straight with you. The FBI will never accept that demand."

Nouri paused. The steady hiss of the propane tank fed the flames. The sound of the ocean drifted through the black forest. Finally, Zahra spoke.

"They'll accept," she said quietly. "Once the State Department hears what we're offering in return."

Jack wasn't sure what she meant precisely, but it was clear enough that they were coming full circle—back to Ava.

"It doesn't matter what you offer," said Jack. "The US government won't buy it."

Nouri answered in a calm but threatening voice. "They'll buy it, because you're going to sell it, Jack. Sell it like your client's life depends on it. And your own."

The threat had a certain cadence to it, and the proverbial light bulb blinked on in Jack's head. "We met before you testified in the Hague proceeding, didn't we, Nouri?"

Nouri didn't deny it.

"That night outside my office," said Jack. "You had a mouthful of cotton or something to disguise your voice. But that was you sitting on my kidneys, wasn't it?"

Still no denial.

"Let's go inside," said Nouri. "We have some rehearsing to do."

CHAPTER 47

J ack rehearsed his sales pitch at the kitchen counter. Nouri was his coach. Zahra was his test audience.

Practice was important. Jack had to present Zahra's demand in a way that was satisfactory to Nouri—that "sold it." At the same time, he needed to signal to Andie that he wasn't speaking of his own free will. And then there was the wild card in all this: if Jack played it just right—"With feeling," as Nouri put it—he might finally find out the truth about Ava Bazzi.

After a couple of trial runs, the third time was the charm.

"That was impressive," said Nouri. "Let's do it."

Zahra laid Jack's phone on the granite countertop, equidistant from Jack on one side and Zahra and Nouri on the other. Jack speed-dialed Andie, and she answered.

"Is Zahra ready to surrender?" she asked.

"We're ready to make a deal," said Jack.

He'd caught her off guard. "A deal? Jack, we're not going to—"

"Please, just listen to me, Andrea."

There was silence on the line. He never called her Andrea. *No one* called her Andrea. She seemed to take his cue.

"Okay, got it," she said. "I'm listening."

"Zahra has specific conditions of surrender, but first it's important for you—for the FBI—to understand where she's coming from. I'm not speaking to you husband to wife. I'm speaking criminal lawyer to FBI agent."

Criminal lawyer. He hoped it registered with Andie—that term he never used, that he always corrected to "criminal *defense* lawyer."

"Understood," she said.

"Let's go back in time to when Ava Bazzi was arrested and 'disappeared' in the custody of the Tehran morality police. The Iranian government claimed that she escaped and fled the country. Human rights organizations all over the world listed her as another victim of the regime. The US State Department never took a public position one way or the other. The question is: Why?"

"Are you expecting me to answer that, Jack?"

Jack ignored the question, sticking to the presentation Nouri had approved.

"Fast forward to when I became Zahra's lawyer. The State Department still had no official position on Ava Bazzi. But behind the scenes, it used all the leverage of the federal government—mostly through you—to make me stop trying to prove that Ava was murdered by the regime. Again, the question is: Why?"

"You're asking questions I can't answer," said Andie.

"There's more," he said, adding his code word for good measure, "*Andrea*."

"I'm listening," she said, still with him.

"At the child custody hearing in state court, Farid showed up with an order from Iranian family court granting him full custody of Yasmin on her seventh birthday. It was a fake, but the judge enforced it because the State Department issued a certificate saying it was authentic. Same question: Why?"

"You tell me, Jack," said Andie.

"It's obvious: when it comes to the disappearance of Ava Bazzi, the State Department has something to hide."

"'*Something* to hide?' That's not very specific."

"You'll get specifics. First, here are Zahra's terms of surrender."

"Go ahead," said Andie.

Jack felt the barrel of Nouri's gun at the base of his skull. Nouri had scripted out the final part of the demand. Jack read the exact words to Andie.

"No criminal prosecution for anything," said Jack. "And Zahra keeps Yasmin."

"That's impossible," said Andie.

"Check your email in about two minutes," said Jack, sticking to the script. "I'm sending you a video file."

"What video?"

"Watch the video. Show it to your ASAC, the director of the FBI, the secretary of state—whoever it takes to get authorization to meet Zahra's demand."

"What's in the video?"

Jack felt more pressure from the gun muzzle. He stuck to Nouri's script.

"If the FBI doesn't agree to Zahra's terms in one hour, the whole world will see it. The file will go viral on the internet."

Before Andie could respond, Nouri pulled the pistol away, reached for Jack's phone, and ended the call with the press of a button.

"Swyteck, you're a natural," said Nouri. "That was perfect."

Zahra looked at him with soulful eyes. "Thank you, Jack."

Jack looked right back at her. The gun was no longer to his head, but it had left him breathless.

"I mean this from the bottom of my heart, Zahra. Do not thank me. Not ever again."

CHAPTER 48

M y husband is with Zahra Bazzi and her daughter, and he's in trouble," said Andie.

She and her partner were on a videoconference with the Miami ASAC. They were in her car, which was still parked in the lot at the nature preserve. Andie's tablet was resting on the dashboard, with the ASAC's image aglow on the display screen.

"How do you know there's trouble?" asked Tidwell.

She didn't even have to use the words *Andrea* or *criminal lawyer*.

"The terms of surrender Jack laid out for his client are criminal extortion, pure and simple. Jack would never do that."

"What are his terms?"

She told him, including the threat to release the video.

"Send me the video and give us Jack's location. I'll take it from here."

Andie used her phone to forward Jack's email with the attached file.

"Video is on its way," she said.

"Good. Now delete it from your phone. What's the location?"

"I'm nearby. Agent Kennedy and I are less than a mile away."

"Give me the location, Henning. I said I'll take it from here."

Andie didn't like being cut out, especially if Jack was in danger. But she'd already blurred the lines between professional and personal. She gave up Jack's location.

"Jack is expecting me to call him back," said Andie.

"I'll handle it."

"What should I do if he calls me?"

"Don't answer. I'm going to contact him on my terms."

It took all of Andie's inner strength to remain respectful. "I'm sorry, sir. I have reason to believe that my husband is in danger. I'm not going to ignore his call."

Tidwell took a moment to reconsider. "Fine. Take the call. But conference me in immediately. And delete that video."

The videoconference ended. Andie glanced across the console at Grace in the dim light of the dash.

"There's a very fishy smell," said Grace, "and it isn't coming from the ocean."

"Which tells me one thing," said Andie.

"What?"

"Ava Bazzi is bigger than Jack knows. Bigger than you and I can imagine."

"What are you going to do?" asked Grace.

Andie reached for her tablet on the dashboard. "We're going to watch that video."

Jack was in the kitchen with Zahra and Nouri. His cell phone lay on the countertop, and his gaze was locked onto the screen.

Zahra shifted nervously in her seat. "I'm not sure I want to watch."

"It's important that everyone see this video," said Nouri, and he hit the play button.

The video was low quality, and the frames jumped around so randomly that Jack had to strain to discern the image.

"It's from a body camera," Nouri explained. "Like the kind police wear."

Jack watched closely. Whoever had been wearing the body camera finally stopped moving. The frame was still. The image came into focus on the screen. The camera—cameraman—was positioned at one end of a long corridor that was lined on both sides with iron prison bars. Hands and elbows protruded through the bars at random intervals, as if the cells were overcrowded, not enough room for all those detained. The hands appeared delicate, Jack noticed.

"A women's cellblock?" Jack asked.

"Just watch," said Nouri.

Two male prison guards appeared at the other end of the cellblock. An inmate stood between them, dressed in prison garb. The prisoner was much smaller than the guards and appeared to be a woman. Jack couldn't be certain. A black hood covered the inmate's head. The guards started walking toward the camera, bringing the prisoner with them. They walked the entire length of the cellblock, past the overcrowded cells, and stopped in front of the body camera.

Jack looked at the screen carefully. Even with the hood, it was now clear that the inmate was a woman.

One of the guards moved his mouth, talking, but there was no audio on the recording. The cameraman's hands occasionally came into view. He was gesturing the way people do when talking, but it was more than just talk.

"Are they *negotiating*?" asked Jack.

The answer came quickly. A wad of cash passed before the lens, from the cameraman's hand to the prison guard's pocket. The guard handed over a plastic bag that, Jack presumed, contained the prisoner's belongings. The other guard then removed the hood, apparently to confirm that they were delivering the promised prisoner.

"Oh, my God, Ava!" said Zahra.

The video turned shaky again. Ava and the cameraman were on the move, walking at first and then running. A steel door swung open to the night sky. They were in a dimly lit parking lot surrounded by a chain-link fence. A car came into view. More running.

The video went black.

Zahra was overcome with emotion. She ran from the room, leaving Jack alone with Nouri at the kitchen island.

"How did you get this video?" asked Jack.

"How do you think I got it?" asked Nouri.

Jack was still trying to wrap his mind around it, but the conclusion was inescapable.

"Ava wasn't murdered by Tehran's morality police. She made it out of Evin Prison, alive and well. With *you*."

Nouri stared back at him. "With me," he said finally.

Jack's cell phone rang, but no incoming number was displayed. Nouri put the call on speaker, and on his signal, Jack answered.

"This is Jack Swyteck."

"Jack, this is Todd Tidwell from the Miami field office."

Nouri hit the mute button. "Who's Tidwell?"

"My wife's boss in Miami. The assistant special agent in charge."

Tidwell's follow-up came over the speaker. "Jack? Are you there?"

"He's not high enough in the chain of command," said Nouri, the call still muted. "Tell him we need someone with complete authority."

Jack unmuted the call. "Todd, are you calling to agree to my client's terms of surrender?"

"I'm calling to give you a dose of reality," said Tidwell. "I don't know what you were trying to prove with that video you sent to your wife, but it's a complete fake."

Jack wasn't sure how to respond, but Tidwell had hit a nerve with Nouri, and Jack was suddenly relegated to the sideline.

"Fuck you, it's *fake*," said Nouri.

"Who is this?" asked Tidwell.

Nouri was steaming, and the look in his eyes was the same one Jack had seen in the "rehearsal," when something had triggered his anger toward the US government.

Jack remembered his words. *It uses people. Puts them in a position where they can't say no, ruins their lives, and then leaves them to fend for themselves.*

"This is Nouri Asmoun," he said, his voice hissing. "I'm sure your friends at the CIA wish this video wasn't real, the same way they wish I didn't exist. I've been abused from the day I bought Ava Bazzi out of prison. My life is fucked. My entire family in Iran is fucked. But the CIA is going to do right by Ava's sister and daughter. I want this deal wrapped up in thirty minutes. If the next call doesn't come from the right person, the truth about Ava Bazzi will no longer be a secret."

Nouri ended the call. He breathed in and out, bringing his anger under control, and then noticed Jack was watching him.

"What are you looking at, Swyteck?"

Jack didn't look away. He had no answer for Nouri. Only a question.

"Who *are* you, Nouri Asmoun?"

CHAPTER 49

From the kitchen, Jack heard sobbing in the next room. It was Zahra. He wanted to go to her, but Nouri was of the mind to "let her cry it out." A few minutes later she appeared in the entranceway to the kitchen with a tissue in her hand, her eyes puffy.

"This has gone very wrong," she said, sniffling. "I need—I think I should speak to Farid."

Nouri was incredulous. "Have you lost your mind?"

"I don't want to go to jail. Look what happened to my sister."

"Stop," said Nouri. "You have to stay strong."

"What good am I to Yasmin if I'm behind bars? If I ask Farid not to prosecute me for taking Yasmin, maybe we can work this out between us."

"Farid is not your answer," Nouri said. "The only way forward is to keep pressure on the US government."

"I think talking to Farid is an excellent idea," said Jack.

"You don't even know Farid," said Nouri.

"Farid came to see me after the hearing," said Jack. "He told me it was Ava's wish that Yasmin be raised in the West. He wants to honor that wish."

"Then Yasmin belongs with me," said Zahra.

"That's what I told him."

"What was his response?"

Jack soft-pedaled it. "You're not his first choice."

Nouri scoffed. "You see, Zahra? You still want to call Farid?"

Jack looked at Zahra with as much sincerity as he could muster. "I believe he could be persuaded."

Her sad eyes glimmered with a bit of hope. "You really think so?"

Jack could see it in her expression and hear it in her voice: Zahra welcomed any sign that Farid didn't hate her. That alone raised more questions about her allegations against Farid, though it wasn't at all unheard of for the abused to seek the approval of their abuser. Jack's more immediate problem was to extricate himself and Yasmin from a bad situation, and he had to exploit any angle.

"I think Farid would be receptive to your call," said Jack.

Nouri's anger rose. "Zahra, he's playing you. Farid is a distraction. The FBI is trying to stall, and so is he. Don't bring Farid into this."

Jack continued to work on Zahra. "You said it yourself. This is all wrong. I'm sure Farid feels the same way. Everyone's options are narrowing. Let's talk to him about keeping Yasmin in the US. Maybe we can work something out."

"That's never going to happen," said Nouri.

"We'll never know unless you talk to him," said Jack.

Zahra seemed torn. Clearly, she didn't want to disappoint Nouri. But for reasons Jack was only beginning to understand, she felt some kind of connection to Farid, and her feelings tipped in the other direction.

"I want to speak to Farid," she said.

Nouri muttered something in his native tongue.

"Please," said Zahra. "I must talk to him."

Nouri glared at Jack, directing none of his anger toward Zahra. "Fine," he said. "Call Farid. But I want it on speaker so I can hear. And don't tell him I'm here."

Farid's phone number was on the initial court filing, which Jack pulled up on his cell.

"Let me initiate the call and break the ice," said Jack. "Then you can take it from there."

Zahra agreed. Jack dialed, and on the third ring, Farid answered.

"Farid, for Yasmin's sake, *please* don't hang up. It's Jack Swyteck."

There was a brief silence, which made Jack think he'd lost him at hello. Then hope.

"I'm here," said Farid. "Is Yasmin with you?"

"Yes."

"Let me speak to her."

Zahra shook her head—a firm *no*.

"She's asleep," said Jack.

"Wake her up. I want to talk to my daughter."

Jack looked at Zahra, who took a moment to respond.

"I'll check on her," said Zahra, and she left the room.

"Zahra is getting her," Jack said. "It'll be a minute."

"Is Nouri there?" asked Farid.

Jack didn't answer.

"I know Nouri is there," said Farid. "The FBI told me."

Nouri seemed to have lost interest in the wizard-behind-the-curtain charade. "Yeah, I'm here, Farid."

"Did Nouri tell you how we met, Jack? He flew all the way to Tehran to tell me that if I filed this lawsuit against Zahra, it would come out in the courtroom that Ava slept with him."

Jack had to prevent the call from devolving into tit-for-tat. "Let's not rehash the past, Farid."

"Nouri even showed me proof that he was sleeping with Ava," said Farid. "He showed me a pair of her shoes. He told me she left them in his apartment."

Nouri moved closer to the speakerphone. "Don't push me, Farid. Or I'll end this call, and you can forget about talking to Yasmin."

Farid was undeterred. "I'll bet you didn't show those shoes to the Iranian government, did you, Nouri?"

"Last warning," said Nouri. "I'll hang up."

"I'll bet you didn't show them Ava's wedding ring either, or any of the other things she was wearing on the day she was arrested by the morality police. Because if you showed those things, you would have to explain how you *really* got them."

Nouri grabbed Jack's phone and, with the push of a button, ended the call.

There was silence in the room. But for Jack, things were beginning to come clear—and the prison video was making even more sense.

"The plastic bag that changed hands in the video," said Jack. "The one the guards gave you when they handed over Ava."

"What about it?"

"It contained Ava's belongings, didn't it? Her street clothes. The shoes you showed to Farid to make him think she had been to your apartment."

Nouri was silent.

"And the wedding ring you put in the pipe you hurled through my office window."

More silence.

"*You're* the one who wanted to keep Ava from becoming an issue in the Hague proceeding."

"Not just me," said Nouri.

"But you, more than anyone, wanted to shut down any public discussion of whether Ava Bazzi is alive or dead."

"I, *as much as* anyone. But not more."

"When you say 'anyone,' do you mean the Iranian government? Or the US government?"

"Isn't it obvious to you, Swyteck? *Both*."

"Then who are you protecting?"

Nouri didn't answer.

Jack pressed. "Whose side are you on, Nouri?"

His eyes narrowed, but it seemed more like resolve than anger. "I'm on Zahra's side," he said. "And Ava's."

Zahra entered the room. Yasmin was half asleep in her arms, and Zahra was struggling to support the deadweight of a seven-year-old girl.

"Yasmin doesn't want to speak to Farid," she said. "Do you, darling?"

Yasmin buried her face in the crook of Zahra's neck.

"That's fine," said Nouri. "That ship has sailed."

Zahra looked at Jack with a mixture of concern and disappointment in her eyes—a little too much disappointment, Jack thought.

"So, Farid is gone?"

"Yes," said Jack. "That opportunity is lost."

"It was never an opportunity to begin with," said Nouri.

"Then what's left?" asked Zahra. "You keep saying that we have to keep the pressure on, Nouri. But what chance do we have against the entire United States government?"

"They'll give us what we want," said Nouri. "Just as soon as that video works its way up the chain of command and lands on the right desk."

"You're fooling yourself," said Jack. "The video shows Ava was alive when she left Evin Prison. That's what the Iranian government has said all along, and the US government has never said otherwise. That's not a pressure point to make them accept Zahra's terms of surrender."

"That video is the tip of the iceberg," Nouri said.

Jack studied his expression. Nouri didn't appear to be bluffing.

"What else do you have?" Jack asked.

"Do you remember the end of the video? The car waiting in the parking lot?"

"Yes," said Jack.

Nouri's expression was very serious. "I know who was driving it."

CHAPTER 50

ndie refused to leave Jupiter Island.

The Miami ASAC had walled her off from any official role in the negotiations with Jack, but the fact remained that it was her husband in that cottage. Andie and her partner stayed in the car, still parked in the lot at the nature preserve. They were less than a minute away if Jack called for help. Or even if he didn't call.

Grace was in the passenger seat, singing the old punk rock classic under her breath: "*Should I stay or should I go?*"

"Grace, knock it off."

Their stint on the sidelines didn't last long. Andie's tablet lit up on the dashboard with an invitation to join another videoconference. She accepted with the push of a button. On the screen was ASAC Tidwell, but he wasn't in the office. He was on the move, inside the FBI's mobile command center, heading toward Jupiter Island. An FBI hostage negotiator and tech agent were with him in the electronics compartment behind the driver's cab.

"There's been a shift in strategy," said Tidwell.

"I'm at your service," said Andie.

"Hold on. I need to patch someone in."

Andie's screen flickered as another virtual box appeared for a third participant. There was nothing to identify him as an agent for the CIA— except for the fact that Andie recognized him as Agent Hartfield, the CIA agent she had met in Bayfront Park.

"I understand the two of you know each other," said Tidwell, dispensing with an introduction.

"Yes," said Andie. "We took a walk in the park and then met another time for coffee. Neither one was pleasant."

"Pardon my stating the obvious, but the CIA has no law enforcement power," said Hartfield. "Nonetheless, we do have a keen interest in the man holed up in the cottage with your husband and Zahra Bazzi. His name is Nouri Asmoun. He was the man wearing the body camera in the video you sent us."

It was a lot for Andie to comprehend, but she quickly understood the ramifications.

"The man holding my husband knows that Ava Bazzi left Evin Prison alive," she said.

"Yes," said Hartfield. "And much more."

"What?"

"The rest I can share with you only on a need-to-know basis."

Andie immediately understood the implication. "You'll tell me if I agree to do what you want me to do. Do I have that right?"

"Precisely," said Hartfield.

"All right," said Andie. "What's the ask?"

"Asmoun is expecting a callback in just a few minutes. We want you to make that phone call."

The ASAC interjected. "Whoa, whoa, whoa," said Tidwell. "We didn't discuss that. Putting Agent Henning on the phone breaks the most basic rules of hostage negotiation. Andie has a personal stake here. She can't be on the phone and create a situation where Nouri could put a gun to her husband's head and threaten to blow his brains out unless Andie gives him what he wants."

"Thank you, Todd," said Andie. "That's exactly what I would have said, though I probably would have spared myself the image of splattered gray matter."

"Right, sorry," said Tidwell. "I was just making a point."

"Both of you are missing *the point*," said Hartfield. "I'm not suggesting that Agent Henning get on the phone to negotiate. She simply needs to buy time until SWAT can breach."

Andie knew the lead hostage negotiator in Miami—knew how good he was. "Your first option is a breach?" she asked, incredulous. "That's insane. There's a seven-year-old girl in that cottage."

"I agree," said the ASAC.

"With all due respect to the FBI," said Hartfield, "you don't know a thing about Nouri Asmoun."

Andie was a step ahead of him, and the CIA's agenda was crystal clear. "Your priority isn't to get Yasmin out safely, much less Jack and Zahra."

"Theorize all you like, but FBI headquarters has already authorized the breach," said Hartfield—which only confirmed Andie's belief.

"Your priority is to *take out* Nouri. To silence him—permanently."

There was silence, then the ASAC spoke. "Who authorized the breach?"

"Isaac Underwood in Washington."

Andie didn't believe him, though Isaac would have that authority as assistant director of the counterterrorism division. If the order was communicated through Isaac, it was really from someone above even him—someone who actually had secrets to hide.

"Putting Agent Henning on the phone is a key component of the breach," said Hartfield. "Nouri would never expect SWAT to breach while she's on the line. Not with her husband in the cottage."

"I'm not doing it," said Andie.

"The breach already has the green light," said Hartfield. "It's happening, with or without you on the phone. The only question is whether you are willing to increase the likelihood of success by adding the element of surprise that comes with you being on the phone when SWAT crashes through the door."

"I stand behind Agent Henning," said Tidwell.

It was the clearest display of leadership Andie had ever seen from the new ASAC, and she was grateful.

"Thank you," said Andie.

Hartfield was clearly losing patience. "Of course no one is going to put a gun to Henning's head and make her do it. But let me add one element to the mix."

"Nothing is going to change my mind," said Andie.

"This might," said Hartfield. "At the end of the video Nouri sent you, there was a car waiting in the parking lot. Nouri was under contract with the CIA to buy Ava Bazzi out of prison and get her into the car. The driver of that car was a CIA agent by the name of Brian Guthrie."

Andie felt chills at the mention of the hostage's name.

"Obviously, things did not go well for Agent Guthrie in this exercise," said Hartfield. "It has taken all this time, but we are on the brink of negotiating his release from the Iranians. The last thing we need at this pivotal moment is for Nouri Asmoun to make good on his threat, release that video on the internet, and say God-knows-what about it."

Andie understood most of what he was saying, but it still left her confused. "But the video shows that Ava Bazzi escaped from the prison unharmed," said Andie. "That should help the negotiations for Agent Guthrie's release. It supports the Iranian position that the morality police didn't murder her—that she escaped and fled."

"As I mentioned," said Hartfield, "things did not go well. Nouri knows what happened after the video ended."

Andie could read between the lines: Ava Bazzi was most definitely dead.

Her ASAC spoke next, gently. "Andie, maybe you will want to reconsider."

Andie's mind was awhirl. The question wasn't just what was best for the negotiations in Jupiter Island. The next move also had to be in the best interest of a high-value hostage in Iran.

"It's a delicate balance," she said, thinking aloud.

"It bears repeating," said Agent Hartfield. "The SWAT breach is happening with or without your help."

Andie's thoughts were all over the map, literally. Thousands of Iranians had been jailed during the protests. Hundreds were killed.

"Why was the CIA so focused on getting Ava Bazzi out of jail and out of Iran?" Andie asked. "Of all the women jailed during the protests, why did the CIA put Nouri Asmoun and Agent Guthrie at so much risk over Ava Bazzi?"

"Perhaps I could answer that question someday," said Hartfield. "Assuming you were to do your part to bring Agent Guthrie home safely."

Andie recalled her conversation with Farid—the thumb drive of text messages he'd discovered in Ava's locked drawer.

"Does this have to do with the network of Iranian women that Ava was part of?"

Hartfield didn't offer a direct answer. "All I will tell you is that Ava Bazzi was a brave woman. How brave are you, Agent Henning?"

There was silence. For Andie, the balance finally tipped, inspired in part by Ava's courage to stand up against her own government.

"Brave enough to tell the CIA to go fuck itself," said Andie.

"Excuse me?" said Hartfield.

"I'm not going to let myself be used as a distraction while SWAT breaks down the door and gets my husband killed. That's my final decision."

Andie exited the videoconference, and her screen went black.

Her partner looked over from the passenger seat with clear shock on her face. "What now?" asked Grace.

Andie reached for her phone. "I need to get through to Isaac," she said. "Gotta get the green light on SWAT back to red."

CHAPTER 51

Jack checked the clock on the kitchen wall. Nouri had given the FBI thirty minutes for a callback from "the right person," a deadline that had long since passed. He was pacing like a caged tiger as Jack and Zahra watched from their barstools at the counter.

"They think I'm bluffing," said Nouri.

"Please sit," said Zahra.

"I'm not bluffing. I'll release this video. They're playing with fire."

"Nouri, please. You're making me nervous. Sit down."

Nouri stopped and shot a look of reproval. "Don't tell me what to do."

The tone made Zahra shrink. Nouri resumed pacing.

Jack could see a transformation in Nouri. It plainly annoyed him that the FBI was dragging its feet. More than that, it seemed Nouri was still stewing over the way Zahra had insisted on contacting Farid, even though Nouri had things "under control." Jack, too, had found Zahra's behavior odd—and revealing.

As Jack saw it, there was the one triangle of Ava/Zahra/Farid, and a second of Nouri/Zahra/Farid. The common leg was Zahra and Farid, about which Jack was certain of only one thing: Zahra had never been straight with him. It seemed that Nouri, too, was fed up with the lies. Jack didn't know why the FBI had let Nouri's deadline pass without a response, but if the bureau no longer saw negotiation as the solution to this standoff, it was time for Jack to take matters into his own hands. He had to convince Nouri that Zahra's fight was no longer worth fighting. The truth about Zahra and Farid was Jack's only point of leverage.

"Do you feel used, Nouri?" Jack asked.

He stopped pacing. "By your government, yes. I was used in the worst way."

"I was talking about something different," said Jack, his gaze drifting in Zahra's direction.

"Are you accusing *me* of using Nouri?" she asked with indignation.

Too much indignation, thought Jack.

"It was your idea to tell Farid that Ava was sleeping with Nouri," said Jack. "I'm surprised Nouri would let himself be used in that way."

"The idea was to get Farid to drop his lawsuit," said Zahra. "How many times do we have to tell you that?"

"Oh, right," said Jack, his voice laden with skepticism. "He would be too proud to go through the court system if it meant making it public that his wife cheated on him."

Nouri said, "If you knew Farid, you would understand it was a good plan."

Jack dropped the sarcasm, his expression very serious. "Except that Zahra had a very different goal," he said, and then looked again at Zahra. "Didn't you?"

She seemed to sense where Jack's questioning was headed. "Don't you dare go down this road."

"I've been thinking about this ever since you called your sister an 'evil woman,'" Jack said, and then he looked at Nouri. "Do you think Ava was evil, Nouri?"

"Of course not."

Zahra started to backpedal. "I didn't mean *she* was an evil person. I meant—all I meant is that she could do evil things."

"Which is why you sent Nouri to lie about an affair—to show Farid that Ava could do evil things, even if it was a lie."

"So that Farid would drop his lawsuit."

"No. You *used* Nouri to convince Farid that Ava was unworthy of him as a wife."

"That's crazy," said Zahra. "I would gain nothing by that."

"On the contrary, you would gain everything you wanted," Jack said, and then he spoke directly to Nouri. "The point she *used you* to make, Nouri, is that Farid made a terrible mistake when he rejected Zahra and married Ava instead."

"That's laughable," said Zahra, adding a nervous chuckle.

Nouri wasn't laughing, and Jack could tell that the seed was planted in his head. He pushed forward with his theory, linking one detail to the next in machine-gun fashion, cross-examining his own client.

"You didn't stop dating as teenagers because Farid had a temper and you broke up with him. In fact, it wasn't *your* decision at all, was it, Zahra?"

She was silent, though it seemed she wished she could deny it.

"Things ended between you and Farid because Ava did an evil thing, as you call it. Ava *stole* Farid from you."

"What? I dumped *him*." Zahra laughed nervously again.

"Ava stole Farid, and you've never forgiven her. That's why you called her evil."

"That's a terrible thing to say."

"Ava was never unfaithful to her husband. Ava and Farid had the perfect marriage and the perfect child—which only made you more jealous."

"*Jealous?* Ha!"

"When Ava was gone, you didn't marry Farid just to escape with Yasmin. Being married to Farid was what you wanted all along."

"That's a lie!"

"The fact that the marriage was never consummated was not for lack of desire on your part. Farid never stopped loving Ava—which must have pushed you over the edge."

"Don't believe him, Nouri!"

"Far enough over the edge to make you want to hurt Farid in the worst way possible—by taking his daughter."

"Stop it!"

"And when he found you and filed the Hague case to get Yasmin back, you answered with the worst trope in the Islamophobic book: the angry Muslim man who beats his wife and child."

Zahra appealed to Nouri, her eyes welling with tears, but said nothing.

Nouri took a step toward her. "Is this true, Zahra?"

"It doesn't matter."

"It matters!" he shouted.

"Farid doesn't want to be happy!" Zahra shouted back. "He clings to the story that Ava could still be alive. He wants to spend the rest of his life searching for the wife he never stopped loving. He doesn't deserve Yasmin. He doesn't deserve me!"

Nouri's anger was palpable, and all of it was directed toward Zahra.

"I came to this country to help you because I felt sorry for you, Zahra. I felt sorry for what happened to your sister. I felt sorry because you made me think Farid was an abuser. You made me think he was an awful man who didn't deserve his own daughter. You made me believe you were in love with *me*."

"I do love you, Nouri!"

"You used me, the same way the CIA used me!"

"That's not true!"

"Quiet!" shouted Nouri, his voice nearly rattling the kitchen windows.

He was seething, and the room was silent, except for the sound of his breathing. He took the gun from his belt but didn't aim it at anyone.

Jack needed to rein him in and steer him in the right direction. "It's time to give this up, Nouri."

Nouri didn't answer.

"Let's call the FBI and tell them this is over."

"You!" Nouri shouted, pointing at Zahra. "You're on your own, Zahra. I'm not sticking my neck out another minute for you."

"Let's just stay calm and put away the gun," said Jack.

Nouri looked at Jack, but he didn't put the gun away. "You asked a question earlier, Jack. You asked me whose side I'm on."

"Yes," said Jack. "You said Zahra *and* Ava's. Stay on Ava's side. No matter how you might feel about Zahra right now, stay on Ava's side and put the gun away."

Nouri shook his head. "No. Now I'm on *my* side."

CHAPTER 52

Andie and her partner were on the move. Grace had taken over the driving duties so that Andie could focus on her phone conversation with Isaac Underwood.

Andie knew Jack's location, and they were heading up South Beach Road in that direction. But with SWAT in motion, showing up on-site unannounced would have been dangerous to Jack and everyone else inside, not to mention deadly to her career. Andie's best bet was to find the mobile command center, appeal to the negotiating team, and get them to rein in the SWAT breach based on "information on the ground." Having the support of an assistant director in Washington couldn't hurt.

"The decision to breach was made much higher than me," said Isaac.

"Someone outside the FBI?" asked Andie.

"Higher than me," he said, giving her nothing more.

"It appears that someone would rather see Nouri Asmoun dead than keep my husband alive. That's unacceptable."

"No one wants anyone hurt. We simply can't risk Nouri going public with what he knows about Ava Bazzi."

"What does Nouri know?"

"Andie, I can't."

"I deserve an answer, Isaac."

"Even if I told you what I know, it wouldn't fill in all the pieces of the puzzle."

"I'll settle for a corner piece."

Humor, however lame, had gotten Andie and Isaac through many a tense situation in Seattle, and her effort seemed to bring out a hint of the old Isaac, softening him a bit.

"The Iranians didn't know what they had in Ava Bazzi," he said.

"I already know about the text-message network. Ava kept text messages from women all over Iran about the opposition to the government."

Isaac paused, and Andie hoped that he would be more forthcoming now that he knew she was already deep into the secret life of Ava Bazzi.

"What you need to understand is that Ava wasn't collecting this information for a journalist or a human rights organization," he said. "She was feeding real-time information about the protests to the CIA through Nouri Asmoun, who then passed on that information to Agent Guthrie. Ava was a key source of intelligence after the regime shut down the internet."

"And the Iranians never found that out?"

"No. Farid found the thumb drives in their apartment after Ava was arrested."

"He didn't turn them over?"

"No. He destroyed them so they wouldn't fall into the hands of the regime."

"Farid was protecting Ava. Is that what you're saying?"

"If he hadn't, we would never have been able to buy her out of Evin Prison. Ava would have been tortured to give up the names of hundreds of women with whom she communicated, and hundreds more would have been arrested. We bought her out of jail before the Iranians learned any of that. Before they could torture her—and then probably execute her."

"So when you say that the Iranians didn't know what they had in Ava Bazzi, that means they still don't know—"

"What they have in Agent Guthrie," said Isaac, finishing her thought.

Andie fleshed it out completely. "If Nouri speaks, and the Iranians find out now, Agent Guthrie might also be slated for execution."

Isaac's silence said it all.

"What would you do if you were me, Isaac?"

"I'd keep my finger right on the pulse. I'd go to the mobile command center."

"Where is it?"

"You didn't hear it from me," he said, and then he told her.

Andie thanked him and hung up. She was about to call her ASAC to let him know she was on her way, but she thought better of it. Tidwell might order her to stay away. She shot a quick text instead and gave Grace the directions.

It was a two-minute drive straight up South Beach Road to the FBI's staging area outside the town hall. There were no streetlights along the road, and the lights in the parking lot at the town hall were out—at the FBI's direction, no doubt. The mobile command center and SWAT van were parked in a forest of oak trees behind the building, under the cover of darkness. Tidwell stepped out of the command center as the car pulled up. The SWAT van was empty, and the team was nowhere to be seen, which made Andie's heart race.

"Has SWAT breached the cottage already?" she asked.

"Not yet," said Tidwell. "But they're in position. Unless you've changed your mind about calling Jack and creating a diversion for the breach, you shouldn't be here."

Andie rolled with it. "I'm considering it."

Tidwell took her inside the command center. A tech agent and two hostage negotiators were in the electronics room. A video feed from the SWAT unit was on the screen. It was Andie's first look at the cottage. Her throat tightened at the thought of Jack inside, surrounded by SWAT.

"We just received the latest audio," said Tidwell.

It was no surprise to Andie that SWAT had planted eavesdropping devices to pick up conversations inside the cottage. The tech agent played a recording of Jack's exchange with Nouri—Jack's repeated requests that Nouri put the gun away, Nouri's refusal, and his chilling words: *Now I'm on* my *side*.

Tidwell hit STOP, and the recording ended.

"What does that mean—'Now I'm on *my* side'?"

"It's not clear," said Tidwell. "We expect Nouri to make a new demand. Something for himself. When he calls, SWAT breaches."

"This isn't protocol," said Andie. "Nouri hasn't made an explicit threat to hurt Jack, Yasmin, or Zahra. You shouldn't give up on negotiation until he does. That's hostage negotiation one-oh-one."

"Headquarters sees things differently," said Tidwell.

"On what basis?"

"Based on Nouri's threat to reveal what he knows about Ava Bazzi."

"That's not a threat to any of the hostages."

"Maybe not *these* hostages," said Tidwell. "But it's a threat on the life of a CIA agent who's being held hostage in an Iranian prison. If Nouri makes good on his threat to go public with what he knows about Ava Bazzi, Agent Guthrie is at risk of torture or worse at the hands of the Iranians."

All of a sudden the pressure Andie had been getting from the CIA and the State Department made sense. It sent her head spinning. It wasn't simply a matter of jeopardizing the US government's negotiations for the release of an American hostage. It was the danger of letting the Iranians discover the true value of the hostage they were holding—and the dire consequences he might suffer.

"So, dealing with Nouri is no different than dealing with a hostage taker who has threatened to kill a hostage in the same room with him," said Andie, putting two and two together.

"That's the way we see it," said Tidwell. "Nouri has effectively threatened to kill Agent Guthrie, who's at the mercy of the Iranian regime in a Tehran prison cell. We have no choice."

"You have to breach," said Andie.

"We have to breach. There's only one question: Are you in or are you out?"

He was asking her again to make the phone call to Jack—to act as the diversion for the SWAT breach. It was Andie's calculation that a breach was more likely to succeed with a diversion than without one, which left only one answer.

"Okay," she said. "I'm in."

CHAPTER 53

Tension was rising inside the beach cottage. Nouri's deadline—*I want this deal wrapped up in thirty minutes*—was ancient history, and Jack's phone was silent.

"They're out there," said Nouri. "I can feel it."

Nouri had moved Jack, Zahra, and Yasmin to the dining room, away from the glass doors and large windows in the kitchen. It was more of a dining area than a formal dining room, rectangular in shape with large openings at the short ends, one that led to the kitchen and the other to the great room. Slatted plantation shutters covered the doors and windows throughout the cottage, and Nouri had closed all of them to prevent anyone from seeing inside. Jack and Zahra were seated at the glass-top table. Nouri had threatened to tie them up with an extension cord if they moved without his permission, but it hadn't come to that. Yasmin lay asleep in the corner on a blanket. The dimmer was on low to keep the chandelier light from waking her. Nouri was standing along the wall, off to the side of the window. Every few minutes, he would peer through a tiny slit in the shutters. Paranoia was setting in.

"Who's out there?" asked Jack.

"SWAT. I know they are. This is taking too long."

"You told Jack's wife that the next call better be from someone with authority to meet your demands," said Zahra. "I'm sure it's just taking time to find the right person."

"Zahra, shut up," he said harshly. "You don't know what you're talking about."

There was silence. Nouri walked to the kitchen entranceway to check for the sound of SWAT outside the cottage, and then to the front opening to the great room.

"You won't hear them if they're out there," said Jack.

"You agree with me, then? They're here?"

"All I know is that this is pointless, and you should give up. The FBI won't agree to your demand."

"You don't even know what my new demand is."

"Money? An airplane out of the United States? Whatever it is, you don't need three hostages. You should at least let Yasmin go."

Nouri glanced at Yasmin, who was sound asleep on the floor. "She's the only reason SWAT hasn't busted down the door already."

Jack couldn't disagree, at least not convincingly, so he tried a different strategy.

"I could probably help you," he said.

"Help me what?"

"Shape your pitch. Give it the best chance of success."

"I can make my own demand," said Nouri.

"See, you already have the wrong focus. It's not about your demand— what *you* have to gain. It's about the quid pro quo. You have to make them understand clearly what *they* stand to gain. Or what they stand to lose if they don't give you what you want."

"The US government knows what it stands to lose."

"That's an assumption on your part. Assumptions are dangerous in negotiations."

"Have you not been paying attention, Swyteck? If they don't meet my demand, the world learns the truth about Ava Bazzi."

"But what does that mean, exactly—'the truth about Ava Bazzi'?"

"They know what it means."

"Do they? When I was a young lawyer, I lost a trial I never should have lost. We proved all the facts we needed to win, but I didn't deliver the closing argument I should have. I *assumed* the jury knew my client should win."

"What's your point?"

"Sometimes, even when people *know* something, they need you to help them visualize what winning means. How are you going to do that, Nouri?

How are you going to make the FBI visualize what 'the truth about Ava Bazzi' looks like?"

Nouri was silent. Jack pushed a little harder.

"Not just see it," said Jack. "How are you going to make the US government *fear* it enough to give you what you want?"

Nouri stared back at Jack, intensely at first, and then his gaze drifted to a place more distant. He seemed to be going back to that night outside the Evin Prison walls, to the end of the video he'd captured.

"Guthrie was waiting in the car," said Nouri.

Jack needed to catch up with him on the timeline, and he got there quickly. They were literally picking up where the bodycam video ended. "Was Guthrie alone?"

"Yes. Alone."

"Did Ava get in the car with him?"

"We put her in the trunk so that she wouldn't be seen."

"Did you get in the car with Agent Guthrie?"

"No. It was my job to buy her out of prison. It was Guthrie's job to get her out of the country."

"Did he get her out?"

Nouri's gaze grew more distant, as if he were looking past Jack. "No," he said.

"How do you know?"

"He called me the next morning," Nouri said in a hollow voice. "From a little town near the Kuwait border."

"What did he say?"

"He told me I needed to come and get Ava."

"Why? What happened?"

Jack's phone rang. It was on the table in front of him, and the screen lit up with Andie's number. Nouri answered it on speaker, leaving it where it lay.

"Nouri, this is Agent Henning," she said.

Nouri glanced at Jack, then spoke toward the phone. "There'd better be someone important on the line with you, Agent Henning. I said the call needed to be from the right person. Someone with authority to deal."

"You're talking to the right person," said Andie. "I have full authority to meet reasonable demands."

Jack knew she was bluffing; no hostage negotiator ever led with "I have full authority" and gave up the ability to say "I need to check with the powers above me."

"You're too late," said Nouri. "My demand has changed."

"Okay. Let's work with that. Maybe I can still help. What's the new demand?"

Jack assumed that her questions were intended only to stall for time. He joined her effort.

"Nouri, remember what we just talked about," he said. "Quid pro quo. What do they stand to lose?"

Nouri looked at Jack with skepticism at first, but as the silence lingered, he seemed to come around and see the value of Jack's advice.

Jack played to it, picking up where they'd left off. "Nouri was telling me what happened after Ava got in the car with Agent Guthrie," he said. "The information he intends to make public."

"We don't want you to make any of that public," said Andie. "That would be very dangerous for Agent Guthrie."

"Guthrie doesn't deserve protection."

"I'm sorry you feel that way," said Andie. "Guthrie had your back as your handler."

"Guthrie was a fuckup."

"That's not the information I have."

Jack didn't know what "information" Andie had, but he knew he was so close to the truth. He wanted to hear it from Nouri.

"Tell me, Nouri," said Jack. "Tell *me* with the FBI on the line. Help them visualize the truth before you make your demand."

Nouri's anger rose as he spoke. "The plan was to leave Ava hidden in the trunk for a little while. Just until they got out of Tehran, away from the morality police. But Guthrie lost his nerve."

"Lost it how?" asked Jack.

"He was afraid of getting caught by the police with Ava in the car, even after they got outside Tehran."

"So what did he do?"

"He kept Ava in the trunk."

"How long?"

"All the way to the border."

"How long was that?"

Nouri didn't answer.

"*How long?*" Jack pressed.

Nouri's voice tightened. "Ten hours. The first hour or so at night in Tehran, not so bad in October. But the last three hours were in the province of Khuzestan. Do you know Khuzestan, Jack?"

"No, I don't."

"One of the hottest places on earth. Every day in summer is more than forty-five degrees. Even in October, over forty in the sun."

Jack realized he meant forty degrees centigrade, which was over a hundred degrees Fahrenheit.

"The morning Guthrie got to Khuzestan," said Nouri. "That's when he called me and said to come get Ava."

"Did you go?"

"Yes. Guthrie left her in the car on the side of the road."

Zahra gasped, which told Jack that she'd never heard these details before.

"What kind of shape was she in?" asked Jack.

Nouri looked at him, his eyes filled with anger. "Ava was dead. She suffocated."

Jack felt a chill. It came as no shock that Ava was dead, but the manner of death was deeply distressing. Zahra covered her mouth to contain her reaction. Andie was silent on the line.

Nouri finished by saying what needed to be said.

"It wasn't the Iranian morality police who killed Ava Bazzi. It was that coward from the CIA. That's what the truth looks like," he said, and then he spoke directly to Andie on the cell phone. "Does the US government get the picture, Agent Henning?"

"Yes, we get it," said Andie.

Jack could hear it in her voice: she too was hearing this for the first time. But she stayed in role.

"Before we meet your demand, I need to know that Yasmin is safe."

"She's safe," said Nouri.

"Jack, is Yasmin safe?"

"Yes. She's right here in the room with us. Asleep on the floor."

"Okay, good. Have you been playing that silly Harry Potter game with her? The one you play with Righley?"

The question was out of left field, but Jack had to assume there was a point to it. "You mean the cloak of invisibility?"

"Yeah, that one. Have you played it with Yasmin?"

In the Harry Potter series, Harry and his friends at Hogwarts could become invisible by covering themselves with the cloak of invisibility. It wasn't actually a "game" that Jack played with Righley, but more of an annoying "daddy trick" in which he became the cloak and smothered her entire body in a giant hug.

"No, we haven't played it," said Jack.

"Well, you should."

Nouri was losing patience. "Enough with the Harry Potter bullshit."

"You should definitely play that game with Yasmin," said Andie.

"I said enough!" shouted Nouri.

"Jack, do it now!"

Jack took her cue, launched himself from his chair, and dove to the corner of the room, "cloaking" Yasmin with his body as a human shield.

In the same instant the glass doors to the kitchen exploded, sending glass pellets and fragments of the wood shutters flying. Zahra screamed at the top of her voice as a SWAT team burst into the cottage and charged toward the dining area.

"FBI, drop your weapon!" they shouted.

Jack heard the crack of gunshot from very close by, probably from Nouri. A flurry of return fire followed, and Nouri fell to the floor beside him.

Yasmin was crying, confused and frightened. An FBI agent snatched her from Jack's arms, and a barrage of questions came from everywhere.

"Are you okay?"

"Is anyone injured?"

"Is everyone okay?"

Nouri was still breathing, but barely. He lay in a crimson pool of his own blood.

"Don't move!" a SWAT agent shouted.

Nouri's eyes blinked open. Jack moved closer and sat at his side. He was struggling to say something.

"My demand," he whispered.

"Don't try to talk," said Jack, but the look in Nouri's eyes drew Jack's ear closer.

"I want what they promised me," he said in a voice that faded. "I want my parents and my sister out of Iran."

The request cut to Jack's core. This dying man, Ava Bazzi's handler, had been used by the US government and then used by Zahra. Jack wasn't ready to forgive him for having put a gun to his head and put Yasmin at risk, but still, he was struck that after all that, Nouri wanted nothing for himself.

Jack wasn't sure if Nouri could hear him, but he answered anyway.

"It will happen," said Jack. "I promise."

Nouri's eyes closed, and he was gone.

EPILOGUE

November was a month of changes.

Jack stopped being Zahra's lawyer the moment they stepped out of the cottage on Jupiter Island. He'd represented worse human beings in his career, but Jack drew the line at defending anyone who lied to him. Even without his help, Zahra avoided the more serious criminal charge of child abduction. As in most cases of "parental kidnapping" in Florida, Zahra faced a single charge of interference with a custody order, a third-degree felony. A federal immigration judge rendered all of it moot: Zahra was deported and sent back to Iran before the arraignment. Jack shuddered to think what life was waiting for her there.

Farid and Yasmin found a happier ending. Farid could have taken the easy road. He could have continued to insist on the legitimacy of the custody order of the Iranian family court—the order that the US State Department had certified as "authentic," that his lawyer had presented to a family court judge in Miami, and that the judge had enforced. He could have relied on that order to claim full custody of Yasmin, packed their suitcases, and taken her anywhere. Instead, Farid hired a new lawyer and initiated supplemental proceedings before the same judge in Miami family court. Dr. Vestry, the child psychiatrist Jack had hired, was a key witness at the hearing. She cleared Farid's name and reputation, testifying that in her expert opinion Yasmin's drawings were the product of Zahra's coaching— parental alienation syndrome—and that Farid presented no danger, much less grave danger, to his daughter.

Jack checked in with Farid's lawyer after the hearing, and she made it possible for Jack to say a proper goodbye to Yasmin. He drove to the airport and met Farid and his daughter at the international terminal two hours before their flight to Heathrow. Their bags were checked, and Jack had a few minutes with them before they joined the long, snaking line through security.

"How long are you planning to stay in London?" Jack asked Farid.

"Forever, I hope," said Farid.

A horn beeped, and an electric vehicle loaded with elderly passengers zipped past them. Yasmin held on to her father even more tightly.

"Did your British citizenship come through?"

"My immigration lawyer says it looks good," said Farid. "In the meantime, we can stay under the Entrepreneur visa."

Jack got down on a knee to bring himself eye-to-eye with Yasmin. "I brought you a present from Righley," he said.

"Righley's nice," she said in a little voice.

"Do you want to see it?"

Yasmin nodded. Jack opened his backpack and pulled out a stuffed bear.

"His name is Paddington," said Jack.

Yasmin extended her arms. Jack handed over the bear, and she squeezed it so hard that Paddington's signature red rain hat popped off. It reminded him of Righley's reaction, two years earlier, when he'd returned from London with the same gift.

"Thank you," said Yasmin.

Farid checked the departures board. "We have to be going."

Jack rose and wished him luck. Farid took Yasmin by the hand, and they started away.

"Farid," Jack said, stopping them.

Farid turned and looked.

"I'm glad you're honoring Ava's wish," he said.

Jack didn't have to explain. Farid knew he meant Ava's wish that Yasmin be raised in a free country. He simply nodded, and the new family—Farid, Yasmin, and Paddington Bear—entered the security line.

It was early evening by the time Jack escaped the traffic and left the airport. Andie had asked him to meet her for happy hour at one of their favorite neighborhood bars, and he drove straight there.

Fox's was a relic of old My-amma, cozy and unpretentious, everything modern Miami was not. Its heyday had been in the 1970s, which was obvious from the most popular items on the bar-food menu: spinach dip, French onion soup, and fried mozzarella sticks. There were no windows, no skylights, no flat-screen TVs, and definitely no shot girls with recently enhanced breasts. Fox's had been at the same location since the 1940s, and after a short hiatus to remove decades of grime, a new owner reopened the bar exactly as it always had been, right down to the brown wood-textured wall panels, which had a certain nostalgic charm but also reminded Jack of a refurbished basement somewhere in New Jersey. Above all, Fox's was dark. So dark that you could barely see the people at the other end of the long bar. Even in darkness, Jack would have sworn that the woman with the blond bob, alone in the back booth, was trying to catch his eye.

He looked away, and the bartender came over.

"What'ya drinking?"

This was not the place to order a skinny margarita. "How about an old-fashioned," said Jack.

"You got it."

Jack checked the time on his cell phone. At that very moment, Farid and Yasmin were somewhere in the air, which made Jack smile to himself. In another two days Nouri Asmoun's parents and sister would be flying in the opposite direction. Their emigration from Iran was the final piece of a larger US-Iran negotiation that had already resulted in the release of five Americans from Evin Prison in Tehran. The names of four hostages were made public, and their reunion with overjoyed family members at JFK Airport was headline news. The fifth chose to remain anonymous. Jack was one of the few to know that it was CIA agent Brian Guthrie.

"Here you go," the bartender said as he set up the drink. "Compliments of that gorgeous blonde over there in the booth."

Oh, boy, thought Jack, and as he glanced in her direction, he saw that she was already coming through the darkness and headed his way. Only when she passed the neon beer sign, three stools away from him, did the realization kick in.

"Come here often?" asked Andie as she climbed onto the stool beside him.

"You cut your hair?"

"It's a wig. It's a different color, too, in case you didn't notice."

"Uh, *yeah*, I noticed. What's this about?"

Andie set her drink on the bar top and swiveled her seat to face Jack more directly.

"I'm going away for a little while."

It took Jack a moment to get a word out. "What?"

She seemed to appreciate the expression on his face. "Sorry, that didn't come out right. I'm going *undercover* for a while."

"Ohhh," Jack said with relief. "So, this will be your new look?"

"Exactly."

"Wait. I thought that was the whole point behind your promotion to the international corruption squad—so that you could stop doing undercover work?"

"It was. But that was when I thought there was a possibility of becoming a single mother."

She took Jack's hand, and he smiled. Things had come a long way since their first marriage counseling session, but this was the first major life decision to confirm the mend.

Andie shed the serious moment and was suddenly playful. "Maybe I'll lose the wig and make this permanent. Take the plunge. Cut and color."

"Whoa," said Jack. "I love your hair."

"I could be like Catherine Barkley in *A Farewell to Arms*. She told Frederic that she would cut her hair short so that he could fall in love with her all over again."

A Farewell to Arms was the one old movie they completely agreed on: the 1932 version with Gary Cooper and Helen Hayes was better than the 1957 release, but neither was remotely true to Hemingway.

"Doesn't Catherine die in that movie?" asked Jack.

"Yes, but only once. It's the cowards who die a thousand deaths."

"Sounds like Hemingway."

"It's actually Julius Caesar, as written by Shakespeare, as interpreted by Hemingway. But that's not the point."

"What is the point?"

She tossed her hair awkwardly, a bit too much neck torque given the loss of length. "The sex was great," she said.

Jack smiled receptively. "Point taken."

ACKNOWLEDGMENTS

My wife has a wonderful mix of friends. Many of them have read my books. A few—I'll never say which ones—have unwittingly shaped a line of dialogue from time to time or, perhaps, loaned a quirky trait or habit to a female character. For *Grave Danger*, it was one of Tiffany's special friends who shared her personal insights into Iranian life and culture, which were invaluable to me as a writer. I am deeply indebted to Sima for the fruits and nuts from the Tehran Grand Bazaar, for the tea served in porcelain cups that have been in her family for generations, and for all the stories that didn't necessarily make it into the novel but informed the character development in critical ways.

I'm also grateful to the Honorable Judy Harris Kluger and Charlotte A. Watson, cochairs of the Practicing Law Institute's presentation "Addressing Domestic Violence: The Hague Convention on International Child Abduction and Its Intersection with Child Custody Law." I'm sure the expert presenters—including federal judge Denny Chin, who is mentioned in the novel—were completely unaware that the most appreciative member of their audience was quietly thinking about his next novel. Of course, any mistakes as to the legal nuances of a very complicated area of law are mine.

Writing can be an isolating process, but a book is really a team effort. As always, big thank-yous go to my longtime agent, Richard Pine; to my editor, Sarah Stein; and to my volunteer Beta Reader, Ann Carlson.

Finally, I want to thank the readers who take the time to connect through email and, even more special, the occasional handwritten letter. I do answer each one myself and appreciate your patience.

—JG, *March 2024*

ABOUT THE AUTHOR

JAMES GRIPPANDO is a *New York Times* bestselling author of suspense and the winner of the Harper Lee Prize for Legal Fiction. *Grave Danger* is his thirty-second novel and the nineteenth in the popular series featuring Miami criminal defense lawyer Jack Swyteck. His books are enjoyed around the world in twenty-eight languages. He lives in south Florida, where he is a trial lawyer and teaches Law and Literature at the University of Miami School of Law.